The Work of an Ancient Hand

THE
WORK
OF AN
ANCIENT
HAND

BY

Curtis

Harnack

HARCOURT, BRACE

AND COMPANY

NEW YORK

for H.C.

The Work of an Ancient Hand

I  The devil in black sits beside me, thought Letitia Kallsen, as she rode the train with her husband across the flat plains of inner Iowa toward their new parish. It was autumn, a time to pluck ripe fruits and rake dead leaves, the gathering together and the laying waste; this was her life, too, and everywhere the ancient pattern: the shape of the world was the larger impress of her own heart.

She looked at Vernon, dressed in black, his hands folded in his lap, his eyes closed restfully. The train rocked him in the cradle of new adventure, and he was awaiting his destiny with calm, as if all the past were truly gone forever and this journey promised a final fulfillment of their lives. After all, he had received "the call," a distant trumpet indeed! A horn winding beyond the walls of that little village of Stilton and the horror which enveloped their lives. Quickly, after the death of Eugene, the church synod had arranged for the Kallsens to leave, though the procedure followed the precepts of Scripture. Like the apostles of old, in order truly to serve, the call must be ringing and imperative—to go to Macedonia, to slip over the Damascus wall and lower yourself in a basket, to preach to the Greeks in the market place of Athens, where, according to the Bible, Dionysius was the first to confess his sins.

In this manner Vernon received his call in September, 1930, to journey to Kaleburg, but the Kallsens pretended between themselves that this had all come about merely by accident, and Letty did not voice her suspicions that the council had heard disturbing reports about their son's death; in order to quiet the people of Stilton and further the aims of the church, the proper moves had been made. Vernon would not admit the likelihood of this, Letty thought, because he feared the Lord might overhear and disapprove—or think him secular in his viewpoint. Some God, Letty felt, who couldn't see into the black depths of his heart but had to rely on wayward lips. Oh, we are all phonies, everyone of us, and deserve what we get. And if Kaleburg turned out to be the filthiest, meanest town in all America, with blackguards of the new sort, who club you with kindness and rob you of self-respect, she would not be surprised. The Kallsens deserved no better—and not because of Vernon, she reminded herself sharply; I, too, am getting my just reward. This is the bed I made and am forever mussing, where I lie down alone.

It will be the same in Kaleburg, she knew, despite new people with strange names and different lives transpiring before her very eyes. She and Vernon would be both actors and observers, and as usual with the clergy, mostly the latter, since the preacher dwelt apart—called in to witness the last gasp, but never a glimmer of truth was really learned before the lips stilled forever and the wild eyes closed, nothing but the old saw, "this, too, shall pass away." She was not awed by it any more. Vernon's stirring words over a newborn babe no longer lifted her heart in wonder; nor did she relish the greasy bits of gossip that showed the human race to be ugly and sinful; nor did her heart warm to the sentimental notion of possible goodness in her fellowmen—an act of charity or unselfishness. She distrusted it all, the whole panorama of life, because she felt she knew it too intimately from the start and was aware of how

fate kept writing with a larger hand behind her, the way a child
with a compass, pencil on both points, enjoys the seemingly
free play of the outer stylus, which writes along, too: a mysterious working, a cabalistic gliding across the page—only no, see?
The words written are the same, the message identical. So, too,
with Kaleburg. She saw it coming. The dark message we reap is
at last our own.

There was, however, Vernon to think of, this other egg in
the basket of their lives. He was uplifted by the new challenge
of Kaleburg; he was Paul on the way to Tyre, unaware of the
prison, his destiny. All is a secluded lesson, he would say, if one
could just find it—even what happened to their son, hanging
with a broken neck from the bough of an apple tree. Was not
Absalom a lesson? He, too, swung from a tree, caught in the
long hair of his vain ambitions, netted by folly.

Letitia Kallsen settled back upon the green plush cushion
of the train coach. Up ahead three rows she noticed a boy and
girl rubbing their cheeks together. Dressed in new clothes, they
were obviously honeymooners on the way to the Black Hills.
Letty sighed, thinking of them, and of the distance between
herself and Vernon. Each to his own. She glanced at her husband's passive, Christian face. If he only knew, she thought,
with all his talk of saving souls, that here beside him sits a
smirking heathen. Do your worst, you man of God, I can take
it. She closed her eyes.

What a relief not to have to face those distrustful eyes of his
Stilton parishioners, Vernon thought. Eugene had won their
hearts and loyalty—won them by ways of the flesh and not of
the spirit. But he quickly reminded himself to stop thinking
about it; that trouble was all behind him. He turned to Letty
and smiled, although she did not notice him. He dreamed of
Kaleburg—what it would be like. There were intimations of
some promise ahead, some wonderful unfolding. He knew

Letty regarded the trip as an ordeal, rather than a chance for a new life. Since her hysteria over Eugene's death, she had been very unstable, although she was now much better than at first, when he had had to keep her locked in her bedroom lest she tear her hair in the streets and shout absurdities. When the doctor's sedatives had worn off, she had scratched on the door, her nails like claws, her sobs uncontrollable. And of course, blame had had to be found, fixed, and delivered. What had happened to Eugene could not be considered an accident, terrible for them both, but responsibility had had to be placed like a bloody badge. And she had fixed it upon him, as passionately as if Eugene had been a child of her womb, instead of an adopted boy, only with them a few months.

He knew himself that it had all been a test of the Lord, and now, bereft of their child, they would be taking on all the children of Kaleburg, with some revelation forthcoming as a result. Thus the ever-moving force behind his life pushed him forward, at each turn revealing a little more. Back in Stilton he had kept a diary to record his spiritual progress. He had taken long walks down empty dirt roads that afforded no vista except monotonous rows of corn on either side—nothing scenic to distract—and how heaven had seemed to pour down straight upon him from above! He had received his most inspiring thoughts out there, and each time he had jotted a few words on a slip of paper, tucking the tab into one of his pockets—later he had fished it out and whole essays resulted. The potent, loaded words, *Dies Irae*, for instance, had spawned five full pages in his narrow-lined notebook. The "shout from heaven" mentioned in Scriptures in connection with Judgment Day struck him as a significant metaphor for the resurrection. He could almost hear that "shout from heaven," and the notion seemed to him more than a childish way of expressing relief that indeed there *would* be a final reckoning. He wrote down his ideas in a spidery script that was so clear no one would ever have difficulty deciphering it.

How far indeed he had come since those days of his child-hood, one of five sons on a northern Wisconsin farm, with a father whose rule was as rigid as his back and a mother as long-suffering as Sarah. From an early age he had been enraptured by the beauty of the spring world, the sadness of death in autumn, and the long grave of winter. There was something portentous in it all, if he could only manage to snatch the latent meanings beyond his reach. The casual unconcern of his brothers for these mysteries seemed puzzling. They flung them-selves indiscriminately about in their lives, marrying in a flash of passion, dropping away into towns and cities to breed chil-dren; they became fused with the cycle, rather than trying to understand it. He felt that his mother realized what he was up to. She suggested the ministry, adding: "We should have one preacher in the family, like the Catholics have a priest—to pray for everybody's sins." When he considered the transgres-sions of his older brothers, his drunken Uncle Timothy, and cousins by the score whose secret sins were unknown, he easily saw a flock shaping up around him.

He expected that the heavy college texts he read for theology courses would provide some of the answers, but he soon learned differently. Church doctrines had to be mastered first. He hoped to be smart enough some day to understand where they were wrong. His teachers thought him too zealous and suggested he eat better. But he had precious little money. He earned his way through that small parochial college by shoveling coal in the heating plant and sleeping in the overheated room above the furnace. There he had a small cot, lean and hard as a monk's pad, and a square desk, straight chair, and a curtainless window that looked out upon the sturdy smokestack which rose aloft like the Tower of Babel—a lightning rod on the top, like a small pin for angels to dance upon.

In that sweltering cell he fought his tired flesh, to overcome it with his mind and spirit. Sometimes in winter when icy winds raged and snow blew thick, the red hot furnaces below would make his room so stifling that even with the window wide open and the radiator turned off, he perspired as if he inhabited one of the lower rooms in hell. In desperation he would strip the clothes from his body, only to disgust the purity of his thoughts by the sensuous infiltration that almost always came, when, naked as a cannibal in some lush tropical jungle, he lusted for a woman to prance with him around the beastly fires of sex. He was consumed by the flames of carnality, until finally he would perch like a loathsome bird upon the windowsill, with the deathly blasts of frigid north wind cooling across his body; then, miserable, disappointed in himself, bewildered by God's plan for him, he would fall sneezing into bed, and in the days of coughing and sore throat and fever, he would whip himself with the reminder that this was the penalty, after all, the wages of sin. He would cough until his lungs ached and tears came to his eyes. Perhaps someday, he thought, God would lose patience, send him pneumonia, and dispatch him promptly.

But he graduated with honors. He was admitted to the seminary on a small tuition scholarship—which filled him with pride. However, by this time his mother was dead, and his father, who now lived in a nursing home, seemed unable to comprehend what Vernon was up to, or why this youngest son was not married and producing grandchildren, like the others. He had sixteen so far and hoped for an even two dozen before he died. He had never gone for religion, much.

Vernon was quite surprised to find himself alone at graduation. It was as if now he were looking around on top of the waters, after swimming for years among the shoals of the deep, probing for the mystery of the world. No one in particular was watching his performance, or cared.

In seminary he discovered that even the church rulers were

not impressed by his struggle to enter the holy doors, despite his obvious commitment and suffering, his bloodshot eyes and scholar's pallor. Confronted with their indifference he struggled even harder. Late into the night he read his history of Christian thought and learned to put down questions that his independent logic continually raised, for he did not wish to annoy his superiors further. He studied the official doctrines as if they had been writ on stone and handed down by Moses himself. He beat Greek and Hebrew into his tired head.

One wintry night his eyes suddenly gave out. Like Saul on the road to Damascus he was plunged into total darkness, and terror flew up his throat. He leapt from his chair, although a strange, new, and holy feeling filled him with spiritual strength. "Ah!" he said aloud, with a rising, triumphant gasp, for a sweet sense of achievement was his—knowing now, as he did, that he had won the battle at last; he had given supremely of his earthly self, and now the spiritual prize was his. Even the seminary deans would be convinced of his worth—and shamed, too, by the black flower of perfect attainment which was his, which would never be theirs, for their faith was not strong enough. A few minutes later his sight returned, common as daylight, and he flicked off the lamp in order to remain for a while in the dark cathedral of his triumph.

"Kaleburg, next stop!" the conductor called, walking down the aisle toward the Kallsens, and Vernon excitedly craned his neck to catch a glimpse through the forward windows; there was no sign of a town as yet.

"It'll be a while, surely," said Letty without looking at him. She felt the precious minutes of uncertainty ebbing away and dreaded the pronouncement of sentence that the parish of Kaleburg, thrown about their necks, would be.

"No, see!" he said, pointing. "There's the town across the fields. I see the steeple!"

Letty looked and shrugged. "Only a Catholic church would be that big."

They stood up and swayed in the aisle, anchoring themselves on the backs of seats, as if they were wading in a swift stream. Vernon tugged at their suitcases overhead, imperiling fellow passengers, who pulled in their heads. Then the Kallsens were ready, with their bags at their feet, but the train had only reached the outskirts of the town.

We're so eager, Letty thought, one would imagine we were approaching the gates of heaven itself. She studied her husband's erect head, his thin, spiritual nose, and his rather pale face. The forehead was always slightly oily, as if just recently anointed. On the whole he had a rather handsomely molded face, especially the strong curving jaw and that interesting cleft exactly in the center of his chin, a kind of dimple, which had fascinated her in the early months of their marriage. She had not been able to kiss that spot enough; he had thought there was something wild or crazy about her, the way she kept toying with him there. Well, she had stopped. Now, all these years later, here was that same sensuous dimple—oddly repulsive.

Vernon smiled excitedly. His wide-apart blue eyes seemed almost to be on the sides of his head, which gave him a vulnerable look, for it suggested compassion and magnanimity—he was open to the world. However, his stout neck should have told her of his stubbornness, and the tourniquet of his cleric's collar cut off the warm blood from ever reaching his brain. But all in all, he has gotten through life better than I have, Letty thought; certainly he carries fewer scars before the world. She despised the unkemptness of her saggy brown suit, the peach-colored blouse with the button missing at the top. She had fixed an imitation silver pin of a nameless, lackluster flower at her throat, and thus held her costume together. Her hair was half gray, and her face, which could never carry a swatch of rouge, was quite wrinkled and sallow. What I am shows all over me, she thought.

"Kaleburg! Kaleburg! This way out!"

" 'This way out' indeed!" thought Letty. Kaleburg would be no way out. She would just be dragged in all over again. But she followed him, as women must.

A tall young man with a round, small head took Vernon's bag, shook hands with both of the Kallsens, and said something, but the train whistle blew and Letty heard nothing. A shrunken, grandfatherly little German seemed part of the welcoming committee, too. He kept grinning at Letty with a crooked smile, and he bobbed his head, as if he were an uncle teasing a favorite niece. She found him rather amusing and couldn't help responding with a smile. His hair was thick and gray-white, the color of winter underwear, and his gnarled hands were huge. As they stood in front of the station and watched the train depart, he said his name was Claus Schneider. He was a farmer and chief elder of the church.

Meanwhile, Vernon was talking guardedly to Bill Wolbers, the tall young man, who, it turned out, was vice-president of the Farmers Savings Bank, although he looked too young to have such a pretentious title. After the suitcases had been placed in the trunk, the four people climbed into a late-model Packard, which was shiny dark green in the afternoon sunlight. Wolbers drove off, explaining things about the town, and now and then pointing his hand out the window. Letty sat in the back seat, next to silent Mr. Schneider, who occasionally turned to her and smacked his lips and shook his head, presumably in reference to Wolbers' guidebook rambling about Kaleburg. They drove up the wide, paved Main Street with its prosperous-looking stores and many, many taverns. Yes, the German Catholics saw no harm in liquor, said Wolbers—and they found ways of getting it. Even the priest liked his whiskey. The Catholics apparently tried to run everything in Kaleburg, "but with you here,

Reverend," said Wolbers to Vernon, "things might change, huh? Our other man just tucked himself in and didn't try to do much."

"He died!" said Claus Schneider suddenly.

"He was old, of course," said Wolbers.

It didn't take long to cruise three blocks through Main Street, even at five miles an hour. Wolbers showed them the dingy post office, the Farmers Savings Bank with its Doric columns of cement, the grocery stores, and the dry goods shops. He swung the Packard past the impressively large Catholic church, and all were silent as they considered the size and strength of their opponent Christians. They scrutinized the brick nuns' home, the handsome house for the priest, the parochial school, and the cave-like grotto. A few more blocks and they arrived at the small wooden church with a slender steeple—like a country schoolhouse with a tower added—and, next door, Letty saw the little box-like parsonage. Not exactly the home of one's dreams, she thought, but painted, and with an expanse of lawn. She could hardly wait to get inside, but Wolbers pulled the luggage from the trunk absently, as he talked on and on to Vernon about the miserable corn prices, the generally dire effects of the depression, and his high opinion of Herbert Hoover. "Now, I'm a banker," he said, "and I know what's happening to our economy. You take the average farmer, he just goes along planting his crops and raising pigs. Then all of a sudden he's stuck and he comes hollering to the bank—we should do something, or somebody should do something. They blame the Republicans; they blame the meat packers; they blame everybody but themselves. It's interesting, ain't it, how people are?"

Vernon nodded, for he was always a good listener. Back in Stilton his theory about getting along well with people was to give them all the rope they wished. In the end he would always tie a spiritual knot. Of course, people expected that from a minister. And maybe greater familiarity wasn't a good idea. He was made uneasy by the pressure of Wolbers' friendship—the jovial hand on his shoulder—for how would it figure in church politics? One would expect strangers to go easy on a first meeting and show a little respect for the new minister. All in all, Vernon had had enough glad-handing back in Stilton to last him a long time.

Claus Schneider took Letty's arm and nodded toward the house. "Come on," he winked. "You want to see it, don't you?"

"Oh, yes!" she cried eagerly.

"I know the door's open," he said, and they started up the sidewalk. Vernon and Wolbers followed just behind them.

As Letty entered, the kitchen floor glared between patches of linoleum with an impossible gloss from new varnish. Wolbers removed his black felt cap; he was bald, and much to Letty's surprise, he suddenly looked older; he sounded less silly with his measured, masculine, authoritative talk. "Your boxes —the goods you sent ahead by rail—came yesterday. And do you know, Mrs. Kallsen, the ladies of the church got together and unpacked everything for you?" He opened a cupboard— there were her yellow dime-store dishes. He stepped aside with a flourish and opened a drawer of the stove to reveal her scarred pots and pans. "Your sheets and tablecloths and towels—that sort of stuff—are in these drawers here," he said, walking into a little hall that led to the living room, dining room, and study. "Your clothes are all hanging in the closets upstairs, getting the wrinkles out. Even your dresser is set up—with all your things right where you can get at them." He smiled. "Carrie Maxwell and Verna Paff thought of everything. Oh, wait'll you meet those two." He rubbed the back of his neck and shook his head.

Claus Schneider began telling about Verna Paff and her two sisters, one of whom had married a neighbor of Claus'. "We all live not far from town. There's a whole ring of us Protestants— with a few Catholics sprinkled in."

Vernon kept walking away and looking around; he did not even pretend to listen. Finally Letty followed him, and the more she thought of Carrie Maxwell and Verna Paff poring over her household goods, the angrier she got. Snoopy creatures! How dare they peer at my slips and mended sheets, inspect my worn-out corset and chatter about the faded towels? Oh, she was tired, tired, tired of this everlasting patronage, the way congregations treated them like orphans and expected gratitude for their charity. How she hated thanking smug parishioners who felt pleased about voting a ten-dollar raise—with the reminder, "Of course, you get the parsonage free and all the food farmers bring in." And if ever they saw a new ornament on her drab Sunday dress, their faces would show peculiar interest, for had not their hard-earned money gone into the purchase?

But Letty said to Wolbers, as she knew she would: "How nice!" though it was difficult to smile.

"Very thoughtful of them, certainly," echoed Vernon quickly, for he guessed her inner rage.

And as soon as the house was cleared of these two outsiders, Letty intended to let fly with her indignation, for was not Vernon responsible, in part, for this everlasting lack of privacy, this rented life they lived? "Now don't get so worked up—they meant well," he would explain. And probably, after she had heaped upon him all the bitterness of her heart, he would go off silently to his study and carry the burden to the Lord. It was just as simple as that! "Are there trials and tribulations? Take them to the Lord in prayer." Once that was done, none of the acid was left within him to eat at his well-being. Oh, no. This was how religion worked.

But after the men left, promising to return soon with the other elders, who were eager to meet their new minister, Letty said nothing at all. What was the use? Now the business at hand was to make this religious hotel seem like home—but how? Oh, there would be fat jolly ladies to thank for deciding to paint these kitchen walls a slimy green, and for brilliantly picking that Virgin Mary blue for the dining room, and for selecting the living-room wallpaper of great nosegays, which made the four walls swim together before her indignant gaze. None of the decoration could be changed, since this was carefully thought out and committed—a deliberate, painstaking achievement of bad taste. This busy-body Carrie Maxwell—and the other woman Wolbers mentioned—were they responsible for this, too?

On the floor everywhere downstairs was a gay marbled linoleum in five colors, predominantly a muddy wine. This well-used covering carefully preserved the hardwood floors Bill Wolbers had talked about so proudly. Yes, there would be many, many more ministers' families coming and going, and this worldly wise congregation, German-thrifty, knew how to preserve its own against undue wear.

At the front of the house a sagging porch had been tacked on by handymen—members of the congregation too cheap to hire a carpenter, preferring to give their tithes this way, and of course botching the job. A gap of two inches showed between the porch floor and front doorsill. The lean-to was pulling away and the floor slanted down—but it was a screened-in porch, another room in summer. Letty knew thoroughly what had gone into their thinking. Every retired farmer likes a spot to face a road of some kind, to see as many people going by as possible, in order to make up for a lifetime of solitude in the country. They had assumed that the minister's wife, too, would appreciate this ideal grandstand spot on Main Street, only a few blocks from the business district. Here on summer evenings they expected her to sit and rock and watch the couples riding to the dancehall and taverns uptown; and she should shake her head and clack her tongue at the sinfulness going on out there in the mainstream of life. This was supposed to interest her— the way people lived out their silly lives—well, it would not;

nothing amazed, shocked, or disillusioned her any more. Not after what I've been through, she thought.

Now with Vernon she continued to inspect the house, and upstairs they entered their connubially arranged bedroom: his suits next to hers; his shirts in one drawer, her underclothes in another. Such intimacy their apparel had not had for lo these many years! She waited for him to speak and comment on this oddly contiguous situation.

"Which bedroom do you want?" he asked, matter-of-factly.

He's too withered to be even embarrassed, she thought. "This is a nice big double bed, isn't it?" she asked wryly, watching his face: those innocent blue eyes blinked with child-like unconcern.

"Since you like it here, I'll go into the next room. The other can be a storeroom—and downstairs will be my study." He walked toward the door.

After all, we're both past forty, she thought, and some things should be put from our minds. But she knew for certain that at times a desire to make love swept over him, too, as with every man, despite those damned warnings in the Bible. "You go where you'll be most comfortable," she said sarcastically.

He paused at the door. "At night I like to read, you know," he said penitently. "The light would bother you."

"Yes, the light—the truth and the light," she said wearily, picking up a comb and flinging it back upon the dresser top, "they both bother me. I like the dark old sins, I guess."

"Letty—remember," he began, his greased brow wrinkled, "we're in a new town, now. And a new house. I just hope we can both be new in our lives here, too."

"As simple as that, is it?"

"No, of course it won't be easy. We have so much of the past to forget—and forgive—in each other."

"Oh, please don't throw empty words at me now. I've got to lie down, or I'll have a headache."

"Things can be better here in a worldly way, too," he said. "These people are rich, and that old Claus Schneider has several farms. They'll take care of their minister—it'll be a matter of pride."

"Yes, *their* pride, but none left for ourselves." She kicked off her shoes and lay down on the bed, pleased momentarily by its softness. The windows were narrow and high, as if begrudging the little cheerful light allowed in. The dresser was a familiar chipped-veneer job, a discard from some family about to purchase a new bedroom suite; the same with the rocker and this bed, she thought—and perhaps even those curtains and the rag rug on the floor, which was like a pool into which a stone had just been dropped.

"I see a new end in this beginning," said Vernon mysteriously, his voice brooding and hollow, as if he were speaking from behind a tabernacle veil.

Letty sat up quickly and watched him walk, as if in a trance, to the window; the afternoon sun fell with a certain radiance upon his shiny face. Oh, what brilliant plan has now occurred to him, she wondered? The last big scheme he tried, back in Stilton, had certainly been a fiasco—that adventure in defrocking himself. One day he had simply decided that he would be everybody's close friend, a regular Joe, a buddy. The final result had been their adoption of Eugene. The boy was supposed to pull Vernon into everyday community affairs, and that, in turn, would pull secular people into the spiritual world. What a mishmash of strategy, ending with Eugene upon the tree! She buried her nose in the pillow and wondered at the capacity of the mind to self-deceive.

She could remember clearly that tattered coat Vernon had affected when he went off to have coffee with the farmers in the local café, as if it would make no difference that he had not sweated in the fields with them. He was going to become "close" with everybody, just because he never had had, in truth, a close friend in his whole life. And his bowling—that was an effort at companionship, too, although it looked at first, when he flung himself about on the hardwood lanes, as if he fancied himself the tail of a comet, for sometimes the ball stuck fast. He could never let go of anything. Then, when he began to realize that his success with the adults was somewhat dubious, he organized a young people's group and went with them on wiener roasts in the woods. He lustily sang campfire songs around a few blazing logs, while his young people were wishing to heaven he would go away and let them neck in peace under their blankets. He was a good fellow in the Grange, too; everywhere except at home.

Vernon at the window looked out upon the town without seeing it, for his thoughts were caught up by a strange feeling that there was something auspicious in his arrival here. He felt it in the very air of the house—this house which seemed rather familiar, almost what he had expected, as if he had dreamed all of this, as if he had shared God's dream, which may be the world. "Letty," he said softly, without turning around, "when the elders come, you let them in, but I'll stay up here a while and make them wait."

Propped up on her sharp elbows, she stared at him intently. "What a fine way to begin! They'll turn sour and begrudge us every penny they give."

He did not turn to look at her. "Oh, no, I think they'll be afraid to deny me anything."

"What makes you say that?" she scoffed.

"Because I'm beginning to understand that familiarity with the congregation should not be the pastor's role. I'm going to keep aloof. If they know me too well, what I say from the pulpit doesn't make a strong enough impression. Back in Stilton I lost some of the respect, some of the awe, that religion must have. And that's what caused the trouble." He spoke as if he were talking to himself. "This time it will be different. When the elders come to meet me, you let them in. And they're to wait. God demands special accord, even the servant of the Lord, a humble minister. It's important to strike a little fear into their hearts." He leaned one hand against the window frame and looked over his right shoulder at Letty. "I only wish—as you do, too—that they hadn't unpacked our belongings, as if we were just any neighbors to be helped! Too bad they had that chance to cut us down to their own level, to make us common as old shoes. That's just the sort of intimacy they naturally want. It makes them feel at ease, unmindful of religion, and it postpones their anxieties about the after-life. They'll want to pull us into their everyday doings. But I'm not going to allow that, Letty. I'm staying out, where I belong. There'll be no dart-throwing in the basement with the men's club—me pitting my skill against the others. I'll wear only black suits and go about the streets of Kaleburg, watching the uneasiness in the eyes of sinners who meet me. No one will know my real thoughts— and not knowing, they will suspect that I know everything. This is how the true ministry is accomplished, by conjuring up the clergy in everyone's heart."

"And what am I supposed to do in all this?" she asked flatly, pushing a bobby pin back into place. "Oh, look," she pointed toward the window, "here comes Claus Schneider already. He must have rounded up the elders. They're about to look us over, to see what sort of purchase they've made."

"No, no—we're looking *them* over. And I intend to make it clear from the start that I'll not accept what they take themselves to be—or pretend to be like them myself."

Hurriedly, before the old man began knocking downstairs, she asked: "But *why?* What are you trying to do? I don't understand. If this is just your way of forcing yourself to forget Eugene and the way you drove him out of the house to—"

"Stop it!" he snapped angrily, his face a sudden scowl. "What's done is over and through, can't you learn that? I told you not to mention the boy. It won't do us any good to go over and over it."

"All I want," she said slowly, looking at herself in the watery, blurred dresser mirror, "is a little peace." Downstairs Claus Schneider pounded vigorously on the door. "Well, what shall I say to him?"

"Tell him to come in. Offer him a chair in the study."

Letty clung to the railing on her way down the steep, short stairs. At the bottom, where heavy drapes closed off the staircase, it was so dark she could hardly see. She hurried out to the kitchen door. "Come in, come in, Mr. Schneider," she said nervously. He was stiff-jointed and proceeded into the house with care, laughing jovially, as if approaching lameness were only something to be amused about, as though he had looked death itself in the eye with composure. His lined face seemed lifted into a continual half-smile; it made one happy to see him. Here is somebody at least, she thought, who has gotten through the years with pleasure. "Go into the study. I'll make some coffee."

"*Gut, gut,*" he said. "The women—they bought you coffee."

"Yes, yes I saw it there on the shelf," she said, faltering now in her grim annoyance at the congregation's patronage. "That was very thoughtful of them." She wheeled around at further knocking on the door, and the old man accompanied her as she opened it to the elders. They filed in, solemn as pallbearers, and Claus began his introductions with a handsome blond farmer named Henry Ketter. Letty found his hand pleasingly rough and sturdy.

"This is Herman Johns," Claus continued. "He's the one I was telling you about—married to one of the Paff girls." Herman was red-faced, easy among men. Next came a thin, sickly man named Myron Koch. "He's the druggist," said Claus gaily. "Sells everything from rat poisoning to chocolate sodas—ain't that right, Myron?"

Claus was still turned, waiting for a response from Myron,

which didn't come, when Hans Albrecht stepped up to Letty and introduced himself. "Welcome to Kaleburg, Mrs. Kallsen," he said, and Letty was surprised by his courteous manner. He wore overalls like any other farmer, but there seemed to be something special, even extraordinary, about him.

Bill Wolbers, bringing up the rear, apologized for those who couldn't come. "But you'll be meeting them before long."

Letty seated the men in the study; they found chairs in a half-circle near the windows. "I can't remember your names— and I might forget your faces at first," she said, smiling, "but I'll come to know you at last." And even as she spoke she knew that the mere presence of these men had already turned her bitter heart half sweet again; she almost hated herself for giving in this easily, for responding to the excitement of new people, a new place, and new stories to hear about them. She returned to the kitchen, where the coffee was steaming on the stove, and then she remembered Vernon. "Ah, if those men only knew what's up *there*!" She lifted her eyes. Then she tried to shut him from her mind.

When she entered the study a few minutes later with the cups and saucers on a tray, Bill Wolbers asked, "Did Reverend go out for a walk?"

"Oh, no," murmured Letty, and she felt her ears grow hot. "There's no milk or cream," she said to all of them. "Will black coffee be all right? I'll bring sugar." They squeaked their chairs and shuffled companionably, turning and talking to one another. Claus Schneider, speaking for all of them, assured Letty that they would drink anything.

"Oh, not 'anything,'" Wolbers said. "At least, not in the parson's house." They all laughed.

Letty excused herself and hurried upstairs to Vernon, who still stood staring out of the window. "Come on down," she pleaded, her voice in a hoarse whisper. "They're asking for you. You're just starting on the wrong foot with your stubborn, silly ideas."

He turned coolly and said: "Make them wait."

His outrageous behavior seemed suddenly too much. "Oh, you think you are God, looking there at me. But I know better." She hurried away from him, feeling dizzy, as if she might topple at the head of the stairs and fall into that black pit at the bottom. In a little while she would have a headache, but now, below, guests were waiting. She moved down the steps, thinking, I'm going to rush through those curtains and into their midst, shouting: "Gentlemen! Gentlemen! The minister is mad!"

But her jaw was rigid as she entered the study; she did not dare look at any of them. "He will be down," she said finally. Her comment seemed to hang in the air, and no one said anything. She felt, as she sat on the only remaining chair, that a suspicion of something strange was moving from mind to mind. Now they were all avoiding each other's eyes and hers, too. The atmosphere seemed thick with ominous speculations and brief, unspoken fears. Then at last they heard the first thump on the stairs. "There he is," said Letty with relief. "He's coming now."

But he descended slowly, step by step—noisily, as if he had a wooden leg. She heard him cross the short hall, saw the green plush drapes to the study tremble; then his long thin hands clutched the edge, and with one sweeping motion, he pushed the curtain aside and dramatically revealed himself to them—a strange glint of triumph in his eyes. The druggist jumped to his feet, then Wolbers; then they all stood, as if a prince were entering.

His scheme is working, thought Letty. Now the masquerade has begun.

II  The very next day Claus Schneider returned to pay the Kallsens a visit. He parked his car in the alley and knocked on the back door; on his arm he carried a basket of eggs. Vernon, who saw the old man from the window of his study, was immediately apprehensive. The farmer was altogether too curious. He was peeping through the curtained window of the door even now, trying to look in. Hastily, Vernon reached for his coat, put on his tie, and brushed his hair; he gave himself a solemn appraisal in the kitchen mirror and turned to answer the door, since Letty was downtown shopping.

Claus Schneider shuffled in, full of hearty talk about the weather and questions about the Kallsens. He glanced inquisitively into the study, where Vernon's papers lay spread out, and then he made himself at home by sitting down on a kitchen chair. "Mrs. Kallsen isn't here," began Vernon awkwardly, "but I know she'll appreciate these eggs. She likes to bake."

That small confidence set the old man off about German cooking: peppernuts with bits of citron, which he liked to dunk in his coffee, apple *Pfannkucken*, fritters rolled in powdered sugar, and even marzipan, which he admired because it was German, but really didn't like. "Tastes too much like medicine —cough syrup or something."

Vernon was wondering how to get him out of the house, for the old man had his hands folded comfortably as if he expected to spend the afternoon in this leisurely fashion, getting to know the parson better—picking up a few stories to tell his friends. Deliberately, Vernon moved toward the door. "I'm sorry Mrs. Kallsen isn't home, but I'll tell her you came."

Claus Schneider looked at him in surprise, his blue eyes alert and questioning; then he bobbed his head and smiled. "Well, I just thought I'd drop by with these," he said, getting up. On the steps outside he paused, tamped tobacco into his pipe, and finally confessed that he had no matches. Vernon hunted for kitchen matches inside, and when he returned, Claus was sitting on the lower step; he explained that his game leg hurt when he stood on it too long. With elaborate puffs and extreme concentration, he managed to get the pipe going. "You have no children, huh?" he asked, tossing the match into the spireas.

Vernon was alarmed. He could not tell from Claus' expression or by the casual tone whether the remark was truly accidental, or whether it was a probing inquiry based upon some rumor he had heard about the mess in Stilton. It hardly seemed possible that in such a short time the story of Eugene's death could have caught up with him, unless the synod had been indiscreet—which was not likely. He replied with deliberate unconcern. "No, but we had an adopted son for a while."

"Oh?" asked Claus at once, the smile lingering on his face.

Vernon decided not to hedge. "He did not live," he said simply, sorrow heavy in his voice. He expected such an admission of grief would make Schneider change the subject.

"*Ach*, I'm sorry," said the old man. "That's too bad." He puffed heavily on his pipe, as if aware that he had blundered upon awkward ground. "I've got two boys myself, good boys— the one just a kid—a sort of late surprise." He winked. "The other's grown up. I've often thought, it's hard to tell how things'll turn out. A fella just never knows." He seemed determined to ease Vernon's self-pity by exploring the whole matter. "You maybe don't realize it, but for a farmer to have sons is awfully important. And not just for the extra hands on the plow, either, though that helps. I mean—you have a place in the country, and you like to think it'll always be there. In the family, you know. Ah, yes, this business of kids—you just don't ever imagine the way it'll work out—or what you'll do wrong or the kid'll do wrong. I've been thinking about my neighbor, John Hendricks. He's an old, stubborn man, and I've known him all my life. Then he had this kid, Junior, and what a time those two had—couldn't get on. They're Catholics—not any of our people—but I know 'em awfully well, the way you do with a neighbor, through the years."

Vernon moved back toward the door when Claus looked up at him expectantly, as if about to say a good deal, but wanting to be sure of his audience. Vernon did not wish to appear unfriendly; he just preferred to draw the line between them securely, and so he said nothing—but he moved his hand on the doorknob.

Claus glanced at him sharply again, this time with considerable unease in his eyes. Vernon was irritated by the old man for trying to be as gossipy with him as with the farmers in taverns uptown—eager to pull even the parson into the daily round of claptrap and speculations, surmisals and judgments. Had the religious life of this town sunk so low that even the chief elder held the minister in such slight regard? There was some dignity needed—someone in their midst had to be above them all, if not in fact (for he knew the dangers of sinful pride), at least in their fancy. "Thanks for the eggs, Mr. Schneider," he said with a cordial nod. "And may God bless you."

The old man got up slowly, putting the pipe which was already dead into his pocket. He turned away absently, for although denied the pleasure of telling the new minister about John Hendricks—a man lucky enough to have a good son but who did not know it—Claus continued to think about the tale himself and how it all had started.

The first Hendricks in Kaleburg had been one of the earliest settlers; he bought land from the Illinois Central Railroad, broke the tough sod with a yoke of oxen, built a house and barn with his own hands. He had one son, John, who eventually took over the place. Although the Hendricks fortune mounted, John and Anna had no children, and they grew older. They were like Zachariah and Elizabeth, with no Gabriel appearing before them to announce good news. The turn of the century came, and their lives seemed to hold no promise; they often talked of how much they wanted a son, and Anna even told the priest, the new one who arrived in 1906. The obliging priest arranged for a special blessing from the Pope, and a few months later Anna was definitely pregnant. "John, maybe a boy it is we'll have," she said, overjoyed.

"Yah, maybe," he replied. For twenty years he had hoped for a son to help with chores, feed the chickens, cultivate the garden, and shovel snow from the feed lots. "A boy it might be," he murmured, strangely unmoved at the prospect. A farmer needs sons all right, but they must arrive early, so that when retirement comes a man can turn from the farm with satisfaction, knowing the land will sustain the new generation, and the next, too. But John had worked the years himself, and the farm had prospered; now, ironically, came the son. *Ach*, John thought, something will be wrong with the child. He'll be overripe, having lain in the womb so long.

Even at Junior's birth he could not match Anna's joy, so filled was he with thoughts of having to lease the farm to renters before Junior would be grown. It would not be long now until John's retirement, and until then Junior would be a toy, a plaything, a diversion; he would not count for anything but a damned lot of trouble.

During all the long years on the farm, Anna had had troubles, but she would not mind this new kind. Her thick cheeks and wrinkled forehead pressed in upon her once-bright eyes; her hair had grayed, her limbs were heavy. On the horizon of her life the massive grove that bracketed the farm stood guard. The cottonwoods rattled in the summer breeze, swarmed black and alive in fall when the grackles flocked, gleamed stark in the winter moonlight. But in the spring the trees pushed out green leaves, and she had never known that joy until April of her forty-first year when Junior was born.

Fatherhood annoyed John. Babies cry, yes, he knew, but not like this one; not day and night. "What's the matter with it, anyhow?" he would shout in fury.

"*Ach*, shut up. He's just hungry," she would reply.

And then more rich whole milk would be set aside. John had always been careful about milk. Right at the beginning he had trained Anna to drink coffee black in order to save cream for the can he carried daily to town; she got used to using skim milk for cooking, or water; and they managed without butter entirely for the sake of creamery checks. Now the little one nipped on a big bottle all day, and Anna gulped down large glassfuls at each meal. "It's what the doctor says," she told John calmly.

"*Ach*, I don't pay that doctor if he keeps talking," said John.

Anna suggested they buy an icebox to keep food fresh longer. "You don't want the baby to get sick on spoiled milk, do you? What do we do when summer comes, huh?" And although John replied, "We never got sick before," she quickly said, "You ain't no baby, though. You don't know how easy a baby gets sick. We ought to have an electric icebox, that's what— like the Schneiders. Claus had the electric run straight to his farm. That high line goes buzzing by and we fall around in the dark still. And don't tell me you ain't got money for it. I know you never give me none to spend and you wouldn't let go a penny yourself—so it must be somewheres."

Old John shook his head, for in a torrent it came, and now Anna sounded like every other woman. She would soon be having him junk the buggy; next she would want an automobile.

"What are we saving money for, huh? If not for Junior?"

He did not try to answer; he walked away. Secretly Anna rummaged through his bureau drawers, hunting for his bank books. At last she found them and sat down with a pencil. The figures, adding up to a row of six digits, made her lean against the bedpost to calm her excited heart. She examined her figures again—oh, she had made a bad error, but the total was still enormous. "Ah, we are rich, rich!" she murmured, thinking of her poor dead mother who had urged her to marry John, those many years ago. "Sure, John Hendricks never cracks a smile," the old lady had said, "but you marry him, Anna, and you'll be rich some day. You see."

She thought of this as she bent over the washboard with diapers, carried kerosene lamps from room to room, and climbed up and down the cellar stairs with milk from the cooler. Then the unbearable pains from milk leg forced Anna to bed. If the chickens were not to starve, John had to feed them, and if the eggs were not to be broken and lost, he had to gather them. If he wanted supper he could cook it; if he liked a clean house, he might sweep it. Anna had brought forth Junior, and with the baby she withdrew to the bedroom.

Beaten at home, John found no solace in Meecher's Taproom, where his cronies still snickered behind their hands and burst into red-faced laughter over jokes he couldn't quite hear. They wondered how he had finally managed to produce the rascal. "Was you gone long from home?"

At last John made only business calls in town and avoided Meecher's, hoping that fresh daily gossip would finally obscure interest in his virility. But when he stopped for a beer weeks later, his neighbor, Claus Schneider, shouted to everybody: "Here comes that hot young steer!" The men at the card tables all roared with laughter.

"Hey, John, where you been?" someone called. "At it again?"

Stonily, John drank his beer at the bar, drained the last drop, and set it down with a ringing thud. Merriment washed him into the street, and he pulled his cap over his ears. Other men sleep with their wives and have children, he thought. Claus Schneider himself had been late in fathering Sammy. Why did people have to pick on him?

He decided to put in more work on the farm. After buying ten new milk cows and additional cattle for fattening, his morning chores lasted until the sun was high. Although John now rose at four-thirty instead of five, he wondered in a moment of self-pity how he would manage during the harvest season. Somehow, he planted his crops and during June plowed corn until the moon rose. Even on Sundays after mass he would pull on his work clothes and march out to harness the horses. In this way he evaded the baby's screams and the smoldering eyes of Anna.

In his absence Junior rollicked and laughed in the house, and Anna sang while she worked. As the boy grew older, they played nonsense games between the rooms, peeping at each other through cracks in the doors and hiding behind coats in the closet. Once John surprised them in the midst of their fun. "What's the matter with you?" he frowned, staring at both of them. And the house grew quiet and sober again.

Junior lived in a world of bright greens over-arched by blue; among the golden flowers Anna planted in profusion around the house, he played contentedly with the dog, cats, and his pet Cornish chicken. But their relationship seemed inverted; it was as if Junior were somehow their pet. Other farm animals were hostile: the horses lifted their manes with animosity when

Junior approached; if he tried to cross an open field, the cattle charged; and the pigs would stampede if he neared. These, his father's animals, put him in his place.

When Junior reached school age, Anna dressed him in new overalls, fixed a lunch box and Thermos containing chocolate milk, and sent him into a world in which she feared he would not fare well. From the first day on, the neighborhood boys, Irving Johns and Robert Schneider, lay in wait for him. Junior's truncated body, the odd flap of his legs as he walked, and the peculiar shape of his head either drew sympathy or ridicule and torture. Miss Beason, the young teacher, pitied and tried to reassure him. In art class she frequently praised his work. "Very pretty, Junior," she would say, looking at his bursts of crayon, his profusion of wild black lines in a blossom of color.

As the years passed, John's powers did not wane, and he did not wish to retire at the customary age. He began to hope he still might have time to train Junior to manage the farm; therefore, each summer the boy trudged at the old man's heels, silently awaiting instruction. Junior never complained; he never dared to ask questions; and he never understood. John might command, "Lift up that tongue, and when I back up the horses, push down the pin." But Junior heard only "back up the horses," and he watched fearfully as the towering thighs and clumping hoofs edged closer; then he would drop the tongue and run. "Damn it, come back here!" John would shout. *"Tuffelbux!"* They would try again.

Summer bondage was predictable, but in school Junior could not count on the outcome of a single day. Once when he had to stay after dismissal to make up a lesson, the older boys lay in wait for him in Schneider's grove. At first Junior tried to fight them off; then he submitted and allowed them to strip off his overalls and run away with them. In the dust of the road he listened to the muffled tramp as they disappeared, laughing, in the mauve, cooling dusk. With just his shirt on,

Junior crawled into a culvert under the road and waited, shivering, until dark. A noisy automobile passed overhead, trembling the earth and sending down a fine shower of dust to melt into mud on his tear-stained face.

After dark when he pushed open the kitchen door at home, both parents were sitting at the bare table, gazing at their knuckles. "*Ach*, you at last!" Anna leapt up, incredulity and relief on her face.

"Come in here," John ordered. Junior cowered behind the door until John pulled him into the light. "My God, where are your pants, huh?" He reached for the razor strop on the washroom hook. "Answer me, huh?"

"Oh, John, don't do it. He's just come home."

John gruffly shoved Junior out the door and down the path to the chicken barn. "I teach you something yet, *dummkopf*."

"John, John!" screamed Anna. "Not before supper, do you hear? Not before his supper!"

Row upon row of murmuring white hens gazed down disapprovingly at Junior's rear end, bared and vulnerable in the lamplight. When the blows began to fall they clucked and chattered, an amphitheatre of spectators cheering the demonstration.

Junior failed the seventh grade entirely. Though he would never graduate from grammar school, state law required that he attend until age sixteen. Luckily, in his final year he made friends with Joe Clausen, a buck-toothed boy who was also victimized by neighborhood bullies. They poked around creek bottoms, dug up mole caverns, and tried to catch pigeons on the metal hay carrier of the Hendricks' barn. However, Joe Clausen's parents were strict Protestants and frowned upon the friendship, for fear it would somehow contaminate Joe. They gave their son extra work, warned him against Catholics, told him Junior wasn't quite right in the head, and suggested he find some other boy to play with. Junior never understood what had happened, for Clausen couldn't think how to explain. There was simply an end to that friendship.

For Junior's sixteenth birthday Anna decorated an angel-food cake. John, who was unusually genial, presented him with a family pocket watch of gold. "You're a man now. You work like a man, too, now." And so the two of them set off to farm together. Junior learned to lean his head firmly against the cow's coarse hide when milking. Entering the pig pen with a bushel of corn, he would kick the pigs viciously and shout to convince them that he meant business. But the pigs only grunted and tried to knock him off balance; they did not keep their distance as they did with John.

Try as he would, Junior could not conform to John's spare pattern of farm management. He won peace from the hogs' malevolence by feeding them bushels too much. He forgot important details, such as sweeping out the oats wagons after threshing was over for the day. A careful worker could gather a quarter of a bushel, feed it to the chickens, and subtract the amount from their usual rations. Junior was not an efficient milker, either, and he was too generous with the cats. They crowded close to his stool to beg spurts of milk directly from the teats, and John quickly discovered why they were mewing and milling about.

When Junior pitched down hay to the horses and filled their oats boxes, he stayed safely on the other side of the stall. While he was harnessing them, his pseudo-commanding, hysterical shouts echoed through the barn, making them jittery. "Cut out that damn yelling," John would shout from another part of the barn. Junior, angry with the horses for arousing the old man, would scream all the louder or poke them with a pitch fork for punishment—until blood appeared for the flies to feast on.

One evening he entered the horse barn alone after plowing

corn with a team all day. He did not notice that the horses were all loose in their stalls. It was dark and he could never say just what happened, only that suddenly he found himself cut off from the door and in a corner away from the mangers where he might have leapt for safety. One of the beasts began kicking the barn wall, exciting the others. When Junior tried to escape, they reared above him; a glancing blow knocked him to the brick floor. He slipped in fresh manure as he tried to get up and caught another blow from the horse's hoofs.

Anna found him an hour later, a side of his face badly damaged; he lay unconscious for seven hours. His eyesight was impaired, and he lost part of his hearing in one ear; but he lived. "*Ach*, he'll never make a farmer," said John to Anna as they sat on the hard bench in the hospital.

"But he's a good son," said Anna. "What you care if he's a farmer or not? You got plenty of money. You got all the money you'll ever need. Once in a while you got to think of that. We could go to California right now and never lift another finger. We could have gone long ago."

Whenever Anna talked like that, John wondered who would run the farm. Everything he had built would go to ruin with that boy running around. But John could not deny that in many ways Junior was a good son. He did not gamble or waste time with girls, nor did he ever get drunk. Sometimes he went to movies in John's new car, but he always came home early and never discussed what he had seen. You could ask for a lot more in a boy, but perhaps when Junior got older he would learn to farm. John remembered that he, too, was aging; and Anna seemed slower all the time, complaining of rheumatism and pains over her heart. *Ach*, what can you do about it anyway, he thought?

One morning John pulled on his clothes in the darkened bedroom, descended to the basement to start the furnace, and when he came up, found the kitchen cold and lifeless. "Anna!"

he called severely, for this had not happened in all the years they had been married. "Anna, get up!" But she did not move, and he went in to find her dead, the blanket bunched in her hands across her breast. And he had lain half the night beside her when she was no more! She had gone without a call, without a hand out to him for help, not even to ask that the priest be called. She had clutched the blanket instead of his arm. He felt betrayed. At first his shock at her response to death stunned him more than the fact that she was dead. And then he leaned against the bedpost and wept. Anna could not see him now, sobbing on the slippery post, nor would anyone, ever.

The notoriety of death brought neighbors to help with chores and women to cook and clean. Claus Schneider's sons, Sammy and Robert, did the milking, while Henry Ketter fed the pigs and gathered the eggs. Neither John nor Junior were allowed to lose themselves in work, for they were supposed to be idle and completely grief-stricken, although actually they were simply stunned and couldn't think beyond their shock. Catholic friends of the Hendricks family stayed late at night, smoking and telling stories. Not until Anna's burial did the kindly strangers quit the farm; death visited other households, and the comfort bearers moved to new scenes of mourning. When the glib phrases, as easily come by as funeral flowers, had died away, Junior began to realize that none of the condolences helped the loss of his mother herself, and grief was new and bitter. Junior felt that he alone bore the sorrow of Anna's death. His inscrutable father showed no sign of torment, no new expression in the sad eyes; his hunched shoulders were no more burdened than when only the land had put its work upon his back.

But John was troubled; he looked out from the mask of his face at his lonely son and wondered how to act and what to do. For weeks an uncomfortable, unspoken groping existed between

them, and each day the uneasiness ended in John's saying simply, "Yah, well, I think I'll go to bed. You get some sleep,
too." And he clumsily patted Junior's shoulder before he retreated upstairs. He had never returned to the bed where Anna
died.

One day in an effort at companionship, John told Junior,
"I'm going to Detterman's to pick up that cow I bought. Want
to come along?"

Junior nodded, curious about the Detterman farm, which
was several miles away. People said that chickens sat on chairs
in the dining room and that one of the eight children kept a
calf in the pantry. When they arrived, Detterman took John
to the barn and Junior was left alone in the yard to gaze at the
run-down buildings. A few pale children glowered at him from
the windows of the house, and just as he was about to retreat
to the car, Dolores, deputy mother for the younger offspring,
walked barefooted to the pump. She did not glance at him.
Silently, he watched her leap upon the pump handle and ride
it down to the ground. Junior felt he should offer to carry the
water pail back to the house, even if she were a Detterman. But
as he moved forward, she snatched the bucket from the nozzle
and hurried toward the house. The white-faced children, transfixed in the windows, looked triumphant.

A half-minute later Dolores came out on the porch with a
dipperful of water, offering it to him, and she smiled. The children at the windows vanished as he stepped forward to accept it.
"My name's Dolores," she said.

"I'm Junior Hendricks."

"No, you're John Hendricks, Jr."

"Yes, that's it," he admitted, surprised that she knew. He
wondered frantically what to say next, for he was certain he
would never get a chance to talk to her again. He had seen her
too often with good-looking, popular young men in Koch's
drugstore. Perversely, his attention wandered across the yard to

his father, who was haggling with Detterman. He knew John had found some reason for knocking down the original sale price.

But Dolores did not seem to notice his discomfort. She asked how he and his father were managing with Anna gone. What was the house like? Did it have many improvements? Flattered by her interest, Junior told how Anna had fixed up the rooms; she had sewn red and white curtains for the kitchen, and the new linoleum covering the floor had always gleamed. "But it ain't that way any more." As he faltered, Dolores again took over the conversation.

A few minutes later John walked to the car, ready to leave. But before Junior left, Dolores murmured, "You miss your ma, don't you?"

Junior turned away with tear-blind eyes. Dolores, of all the people who had offered sympathy, understood most truly.

Fearing she would surely scorn his attention, Junior did not wish to see her again; but after mass the next Sunday she stopped him outside the church door. "Hey, what's your hurry?" Her hand, raised to anchor her pink hat, seemed to be waving at him in greeting. They talked briefly while the strong March wind flattened against them, and Junior, conscious of the crowd observing them, was irrepressibly proud. But John had gone to the car, and he honked the familiar horn impatiently.

"Let the old man wait," Dolores said, when Junior started to leave.

He stopped. "Yah, why not?"

"He ain't got no place to go but home," she said, and they both laughed.

In early April Junior bought a second-hand car with his savings, and he courted Dolores almost every night. Grooming carefully before leaving the farm, he would stand in front of his dresser mirror, his face turned slightly sideways, in order to obscure the dented forehead. Even without his glasses he could see that his features were regular, his chin strong, and the total effect almost handsome—especially since he had become more muscular in the last few years. He usually put on a suit, and for special dates, rubbed a little perfume on his chin from Anna's old and almost empty bottle.

Each time he drove into the Detterman yard, Dolores came fleeing from the house. Never did she invite him in, nor did he wish to see her surrounded by Dettermans; Dolores was so different. He did not take her to the Hendricks' farm, either, until one day when John had gone to Missouriville to buy fattening cattle. Junior noted her eagerness as they drove into the yard, and he was proud to show her his house. She surveyed it carefully, and when she had seen it all, said: "Yes, I feel at home here. I think maybe you'd better ask me to stay." Junior put his arm around her and they kissed, standing in the middle of the yard with the dog and cats looking on. As they broke apart slowly, Junior heard the crows calling back and forth across the grove.

"But—but I don't want to tell *him*," Junior said slowly.

Dolores seemed unconcerned. "Okay, let him find out when he hears the banns read."

"I don't think I should wait that long."

"You're of age, ain't you? You can do what you want."

"Yah, I can do what I want all right," he replied.

But before the official announcement, news of the engagement spread widely. Although friends of John wondered if he had been told, they were too embarrassed to say anything. They thought it merciful that Anna had not lived to see her son disgrace the family name. Since age fourteen Dolores Detterman's romantic career had seemed destined to end in an abrupt marriage and a baby a few months later. She had been out with the town's fastest men, with married men and scoundrels. Her alliance with Junior could only mean that she was angling for the Hendricks fortune; they could not believe Junior had gotten her into trouble.

Junior did not sit with John on the Sunday the announcement was made, but his father accosted him outside the church door. His fingers trembled with rage as he lifted his hand to admonish the boy. "What money you got to get married on, huh?" Now no Anna restrained him. Let everyone know how he felt about it so that none should think less of *his* honor. "Yah, you think you're old enough to get married, but how're you supporting a wife, I ask you?" He clutched Junior's arm. "You think I take her on, you got another think coming!"

Dolores intervened and pulled Junior away without looking at John. The newly engaged couple did not wait around for customary congratulations but hurriedly got into Junior's car. "What did he mean, you ain't got any money?" she asked. "The Hendricks have lots of money, and I guess you can support a wife if you want to."

But Junior confessed that he had no money of his own, except what Anna had left him from her father's estate. "I don't know how much there is." John had invested it in savings bonds.

"You just better find out about that," she said excitedly. "How do you know he didn't take care of your money so well that it's all *his* now?"

Junior stared in surprise at his future bride. The Hendricks didn't quarrel over money among themselves like some families did, he thought. Not like maybe the Dettermans would. Her hard bright eyes looked oddly alien; the fine-boned, un-Germanic face was that of a stranger. He wondered what he was getting into. Sensing his coolness, Dolores brought up the memory of his mother. "She slaved and fed him all her life, and what did she get out of it? You think the old tightwad made things easier? He didn't care nothing about her, and he don't care nothing for you, either. It's only him he thinks of, and always has."

"I'll stand up for what's mine," Junior said. "You'll see."

But courage was not needed, for John turned over the bonds without argument. "You're a damned fool to go cashin' them in before you need to," was all he said. He did not realize the extent of the wedding preparations. The expenses for Dolores' trousseau, the bridesmaids' costumes, flowers, and refreshments for the reception were all falling to Junior, since the Dettermans had no money. He had also engaged a danceband and had rented the Cornflower Ballroom for the traditional public wedding dance.

John assumed complete indifference to the proceedings, even on the very morning of the wedding. Before they started chores, Junior asked, "You're coming to church this morning, aren't you?"

John replied, "Hell no." He marched abruptly to the barn, the milk pails clanking at his sides.

Junior lifted his head to breathe in the cool dawn air. His secret fear of a last-minute obstruction evaporated with the dew, and now he reveled in wedding bliss. After the honeymoon he would bring his bride home, and they would share the big master bedroom upstairs that had always been a spare room. Since Anna's death John had been sleeping there, but Junior had persuaded his father to exchange rooms with him. "The double bed you won't be needing anyhow." Now with sudden urgency, he hurried upstairs to wrestle with the sheets in making the bed. He tucked in the corners neatly, tossed the patchwork quilt across, turned down the top, and in an agony of anticipation, threw himself upon the bed, mussing all his careful work. He lay there, staring at the ceiling, filled with a mastery he had never known before. A few minutes later he sprang up to seek his image in the mirror, yearning to confirm his joy.

Then he raced down the stairs to slop the hogs before his father noted his absence.

Of the wedding itself, only the priest's white hands, the crimson runner down the aisle, and Dolores, mysterious behind the white lace veil, penetrated his dazed senses. Then they were chauffeured with horns blaring through the streets of the town, and he sat erect beside Dolores in the back seat of a festooned car. They were toasted at the wedding breakfast held in the church parlors, and afterwards, Dolores showed Junior the array of presents on card tables, while a ring of people exclaimed at proper intervals. Through a window Junior saw men clustered on the lawn outside, and by their rapt faces he knew they were telling lewd stories.

That evening Dolores led Junior onto the glazed dance floor, and as the band played "I Love You Truly" in waltz-time, his feet stumbled around under her voluminous satin gown. They were all alone on the wide floor until the best man broke from the rim of watchers to cut in and pin a dollar on her skirt. Then the ushers, each in his turn, bestowed a dollar bill, and soon everyone was cutting in. The music increased in tempo, the hall echoed with the shuffling throng, and Junior watched the men flock to dance, if only for a moment, with his newly won bride. He was proud of her popularity but gazed rather somberly as some partners embraced and kissed her. Several five- and ten-dollar bills fluttered from her gown, and he wondered what they signified.

After waiting until they had all had a chance to honor her with bills, Dolores said to Junior, "Let's be on our way." They left town with Dolores counting the sheaf of greenbacks in her hand. "Just think, one hundred and twelve dollars!" More booty than any bride had ever received.

Junior remembered uneasily all the men who had taken a kiss after pinning on bills. "Just think how much that band cost," he said. "And rent for the hall took it up to three hundred and fifty dollars. So I guess we don't have anything to feel so good about."

Once settled in their guest lodge in the Black Hills, Junior knew that two weeks was not enough time. He did not wish to return to the farm, ever, and he told Dolores as much. He meant it as a compliment to her and their married bliss, but she reminded him of his duty almost at once. "*Ach*, you're like the old man," he teased.

Dolores was restless, eager to start fixing over the house, anxious to cook in her own kitchen. "And it'll be so good, not having to look after all them snotty kids. You don't know what it was like—even if they are my own family."

Junior's dread of returning sharpened with every mile on the way back. When they drove into the familiar farmyard, the strange quiet of the place disturbed him; he remembered he had not spoken to John about taking care of the livestock, milking the cows, or anything—he had simply left. An image of starving, gasping animals in the barn filled his head so powerfully that he forgot to carry his bride over the threshold in his haste to run to the barn. He flung open the doors and leapt in; the animals, never fat, stood contented, insolent, and inquisitive as Junior gaped at them. The udders of the milk cows were slack.

As Junior came out of the barn he saw the kerosene light glow warmly behind the curtains in the kitchen. With sudden panic he imagined his gruff father confronting Dolores, or stepping furtively toward her out of the dark shadows. He ran to the house and threw back the kitchen door. Dolores looked at him casually and lit another lamp. "He's not here?" Junior asked.

"The old man? I don't know. The house seems empty."

They searched upstairs and found none of John's belongings.

The single bed in the little room had been stripped of blankets and linen. "He's moved out!" she smiled.

"He's gone all right," Junior replied, subdued, for the victory had been won too easily. He carried the suitcases in, and after guiding Dolores to the bedroom, closed the door firmly and took her in his arms.

The next morning in the barnyard, old John, who had driven out from town, only nodded a greeting. "Don't give the cows any more silage," he said. "I fed them plenty already."

They both planted corn in the field that day, crossing near each other as they moved up and down the long rows with slow teams; but not a word was said. When they watered the horses at noon, Junior suggested to his father, "Why not come on up to the house for dinner?"

"Yah, you think I wouldn't? You don't get rid of me that easy."

During the meal Dolores asked John about farm affairs, and she didn't take offense by his curt replies. She learned he was living above the Gambles store in town. "That's nice and handy to Meecher's Taproom," she said.

"You think I want to spend all my time drinking in there? I ain't that way yet."

"You want some more coffee?" Dolores rose to get the pot.

"Naw." The old man hunched closer to his plate, his hand splayed across his cup.

Although no open quarrels developed, Dolores complained to Junior that his father was depressing. "If he's retired, why does he come poking around here for?"

"Well, it's his place. I just work for him."

"It's yours, too," she said. But as Dolores questioned further, Junior told her he had made no specific salary arrangement with his father.

"When we need money, we just got to ask him for it," Junior

said. In fact, since he had only a few dollars left in cash, Junior planned to request money for grocery buying on Saturday.

But when he approached John, the old man asked coldly, "How much you need?"

"I don't know. How much do groceries generally cost? You always paid for 'em."

"Well, now you'll find out, won't you?" He smiled bitterly as he doled out a few dollars—much too little, as Junior and Dolores discovered when they got to Schmidt's store.

During the following week a settlement was reached. John agreed that Junior and Dolores could have all income from the produce, and the more frugal they were with cream, butter, and eggs, the more money they would make. In this way John felt that the girl would be trained to cook more sensibly, and he was in fact doing his son a good turn. Although Dolores objected, she took up the challenge, and pinched, saved, and carefully marketed everything she could. However, prices were poor, for the depression was becoming severe, and she had nothing left to put aside. "We've got to look to the future," she kept telling Junior. "We can't go on from hand to mouth. If he had a hired man he would have to pay regular wages, so why don't he pay anything to you?" In fact, she deliberated, since Junior was his only son, the least John should do would be to share-rent. Then if crops were good the profits would be high; if they were bad, there would be no money coming their way anyhow.

But when John heard her scheme he shouted, "*Ach*, what next? You don't fool me this easy." He scowled at both of them for days and refused to talk. At meals Dolores cheerfully carried on a bright conversation, and unlike Anna, was not daunted by the tension. She purposely served the old man small portions of creamed corn-and-liver, knowing he liked it but would be too proud to ask for more. A week later with no warning, John abruptly announced, "All right, we go fifty-fifty if you want. I didn't give no wedding present yet. This'll be the wedding present from me."

One Sunday after church a friend said to Junior, "Don't see you very much. How're you gettin' along? I see you're puttin' on weight, so I guess married life agrees with you."

He told Dolores what had been said and teased her, observing that she, too, was putting on weight. "Shouldn't eat my own cookin', I guess," she replied.

They joked at mealtimes about reducing until Dolores uncomfortably changed the subject. Like all women, Junior thought, she didn't want to be told by her husband that she was losing her figure. Still, he did not want her to get big so that they would look funny together as a couple. Of course, it occurred to him that Dolores's size might indicate something else. He didn't know how to ask. It was the wife's job to tell things like that, to start knitting and hint around. He remembered that several times soon after their marriage, when she was washing breakfast dishes at the sink she had taken ill and rushed off to the bathroom. He had thought nothing of it then, and Dolores had only said, "It ain't anything to worry about. Something I ate, I guess."

Lately, she had been taking afternoon naps, and he encouraged her to rest. "You got to take care of yourself, you know," he said significantly, waiting for her to admit that she was with child.

"I'll get along," Dolores simply murmured, and he finally left her.

When silage-cutting season arrived in September, Junior suggested to John that this year all the neighbors should go home for supper, instead of eating where the day's work had been done. "You get to do your chores while it's light, then. And nobody cares that much about eating supper away from home."

Since the Hendricks were scheduled to have their silage cut

first, John would have to broach this inhospitable suggestion to Claus Schneider, Herman Johns, Henry Ketter, and the other neighbors. He scowled. "We always eat supper where we are. I never heard anybody before say we shouldn't."

Finally Junior came forth with his real reason. "Dolores ain't feelin' too well these days. I don't see why she should have to get big suppers ready."

"Yah, and I notice she ain't lookin' so thin, either," John replied.

"It's none of your business," Junior said hotly, sensitive to the ridicule that lurked behind his words.

"Yah, I guess she couldn't have silage cutters," John said sarcastically. "Havin' a baby any day now, huh?"

"And so what to you?"

"The fastest breeding I ever heard of, that's all."

"Yah, I don't waste no time." Pride of coming fatherhood made him boastful. "I don't waste time—not like you!" It came out almost before he realized what he meant.

For a moment John was stunned and did not move. Then he slapped Junior across the face. "Damn *Kind*, you forget your mother's memory quick. But I don't."

"I don't forget nothing," Junior shouted, stepping back. "And I won't forget this." He rubbed his cheek. "We have a baby and it's none of your damned business. And if we have one right away I'm glad, by God!"

"*Dummkopf*, you don't know what you're all about. You can just get off the place with that woman. And you better think of where you're going, because you're not stayin' on this farm after March 1. I'm hiring new renters. I have enough of the both of you, by God."

When Junior told Dolores about the flare-up, she finally admitted that indeed a child was on the way. He was careful not to mention how harshly John had spoken of her, nor could he understand the severity. "The old man must be gettin' cracked, that's all I can figure." Although all farm leases expired in spring, Junior almost wished that they could leave now.

"Sure, you don't pay any attention to him," said Dolores. "He's sour about everything."

"I'm glad we're going to have a baby, and I don't care who knows."

But Dolores was not so proud, and the more evasive she became on the subject, the more tenderly did Junior help her with household chores. He knew she was sensitive about her size, for she kept telling him that some women get big awfully early and stay that way the whole time. "I don't mind," he said, smiling. "I don't mind in the least. Just so long as I know it ain't the cooking. Else I'd be having to buy new overalls for myself."

They did not speak of the future, where they would go after March 1, or how they would afford the child. During corn picking the men worked late in the fields, and Junior was too tired at night to want to talk much. But whenever they were alone, Dolores' dark eyes widened if he neared, and she would try to get away, as though fearing he would molest her. Her behavior was part of the peculiarities of pregnancy, he thought, and did not brood. But once, after she had gone up to bed alone, he did not allow enough time to pass before ascending the stairs. She was half undressed when he opened the door, and she screamed, "Get out of here! Get out!"

He did not enter the room at all that night. As he lay on the couch in the living room, the old awareness of his physical repulsiveness came back to haunt him. He wondered again how Dolores, who had been so beautiful, could have accepted him in marriage. Surely pregnancy with its illness and anxiety had awakened her regrets. And so the product of the love they had enjoyed these last brief months would come at last to split them. The child would mark the end and not the beginning. He tried to stop his thoughts. For the baby's sake he must not predict these things. He would think, rather, of joy for the coming child; he hoped, above all, for a son.

One noon before the end of corn picking, Junior returned to the house to find Dolores writhing on the bed in labor. "Oh God, call a doctor!" she shouted.

He raced downstairs to tell John he would not go to the field that afternoon. His father sat at the table, hands folded on the oilcloth. The old man was not excited by the news. "You call the midwife and it'd be more like it."

Junior grasped the back of a kitchen chair in sudden rage at the obdurate old man. "Get out of this house. You go get your dinner in town!"

John rose slowly to his feet. Only his eyes, quickened in anger, betrayed his emotions. "I hear no more of this talk! You let her have the bastard right upstairs and you tell me to get out of my house. You think because I'm your father I got to put up with you. Well, I don't. I tell you now I don't think of you any more. I don't care where you go or what happens to you or how many bastards that woman tells you are yours." John stepped forward, and a sudden tremor ran through his body. He leaned heavily against the table and said more quietly, "Dumb-ox, can't you hear her scream?"

Junior reeled with numb steps toward the stairs. He knew he must hurry to the hospital; the rest could all come later. John had gone when he re-entered the kitchen with Dolores. He half-carried her to the car and then drove hard all the way to the hospital, with only Dolores' low moan speaking the agony of the moment.

"It's premature," he apologized to the nurse when he brought in Dolores. The nurse's professional glance stopped him from further comment, and Dolores was rushed to the delivery room.

Finally, with hours of empty waiting ahead of him, Junior abandoned all attempts at self-deceit. The truth was a fact that would parade before the world this afternoon. But no feeling of anger or revenge stirred within him. He knew he should hate someone, himself most of all, for failing to heed warnings from his father and friends. Disregarding all, he had married her and reaped an interlude of happiness, an idyl falsely come by and now already past. He knew himself again, the old familiar self alone in an anchorless haze. Now he had come home.

He thought of all the people in Kaleburg meeting in taverns, parked cars, and grocery-store aisles, their heads together as they counted the months on their fingers. He saw the snap and flick of each finger as it sprang from the closed hand to shame him. And he heard them: "She knew it all along. She must have. Wasn't it March when she first latched on to him? No wonder they went to the altar in April, when there wasn't no time to waste."

Some would laugh and slap their thighs, "That poor son-of-a-bitch! How do you suppose he felt when he found out?"—not knowing that in the waiting room of the hospital he sat calmly empty of hate or anger. Since he had not felt happiness to be his right, he could not protest its loss. All the time at the base of his foolish dream had lain the dormant knowledge that it couldn't be true.

Thinking of the men in Meecher's Tap, chuckling over the news, he wished the ridicule were his alone, for he could bear it; but he cringed for his father's sake, for the smirched Hendricks name. Some of his mother's old friends, with sad but kindly looks, would indicate that though this had happened they still stood by. The thought of their pity angered him.

It was Dolores he should hate, not friends who forgave. She had kept the secret hidden for months behind her dark eyes. She had in fact spared him her confession and deceived him with joy. Each day she had been bound by her guilt he had been free to love. How could he hate her? If she had told him of the child before the wedding, would he have married her? He knew the Hendricks' pride too well. It would not have happened; nothing would have happened; there would only have been corn, cattle, and the empty house, and John laboring all day long without stop: that would have been his summer, not the quiet nights on the screened-in porch.

Two hours later the nurse touched his shoulder. A boy, she said. Seven pounds, one ounce. She beckoned him to follow, but he had no desire to see the child, no wish to have his mock-parenthood thrust upon him. "This way, please," the nurse insisted, and he complied.

Junior approached the glass partition indifferently, for the child seemed almost irrelevant—until he saw the red, raging infant, and then unexpected, uncontrollable pity overcame him. The nurse held up the basket, nodded and smiled, but Junior turned away and began to weep: the terrible sadness of birth, the old, old wrinkled pain on that screaming face. Now it would all start for this child that was not his son, but part of him, still. And Junior knew what John must have felt as he looked through this same window twenty-two years ago with sorrow.

Had Dolores' moment of pleasure been worth all this? A slow anger uncovered itself within him as he pictured her, thoughtless and wanton with someone he did not know nor cared to know. Who would speak for the child who had been the outcome? Junior rubbed his eyes, straightened up, and compassion for Dolores passed from him. Nothing she had endured, or Junior now endured, equaled what the child would have to endure and never understand.

The nurse told him he could see his wife now, and he followed her down to the maternity ward with no notion of what he would do or say. Dolores lay buried in the sheets, her dark hair long and straight against the white pillow. Her nervous animal eyes watched him with fear. "I saw the baby," Junior said, stepping close to the bed. Feigning weariness, Dolores pulled the sheet over her eyes, but Junior knew that neither of them could ever hide from the existence of the child. He drew back the hem and faced her without enmity. "He's a nice little boy," he said deliberately, "our son."

At first her wan face revealed no comprehension, so stunned was she by his response. Then relief focused into a smile and she struggled to free her arms from the sheets. She stretched up to embrace him. For a moment he hesitated—from this side of the bed the scar tissue of his caved-in temple lay naked to her gaze. His impulse was to draw back. Suddenly he bent closer, with confidence that she would not be repulsed—now or ever—and acknowledged the gratitude in her eyes with a kiss.

Although John settled on a new renter to take over the farm the next season, he learned in Meecher's Tap that Junior had not leased another place. The boy appeared to be unconcerned, wrapped up as he was in the new baby and helping Dolores in the house. During the winter John spent less time on the farm, but he did not intend to let matters go along entirely unwatched, for Dolores might get Junior to sell cattle on the side or ship some chickens to market before they left. When February ended and no moving van arrived, John began to wonder if they really meant to go. For one indecisive paternal moment he almost changed his mind. But the new renters would move in next day. What had been done was done.

He lurked around the barn late in the afternoon and watched Junior and Dolores pack the car with personal belongings. He had intended to stand close by to see that they didn't load up any of Anna's things, but he did not. The job only took an hour, and when they were ready, Dolores with the baby climbed into the front seat. Junior looked around and saw John standing in the barnyard. His father took a few steps forward, then stopped. After pausing uncertainly, Junior waved his hand like a child saying goodbye. He got in, the car lurched forward (Junior always threw in the clutch too quickly), and they were off. Long after the sound of the automobile had died among the hills, John remained where he stood. He had just seen a Hendricks, his own flesh and blood, leave the land where he had been born and raised. At last John spat upon the ground and went off to put away the horses who stood near, watching, too.

John showed the new tenants around next day and was impressed by their business-like ways. But in succeeding weeks they complained about everything: the man wanted better machinery, the woman a modern house. Late in May after an absence of several days, John discovered with shock that the tenant had plowed up the ten acres of virgin pasture land south of the stockyards. Already half of it was planted in corn. This last acreage to be ravaged by the plow had been set aside by John's pioneer father to be used as pasture for the livestock. Where would the animals go now? With rage and dismay, he stumbled across the moist black earth to the man planting corn. "Stop it! Stop it! What're you doing to my land?" he shouted, even though he knew it was all too late.

The tenant laughed and promised to grow corn ten feet tall on this strip. "It'll be the best damn corn you've ever seen. Just wait."

"*Ach*, I waited too long to tell what I think of you. First this is wrong and then that. You got no more sense than— than I don't know what." Junior would have known better; the boy had done some crazy things, but none of it had mattered much. Not like this, which could never be undone. "I don't want you back next year, you hear? And that's the end of it."

"What makes you think I'd want to come back? I've had more trouble with you than any man in the county. And if you think you'll get another renter easy, you better think again. After what I'm going to tell 'em!"

"*Ach*, I'll get my son."

"You had him once," came the snickering reply.

John turned away abruptly, for what did he care if rumors had gone about? Dealings with his son remained his own business, and all the talk in Kaleburg couldn't stop him from getting his son back on the farm, if he wanted to. But the more John thought, the more uncertain he became that this would be possible. He had no notion of Junior's whereabouts and no way of finding him except to let others know he was seeking the boy.

Stifling pride, he casually asked the men in Meecher's next day if they had heard any news of Junior. Claus Schneider remembered having seen him in Missouriville some time ago but did not know if he were living there now. John hung around the tavern more in succeeding days, and at last John Leech reported that Junior was working in a ball-bearing factory in the city.

John, who had never seen the inside of a factory, couldn't imagine Junior in such a place. "That so?"

"Yah, and he's joined a union, too," added Leech. "You know that?"

"Making pretty good money, huh?" John asked.

"I guess! You know what them factory workers get." A rumble of assent passed around the card table. Junior was obviously doing well.

Making good wages, being on his own, why should Junior ever want to return to the farm, John wondered? And then there was Dolores—and the baby. He dropped his hands and walked slowly out of the tavern, despondent at the thought of trying to revoke the past. It was like wishing Anna back, or Junior a boy again, or that this day be like the old days.

Abandoning hope of reaching Junior, John spent an inactive summer in town, and he noticed that even the calluses on his palms were turning soft. The brown stain, burnt into the backs of his hands by years of summer sun, began to fade. Still, he preferred to ignore what was going on at the home place rather than fight with the tenant again. To John's surprise the oats yield ran high, and after threshing season the renter efficiently presented his accounts and paid John the half due him. John endorsed the check, deposited the money in his savings account. The whole transaction took less than an hour— this was his only contact with the harvest. In the fall would come silage cutting and then corn picking, but John would experience them only from a distance. The reaping of crops was no longer something to anticipate, for it had little connection with his life. Impulsively, he withdrew the oats money he had just deposited in the bank and gave it to the church.

The priest, in accepting the check, had this advice: "Now you must make up with your boy. You're getting to be an old man, and the sun should not set on your anger."

With an ancient premonition, John knew the import of the priest's words; his heart fluttered in protest, but only for a moment. On this earth all living things are born, grow old, and die. "Yah, but the boy is gone," he said slowly.

"You try to find him," said the priest.

Upon leaving the parish home John stood for a moment at the bottom of the steps and watched a group of children playing on the bare ground of a field next to the parochial school. How they shouted and ran, laughed and fought, as they scrambled after the ball! And if in the heat of the game they surged toward him, they would run him down without thinking; and wasn't all of life like that? He found a certain pleasure just in watching their restless movements, as if he would warm his own stiff limbs over the fire of their energy. He clasped his soft hands together, but he hated the weakness he felt in them. The freshly ironed overalls he wore were almost a sacrilege, too—

a work garment that would never be soiled by work, as silly as the miniature suits boys wore, like little businessmen on the way to make-believe stores.

Wearily, he walked toward Meecher's, knowing already whom he would find there, what each would say, and how all would avoid recognizing the fact that they were bound together in a gentle day-by-day killing of time, which seemed ironically to be the one thing they had left in great abundance. But if John could find his son, install him on the farm, and help him get started running the place—that would be a mission to fill the precious days he had left.

In the afternoon he drove to Missouriville and stopped at the LeHigh plant. Conquering timidity, he entered the large brick building with its windows painted blue and asked in the personnel office if he might speak to Junior Hendricks. A clerk checked the name on a spindle and sarcastically emphasized the "Junior" as she asked twice for the spelling. "I'm sorry, he's not on the payroll here. Let me check the records." She found that he had left three months ago, leaving no address. "We closed down part of the plant then. You might try the Lendux company down the block. Some of the men found work there."

"Yah, I'll try," said, John, shuffling out.

But at the nearby factory he learned nothing. A kindly secretary suggested he look in the telephone book for Junior's home address, and John found a Carl Hendricks and a Myron Hendricks, but no Junior. Could the boy have changed his name entirely, in his disgust? On an impulse he checked "Detterman," but there was none in the book. Perhaps he did not have a phone, or he might live in one of the suburbs across the Missouri River. John drove around to all the nearby towns and checked phone books, but by evening he still had no clue, and he was very weary. He did not like to drive at night, and so instead of returning to Kaleburg, he took a room in a downtown hotel located next to a large department store. Shoppers in town for the day always sat in the lobby and waited for each other. Many times in the past he himself had arrived from the stockyards to find Anna there, ready to go home. That evening he remained in the familiar lobby until quite late, and one man who visited with him for an hour suggested he try the post office in the morning; they might have his son's change-of-address card on file.

But when the post office opened, John was told, "Try the police."

"He won't be on their books," John affirmed sternly, certain that Junior had done nothing wrong. These city people had strange ways; they would as soon spit on you as speak.

The postal clerk laughed. "Missing Persons Bureau, I meant."

"Yah, that's a thought," said John, and he walked down the street to the police station.

He passed from an ordinary uniformed cop to the gray-haired chief sergeant, but none of them could quite understand what he was after. "Are you bringing charges against this Junior Hendricks, or what?"

"Oh, no, no charge," said John, solemnly shaking his head. "I'm his father." They obligingly looked through their records, but they could not help him. John thought to himself as he headed back to the hotel that probably in the end he would be on his own in this search. He viewed the hotel lobby as a kind of crossroads for the whole surrounding country, and sooner or later everyone passed the corner. If Junior were anywhere in the vicinity, at some time or other John would spot him, provided he were patient and kept an alert eye. He bought a razor, brush and soap, and a few clothes; his daily needs were simple. He planned to stay at the hotel indefinitely.

In the weeks that followed, many Kaleburg people stopped to ask him what he was doing; they feared he had lost his senses and urged him to return to his room above the Gambles store, where at least the village could keep an eye on him. But he shook them off, one by one. He began, finally, to see Junior in every other departing shopper or behind the wheel of a car going slowly by. Several times he rushed out to stop a passer-by whom he thought was Junior, only to return to the lobby, feeling foolish and depressed.

When at last he gave up his watch and returned to Kaleburg, it was because he thought Junior and Dolores might turn up there. He discovered that everyone in town knew he was seeking his son, and any wisp of news would surely reach him. In the meantime, he changed his will, leaving everything to Junior except two thousand dollars in bonds for the church. At confession John felt easier, although he told the priest nothing of the change in his will. How unhappy Father Dohlman would be to learn of that!

Then John questioned Dolores' family, but since only the younger children could read or write, he was not surprised to discover that they had received no word. Each day contained the hope of news; he arose from his bed as easily as if cows were waiting in a dark barn to be milked. He spent his mornings among the players of pinochle and hearts in Meecher's, and in the afternoons he sat on a bench in front of the Farmers Savings Bank and carefully scrutinized each passing car. Not only would he spot Junior should he pass, but any person having heard some news could easily stop and tell him. John Hendricks became as familiar a fixture on Main Street as the barber pole or the café signs; and he looked eagerly into each face he met, waiting.

III 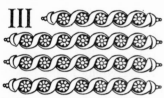 Every day as the time neared for Reverend Vernon Kallsen's walk to the post office, a strange anticipation seized him; no sooner did he leave the parsonage than he began to narrow his eyes and peer nervously down the street to catch sight of the bedraggled man on the bench in front of the bank. He never spoke to John Hendricks, who seemed hardly aware of his presence, beyond the simple greetings of "Good morning" or "Good day," and although Vernon was tempted to linger, he never sat down.

He and Letty had lived nearly two years in Kaleburg, but until this time he had not really felt himself in danger of succumbing to Letty's persistent torment over their past in Stilton and Eugene's death. Though Vernon tried to shut his ears, he learned the story of John Hendricks' estrangement from his son—and the moral lesson it was to all. Letty was relentless in her campaign to bother him because she herself wallowed in the misery of the past; she could not bear to have him free of it—and he was trying to be.

"You see him there? John Hendricks!" she would say whenever they passed along Main Street. "He killed his only son."

"He did not."

"He drove him out—out and away and gone forever. And look how it's killing *him*."

"We don't know anything about it."

"Oh, yes we do—both of us," and her lips would curl in a sly, sadistic smile. "Or don't you think of Eugene any more?"

Again he would tell her, though endless repetitions unfairly seemed to dull the sincerity of his words, that bygones must be bygones; they were here in Kaleburg.

"You think nobody knows what happened? You expect to get away with your crime?"

"Nonsense, and you know it!"

"Oh, we won't try adoption again—I guess not!"

"No indeed, not with you the way you are."

"Yes, turn attention on *me*. Say I'm crazy, but at least you can't say I didn't love Eugene and do everything in my power for him."

"We were both doing our best, trying as hard as we could."

"But you whipped him every other day."

"He needed disciplining for his own good." Then he would point out again, for the hundredth time, that an accident of life—or of death—was not to be misread. There was no point in trying to entangle the survivors in a hopeless web of guilt. Only misguided reasoning could carry her so far as to suggest that he was responsible for Eugene's broken neck.

The trouble was that even as he argued Letty saw through him. She knew he could not actually bring himself to think about the catastrophic end of their boy. And yet the horror of that afternoon two years ago lay just beyond the rim of his mind, like some smoldering granary fire glowing in the night and sending a cloud of ugly smoke across the fairest days. Knowing this, she would be sure to say, each time they saw John Hendricks: "You'll be like that old man there some day —maybe not tomorrow or next year, but eventually. Mark my words."

"Your words as usual outrun your thoughts."

"And your thoughts? Where are they?"

"On my work," he lied. "On all that we have to do here in Kaleburg." But he knew that neither of them had done much. And a call to Christian duty never stopped her; rather, it unleashed a whole set of biting prejudices which were further intended to arouse him, to force him into a posture of clerical absurdity, of stiff-necked self-righteousness; and then she would destroy him with a rattling, mocking laugh.

Vernon did not dare reveal to her the real current of his inner griefs, and she could not forgive him because he did not try. The notebooks in his study were as carefully locked away from her prying gaze as were his daily thoughts. Otherwise, she would have known that he recognized the effect of John Hendricks upon this town and himself. Everyone who sorrowed over missing loved ones saw in John a public image of himself.

One Sunday Vernon contrived a sermon which came perilously close to mentioning the old man specifically, but Letty, if she saw the connections he strove for, said nothing afterwards. It was based on a line from Galatians: "Every man shall bear his own burdens." And Vernon Kallsen knew full well what were his.

At last John Hendricks fell ill with a cough and fever, but he refused to go to bed in case he should miss possible news about Junior. He developed pneumonia and died in four days. After a time the local attorney, executor of the Hendricks estate, offered money for information concerning the whereabouts of the lost heir, but it was several months before the reward was collected. Dolores sent her parents a message from Seattle, where Junior was a welder. It was simply an announcement of the birth of a child—another son—and his name was John.

*

The new tenant who took over the Hendricks farm shortly before John died was Tony Nisson, and it soon became clear that there was not a worse farmer around Kaleburg. Everyone said old John must surely be stirring in his grave. Weeds were thick in all the fields, crops were poorly harvested, the machinery was falling apart, and the house was overrun by children. Junior Hendricks in Seattle received his small yearly rent and let it go at that. The Nissons, it seemed to neighbors, had found a soft berth at last, and ironically they were now settled on good land and living with almost as much security as people who actually owned their farms.

Protestant neighbors were pleased about the eight Nisson children, who kept the country schoolhouse open, for since Tony Nisson was an indifferent Catholic, he did not heed Father Dohlman's suggestion that the children attend parochial school. Vida Ketter happily continued sending her older boy, Paul, to the nearby schoolhouse, rather than having to drive him to Kaleburg, where she herself had been educated. Her husband teased her about this, because for many years Vida had proudly maintained that she was a city person at heart; now, when it was a matter of keeping her children close around her, she was eager to take what the country offered.

In the autumn of 1933 Paul Ketter and Velma Nisson were the youngest of Miss Beason's ten pupils and alone in the fourth grade. They were allowed extra play time and were not burdened with duties, such as sweeping the floor or pounding chalk from erasers. All of their hours were spent together: studying at their desks side by side, reciting on the gray bench in front of the room, and running about during recess. With such constant companionship, Velma felt clearly life had destined them to be mates, and it seemed to Paul, too, that they were in love. All through September they walked the dusty mile to school with arms entwined and lunch pails dangling.

Velma began calling him "Darling" in front of the others

and privately urged that they marry while young. At first the
talk of marriage was almost a joke between them; and then
they pretended they were serious about it. Before long it didn't
seem to be make-believe. Paul Ketter studied Velma's small
triangular face and looked deeply into her eyes. The girl was
very thin and shorter than he was, but in all probability she
would grow up to be beautiful. In looking ahead, he could
think of no girls his age in the neighborhood who might some
day be his wife, and so finally, Velma convinced him that fate
had played a mysterious hand in this, their early romance. The
other children, especially Velma's older brothers and sisters,
quickly began making fun of the "lovebirds," and in that way
word got around, even to the older people.

During silage-cutting season in September, Joe Clausen was
helping Henry Ketter, and he was invited to eat all his meals
with the Ketters. Since his parents' deaths Joe was a bachelor
farmer left alone, and Vida invited him frequently to sample
her cooking. Joe was buck-toothed and genial, and he acted
younger than his years when he and Paul did chores together.
Clausen had had no real friend since his schooldays companionship with Junior Hendricks. Now he learned of the puppy
romance of Paul and Velma, and he was persistently eager to
hear more about it. "Come on, Paul, tell me about your sweet-
heart," Joe urged, his eyes bright with laughter. But Paul refused to talk, for he got enough teasing from his schoolmates
without taking this extra banter from Joe.

One evening Clausen returned from the fields with a wagon-
ful of silage and found Paul in the barn gathering eggs. "I saw
you from the cornfield," Clausen began, his voice rising, "you
and that little Catholic girl." He laughed and rubbed his fore-
fingers together, a gesture Paul didn't understand. "You had
your arm around her."

Paul said nothing. He carefully removed one white egg after
another from nests under the mangers. "You shouldn't be hang-

ing around that girl so much," Joe continued. "You'll be getting into trouble."

Paul did not look up. He had heard that phrase at school in connection with scandal, and he thought he understood what it meant. It was frightening to think that he and Velma were close to getting into trouble, but he was also a little flattered. He hitched his overalls strap one notch higher. "You mind your own business."

Clausen's toothy grin fell away. "Don't be such a sissy, playing with girls all the time."

And now Paul was completely confused. It was true that the other boys were contemptuous of girls because they were full of giggles and unable to throw a ball from outfield to homeplate. It was the worst sort of luck to end up with a lot of them on your team. But men and women certainly liked each other well enough to marry and spend a whole lifetime together. He did not understand this business, but he said nothing more to Joe.

Next morning when Velma put her arms around his neck and kissed his cheek, Paul pushed her arms away and ran down the road with the Nisson boys and Chuck Albrecht. He raced along, happy to be free, and Chuck slapped him on the back approvingly as they all paused to catch their breaths on the crest of a hill.

When Velma arrived at school and slipped into her seat next to Paul, she refused to speak to him. At first he didn't mind, but gradually her silent rage unnerved him. She glared him down when he asked to borrow a pencil. Completely unsettled by her cold fury, Paul could not concentrate on the phonics lesson a few minutes later. He saw it was his turn to recite, but he could not put the syllables together. "What's the matter with you, Paul?" asked Miss Beason. "Can't you think of anything but Velma?" The students began to titter, and he blushed deeply. Then it was Velma's turn, and since her performance was perfect, Miss Beason praised her. The two women seemed in league against him, and he longed to join the boys at recess.

But at ten-fifteen when he ran outside with Velma, she demanded an explanation for his having deserted her on the way to school. Paul confessed that Joe Clausen had talked to him the night before and made fun of him for being a sissy and hanging around girls.

Velma scoffed. "Why listen to him? Joe's the sissy, not you. I heard my sister Luella say that Joe Clausen wouldn't know what to do if a girl loved him. He doesn't even take out girls. He doesn't know anything about this business. With us it's different."

The more they talked together, the more Paul came to understand that the two of them were probably more grown-up than those who laughed at them. After all, he and Velma were going to be married; none of the others in school had settled that question yet, and Joe Clausen wasn't even trying. On the way home after dismissal, Paul and Velma made an extravagant display of affection. They no longer cared in the least about the opinion of the world.

But several days later when Paul was in the kitchen alone with his mother, she asked suspiciously, "What's this I've been hearing about you and Velma Nisson?"

"I suppose Joe Clausen's been blabbing," Paul replied angrily. "Why doesn't he stay on his own farm, instead of coming around here?"

"Your father needs him, that's why," said Vida sternly. "I asked you about Velma."

"What about her?"

"Those people are trashy, and you shouldn't listen to the things she says. The Nissons are hardly the sort I'd expect you to have much in common with. And I wouldn't be surprised if that Velma grows up to be the worst of the lot. I don't like the look on her face."

Paul could hardly swallow his piece of cake, for he was alternately ashamed of Velma and loyal to her. In the end he said nothing, and Vida ended the conversation by warning: "I'll speak to your father about this silliness if it goes much farther."

After much reflection, Paul resolved never to let anyone know what he and Velma were doing; they would hide their love. He hated the thought of being too young and not knowing anything. At least with Velma he could be grown-up. And in the end he would prove to them just how old he really was, when, later on, he and Velma married and had children.

The next day at recess while everyone else was thoroughly absorbed in ande-ande-over, Velma and Paul fled for cover in the chokecherry bushes located in a far corner of the schoolyard. Secluded in their green sanctuary, Velma showed Paul a small ring with a blood-red stone. "Now we can get married," she said. "I stole this from my sister's dresser."

Warmed with excitement, Paul reveled in the wickedness of the whole thing. What would Reverend Kallsen think if he knew Paul was engaged to marry a Catholic? All the Sunday-school classes had been told about Catholics, and how they're always out to snatch unsuspecting Protestants, especially through marriage. But Velma did not seem a strong Catholic, or else she would not repeat those stories she had heard from her sisters about the nuns who were naked under their black robes and the priests who whispered naughty words in the confessional. Paul had no doubt but that Velma would turn Protestant when the time came, if he asked her.

Together they laid their plans. On the way home one night they secretly lingered behind the others; they watched the laughing, self-concerned heads disappear behind a hill, and then they scrambled under a bridge. Wooden beams with swallows' nests were overhead; it was dark, cool, and private on the dry bank of this gully, which was seldom a creek. Paul was quiet and slightly frightened.

Velma suggested they kneel together. He slumped down, and then to his astonishment, she began to repeat the marriage ceremony—at least she came close enough to the real words so that Paul felt the pact was binding. He had expected nothing as final as this! But he slipped the ring on her third finger, which she held out to him. She bowed her head. "Holy Mary, Mother of God, bless us now and at the hour of our death. . . ." Faster and faster she spoke, mumbling what to Paul in his mounting terror seemed a kind of witch's spell. He was filled with remorse for what he had done. And Velma with her head lowered seemed so changed—she had become a Catholic completely. He saw her hands moving, then spotted the rosary, like black ants crawling in her palm. He knew that he was lost.

At Sunday school Paul crept gloomily into the classroom in the church basement; he dreaded the first glance of his teacher. But she was ill, and Reverend Kallsen told the class to join the Bible study group, which he taught. Today they were concerned with Genesis, the section telling of Jacob's labor for the hand of Rachel—how he worked for Laban seven years, only to have the old Syrian slip his first-born into the marriage bed instead of Rachel. While Vernon solemnly discussed the passage, he was aware of a few giggles in the back row. One of the older boys went so far as to ask specific details about this Biblical domestic set-up. "Then Jacob kept *both* Leah and Rachel?"

"And two handmaidens besides," said another with a snicker.

For a moment Vernon did not look up from the text, and then, mustering complete calm, he began his explanation. "According to the old Hebrew law, a man could have more than one wife. It was important in those days to have a lot of sons.

You notice that Jacob really loved only Rachel, who was to be the mother of Joseph and Benjamin, the ancestors of David, into whose family Jesus was born. This was the Lord's intention. It was the wise hand, the ancient hand at work throughout the Holy Scripture. God had it all planned out—as He guides our own lives. Then it is our duty to try to understand His scheme."

Paul, who was made bold by his own involvement with a woman—and tricked into it at that—raised his hand. "Why didn't Jacob give Leah back when he found out she wasn't Rachel?"

There was a guffaw in the back row and a restlessness among them all. This always happened, Vernon reflected, when things of such a nature came up. Usually he tried to pick Biblical readings with an eye to avoiding sex, but in the Old Testament this was difficult. "The reason he couldn't give Leah back is that he didn't discover the mistake until morning. He had already humbled her." Purposely Vernon used that curiously apt term from Deuteronomy, and he believed that everyone but the youngsters would understand. Later on the boys would explain the business to Paul Ketter in words he could comprehend—if, indeed, a boy that age sensed anything at all about the compulsions which would beset him in later life.

On Monday Paul returned to school, and since during fair weather in autumn and spring Miss Beason allowed the youngest pupils to remain outdoors following afternoon recess, Velma and Paul were left alone to make love. Velma prepared a bed of leaves in the chokecherry clump, while Paul, watching her, became more and more uneasy. She put her arms around him, but he broke away, saying he must hunt food for their household. He promised to return soon but took a long time as he dawdled along the fence rows. When he finally came back, his prize booty was a pocketful of plump seed pods from wild roses, and in his hand he held tenderly intact a puffball, which he knew Velma would delightfully collapse.

"We must kiss and love," she said, putting his gifts aside.

Although he wanted to, he was afraid he didn't understand everything she intended, and he wondered where this kissing might lead them. "They'll be getting out of school any minute now," he said quickly. "It must be nearly four o'clock."

"You're not afraid?" she asked. "You're not like Joe Clausen or those sissy boys?"

"Oh no, we're married," he assured her in an unsteady voice.

"Then come on."

"But if school lets out they'll catch us. Let's wait till to-morrow." He clenched and loosened his moist hands. "Look— look!" He did not disguise his relief. "School's out. Time to go home." He scrambled up and ran from the bush.

Velma took the delay good-naturedly, for tomorrow promised certain success, although Paul warned her that if the weather were bad they would have to postpone it again. She didn't think it would rain or that they would have to stay indoors. She never liked to stay inside. In fact, as they walked slowly home, she told him about her grandmother, who did not live in a house at all. She had never mentioned her grandmother before, nor had any of her sisters or brothers, and Paul goaded her by saying he didn't believe a word of it.

"I *do* have a grandmother. She lives in a cave in the alfalfa field."

"Huh!" he said scornfully. "And who put her there?"

"The priest did—after she threw up seventeen dishpans full of devils. They had an awful time with her."

Paul was suddenly interested. The Nissons were a strange tribe, and almost anything was possible. He asked if Velma had actually seen the devils—for that was something no Protestants ever got to see.

"No, this all happened a long time ago. But it's true."

"You're sure she's in a cave?"

"I see her lots of times and bring her food."

"I want to see her, too." He still didn't really believe any of it.

"Only our family visits her."

"Well, I'm your family now. We're married. I just want one look, that's all. Otherwise, I'll think it's all a lie."

"All right," said Velma. "You'll see."

That evening Paul wanted to share the tale with Joe Clausen, who sat around long after supper, unwilling to go home to his empty house; but he knew Joe would make fun of him for even wondering if the story were true. Yet, how could anyone really know that Velma didn't have a grandmother in a cave unless the alfalfa field were explored? Paul imagined the old woman out there, summer and winter in a dark cave with devils leaping. He saw Velma creeping close to the mouth of the hole and touching hands with the old woman as she passed over food. But when he tried to imagine the Nisson grandmother, all he could see was old Anna Hendricks, long since in her grave; she had once given Paul a raisin cookie.

From the Ketter roadgate next morning, Paul saw the Nisson alfalfa field: thick green with a late September crop. He searched for the darkness of a yawning cave when he started for school, but he saw no sign of it. Once at school he nearly forgot the matter, for he was worried about the afternoon tryst with Velma that he had promised to keep. While sitting at his desk, he felt confident that he would manage the affair well— and how proud and relieved he would be when it was over, although he couldn't tell Joe Clausen, or anyone. Just to do it once, he knew, would settle the business for good, and then they could go back to playing with the other children.

After recess when they were alone on the playground, Velma suggested that they go to the girls' side of the outhouse, if Paul didn't think the chokecherry bushes were private enough; but he wouldn't hear of it. No boy ever did such a disgraceful thing. It even smelled different in there. Anyone could tell that the separation of the outhouses was definite, not to be lightly altered.

Velma, convinced of his reluctance, said she wouldn't mind going with him to the boys' side. Somehow, this struck Paul as even worse. "What if a boy in school asks to leave the room? We can't hook the door from the inside. And even if we could, the boy outside would wait and see us as we ran out."

Of course, the coal bin located in the middle of the shed might do, but after investigating the padlock, which only Miss Beason could undo, they eliminated that dark chamber as a possibility. Velma became more and more anxious as time slipped by. Soon they were back home in the chokecherry bushes, but Paul again complained that it was too public.

Then Velma had an irrefutable idea. Just on the other side of the high fence marking off the school ground lay a thick, anonymous cornfield. They could run down the rows deep into the field, far from the schoolhouse, the road, and any prying eyes. There, only the skies looked down; blue, brilliant, and silent. Velma started over the fence at once, but Paul stopped her. A panic gripped him. Once he climbed over, there would be no turning back. "I—I won't do it until you show me your grandmother in the cave."

Velma paused, her leg suspended in mid-air. "All right, I'll show her to you tonight." She dropped into the cornfield. "Come on."

"No, no—I want to see her first." He looked through the mesh fence at her. "I won't go in there with you until I see your grandmother's cave."

Velma scolded him for going back on his promise; they had their first serious quarrel. At last the older students were dismissed from school, but even then Velma didn't come out of the cornfield. Chuck Albrecht had hauled down the flag and most of the pupils had started for home before Velma climbed over the fence. "All right!" she said sulkily. "We'll go to the alfalfa field right now."

Because they didn't want anyone to see them hunting for the cave, they agreed to meet on the edge of the Ketter grove after the others had gotten home. Paul saw, upon entering the kitchen, that his mother had made doughnuts, but he was so excited that he could hardly stuff them down. In his nervousness he made several trips to the outhouse. At four-thirty he slipped quietly out the back door and into the orchard. He loped through the grove on the balls of his feet, Indian-careful. Velma startled him as she stepped from a hollow tree. "What took you so long? *I* never went home at all."

"Your folks'll wonder what happened to you."

"I don't care!" she said with an abandon that struck Paul as ominous. They climbed over fences hastily and headed for the alfalfa field, but now he noticed that Velma lagged behind. "Remember," she said suspiciously, "you promised, and this is final!"

"But show me your grandmother. We're going to see her first." As Paul had it figured out, they would be occupied with her so long that they could not go to the cornfield until to-morrow afternoon. Soon they had covered the whole length of the field, and there was no trace of a cave or a grandmother. "You tricked me!" Paul turned on her. "You just wanted to get me out here. Well, I'm not going to do it, I tell you. You promised the grandmother first."

"All right! You don't have to get so mad. We'll see her. She's in that cornfield right there. It was planted to alfalfa last year; this year it's corn. I haven't been out here all year, so I didn't remember."

Reluctantly, Paul followed her into the tall brown-and-green cornfield. Half the leaves were dry, and the ears hung heavily on the stalks, golden tips showing. Velma turned her head first one way, then another, as if listening for something. Paul stopped once and listened, too, although only cattle lowed in the distance, and Sammy Schneider on a neighboring farm was calling hogs. Paul sensed that they were walking in a circle, rather than in any particular direction. He held her hand and neither of them spoke. Finally she stopped, her face filled with excitement. "Now! Close your eyes and don't move."

Paul obeyed without thinking. The wind rustled above him in the tops of the cornstalks; the slow minutes dragged on. He thought he felt the presence of Velma close by—at least someone—perhaps the grandmother! "Velma!" he whispered. "Is that you?" There was no answer. Suddenly he was certain that it was the grandmother and that Velma had run off. "I'm going to look—I'm going to look now!" he said aloud.

"Wait!" It was Velma's voice. "I'll count to ten."

Paul forced himself from peeking during the long seconds. At nine his lids were parting; at ten his eyes were open, but he saw no one. Then he glanced around and found Velma sitting on the ground in the next corn row. Her underpants of faded flour sack hobbled her ankles. "All right, kneel down," she said. For balance, she gripped the base of a cornstalk. "Come on."

He seemed rooted himself, firmer than the cornstalk. He could not think what to do. How strange it must feel to sit naked on the ground, he thought, although Velma didn't seem to mind. "No—no," he said quickly. "I don't want to." He longed to flee, but he knew he had to stay. He reluctantly dropped to his knees several feet from her. Digging up the ground with his bony knees, he inched closer through the turf. She encouraged him, saying it was all right, for they were married and in love forever.

But as a practical matter, he realized that he could not proceed. He could have explained why he stopped. He might have told her that if she hadn't tricked him into the cornfield this afternoon—if they had waited until tomorrow—it would have turned out differently. Then he would have planned for it, drunk a lot of water and not gone to the outhouse for hours, so that when the time came for him to be a husband, he would be ready—not in a fix like this. But he was tired of explaining and making excuses. For weeks now he had been ruled by Velma's wishes, and he had earnestly tried to keep in good with her. He'd had enough. He rose from his knees, straightened his clothes, and as far as he was concerned, the business was over for good, marriage or no marriage.

Velma scowled. "Hey, what's the matter?"

Before she could say more, he snapped back: "I *knew* you didn't have a grandmother in a cave."

"She'll never come out now," Velma answered. "Never! Not for you!"

And in truth, she never did.

IV 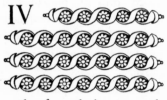 After Bible class, church service, and dinner, Vernon Kallsen faced one of those dreadful Sunday afternoons. Despite the beautiful autumn weather, the rustle of maple leaves on the walks, and the glistening spiderwebs in the air, he was confined to the house. He was a prisoner by his own will; he was living out a sentence self-decreed. Letty was somewhere visiting friends—she hadn't told him where—and even though he longed to escape the oppressive silence of the parsonage, he knew that ambling through Kaleburg would be a public promenade. He felt keenly a harsh edge of awkwardness between himself and all others, and though he had purposely created this distance and cultivated aloofness since the time he arrived in Kaleburg three years ago, there were periods when loneliness was agony.

Today the mocking laughter of the Bible class and their rowdy questions about Rachel, Leah, and Jacob continued to haunt his mind. The incident so clearly revealed a latent rebellion against *him*. He had to defend every part of the Bible as if he himself had written it. As St. Augustine observed, there was nothing holy or innocent about childhood: gluttony, beastliness, and all the animal vices have free play. Surely this had been the case with Eugene—and part of the trouble. In every human being the spiritual sense was late developing. The Bible class students, averaging sixteen years of age, seemed to have nothing but sex on their minds most of the time. Had he himself been this way? As he thought back, he realized that normal passions had pulsed within him but that from an early age he had understood his responsibility for controlling them, for subduing himself.

And yet, like St. Augustine, "bound with the disease of the flesh, and its deadly sweetness," he had desired marriage. For a time after the wedding he felt released from the pressures of lust, and part of the pleasure he and Letty first had in marriage came about because it was not only permitted by society but blessed by God. They found the featherbed in the Stilton parsonage a fine, soft place for making love.

The trouble that grew up between them came partly from the outside—from the congregation itself. They were such a lax, hypocritical bunch that Vernon simply could not stir them. Some preacher from New England, imbued with New Thought, had held sway over them earlier, proclaiming that they were all good, their impulses fine, and that they should love themselves and others, for there was no sin. Although this dazzling minister pushed on to California with his happy philosophy, the people of Stilton continued to be comforted by the memory of his words, and they stayed away from Vernon's sterner brand of Protestantism.

As his failure to be an effective pastor became more and more apparent, Letty tried to help him by patient encouragement, by telling him again and again that she believed in him and his abilities. Oddly enough, he was not bolstered by her show of concern. She was irritating, and he finally became angry. Was not this difficulty in Stilton something personal that he himself had to see through to the finish? Despite her words of love, he sensed that her good opinion of him was slipping rapidly—but what could he do? They did not always make up their quarrels in the dark bedroom when their bodies touched in the featherbed. In fact, the charm and success had left this part of their lives, too. It was better to stop love-making altogether, rather than court the agony that came from half-hearted, abortive attempts to achieve their former physical union.

Then, quite without a warning of the danger, Letty came down with the flu, which developed into pneumonia, and she very nearly died. For months she lay in bed and Vernon nursed her; he felt that their love grew healthier because of this tender relationship. Gently, he would kiss her cheek, and should desire stir within him he quickly drew away. He began to understand why Letty's illness had intensified their sense of love for each other: it precluded the blind, gratifying struggle of the sex involvement. It allowed them to appreciate each other as they were, without that film of passion which distorted them both—for in the throes of intercourse, she became as base a creature as a bitch in heat, and he himself, with his teeth bared on the tendons of her neck, ready to destroy her with every part of himself—he, too, was nothing but a beast. Why had this business ever been dignified with the name of love? It was something they did together in the dark because they were married and devoted to each other, and silently forgave and forgot in the daylight.

One afternoon as he brought her tea, he realized how innocent and untouched she seemed in her illness—their love was purged of impurities. "I've never felt so close to you," he murmured, picking up her satiny hand—smooth-skinned, long absent from housework—"nor has our marriage been better."

"Darling," she murmured, smiling, pulling him down to her. He lay beside her outside the covers.

Almost immediately the old whirlpool began, and what started as kisses of respect and devotion, turned into the hot kind. He flung aside the bed linens and pressed his body against hers. His admonishing mind tried to brake his passion, reminding him of her illness—but reason had never succeeded in the past, nor did it now.

Thus it was their child was conceived.

As the pregnancy developed, the doctor prescribed a diet of red meat and milk to build up Letty's strength. She was in and out of bed most of the time, and Vernon's anticipatory feelings about approaching fatherhood were dampened by his sense of guilt for having caused her vomiting, dizziness, and general malaise. If anything should happen to her, he knew he would be to blame.

In her fourth month disaster struck. While Vernon was in his study, Letty fainted, hit her head on the edge of the cook stove, and later, in the hospital, had a miscarriage. Death moved close, but she struggled to live. Again there followed long months of ailing, during which Vernon managed the house, nursed her with loving care, and filled his sermons with angry exhortations against all who sinned.

Eventually the intimacy of their lives renewed their sexual life—this time at Letty's insistence—and surprised though he was, grateful for her acceptance of him, he realized, even while their bodies surged together, that this time he would not be responsible for the consequences. After that their love-making occurred frequently, and at last she was pregnant again. The doctor warned them of the dangers; Letty was still in poor health, and after a month she miscarried. At least for the time being, the physician suggested, they should use contraceptives, and with both of them blushing, he went into details concerning the use of the diaphragm. But Vernon knew that he and Letty could not use their bodies for carnal pleasure, contrary to the will of God, for the Old Testament clearly stated that no seed should be spilled upon the ground. To make things easier for both of them, they began to sleep in separate bed-rooms.

Along with these personal difficulties came the increasing conflict they felt with the times. They were poor when everyone seemed rich: farmers were buying twenty-dollar silk shirts, and townspeople were building new homes. They felt sober when gaiety prevailed. They shunned sex when even women talked about it more freely, cigarettes hanging from their lips. Every-where, the concern about Judgment Day and the after-life was woefully weak. Vernon did not spare himself blame for the rotten condition of local religion. He had failed to make his congregation spiritually aware, and he began to talk unceas-ingly to Letty of his ineffectiveness. Thus purposely weakening himself in her eyes, he took the scourge of her despisal—which she gave at last, reluctantly. Her voice had grown sharp, her body rather shapeless and hard. She told him it was all his fault—everything he said to denigrate himself was true—only worse. "You've made me into an old hag! Look what you've done to me—and why? What's it all for?" She began insulting him in public, calling him a fool, laughing outright at him—all of which only added to the thorns already pricking him. In front of the congregation his Sunday-morning prayers became frenzied displays, and the congregation stirred with embarrass-ment. They wondered what lay behind the veiled words; what trouble was afoot. Of course, he knew they were wondering.

One evening he fabricated an excuse to enter Letty's bedroom after she had already retired. He sat on the edge of her bed and attempted to open up again the whole subject of their loss of companionship, the absence of tenderness. With a weary hand he slowly began to caress her shoulder; then he ventured to put his lips lightly on her neck. But suddenly she erupted. "Get away from me! Why are you coming here *now*? What's the matter with you?"

"Can't there be any affection between us?" he asked forlornly.

"No, no, no," she said, turning her face to the wall. "You're like spoiled meat to me."

Towards the end of the 1920's, with his church membership at an all-time low, Vernon read an article by a minister who suggested using business methods to win souls. It was time Christianity started a selling job. With old-fashioned ways, religion could get nowhere. In the future the smart pastor would picture the church to his young people as a place for fun and fellowship—a kind of club for men, a social arena for women.

Vernon decided to try this new radical approach, and although Letty warned, "You'll make an ass of yourself," he shed his somber black robe, told jokes one Sunday in church, organized the young people, joined the Grange, and in every way tried to "step down from the pulpit." As his experiment met with some success, Vernon saw how much children held the local focus: their triumphs in football, their roles in drama productions, their courtships—these were of vital concern to everyone. And so he suggested to Letty, as casually as he might have brought up the subject of a new lawnmower, "Perhaps we ought to adopt a child."

"But I thought you—" she began, then stopped. "All those old objections—I mean, about the child's not really *seeming* ours—they don't matter, do they? The thing to do is make it all natural and ordinary."

She added the last, Vernon knew, because in prior discussions she had always complained of the twitch of fear about his eyes and his general unease when adoption was mentioned. He abhorred the unnatural, and there seemed to him, always, something contrived and even pathetic about the little families so consciously fabricated. He preferred taking the judgment of the Lord, which clearly seemed to pronounce barrenness to their union. Now he was beginning to understand that this view stemmed chiefly from his embarrassment. Such a bias dissolved with increasing years—yes, especially with a stalemate in their sexual relations; it was odd, but now that he felt himself beyond the reach of a young man's torment, more nearly out of the grasp of carnal attractions, he could broach this subject of adoption calmly, as if it were the first time they had discussed it. "Our church orphanage in Davenport—you know how many children they have there and no suitable homes," he began. "It would seem—"

"You're serious then? You really are?"

"Don't you see, this is a way of helping the cause? Of getting under the shell of this town."

Letty looked at him oddly. She didn't like his reason. She had never been willing to put the concerns of the church above her own private wants. He supposed this was to be expected in a woman, but one could hope for less selfishness in a minister's wife. Perhaps it made no difference, provided—as in this case— their desires settled on the same thing. She wanted a child very much, and, not wishing to upset him or send him into an angry reconsideration, she handled their discussion tenderly. This little hold he had over her amused him. He intended to use it to get precisely the right child when they made their trip to Davenport.

In the days that followed, Letty was buoyed up by an ecstatic expectation, and she could not help but share her excitement with Vernon. He was touched by her eagerness, and curiously enough, what may have begun as a calculation ended in genuine enthusiasm vigorously shared. Perhaps long ago they should have done this, he realized.

For a minister's family adoption would be simple—none of the usual long investigations. A favorable report on the domestic situation was automatic. Vernon and Letty decided to adopt a boy, for, as Vernon pointed out, a son would very likely play a more prominent role in the community than a girl would be able to. The boy would have one of the rooms upstairs, and Letty said she would paint it blue, "a good masculine color." She would sew new curtains and buy new furniture for him. As their plans spun out, they felt as if they were creating the child. An old sense of intimacy returned, and even the meals were better prepared.

On the day in September, 1929, when he and Letty took the train to Davenport to visit the orphanage, the weather was unseasonably hot, the earth dry, and through the coach windows they saw endless fields of parched corn and burnt pastures. Even though the sky itself was brown, they were not depressed, for this project of adopting a son united them in what could only be called love. Letty put her hand on his arm. He felt at peace and happy.

They took a taxi from the depot to the orphanage, where they were expected. The institution was an imposing brick mansion, formerly an insane asylum, which the church had purchased cheaply. "I'm afraid I look a sight!" said Letty, brushing her clothes with her fingertips and thrusting new pins into her hair.

Vernon hardly heard her, for he was watching a group of boys playing touch football on a barren stretch of ground. "Look, some of the children. It's nice they let them out on a day like this."

"Why wouldn't they?" Letty asked.

Vernon did not reply. After paying the driver he stood where he was and gazed at the boys. The football was snapped from center, and the teams scuffled together in a rising cloud of dust. Soon they were all shouting and arguing, with no referee around to settle the dispute. But one boy, much larger than the others, bullied them into continuing the game. His masculine voice rang out above the piping chatter of the younger players. His chest was tanned a deep brown, the same hue as his overly long hair. As he carried the football around left end on the next play, he cruelly stiff-armed all who tried to catch him, sending them reeling into the dust.

"Come on," said Letty. "We're late."

"Let's see just one more play," Vernon replied, standing there with the sun hot on his shoulders. Next there was an attempted pass, but the big boy, who had been unable to get his pass off in time, argued that the other team had been off side. The opposing team in an angry gang immediately surrounded him, as if they were about to drag him to the ground and trample upon him. But he stood there, contemptuous of them all, and thrusting up his right hand, he made an obscene gesture with his finger.

"Come on," said Letty, who was already standing with one hand on the door. "The boys we're supposed to look over are probably waiting."

But Vernon realized, as he turned away, that he had already made his choice: they would adopt that young ruffian—that dirty, overgrown, incorrigible teen-age boy. And that mocking, obscene gesture: how much it resembled Vernon's own hand movement at the close of each church service, when, the fore-finger of his right hand erect, he drew in the air the sign of the cross.

V 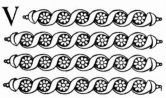 As Claus Schneider proudly told Reverend Kallsen, soon after the minister arrived in Kaleburg, lucky was the man blessed with sons. It seemed as natural a desire as one's will to live, but it was only really talked about in case there was trouble of some sort. With Claus Schneider's own sons there was seldom any serious difficulty, and much of the time the old farmer did not question his two boys about where they went or what they did.

Sometimes Sammy, the younger son, would disappear and not show up for hours. He would slip through the mulberry grove and angle down a long lane to visit Joe Clausen, whose land lay on the opposite side of the section. Sammy was already tired of his brief career in farming, and he fully expected to abandon Kaleburg for the excitements of the larger world; were it not for the depression, which was still severe in 1934, he would have wandered long ago. Although he dreamed of extravagant adventures, even simple diversions amused him, like bottling up a flicker in a hollow tree by putting his fist over the hole; or chasing winter-slow rabbits on foot, shouting for them to run faster; or taming a baby crow and teaching it to talk and sit on his shoulder like an evil spirit; or seducing girls, which in the last few years had become his favorite pastime. But Joe Clausen was another amusement, for he was a virgin bachelor, homely as a grade-school puppet, and he was definitely odd.

Sammy did not run down the lane of cottonwood trees and cross Joe Clausen's back forty simply to spy on the queer bachelor, nor did he sneak through the thicket of grove or slip close along the apple-tree trunks in Joe's orchard in order to watch Clausen kissing his dog Betsy, for the bachelor's relationship to his bitch was quite an open one, and Sammy could get the full pleasure of this entertainment by pulling up a kitchen chair. Sammy had to admit that Betsy was attractive, with a cute little pink nose and the kindest brown eyes one could wish for, even in a woman. Her coat was tawny, lustrous, and her legs were as white as if she wore silk stockings, like a nurse. Betsy's tail, however, was the most wonderful thing about her, and in pride and affection Joe would run his fingers through the silky plume she lifted aloft, and actually, Sammy could see, it was hair as clean and beautiful as any he had fingered on girls in all Kaleburg. "She's a beaut, Joe," Sammy would say, laughing, and Joe Clausen with a wide grin, his buck teeth exposed like a mule trying to get rid of its bit, would fling his arms around Betsy's breast and bury his ear in her soft neck. The dog would look at Sammy, who could hardly contain himself, with the soberest kind of pride, as if she were saying, we have found in each other an end to loneliness.

Besides Betsy there were two other dogs on the farm, for as Joe told Sammy, "Somehow, I'm lucky. The dogs just seem to come here." They did not even have names, however, and Clausen referred to them simply as Hound and Dog; they slept outside under bushes in summer, stretching their half-naked stomachs along the cool earth hollowed like saucers under them. One was small and fox-faced, of the rat terrier breed, and was excellent for worrying milch cows along the shifting narrow

cowpaths in the pasture; the other, Dog, was sullen and sometimes fierce, especially to strangers, and Joe used him for hunting pheasants in November.

Betsy's role was that of companion. She followed him everywhere on his daily chores, beginning with the milking at sunrise. Hound snapped at the bony, angled back legs of the Hol-
steins until they leapt over the sill and lumbered into the barn,
while Betsy wagged her silken tail, welcoming them coolly
like a hostess, watching them find their familiar stanchions, and
then Joe locked them into place by snapping kicking chains
on their rear legs. Betsy also swayed majestically through the
mewing cats, and simply a lift of her aristocratic snout was
enough to discipline a mangy cat that got out of line or was
overly greedy about begging spurts from the cow teats. Betsy
never deigned to chase or snap at the cats; they seemed to
recognize her authority with no theatrics of that sort necessary.
She handled the pigs with equal ease, accompanying her master
into the mire of the pens when he flung the largess of shelled
corn at them; on her delicate feet she pranced along in the
clean, golden corn, as if to put her individual stamp on it before
they should move in to devour the food.

But what amused Sammy most of all about Joe and Betsy
was that neither of them realized they made a strange couple,
nor did Joe seem to guess that Sammy was laughing and teasing
him half of the time. Betsy always cleaned Joe's plate after a
meal, and when he held the glistening white plate for Sammy
to see what a fine job she had done, Sammy said, "Do you
know, you've got the best dishwasher there in the world? These
men who have wives washing their dishes with soap and old
greasy water, they get a coating of lye in their stomachs. When
they get old they wonder why they can't eat, why their bellies
ache all the time. But you've got Betsy to wash dishes, and
everybody knows a dog's saliva is a healthier cleanser than any-

thing you could buy. Doctors say you get fewer germs embracing a dog than you do from kissing a woman."

"Is that a fact?" asked Joe, his voice peculiarly high, as if his vocal chords, unused to regular use, were tight as piano strings.

"But I never think of germs when I kiss a woman," said Sammy, launching into his favorite subject—and this was the real reason he came so often to see Joe Clausen. He had been making love to girls around the countryside at such a rate that someone ought to know about it, just to appreciate sporting possibilities. Sammy couldn't talk about this to his stern older brother, Robert, and it was unwise to boast before companions, for the sake of future encounters with their sisters. He had learned that his favorite activity admitted no confiding whatsoever, but he felt a need to share his dream. Life was so dull for most people that he felt obliged to add his bit in order to relieve the general boredom. But alas, Joe Clausen, who had never known a woman and who had no friends, was the only safe person to tell. If Sammy had been born a Catholic, he could confess every intimate adventure to the priest—but certainly Reverend Kallsen was no substitute. Nobody in his right mind would take a real problem to him, for it might turn up the following Sunday in church, thinly disguised, used to point up some moral lesson.

Unwilling to view himself as an out-and-out boaster, Sammy insisted that he was instructing Joe in the art of human love, and although he dwelt with too much relish on odd approaches and unusual twists, the aim, as announced to Joe, was simply that "some day you're going to get a wife, and these things you have to know to keep her happy." Occasionally, Sammy thought he saw an admonishing look in Betsy's eyes as he talked so matter-of-factly about Joe's matrimonial future. "I mean, Joe, you can't just stay a bachelor."

Frowning, with worry clouding his eyes, Joe would say, "No,

I suppose not. But I'm pretty happy the way things are—I guess."

Such a remark opened up for Sammy a chance to relate recent moments he had had with women, until Joe's face showed a silly smile and his eyes slightly popped from too much attention, for, unused as he was to ordinary conversation, he over-reacted to Sammy's talk. "No!" "You don't say!" he would shout and slap the table, his knee, or Betsy's back. If he hit the dog she would look over her shoulder at him with wounded eyes. "By golly!" or "That's something, all right!" would tumble out in various keys, generally in the upper register, and sometimes as he lifted his head, his Adam's apple bobbing like a valve, his exclamations became strangely inhuman, as if he were a dog himself, struggling for human speech. In a way, Betsy took the whole thing more calmly. And finally, when Sammy had relished himself fully in the role of lover, most of the tales enormously exaggerated, he would sit back, spent and at ease, while Joe continued murmuring and shaking his head with spasms of reflection and astonishment, almost like the after effects of love-making.

But despite the intensity of Joe's interest and the way both of them became utterly absorbed in Sammy's tales of female exploit, Sammy always came back, as if he were swinging on a familiar limb, to that old observation: "But Joe, why haven't you ever tried it?" He asked the question again one day near the end of winter.

Joe confessed that indeed he was missing a lot, but even while he talked his hand slipped comfortingly around Betsy's neck and occasionally her deft pink tongue slurped to his cheek as caressingly as a love pat. Sammy pressed to find out just what Joe's ideal woman would be like and was surprised to learn that this red-faced scarecrow of a man not only insisted that, if he married, his wife be a virgin; she should also have silky hair as fine as Betsy's plume, a sweet and docile temperament, a graceful body and flawless face—in short, she was beyond reality. "The trouble with you, Joe, is that you haven't seen any women in the flesh. You don't get out enough to look 'em over. Next Saturday night why don't you come with me to the Pentecostal revival meeting?"

"Why should I go there?" Joe asked. "Those banjo players don't preach our kind of religion."

"I wouldn't miss revival time," said Sammy. "You just don't know how exciting it can get, and all sorts of girls come. They stand up front and confess their sins, and when the preacher shouts 'Go and sin no more,' there I am, waiting outside for the prettiest, worst sinner of the lot."

"But to look for a wife in such a place—that's a different thing." And then he told Sammy a few more things he hoped for in a spouse. "I guess I'd prefer a tall girl, because the rooms in this house are big, and since she could easily get through the doors without stooping, no sense having a little short girl and wasting all that space." He winked slyly. "Then, too, a tall woman can carry milk pails easier. They won't dangle around her ankles. She ought to have good teeth, too, because dentist bills can be awful."

The more Joe talked, the more Sammy realized that finally, indeed, dreams of matrimony were spinning about the farmhouse even when Sammy was not there, for upon his arrival Joe began introducing the subject of women, not Sammy. Once when Joe was talking excitedly, daring himself to visit the Cornflower Ballroom and stand in the stag line, Betsy climbed into his lap and stepped unthinkingly upon his groin, as a dog will, and Joe gave her a slap that sent her reeling and yelping against the wall. "Damn bitch, climbing all over a fellow!"

But Joe was reluctant actually to commit himself to a night of courting, in case he failed. He attended a movie in Kaleburg with Sammy one Saturday night and afterwards hung around Koch's drugstore while Sammy flirted with high-school girls.

Joe felt shy and was eager to dissociate himself from Sammy, who, now in action, laughed and pranced in front of the girls like a jester and seemed impossibly young. Joe hid behind a magazine rack and busily turned pages of a screen publication. In his yellow tartan sport shirt he felt uncomfortably clean, and his stiff, little-used trousers seemed oddly not his own. He was miserably aware of his homely wind-burned face, which above the strange clothes seemed tenderly exposed, unnaturally naked before the world, as if his clothed body had squeezed out this top like a tube of toothpaste.

"C'mon Joe, what're you doing back there? Buttoning yourself up?" Sammy called cruelly, now finding Joe handy to use as a butt in order to win the laughs and smiles of the girls for himself. "Sit with us!" he implored, knowing that every time Joe Clausen opened his mouth, Luella, Evelyn, and Joyce would have a merry time laughing among themselves behind paper napkins, with knee-nudgings and secret looks. He did not care about Evelyn or Joyce, who were scrawny despite their built-up brassières, but Luella Nisson's arms were plump and her breasts fully formed, and Sammy was filled with desire and determination that she should be his. In his concentration, he almost forgot his past ties of friendship with Joe. He simply insisted that Joe sit down with them, partly because, in order to make room, Sammy would have to squeeze against Luella, and he intended to press his thigh against hers and communicate his intentions, a maneuver which had worked in the past, especially in movie theatres.

"I'll just have a soda by myself," Joe replied with stiff formality, his eyes rolling upward to gaze at a fresh, brightly painted Coca Cola sign depicting handsome, uncomplicated people. The girls giggled just loudly enough for him to hear. Joe climbed upon a swivel stool, rested his elbows on the marble counter, and stared straight ahead at himself in the mirror behind the row of malted-milk mixers. He longed for the release and solitude, the wide freedom of his farm. Half an hour later, when he abruptly departed, he drove down the long lane of plum brush to his isolated farm buildings set in from the road, in the cleft of two gently rolling hills. Betsy, recognizing the sound of his Ford, stood boldly in the glare of his headlights, her silken chest uplifted, her head high, as if she were welcoming the arrival of the sun, shining full into her unblinking eyes. For Joe it seemed good to be home.

When days passed and Sammy Schneider did not come for a visit, Joe assumed that his young neighbor had given him up, disgusted by his failure to mesh with the local girls that Saturday night after the movies. In his mind, Joe built elaborate explanations in case his behavior were called to account by Sammy. He would frankly admit that the early stages of romance with all its uncertainties and possibilities might be fun for someone like Sammy, but Joe preferred to know where he was at all times. He felt confident that if a woman turned up on his doorstep like a stray dog and there was nothing else to do but take her in, he would work out a relationship that would be just fine. But as for bothering the young girls at the Cornflower Ballroom and whipping up his enthusiasm to ask one of them for a dance, all of that was impossible for him now; he was in his mid-twenties and ought to act his age. Perhaps it would be best if the subject were closed for good, now and forever—although, of course, he would always enjoy Sammy's accounts of his amorous adventures.

In April after seeding the oats fields, when the pastures had all turned brilliant green and new leaves on the trees half hid the house, Joe saw Sammy with a magazine in his hand climb over the dry tangle of the old grape arbor; his smile was as bright as ever. "Oh, Joe, I've got a fine idea for you. Just come here and look at this farm magazine."

It was the noon hour and very still, except for robins overhead building a nest in an ash tree and announcing their troubles and exultation to the world. Joe and Sammy sat down on the smoothed stump of a tree which had been sawed off two feet from the ground, and they examined the advertisement section of the paper. "Matrimony in mind? Horizons limited? We act as a clearing house. In no way recommend or judge applicants. Send two dollars, along with picture, circumstances, and kind of mate desired."

"There," said Sammy, pointing his blunt forefinger at the fine print. "When I saw that I thought of you. Just the thing, since these local girls don't interest you much. I know darn well you're not about to go off somewhere and find a woman who *will* do."

Joe nodded. "Not in spring planting time." He was relieved to discover that Sammy did not value him less because of his social failure, and he hardly paid attention to the advertisement.

"Well, are you going to write in or not?" asked Sammy. "What's two dollars to you, Joe? You're rich, and this is a female grab bag, so why not?"

Joe lingered over the phrase "mate desired," and a curiously pleasant warmth crept along his loins. Sitting there in the benevolent April sunshine, after the long, cold harshness of the Iowa winter, he began to wonder if he should not take a wife after all, to live with him in this house vacated by his dead mother and father. "Sure, I'll write in," he said finally, rising, and together they went inside to the kitchen and made room to compose the letter by pushing dirty dishes on the table aside.

Sammy, who had never had occasion to write love letters since his girl friends lived nearby and could be reached by telephone in ten seconds, relished this chance to try his hand at courtship by pen and paper. He paced up and down with his hands thrust deeply into his striped overalls pockets and dictated what should be written, losing sight of Joe as ardor overcame him. "My beloved, whose eyes I know not the color of, whose cheeks and hair have not felt my lips, hark to my plea and heed my anguished suit. 'Thy breasts are like two young roes that are twins . . . thou hast ravished my heart . . . behold thou art fair, my love.' "

"No, no, that kind of talk will scare her away."

"That's the Song of Solomon," said Sammy scornfully. It was the only book of the Bible he really knew. "There's nothing more beautiful. If you want to win her heart, Joe, it'll take some singing."

Frowning, slumping forward on his elbows, Joe had a good mind to forget the whole business, for no crow like him could pretend to be a warbler, and any fancy talk he borrowed from Sammy now would have a day of reckoning when this hypothetical wife confronted him in person. "I've got to be honest, or it just won't work."

"You don't know the first thing about making love, or you wouldn't say something stupid like that. Keep on writing, Joe. 'I am a man who tills the soil, reaping rich harvests for my diligence. I work in the Lord's vineyard, one might say.' "

" 'But I'm not very religious,' " Joe added. " 'I'd prefer a Protestant or nothing woman, but it don't matter much, as long as she's not a Catholic.' "

" 'I am in the prime of manhood, sturdy of limb, strong of character,' " Sammy continued, " 'and my beloved, my Rose of Sharon, with lips like a scarlet thread, must be of sound health in order to live fully the rich life in store for her on this one hundred and eighty acres of top-quality land, debt free.' "

" 'Must be reasonable-looking,' " Joe wrote, " 'with decent teeth and limbs. Only virgins need answer.' "

"Oh, come now, Joe, you'd better not say that. How will you be able to tell anyhow, until after you're married?"

"Just as a warning."

"All right—but now, what have we left out? 'Wanted, for immediate marriage. Supply picture and give details of person and habits.' What about you, Joe? Do you have a snapshot?" The picture would be reproduced and sent out to the agency's clients.

Upstairs in his dresser drawer, Joe found a brown-tinged photograph taken by himself on the Midway of the Iowa State Fair three years ago. The picture had been snapped before he had had a chance to set his features rigidly and eye the dark camera hole with stern defiance. In fact, as he remembered, he had just reached out to snap the curtain shut, so that people wouldn't notice him in there and wonder why in the world such a homely man would want his picture, when the fool contraption had gone off. The result was this profile shot, a little blurred; his heavily muscled arm reaching across his chest gave an air of decisiveness and manly strength. It was fantastically flattering, but Sammy, although his eyes widened slightly in surprise, made no comment other than, "Oh, this is fine. Just the thing. We'll put it all in the mail tonight. I guarantee this'll be the most interesting two dollars you've ever spent."

Three days later Joe received word that his application was on file and at the disposal of the bureau's correspondents. A week later he received three letters, all of them warm and frankly interested. "What do you think of that!" Joe said aloud, looking at Betsy. "Not just one good-looking girl, but three of them!" They were all brunettes; one wore glasses; all were under thirty; and they were Protestant virgins—or at least, they each mentioned filling his requirements. In high excitement he telephoned Sammy, urging him to stop by and help him choose a wife. But Sammy had a date to a wedding dance, and he could not come over until the following day.

When Sammy entered Joe's kitchen the next afternoon, he saw a stack of letters on the table. "Fifteen in the mail today— three yesterday!" exclaimed Joe. "What do you think of that? They're all ages, nationalities, and religions. By God, I've never seen the like. To think, all these women will offer themselves to a perfect stranger. It almost makes me so disgusted I don't want any of 'em."

"Now, now, calm down, Joe. You've hit the jackpot. For once in your life the women are waiting for just the littlest crook of your finger. You be smart and make the most of it."

"What do you mean?" asked Joe, confused by Sammy's sly look. "I take the one that seems best, of course. That's what we've got to figure out."

Betsy, always sensitive to her master's moods, was greatly agitated by the commotion. She flopped down behind the stove on Joe's blanket-lined jacket, only to rise a few minutes later to seek the comfortable odor of Joe in the big easy chair. Nothing suited her long while the men marched around the kitchen and talked excitedly.

Sammy arrayed the women's photographs like a rogue's gallery, pointing his finger at suspected photographers' tricks, detecting latent shrewishness in the eyes of one girl, unfaithfulness in another; he saw naïveté and treachery, fertility and barrenness, brains and stupidity, disease and blooming health, Protestant and Catholic, loving and unloving—all revealed in those photographs, which to Joe's untutored eyes were inscrutable.

"Sammy, how can you tell all them things?" Joe asked.

"Comes with experience," said Sammy modestly, sitting like a judge before the upturned faces. He launched into the paperwork next, analyzing handwriting for character. He read between the lines of carefully guarded phrases such as, "Some people think I'm a little out-sized for style, but others find me just wholesomely healthy."

Sammy made a face, found the girl's picture, and squinted slightly, as if gazing into a crystal; he shook his head. "She weighs two hundred or more and eats chocolates all day."

Another suspicious comment that occurred several times,

with variations, was the half-hearted apology for having to resort to this means of getting a husband. "I've had dates all my life, but the One And Only just hasn't come along. Maybe I've been too particular, but—"

Sammy, reading this aloud to Joe, stopped and shook his head, then tossed the letter aside. "She'll never do. The frigid type. After all these years of bachelorhood, Joe, you'll want somebody to make up for lost time."

"I just don't know what I'd do," said Joe, grinning, wiping his sleeve across his buck teeth, as if to shine them up, "if I didn't have you here to advise me."

"It's a pleasure," said Sammy soberly. Indeed it was. He noted the addresses of some of the women who lived fairly nearby and had a vague notion of asking Joe for dibs.

At eleven o'clock the field was finally narrowed and the winner chosen. She was a Swedish Lutheran who had been only three years in this country and was now working as a maid for a wealthy family in Missouriville. The foreign flavor greatly attracted Sammy, who had never slept with a girl who spoke with an accent, and he convinced Joe that this strong and healthy little maid from the old country would be a grateful, ever-loving wife.

Joe demurred, anticipating the difficulties of trying to get along with an ordinary girl, let alone a Swede who wouldn't understand what he said half the time. "I'd better not make up my mind tonight. I'll sleep on it."

This eased Sammy somewhat, too, since in working up enthusiasm over the girl he had become mightily interested in her himself and was beginning to think that this blonde, blue-eyed goddess was altogether too charming to waste on somebody like Joe, who would take almost anything, really. Perhaps Sammy was carrying friendship too far, giving up perfectly fine prospects like this one, a girl who lived just thirty-six miles away—not a long trip for a Saturday night.

On the following day the mailman drove down the long muddy lane toward Joe's house because the tubular mailbox on the road could not hold the twenty letters addressed to Clausen in flowing, female handwriting. The dogs all barked, announcing his arrival, but Rusty McIverson did not stir from behind the wheel; after all, he had been a mail carrier for twenty years and he knew better. People always came running to see what he had brought, forever curious; he was a kind of year-round Santa Claus for half the farmers of Kaleburg. These letters for Clausen puzzled him, coming on top of yesterday's extraordinary batch. Nothing like it had ever happened before that he recalled. "Well, Joe, got quite a bit of mail for you," he called through the open window to the farmer at the garden gate.

Clausen began making clucking noises behind his tightly closed teeth, for although he was smiling, he seemed awfully upset. McIverson was not surprised, however; he was used to rusty croaks from farmers in outlying areas who didn't have a chance to talk much. He merely watched Joe's protruding eyes as he passed over letter after letter. Joe tucked them into his jacket pockets, under his arms, wedged them inside his belt, and held them between his knees. Finally, at the end, he asked, "Any more?"

"My God, Joe, what do you expect?" As the mailman spoke, Betsy leapt up, putting her feet on the door handle to look hostilely into McIverson's face. "What's going on? Why're you getting all these letters from women?"

"I got more friends than I figured, I guess," he murmured, blushing.

The shrewd mailman sitting indolently behind the wheel guessed that a matrimonial bureau was behind it. "Put out a few feelers, huh? Made a few public offers? Haw! You don't pull the wool over my eyes, Joe. I know what you're up to."

But Clausen, looking ahead to the time when his theoretical

wife might have to retrieve mail from this same nosy carrier, would admit nothing nor in any way explain. How would it be to have his woman teased forever just because she had clamored to have her interests heard in the midst of a few dozen other women? The world was always looking for gossip to noise about the taverns and stores, and he intended to keep his affairs secret.

After the mailman drove away, Joe rushed into the house and ripped open the envelopes. The lovely Swedish girl he had been dreaming about all morning vanished from his thoughts, and he hastily scanned the photographs of the new crop. He was startled out of his wits, momentarily, when a snapshot of movie actress Jean Harlowe tumbled upon his blue-checked tablecloth. He quickly read the letter with the photo—written by some prankster, that was all; she ended up by preaching a little sermon about beauty coming from the inner light, not the outer visage.

This day he did not rush to call up Sammy, for now with two days of experience behind him, he felt himself a fledgling connoisseur in his own right. First he arranged a pyramid of beauty (with Jean Harlowe watching from on top of the sugar bowl), and then he sorted the letters according to religions. Baptists were doing very well in this contest, with Lutherans and Methodists a close second and third. Presbyterians were next, followed by splinter groups of which Joe had never heard —and several persistent Catholics who tried to win his heart despite his warning against Popery. He thought they were only interested in converting him and pushed them all into limbo behind the coal bucket.

Joe could hardly tear himself away to milk the cows and feed the pigs and steers, although Betsy, reminding him that twilight was hastening on, paced the porch with her toenails tapping, impatient for the fun to begin. "I've some beauties there, all right," said Joe to the dog as he swung the clanking milk pails from a peg outside the kitchen door. "Even a city girl might not be too bad, you know?" he said to Hound and Dog, who joined forces at the gate. "There's too much of the farm about farming, the way things are. Be good to have a lady around."

He cooked his own supper with a sharp sense that in the near future this drudgery might be over for good. All of those girls seemed to be looking at him no matter where he moved in the kitchen. He turned around frequently to glance at his phalanx of followers, and there they all were, smiling at him. He sat down to eat feeling like some maharaja with a harem. First he fancied one, then another. He was getting as critical as Sammy. This is what happens, he thought, once you start to play the game.

In the evening, just after Joe had turned on the radio, Sammy came knocking on the door, thrust in his head, and immediately exclaimed, "I thought so! A whole new batch. This is the best bargain I ever heard anybody get for two dollars." He swung into the room, and scarcely glancing at Joe, pounced upon the photographs with great relish, picking up each one.

They had a fine time for two hours, with Joe now feeling himself Sammy's equal and arguing every point. Finally he flung his arms wide. "All right. You take any of 'em you want, Sammy. Sure, take their names and addresses and anything else. Take their pictures. When I settle on that particular one, the others will just end up in the coal scuttle."

"Aren't you going to write notes of consolation? Not even a postcard to all of these?" Sammy asked.

"It's hard for me to write letters. You do it, Sammy, if you want. I don't care. The important thing for me is to make the choice."

"Without waiting for tomorrow's mail?"

"It'll only get me more confused. I don't need even this many women to choose from. I'm not that particular—at least, I wasn't two days ago. Why, last week one of those Catholics probably would have been good enough, if she'd come to my door. Anything in tomorrow's mail you can have, in appreciation for all you've done."

"You sound like a man who's made up his mind."

"I have," said Joe, his chest high, his face sober with the importance of this moment. "She's right there under your left hand."

"Marygold?" asked Sammy, smiling, for she had a sweet round face, soft frizzy hair, and in discussing her with Joe, he had decided that everything pointed to the probability that she was docile and good-tempered. Having been raised in an orphanage and thus used to a hard life, she would appreciate Joe's love and willingly bend her back to provide him with a good home. The choice of Marygold did not surprise Sammy, for he knew that when a man felt himself in danger of being hurt, he took the safe course rather than risk the greater excitements of uncertainty and adventure. For himself, he liked women who were wild and wiggly, hot-tempered and unpredictable, but he could understand Joe's affectionate glance at this benevolent face.

Thus the correspondence began, at first directed by Sammy, but two weeks later Joe was on his own, and Marygold, having given up her waitress job in Dubuque, was on the train for Kaleburg. She was moving into his arms more quickly than Joe had expected; her train was due in Kaleburg shortly after lunch, but he had made no arrangements about where she might stay. The only hotel in town was not a fit place for ladies, since rooms were rented primarily to couples looking for illicit privacy. He had no friends, other than Sammy Schneider, who might take in Marygold as guest while he became acquainted with her. Too shy to mention his predicament to Sammy, he met Marygold's train without a plan in mind. A certain amount of secrecy in this matter was highly desirable, for although

McIverson suspected the mail-order nature of his courtship, Joe still hoped to fool the general public.

Fortunately, on this bright May day the farmers were all busy in their fields and housewives were in their gardens; only the station agent was at the depot to meet the train. Marygold was the single passenger to disembark. She lumbered slowly down the steps from a far coach, which was nearly out of the railroad yard. Had she been riding first class in the observation car? Joe feared the revelation of an extravagant nature, here, at the first meeting. He hurried down the cinder path toward her and the porter. If she was surprised to view him in the flesh, she did not show disappointment, only a flustered uneasiness as they confronted each other. She was much, much heavier than he had imagined, and as if in explanation, she made fleeting references to the fatty foods in the restaurant where she had been working. There was a purity about her voice, which was small, dainty, and pleasant to hear, and a curious innocence in her eyes; Joe found her immediately appealing. He hoped that as she watched him tip the porter and gather up her luggage she would delight in the masterful way he was already taking care of her. He settled her in the car and closed the door.

As they drove up Main Street, Joe pointed at the restaurants, taverns, banks, and churches—naming and explaining the landmarks in a great rush, as if she would surely feel lost, not understanding the significance of these places. She said little but kept a sweet expression on her face, a reserved smile on her lips, and she looked at the surroundings more than at him. They turned down a dirt road toward his farm, and Joe was happy that the meadow larks sang so sprightly, that the bright green of early summer pastures looked so cheerful, and that tiny new cornplants were already growing in some fields, like the stitching of green thread. This was an auspicious season to begin their life together. "And here is my farm," he announced, as he turned down the long lane lined with flowering plum trees.

The house was thoroughly clean, and he kept Betsy outside, although she scratched on the screen door, betraying her former habits. Marygold, however, paid no attention to the dog. She busily inspected the old-fashioned kitchen, which had a hand pump over the sink, instead of faucets, and a wood stove for cooking, even in summer. "Let's go into the living room," said Joe, formally conducting her into the little-used parlor. It was usually sealed shut to prevent dust from entering and begriming the doilies which his mother had crocheted many years ago; the grey antimacassars were like webs on the stuffed furniture, and the room had the smell of an attic.

"Where will I stay?" asked Marygold, settling herself into a leather rocker with care. Despite her weight, her movements were calculated, and she seemed graceful, the way a fat girl on a dance floor often is the lightest partner.

"Oh, upstairs," he said casually, although blood began to pound in his head just at the thought of having a woman across the hall from his own bedroom.

"But I mean now, at first, where will I stay?"

"There ain't no other place, Marygold, but upstairs." The downstairs guest room was too far from the bathroom to be considered.

She frowned and struggled to her feet, as if she feared a spider had lured her into his dark den. "But I mean, I won't have this, Mr. Clausen."

"You can call me Joe," he said, smiling nervously.

"This is against the rules of the agency," she complained.

He smiled, hoping to set her mind at ease, but since he was unable to think of words, Marygold misinterpreted his grin. With mounting alarm she said: "This isn't decent, Mr. Clausen. You take me back to town."

"Now, now, Marygold, I'm not going to hurt you. Just sit

down, and I'll get you something to eat." He thought, probably, that this would please her most. He was right, for at the mention of food she was immediately somewhat placated.

"All right. What do you have?"

"Home-cured ham and fresh bread I got from the bakery." They moved companionably into the kitchen, and while Joe fixed sandwiches and poured milk for her, he explained that he would be on his honor not to molest her until the marriage ceremony, that she should rest content in the safety of her presence here as a guest; as Marygold began to eat, Joe sensed that she was relaxing.

They talked all afternoon, and although Joe's attention wandered at times from her accounts of the orphanage, various jobs, companions, and employers, he quickly came to see that she was as beautiful as he had hoped—very feminine and ladylike. She would keep him shaved, bathed, and cleanly dressed, and together they would go out evenings to card parties around the neighborhood. This would be a whole new life, and the prospect pleased him immensely.

"But what will people say, me here in the house with no chaperone? It don't look good, Joe, that's all. We got to think of the impression we make on people, and I certainly don't want them to get the wrong idea."

"Then I have it! Let's get married at the parsonage right away—oh, I mean," he added hastily, noticing alarm in her blue eyes, "we'll prevent gossips from talking by having it all legal right from the start. Then we can get acquainted at our leisure, if you know what I mean."

She did. After some reflection, it seemed a sensible idea, especially now that she began to feel sure he was trustworthy. They drove to the county courthouse that very afternoon and procured a marriage license; then they returned to Kaleburg. It was nearly six o'clock, an inconvenient hour to bother Reverend Kallsen, but Joe realized that it had to be done, and a minister like a doctor must expect to serve when called. He went to the door of the parsonage alone, leaving Marygold in the car. Hastily, Joe explained the situation to Reverend Kallsen, who seemed quite shocked to learn that Joe had found a bride through the mails. "Is she a Christian, Mr. Clausen?"

"Do you think I'd pick a heathen?"

"No, I mean, has she been baptized and confirmed in our faith?"

"In her letter she said she went to services at a church called God's Word." He certainly thought that sounded religious enough to suit the minister. He was getting hungry, and all of the excitement had made him suddenly tired. He wanted the ceremony to begin and be over with.

"God's Word? What in the world can that be? Some evangelistic group, I suppose." He turned meditatively to Letty and asked if she had ever heard of God's Word.

"Yes, all my life," she answered wryly and rattled a pot on the stove.

"You can marry us, can't you?" asked Joe. "She can come to church with me later," he promised—a hollow resolution, he knew, but something had to be done to get the ceremony going. For all Joe knew, Marygold, left to herself, might be having second thoughts. All she would have to do would be to say no. He had no hold on her yet. The thought of his precarious situation drove him to distraction. "Please, Reverend Kallsen, let's *hurry!*"

The minister blushed and gave Joe an odd look, which he suddenly understood; Reverend Kallsen thought him so hot that he couldn't wait. Joe was shocked that the minister would have such an idea, for Reverend Kallsen, he assumed, kept his thoughts far from the carnal, though he dwelt much on sin in others. There was no explanation Joe could make. "We've got to get some witnesses," he said, his voice sailing out of control. "Let's get going on this."

"I'll be a witness!" Letty Kallsen raised her hand. With a smile she took off her apron and smoothed down her hair. Women were always that way about weddings, Joe thought.

"But—but we'll have to have another," said Vernon.

Joe immediately thought of Sammy, and after asking permission, he rushed into the kitchen and cranked the wall phone.

"Well, *I'm* going to invite the lady in," said Letty, glancing in disgust at Vernon, for she felt he looked as if a holy sacrament were being raided—and at what an unfortunate time, just when the roast was done and the supper table set.

"Yes, yes. Go and speak to her," said Vernon absently, rubbing his moist forehead.

Joe shouted into the telephone, for with half the rural line listening the connection was weak. "Can you hear? Sammy, this is Joe. I can't explain over the line, but you've got to come to town right now. To the parsonage. Yes, quick as you can. This is one favor—the last favor, if you know what I mean. Tell your father it's an emergency. Yes, life or death."

At these words Vernon stepped closer to look at Joe, whose face was toward the wall. Who would have thought this silent farmer had so much passion in him? Would the girl in the car be able to cope with him—a man gone half wild with the notion of marriage, which had been too long deprived him— now raving incoherently on the brink? Perhaps the ceremony should be delayed, for the sake of the bride, until Clausen calmed down. As the farmer hung up, his flashing eyes had a peculiar look of insanity, which further alarmed Vernon. But if he refused to marry them, Clausen would rush with the girl to the Justice of the Peace and Vernon would lose the five-dollar fee customary on these occasions.

When Letty brought Marygold into the kitchen, Vernon's fears were somewhat eased, for she seemed a sensible, immovable girl, surprisingly hefty and earth-bound, and likely to keep Clausen under control, no matter how crazed with passion he became. Joe paced around, slapping his hands together and peering through the lace curtains for a sign of Sammy's car. The women talked pleasantly of the weather, and Marygold told a little about her background. Vernon flung shut the heavy plush drapes, which closed off the study and made it a private chapel. Talk ran out, and Joe could not sit still, although several times Vernon suggested he rest.

"There's Sammy!" Joe shouted when he heard a knock on the door. Letty got up quickly to let in Sammy, and when he appeared, still in overalls and unshaven, he looked nervously at them, taking no comfort in the minister's words of good fellowship. Sammy knew on which side of the devil he had been playing, and although Reverend Kallsen seemingly held out a friendly hand, he was in reality an enemy. "You'll be my witness," said Joe proudly.

"Witness?" Sammy asked blankly, pretending he knew nothing at all about Joe's love affair through the mails and couldn't possibly guess who this large, strange woman might be. As far as Sammy was concerned, he washed his hands of the whole affair; so she *did* turn out to be fat and ungainly, was that any reason for Joe to call Sammy in to give an accounting? Witness, indeed! He would admit to nothing. From the very start he had made it clear to Joe that whatever came of all this, the responsibility would have to be borne by Joe alone. Sammy had only suggested the bureau of matrimony as a last resort, since Joe's local prospects were so dim.

"I guess it's right to have a best friend stand up for you when you get married," said Joe, as they all got to their feet.

Vernon, standing with an open prayer book in his hands, motioned for them to gather closer. "Let us begin."

"Sure—sure," said Sammy, turning to Joe and laughing foolishly. "You darn right, old man, only I didn't expect to be called in so soon." He winked broadly and slapped Joe affectionately on the back. What kind of charm, unknown and

untested, did this homely bachelor farmer have, anyhow? Alone
with a strange woman for a couple of hours, and she was ready
to go to bed with him that night. It almost outdid any record
Sammy himself had set—unless, of course, this girl was altogether too easy with men, which was unlikely. He studied both
of them with new respect and interest, and for the first time
had a suspicion that there was much he still had to learn in
matters of love-making.

The ceremony over, Sammy signed the certificate and asked
Joe, "Where're you going on the honeymoon?"

"We'll take that later, after corn planting. Right now we're
heading for the farm."

Again Sammy was struck by Joe's decisiveness—it was as if
he had everything figured out far in advance. The girl meekly
followed behind Joe, as a woman should. He congratulated
them both and wished them happiness, then departed in his
car. Vernon Kallsen shook hands with the newlyweds. "Blessings on you both. The Lord said, 'Be fruitful and multiply.'"

"Thank you, Reverend," said Joe, slipping him five dollars.
"We will."

In almost every way Joe's new life was a happy one, for
Marygold was an excellent cook and housekeeper, and he loved
to hear her humming while she washed dishes. He did not
mind her gentle scoldings when his table manners lapsed or if
he tramped into the house with muddy shoes, for after all, the
house was her domain, and gladly he gave it to her. Looking
back upon his solitary life, he was appalled by its emptiness.
"You'd hardly believe it, Marygold, but that dog Betsy was
about my only companion."

"Well, those days are over," she said, smiling.

But in the darkness of the night in his single bed, Joe tossed
and shifted uncomfortably, for the old days were not completely over. He was sharply aware of the vague perfume and

powder odors in the upstairs hall and the scented soap in the bathroom, but he was awfully backward about showing her how much her presence affected him. Late one night when he heard her pad back to her room after taking a bath, he leapt from his bed, threw open the door, and grabbed for her. Marygold let out such a frightening blast that all three dogs were roused to a fervor of barking and howling. Back in his bedroom, passion having subsided quickly within him, supplanted now by a hot sickening shame, Joe listened to the mocking dogs and their chorus of admonishment.

When would there be an end to this waiting? She was his wife, wasn't she? How long would it take her to get used to the idea? With mounting apprehension, he realized that the marriage ceremony performed a very practical function, giving public sanction to intimacy. In his peculiar situation there was no fixed time at all, and he regretted that they had not set a date when they would have their own private ceremony. Now he must work out some plan, and there was no possibility of aid from Sammy, who had clearly assumed Joe's success on the first night.

When they went to movies, church services, and shopped together on Saturday nights, Joe felt that their false marriage must be apparent to the whole community. Marygold looked so virginal, and he hovered so clumsily about her, blushing when anyone offered congratulations, wondering if veiled ridicule were not behind the friendly words. Marygold was serene on their public appearances and made no slips as she talked with Kaleburg neighbors. She intimated that she had known Joe for some time and even suggested that they were vague relatives, cousins several times removed. Considering how physically removed they actually were, these incestuous comments from Marygold only deepened Joe's concern. Before long, he feared, she would claim they were brother and sister. During all of the two months that elapsed in this uncertain way, what troubled Joe most of all was that Marygold seemed content and in no hurry whatsoever to establish a closer connection. Perhaps she was indifferent to the business entirely.

He persisted in showing her attention, and he kissed her often on the cheek. Occasionally, she seemed to respond to a hug, but Joe could never be certain that it wasn't his fevered imagination. He bought boxes of candy, bright ornaments for her blouses, and even a tall rose-colored bottle of cologne, which Myron Koch, the drug store proprietor, had recommended. She was delighted with these gifts and told him what a fine husband he was; but Joe was cast into gloom by this praise, for he knew that so far he was a miserable failure as a husband.

He began to hint more strongly about his unhappiness: his mattress was lumpy, while hers was soft (she suggested he buy another); the summer heat hovered in his room, and how much cooler it was in hers (she promised to keep the shades drawn in his bedroom all day); he complained that he was restless, and with the hard work of harvest facing him, couldn't seem to sleep (she suggested he take pills); he said that he certainly hoped they would have a lot of children, for he especially wanted some boys to help him with farm work. She replied with only a wistful smile that he could not fathom.

Then, on a rainy day in August, Joe stopped at Meecher's Tap and found Sammy playing pinochle at a back table. Gulping down two beers, Joe waited at the bar until Sammy finished his hand. He had decided to make a complete confession, and although Sammy might ridicule him, he would also offer advice. Joe felt himself at his wit's end. When Sammy finally joined him and companionably they cocked a foot on the brass rail, Joe was disheartened by Sammy's jovial speculation about the bliss of newlyweds. "You set a record, Joe, I must say. I haven't told anybody, but I'm still remembering how you moved right in and took that girl to the preacher. No funny business about it—that's the way to treat 'em." Sammy grinned and smacked his lips; he drained the glass of beer and wiped his mouth. "Of course, I could tell when I first saw her, she'd been around." He looked at Joe with a sophisticated smile. "Been showing you *plenty*, I'll bet. More'n you ever dreamed of, right?"

Joe's throat began to tighten. He stammered, "Wh-what do you mean?"

Sammy half-coughed and hunched over the bar, as if he thought the whole matter so amusing that he could scarcely contain himself. "When I think of the way you were so particular—'virgins only need apply'—I just bust out laughing."

Joe's face flushed and he clenched his hands into fists. "Now just a minute. You can't talk like that about—"

"Ah, Joe," interrupted Sammy blithely, pushing his arm against Clausen's chest. "What kind of women do you think sign up to meet unknown men? Oh, brother! Did I find out! You know all those women who wrote you? I've been looking 'em up, one by one. That Swedish maid in Missouriville, remember her? Did I ever have a time with that! No language barrier between us, I guess not! And when I told her how close she had come to ending up in your bed instead of me in hers, we had a good laugh. They were all just doing it for kicks—all those women. Remember Susan Sampson from that little town of Dudley? Well, I drove down there about three weeks ago, and let me tell you, she's a half-wit. With her it's just anybody who comes along—the damnedest experience I've ever had. Then I tried that Marian Babson, remember her? The one who said, 'I love a good strong man'? It was all nonsense; she didn't want a man at all. So then I thought, why not look up this blonde babe who said she was a widow? You know, experienced! Maybe got money and all that. Even though the trip was eighty miles both ways, you never know. I got into my car and—"

"Stop! Stop it!" Joe shouted, pushing his arm out so violently that he knocked Sammy off balance.

Sammy caught himself just before hitting the floor and staggered back upright. "What the hell's eating you?" he asked angrily. "I thought you'd like to hear. After all, you and me were in on this together." He straightened his rumpled shirt and ran a comb through his hair, as he glanced over the whiskey bottles at himself in the bar mirror. "Unless," he began that undertone of teasing again, "she ain't what you bargained for."

"You just shut up," Joe replied hotly. All of this awful talk sickened him. It was as if Marygold's sisters were being slandered. And Sammy seemed on the verge of uttering something monstrous about Marygold, too. "You keep your nose to your own affairs and leave me to mine."

Then slowly Sammy began to chuckle, a derisive merriment beginning deep in his throat and erupting into a broad horse laugh. "Oh, ho, ho! I get the picture. All that fat and not a shimmer!" The notion convulsed him, and he hunched over the bar again to laugh himself out.

Joe swung with all his strength, striking Sammy's nose with a half-clenched fist. Sammy instantly sprang back, his nose spurting blood, and then he lunged at Joe. They stumbled into a spittoon and fell to the floor. "Hey, hey!" the bartender shouted. The card players in back rushed forward to pull the men apart.

Sammy, angered and disgusted, walked out of Meecher's, ready to spread the word to everyone that Joe Clausen had gone berserk and would probably end up killing that new woman he had gotten through the mails.

And Joe, clinging unsteadily to the bar, was still dazed by what he had done. He explained nothing to any of the men who crowded around him. His face was cut and his forehead bruised. He kept drinking whiskey until he felt he had control of himself, shaky though his knees were. Well anyway, by

God, I'm rid of that Sammy, he kept telling himself. He was quite drunk when he started home in late afternoon. By this time the fight had given him great prestige, and he saw new respect in the eyes of the farmers who moved in and out of Meecher's.

He drove along the dirt road in second gear, for he did not trust his vision. Just before reaching his roadgate an oncoming car unnerved him so greatly that he slipped too near the ditch. The Ford, like a large beast, nuzzled against the bank; the motor died. Somewhat shaken but unharmed, he realized he could not face dear Goldie in this condition. As he walked down his driveway and followed along the plum brush, he laughed aloud, thinking of how he had certainly done up Sammy properly for making those disparaging comments about his wife.

He did not go up to the house immediately, but instead, ducked his head in the horse tank and shook himself like a dog after a swim. Was he any more sober? He didn't think so. The world looked too green and bright, the sky too blue, and he had never felt stronger in his life.

He wandered into the barn, hoping his head would soon clear. Tomorrow he would worry about the car in the ditch, not now. He slumped down on a shelf of the cement foundation in the empty horse section and stared at the streams of sunlight that came through cracks and knotholes.

When finally he walked from the barn, slightly more sober, his face ached, his clothes were soggy, and he still reeked with whiskey. But with an easy confidence he shouted, "Hey, Goldie! Goldie!" He called her by his private name, which he had never done before. "Come on out, Goldie. I'm home."

She opened the screen door and let it slam behind her, for she was shocked by his appearance. "What happened to your face? An accident? Where's the car?" As he began to speak, she was immediately full of comfort. She took his hand and put her arm around his waist.

"I know I'm drunk and I've been in a fight, but nobody can talk about you that way." And then he told her everything. Inside, while she washed his face tenderly with cotton swabs and warm water, he kept on talking. "Not about my wife, he can't say those things."

"Yes, Joe," she said soothingly, "he's a smart aleck, but why pay attention to him? Sammy's just a boy."

"He may look like a boy, but he's been a man with an awful lot of women."

"Or so he says," murmured Marygold, as she put aside the wash basin. "There? That better?" She smiled and kissed his nose suddenly; briefly, she squeezed his shoulder and turned away. All these weeks she had been enjoying his ardent pursuit of her, his hungered look, his absolute attention—for didn't every girl want some kind of courtship? Who ever knew what the future might bring? So many husbands and wives tired of one another, once they succumbed to the habits of marriage and took affection for granted. Now she felt partly guilty for having caused this rumpus, but also, strangely pleased. She was in love with him, and he with her, despite the vulgar, mail-order origins of their acquaintance.

Joe, noticing her lingering gaze, took her in his arms and kissed her cheeks and lips. "I'm feeling fine now, Goldie. I feel best when we're like this." He pulled her even more tightly against him.

"Don't you think you'd better lie down?" she whispered.

The very roots of his teeth ached, he desired her so much; and the route to their bedroom by way of the stairs and upper hall seemed too long a journey. He opened the guest room and guided her to the bed. When he threw back the covers, his head throbbed, and he put his hand to his brow. She helped him untie his shoes; he sat there, master of his house, while she bent to her task. As he watched her, he felt the effects of the whiskey drop from him; he put his hands on her shoulders, caressed her cheek with his fingers. Then he pulled her into bed with him. "My sweet Goldie," he said. "My wife."

Even as he made love to her—blinding and absorbing though it was—part of his mind kept thinking yes, yes, this is as wonderful as Sammy said. Then it was over, and as he sank away, heart still pounding, he suddenly realized that indeed both of them had been virgins. It had all gone according to plan; and then he slept.

Later, when he arose, he told her to lie in the dark a while, if she liked. The milk cows were lowing uncomfortably in the barn, and it made him nervous. Betsy was waiting on the front porch, a puzzled look in her familiar eyes, for the sun had set sometime ago. Although he felt at peace and a certain joy uplifted his spirits, there was an edge of sobriety, too, with his new knowledge. At first he could not understand it. This lovemaking, this consummation of his marriage—was it the achievement of this he had actually desired all along, had talked about with Sammy, had speculated and dreamed about? Sammy would have one think that this business of possessing a woman was the end of all desires and the aim of life, the one final moment of unsurpassed bliss. But Joe knew now what Sammy had thus far not discovered.

He imagined that moment an hour hence when he would finish milking and approach the house. The kitchen windows would be glowing with light, for Marygold would have started supper. And as he opened the door, she would turn, and they would look into each other's eyes with a new understanding, for now they had a common footing; now they had begun that process of involvement with each other which they had both left celibacy to attain; now they could begin to love.

VI

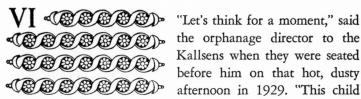 "Let's think for a moment," said the orphanage director to the Kallsens when they were seated before him on that hot, dusty afternoon in 1929. "This child you wish to adopt—don't expect too much. Don't think a mere adoption will make everything rosy for you."

Vernon squirmed uneasily in his chair, embarrassed to be subjected to this kind of instruction, as if he were a twenty-one-year-old bridegroom about to undertake the vows.

"I'm a good deal older than you two," said the white-haired former pastor, "and that gives me a right to speak frankly. You realize, I've seen many prospective parents sitting just where you are now."

Letty turned to Vernon and smiled sentimentally. He saw her out of the corner of his eye but did not turn from the director.

"Always—like you two—the people who come here can think of nothing but the future and the child. Well, now," he cleared his throat, "I'm suggesting a brief look at the past. Mind you, I'm not prying—just suggesting you ask yourselves, 'What brought us here?'" He noticed Vernon's frown and hastily added, "Oh, I'm delighted, you understand. And since

I'm a minister myself, I feel especially pleased to see you here. But what I'm talking about is the child's real position in your home."

"We'll do anything for him," said Letty dutifully. "We always wanted a boy, didn't we Vernon?"

"And our house is big enough," he added.

"That's not the point. I'm asking you to think of something else. When the Lord blesses a union with offspring, motives in wanting the child can't be raised. And yet I think they really should be. Nothing could be worse than an unwanted child, or a child whose presence is desired for ulterior reasons—to cement a marriage or something of that sort." He cleared his throat, smiling. "I'm just mentioning this, you realize, because these young people are in my charge. If they're to leave here and be placed in some home, then in their new life they must be loved for themselves, not for what they can do to improve things between parents. Not for extra help in running a farm, say. Not as a rallying point in disputes between husband and wife—all these things. Perhaps you read my article, 'Who Should Adopt?' in our national church magazine?" He picked it up and offered it to them.

"No—no, I missed that," said Vernon pleasantly, and he stood up to accept the copy. Letty's glance, as he sat down, was furtive but not accusing. If she remembered that Vernon's idea about adoption arose because he wanted to blend the parsonage into the Stilton community, she was not going to risk trouble now by openly accusing him. She, too, was eager for a son. Vernon hastily glanced over the pages. "Very interesting. Very fine."

"You see, all of this is merely a question of love." The director smiled somewhat sanctimoniously.

Vernon blushed. Homilies of this sort always embarrassed him.

"Oh, we'll give the boy plenty of love," said Letty.

What bothered Vernon at this moment was Letty's probable mental image of a three- or four-year-old, dressed in a natty sailor suit. They had never gotten around to discussing the question of age specifically, but Vernon thought a fairly grown-up boy, active in high school, would best fit their needs. The rough youngster he had seen outside on the playing field, bullying all his companions, this boy—without any logical reasoning behind the choice—was the one Vernon wanted.

"Perhaps I ought to mention," Vernon began, "the type of boy we have in mind is—say—a thirteen- or fourteen-year-old."

"Oh, I don't—" Letty interrupted.

"Let me explain," Vernon said firmly, looking at the director. "We're both thirty-nine years old. Perhaps we don't look it, but we are. And if we'd had a boy when we were first married, he'd be about thirteen or fourteen now, wouldn't he? That's all I meant."

"But he needn't be quite *that* old," Letty insisted. "Maybe six or seven."

"At our age? Don't be ridiculous. Let's not forget our gray hairs." Again he turned to the director. "I was wondering about a boy we saw just a few minutes ago on the playing field." Vernon quickly walked to the window behind the desk. "See him there, carrying the football? That lively youngster."

"No, no—Eugene would never do," said the director tiredly. "Why does this always happen? Parents come in here and ask for the impossible. There'd be no sense in adopting a boy that old. Anyhow, Eugene is simply not suitable. Let me show you his record." His head flushed bright pink as he bent over the file cabinet drawer and withdrew a Manila folder. "Listen: Born out of wedlock, father unknown. Mother sixteen at the time. River people—lived on the flats along the Mississippi. Sort of Southern hill people who came up the Mississippi on barges. They're nothing but a nuisance for every town along the river. Eugene has been in pretty good health, but bad blood can't be overcome. Up close you'll see it in his face—something seedy and outcast about him. From the very beginning he's been trouble for us. Stole food from the kitchen when he was six, and ever since he's been behind most dormitory rumpuses. I've personally whipped that boy more times than I care to remember, but nothing fazes him. He can take any amount of physical punishment without a yelp. I suspect his I.Q. is fairly high, but he fails most of his schoolwork. He's crafty, shrewd, and impossible—and naturally, is one of the most popular boys."

"Sounds as if he would benefit from a truly Christian home," said Vernon enthusiastically.

"Nonsense," said the director.

"And think of the challenge." Vernon turned to Letty, who sat stunned. "Taking in a bad boy and making him into somebody good—*that* would be a worthwhile venture."

"Maybe the best thing to make you change your mind is to see him up close. I'll have him called."

The Kallsens waited nearly an hour in an austere Victorian drawing room, and when Eugene came in at last, they jumped to their feet. The director made introductions, then left, and the three of them looked each other over. The boy was as tall as Vernon; his hair, still wet from a shower, clung together in tufts. He wore jeans, T shirt, and tennis shoes without socks. They sat down on chairs close together, and Letty began talking slowly about their trip to Davenport. She asked Eugene about the orphanage food, where the children slept, and how much time they had for play. Vernon studied the boy's brown, rather pimply face, but at first he could think of nothing to say, for he was strangely fascinated. "Do you like it here?"

Eugene's level, unguarded gaze fell upon Vernon. "I don't care." He shrugged his shoulders.

"Would you like to have a real home?" Letty inquired.

"I don't care," said Eugene with an incomprehensible smile. A thin, scraggly mustache shadowed his upper lip.

"Don't you care about anything?" Vernon asked.

Eugene, instead of replying, glanced at other sections of the room. Letty struggled to keep the conversation going; and finally, much to everyone's relief, the director came and took Eugene away.

Letty sighed, after the door closed. "He won't give an inch. Such a stubborn, independent boy. I'm a little afraid of him."

"Oh, he'll come around." Actually, Vernon found himself more interested than ever. "This is the boy we should take."

"He would be so difficult," protested Letty. "Just getting used to him. I mean—someone with a sweeter temper—perhaps a *little* boy."

"No, no, there will always be something wrong. Nobody's perfect. The real issue here is whether or not we can meet this challenge. If a parson's home isn't a good place for an orphan, and if we as foster parents can't handle him—why, then, then we might as well call it quits. I mean, we're miserable failures in every way." Letty said nothing, and during the pause a longing and determination swept through him. "If we don't take that boy, I'll never forgive myself!" He was amazed to find his throat choked with emotion—he was close to tears.

They were allowed Eugene on trial. After an orphanage counseling program intended to ease his transfer to family life, Eugene arrived by train in Stilton. All of the town's five hundred residents knew he was coming, and most of the surrounding farm families did, too. Eugene was the only passenger to disembark, and Vernon's was the only car on the station platform. He shook hands with the boy, picked up his suitcase, and put it in the trunk of his Model T Ford.

"This all there is to this burg?" asked Eugene as Vernon drove over the railroad tracks toward the parsonage. "What do people do with themselves, anyhow? Go crazy?" He squinted, looking right and left.

"You'll find out," said Vernon, smiling.

Letty waved to them from the front door, then came down the walk. "Your room's upstairs, Eugene. I'll show you." She was so excited that she ran ahead into the house. She was eager to see his reaction to the new maple furniture and her blue denim drapes.

Eugene's eyes widened as he entered the room. "This for me? Hey, it's all right!" He inspected the closet, then pulled out the top dresser drawer. "These mine, too?" He withdrew a shirt, pair of socks, and underwear. "How'd you know my size? Bet they don't fit."

"Well, try on a shirt and see," said Letty. She and Vernon sat on the bed while Eugene flung his old shirt into a corner, drew the pins out of the new, and pulled it over his brown shoulders.

"Yeah, it's okay," he said, admiring himself in the mirror. "Yeah, it's fine."

"Come now, supper's ready," said Letty.

Eugene ate eagerly of the roast beef and mashed potatoes, but Vernon found that his appetite had gone. He tried to think of things to say, but each conversational bit fell short of interest. Eugene ignored him and ate happily. Finally, without danger of meeting Eugene's sharp counter-gaze, Vernon studied the boy's narrow, rather handsome face, his rangy shoulders, long arms, and large hands. And shortly after supper they all went to their separate bedrooms.

During the dark hours, although Vernon could not actually hear Eugene's regular breathing in slumber, he distinctly felt the third presence in the household. For so long there had been just the two of them—everything divided in half: one bedroom hers, one his; a study for him, a sewing room for her; his shirts and her blouses; his "V" marked bathtowel and hers with an "L." Now suddenly they were a houseful, just with the addition of Eugene. He liked the feeling but couldn't sleep for a long time, thinking of how their lives would change.

In the morning he slept later than usual, and when he came downstairs Letty told him that Eugene had been up since sunrise. "Out roaming the streets, looking everything over," she said, pouring his coffee.

A vague alarm ran through him. "All alone?"

"Of course. I heard him get up, but I didn't want to start breakfast that early."

He imagined Eugene loping through the town. "And is he still out somewhere?"

"I gave him breakfast around seven, and then he left again. At the orphanage I'm sure he couldn't just walk out the door. He's probably enjoying his freedom."

"I wonder where he is now—you know, school starts at nine."

"Oh, he'll show up."

Vernon bunched up the paper napkin. "But maybe he's run off."

Letty paused, spatula in her hand, before the stove. "Why should he do that?"

"Such a good chance."

"But why do you say that?"

Vernon hastily gulped coffee, although it was scalding. He didn't know why he had said it. There would be no sense in anticipating trouble, and yet, far back in his mind, he knew it was coming. "We've got to be strict with him, that's all, or he'll run right over this household. He's been under the discipline of the orphanage, don't forget. If he gets the idea there're no laws here, he'll simply take over. We can't go soft-hearted."

"But I thought the idea was to give him some love, and—and a home. Isn't that why we're doing this?"

"Well, yes, it's all right for *us* to feel that way. But you know how kids are. If they find out their parents can't resist them, can't deny them anything, they just run roughshod over them. He should know he's on trial and ought to be a bit careful how he treats us. Before we fall all over him—giving him love, as you say—we'd do well to engender a little respect. First of all, he's got to look up to us. I know the type."

"But this is the boy we *chose*!" Letty said. "You were all for him!"

"It would be the same with any boy."

"I wonder about that! If you're spoiling for a fight with him, I can tell you—"

"Shhhh, there he is on the porch."

Eugene paused, the screen door half open. To Vernon and Letty in the kitchen he was a tall silhouette—and he hung there in the doorframe, eerily still.

"Well, come in, come in," said Vernon testily.

Eugene stepped into the room, glancing at both of them, as if he knew full well that they had been discussing him.

"Did you get a good look at the town?" Letty asked brightly.

"Yeah," Eugene answered, tentatively. The Kallsens waited a full minute before he said the rest: "I wish I was home."

Within a week Eugene stirred up disorder in the school. He was leader of a rebel army that lobbed spitballs over the fortification of books on the teacher's desk. He infiltrated the ranks of the American history class, and no serious discussion could take place. Unaccountable disturbances broke out everywhere. The English teacher diagramming sentences on the blackboard suddenly found impudent words among the chalk branches of what only a moment before had been a perfectly respectable sentence. There was a rash of giggling in the study hall, jostling on the stairs, and scuffling at the lockers.

The superintendent spoke to Vernon, reporting the teachers' complaints. "Every day is a fight, and nobody's learning anything. That new boy of yours is behind it—a real wild one, he is. I put him in the freshman class, because he's too big for the eighth-graders. Later on I'll have him come out for basketball —maybe that'll work off some of his steam. The whole trouble is, he's a natural leader. The kids would follow him to damnation, if he led the way."

"Yes—yes, I suppose so. But I don't know what can be done." He would certainly not admit that Eugene was on trial from the orphanage and could easily be sent back. Though each day with the boy seemed more difficult than the last, Vernon was unwilling to accept defeat this soon. His nerves were raw from sleepless nights, and Eugene, who had a curious talent for sensing weakness, would deliberately try to startle him by sneaking up quietly from behind. Suddenly he would speak loudly or walk with heavy feet, and when Vernon jumped—and once even gasped aloud—Eugene would laugh and ask, "Didn't you hear me?"

Meanwhile, Vernon prescribed a rigorous breaking-in course. There were rules for everything from table manners to breaking wind. Eugene ignored them all, was reprimanded, but never listened. Vernon kept him in at night, denied him dessert, sent him to bed, and scolded him in public. But laughing gaily, Eugene followed his own ways—he became known as The Joker—and through it all, the town was set on its ears. Nothing as fascinating as this had happened since the great fire of 1910.

Rumor spread that Eugene was not actually from an orphanage in Davenport but from the boys' reformatory at Eldora, and when Letty reported the story to Vernon, he sank into a chair as if he had been kicked in the stomach. "Well, of course, he acts like a convict—it's no wonder they think that."

"But Eugene has been the one—*he's* spreading the story. It's another of his jokes, only people haven't got the sense to realize it. Why don't you speak to him and tell him to stop— that's all. You know how boys are."

"Oh, Letty, how innocent of you! Why do you think he would deliberately do this?"

"To stir up excitement."

"Can't you see it's all to undermine me and the church? He knows good and well what a minister's son should be—and he'll be the opposite! He's bad, Letty—really wicked to the core. And if ever there was a struggle on this earth between good and evil, it is right here under this roof. I mean, the very feeling of a Christian household seems to call up the devil in him."

"Don't you make too much of this," Letty warned.

"I'm just saying, the struggle is deepening. We've either got to break his wild spirit, or he'll break us. We can't go on mincing around with each other."

"But what do you plan to do?"

"You'll see. There, he's coming up the walk. Go into the kitchen, and don't interfere with us."

"Vernon! What are you going to do? Tell me, do you hear?"

He grabbed her wrists and forcibly pushed her in the direction of the kitchen. She resisted, and Eugene stepped across the threshold and saw them there, locked in a rigid embrace. With embarrassment, they drew apart immediately. Now alone with him, Vernon began at once. "I hear you're spreading lies around town about where you came from. The boys' reformatory in Eldora, is it? Do you know how they treat boys at the reform school?" With his face set sternly, Vernon stepped closer.

Eugene did not move back. He smiled, hooked his thumbs in the loops at the waist of his jeans, and widened his stance.

"You're a liar!" Vernon swung out quickly with the flat of his hand, and though Eugene ducked in surprise, the blow landed on his neck.

"All right, that's enough," said Eugene with cool self-control. Anger flashed in his eyes as they studied each other like two cocks in a barnyard.

Letty rushed in. "Come to the kitchen, Gene. I've got milk and cookies." And after he walked by, she gripped Vernon's forearm with claw-like fingers. In a husky whisper she asked, "What's come over you? You're going to the devil!"

Gradually, just as Vernon had predicted, through Eugene the Kallsens became more involved in the community. Every father had some suggestion about how best to curb the wild boy. The farmers generally thought extra work would wear him down and advised corn picking. The old blacksmith gave Vernon a buggy whip, saying, "Try this!" with a laugh. Vernon hid the ugly black coil in his bedroom closet and did not mention it to Letty. It was the school superintendent who was most certain about how to handle Eugene—and most successful, for when basketball season began in late October, Eugene came home tired at six o'clock; after supper he took a brief look at his books and went to bed silently. Even on Saturday and Sunday afternoons he practiced for hours in the gym—shooting baskets from far out, dribbling rapidly, and rushing in to push the ball through the iron hoop.

The final adoption, which took place in November, was easily accomplished.

And then the basketball games began. Eugene was an immediate sensation. He made thirty-five points the first game, forty the second, and his name appeared in newspapers throughout the state. Vernon and Letty attended the first home game and sat in amazement as the gym vibrated with cheers. Eugene deliberately played to the audience by executing fancy passes over his shoulder and through his legs. "Isn't he fantastic?" Letty kept saying. "I wish I understood the game."

Vernon felt painfully self-conscious. During half-time people kept rushing up to congratulate him—even Catholics—and he could think of nothing to say. One by one the teachers stopped by to tell the Kallsens that they should be very proud of Eugene —and to Vernon's mind, the stern old-maidish English teacher, envy in her eyes, was the silliest of the lot. The village of Stilton was opening its heart to the minister at last, but what an embrace!

As Eugene romped through game after game there was much speculation on whether the team would win the state championship in the class C division. The Joker was such a hero that grade-school boys followed him around, shined his shoes, and ran errands; the merchants gave him food, cuff links, and clothes. Most of the high-school crowd gathered in Mrs. Blount's general store, and when Eugene shoved dress racks on rollers from one end to the other, she only smiled tolerantly. Vernon noticed The Joker getting cockier by the day, but nobody, not even Letty, seemed to mind. And what was happening to the religious sensibilities of the town as the basketball frenzy increased? The minister's adopted son was undermining the little spiritual headway being made. The people of Stilton were worshipping a false god, and the graven image was housed in the parsonage itself—infamy of infamies!

A week before Christmas, vacation began, and there were no more basketball games. But Vernon sensed at once that the gap was quickly filled by everyone's preoccupation with buying presents and getting food for the holidays. Letty's cheerful bustling about and her extensive preparations annoyed Vernon extremely, for she did not seem to realize to what extent she had fallen into the secular trap.

As long as the basketball season lasted, an uneasy peace reigned in the parsonage, for Eugene was out of the house most of the time. Meals were invariably emotionally tense because Vernon insisted that Eugene conform rigidly to certain table manners. Frequently he was sent from the table, as if he were a child of eight, but missing dessert never seemed to bother him—and Vernon suspected that Letty slipped him pieces of cake and pie on the sly.

In February, during the early rounds of state competition, Eugene fell ill with the flu and couldn't play; Stilton lost, and the basketball season was over. It coincided almost exactly with the start of Lent—always a difficult time for Vernon. He preached mid-week sermons, in addition to Sundays, beginning with Ash Wednesday. Each year, as he became involved again in the tale of Peter's ear, the pieces of silver. Pilate's "What is truth?" and the gall and wormwood, he had difficulty finally extricating himself from the age-old sorrow. Easter never saved him. It came too suddenly after the louring skies of Good Friday and the trembling earth. No hallelujahs or choral repetitions of "He is risen!" could awaken him from the dark depression of those long days of Lent. Not until spring itself came and he could walk outside in the reality of May sunshine and observe the green leaves and dandelions did he finally relax and cast off the old winter weight.

One day during the middle of Lent, when the earth was still brown and showed no promise of reviving, Vernon received a call to attend the sick bed of one of his parishioners. As he opened the garage doors, car keys in his hand, he noticed the quick, covert movements of three figures—Eugene and two boys. They lurked behind a stack of old tires and an oil drum at the front of the shed. "What are you kids doing in here?" he shouted angrily, although by their guilty scrambling he knew at once what they had been doing. He was worldly wise enough to know that boys of a certain age had their little orgies in secret. In addition, he saw a faint cloud of blue cigarette smoke, and he sniffed.

Where would this burst of deviltry stop, this spiral of wickedness that was engulfing the household and town? In another year Eugene would be seducing the cheerleaders—if he had not tried that already—and drinking liquor and stealing automobiles. "Now you two," he shouted to the boys crouched behind the tires, "get out of here this minute! Eugene, don't you move." The companions fled, faces averted. "I'll be right back," Vernon told Eugene, then closed and padlocked the door. Yes, put him in jail where he belongs, he thought.

Knowing what he was about to do, a giddy relief filled him— the long wait was over. He quietly entered the front door and slipped upstairs to get the whip. Letty in the kitchen did not appear to notice him as he crept down a minute later, the black coil in his hand.

But while unlocking the garage door, the wave of eagerness and excitement suddenly left him. He was a little afraid of what Eugene might do—there were cases of sons who simply struck down their fathers in open rebellion. He twisted the padlock and pinched his finger. Suddenly the pain urged him on. He flung open the doors with a wild strength. "Where are you?" he called, unfurling the whip. "Where are you?"

Eugene moved in the dusk behind the stack of tires, and Vernon swung the whip. The long black strand cracked harmlessly against the wall. He pulled it in again, awkwardly aware that he did not know how to use it. He had never whipped anyone in close quarters this way—only the rumps of horses on the open road.

Again, the tavern odor of cigarettes assailed him, and the sight of Eugene hovering in the dark reminded Vernon of the secret, dirty acts committed here, under the very wing of the Lord, within the shadow of the church steeple. If ever there was foulness in the Temple, if ever sinners needed to be swept from the Lord's house, now was the time. He flung the whip through another sweep. The slithering tip cracked against an upright beam and wrapped around it. Eugene, three feet away, laughed.

Angrily, Vernon jerked the whip free and swung again, this time hitting the wall with an explosion like a firecracker.

Eugene laughed again—an annoying little cackle, accompanied by a smirk. Vernon tried again, and this time he shattered the window. The glass tinkled like harness bells as it fell. Eugene's laughter bubbled through the air. He half-collapsed in mirth upon the pile of tires, but he rolled aside just in time as the whip swept over him. The black lash kept missing its mark, for Vernon was unable to get a full swing in the narrow space between the car and the wall. Desperately, he tried coming down with the whip, after lifting it high. He hit the rubber tires and dust flew up. In the recoil, the tip lifted erect and wavered in the air like a mocking asp. The next time he hit the hood of the car with the sound of an enormous drum. All the while, Eugene danced impishly from the pillar to the tires and back again, his Joker's mouth wide open, his laugh rising and falling in exaggerated squeals.

"You devil!" shouted Vernon, pale with rage. "You devil!"

Behind him the garage door scraped open, and before he could turn around, a furious beast leapt upon his back—Letty screamed and grabbed for the whip. "Stop it! Stop it!" She crooked her arm around his throat, and the force of her attack toppled both of them. They fell upon the inch-deep silt of the garage floor.

Immediately, anger left him; Letty no longer pummeled him, now that the whipping had ceased. They lay immobile and entwined for half a minute as the full horror of what they were doing came over them, as realization of their hatred and agony spread its enervating influence through their limbs. Then slowly, as if tired after great physical labor, they unwound from each other; they were still breathing heavily. They looked into each other's eyes with dumb astonishment. "What's to become of us?" Letty whispered.

"Oh, Lord help us," said Vernon fervently. He turned and saw Eugene, who crouched satyr-like upon the cylinder of tires; his brown hair was a thatch down the center of his forehead, and his eyes glittered. He was inscrutably watching them both.

"Let us pray," said Vernon softly, turning to Letty.

"Eugene, come here," said Letty. "Come," she added when he did not move. Slowly, he shuffled forward. She drew him down to kneel beside her, on the far side from Vernon.

"Dear God, have mercy upon us in our afflictions," began Vernon, with his eyes closed, his hands clasped at his chest, his knees in the dust. "Lead us toward the paths of righteousness, for His Name's sake."

All three of them were in a row by the rear bumper of the Ford: Letty with her hand gripping Eugene's arm, Vernon with his face tilted back, his eyes now open as he stared up, as if he could look through the roof into heaven itself. Only Eugene's face was dumbly ill at ease. He watched them both.

" 'For we wrestle not against flesh and blood, but against principalities, against powers, against the rulers of darkness of this world, against spiritual wickedness. . . .' "

VII 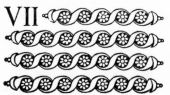 Paul Ketter was the first to see what was happening. He stood at the window of his farm home after breakfast one Saturday morning, early in November of 1936, and watched the first snowflakes of the season scud across the feathered clouds and settle in the grove, on the lawn—and, he knew, in his father's unpicked cornfields. He was sorry not to be in the schoolhouse, secluded from the weather, for he realized what concern and trouble here on the farm the snow would cause. "Look, Dad," he announced at last, "it's snowing."

Henry Ketter glanced in alarm at Vida and murmured, "It can't be." He did not even get up, at first, though Vida rushed to the windows.

She parted the red-checked curtains and saw the snow. "Oh, yes." Smiling with incredulity, she shook her head over this bad luck, for the corn had been left in the fields this late only because Henry hoped to share Hans Albrecht's corn picker. It was the first year he had not picked his fields himself, by hand with a team and wagon. This grim turn of fortune, Vida felt, was only typical of recent events; the snow was a white laugh in their faces for what would likely be their last winter on the Kaleburg farm.

She wished longingly that they could pack up and leave to-day. Unpredictable rural life had never really suited her small-town temperament, although she had tried her best to make a go of it, for Henry's sake. Vida had grown up in Kaleburg, among townspeople who saw each other daily and didn't become queer from being alone too much. When Henry was courting her, she had listened to his prophecies about future farm life—everything to be different from the old-time drudg-ery. The fact was, however, Vida had seen nothing but the stooped earthen look of country women, who seemed to bend closer to the soil which was making constant demands of them —and finally took them entirely.

"Let it snow!" shouted Henry. He rose and walked to the window, leaning his elbows on the frame. "Snow, snow! Who cares?" He laughed and turned around, hoping to have cov-ered his true despair. He had adopted great casualness about everything, once Vida's eagerness to leave the farm developed. Henry, the only Ketter son, had inherited this farm mortgage free, but in the last year he had slipped off the deep end buying cattle, and he would not rise again. There was some hope that Bill Wolbers at the bank might be able to extend the time on the note that was due, but Henry did not expect it. And just when would he *ever* have the money, even if given extra time, the way crops and prices had been running?

In order not to brood about the almost certain loss of his farm, Henry tried to ally himself with Vida's hopeful feeling about their future in some city. He was not dour by nature, nor would he allow his betrayed ancestors to rise from their graves in his imagination. Other things were important, too: his family's happiness and their general well-being; he had to provide as best he could. After all, he was still comparatively young, and there was a lot of strength in his six-foot body. Furthermore, Henry expected to get along well in the city, for he was quite handsome—blond, with the fair complexion of

North German stock—and people took to him easily; that whole angle, he gathered, was important in urban life. It would be comforting, too, to have a weekly paycheck. Sometimes, warming to Vida's enthusiastic dreams of shaded city streets, streetcars, garbage collectors, and department stores, he almost looked forward with pleasure to their move, March 1. On that date the bank would officially own his farm and put it up for sale.

The first snow fell four inches deep, and little of it melted before another two inches descended from low, wool-colored clouds. Throughout November Henry tried unsuccessfully to pick the corn that lay golden and incongruous in the snow. The brown, soiled stocks, long outworn, sagged under the delay. Since the corn picker could not maneuver the clogged fields, Henry made little forays into the corn rows with his wagon and horses. By December he had managed to pick, with fingers numb from the harsh wind, nearly half the crop. But a brief warm spell did not materialize into a stay of grace. New snow came to replace the hard, flattened snowbanks, and Henry reconciled himself to the thought that part of his crop might not be reaped at all.

Throughout December, intermittently, the snow kept falling, smothering the atmosphere with flakes which, on blizzard days, became fine white sand that crept under doorsills and between the windows. No tracks, no animal traces, no human footprints resisted the great obliteration of the snow. Even sturdy black-green firs were staggered and subdued; the snow was a mask clinging to the face of the world.

One day after chores Henry tramped into the house, his face tingling from the cold and his spirits very high. "There's never been a winter like this!" he said to Vida, smiling excitedly. "Nothing even Granddad went through was like this." To parry the season, to accept the splendid challenge—this excited his manhood. Henry heard with loathing of two farmers who had committed suicide, caught, like Henry, by the bad prices and poor crops. One had turned a shotgun against his head while he stood in the cow barn facing his mortgaged fields, letting his wife and children pick up the legacy of the bankrupt. The other had driven his car into the garage and, with the door closed, sat with his foot on the gas pedal to take him to damnation. No wonder the Catholic Church tossed those souls to outer darkness! A man had to recognize the difference between a challenge and a judgment and thus gauge the import of a storm.

The whole family kept alert ears, listening for the distant anger of the snowplow opening the roads, and finally, the weekend before Christmas, the orange county plow furrowed the drifts. Upon driving to Kaleburg, Henry and Vida began gift-buying, while the two boys attended Reverend Kallsen's Christmas-pageant rehearsal at the church. Winter had been upon the land six weeks, and farmers who were usually mute now heartily greeted each other with tales of the weather. Old men at the card tables in Meecher's Taproom told of thick fur on rabbits and foxes, which indicated a long, severe winter. "Wait'll we get to January!" They shook their heads wisely.

The heavy sky was slate, the color of junco birds, but the storm held off. On Christmas Eve the Ketters arrived early at church and obtained good seats. Floyd in his year-old Sears Roebuck suit displayed himself prominently, for he was the only pupil in the Sunday-school primary class sure of all the words of "Tannenbaum," which they sang with faces uplifted to the tree. Since Paul was very large for his age, when his turn came he spoke loudly, soberly, embarrassed lest the congregation have the slightest anxiety over his recitation. There was no fidgeting or giggling from either of them.

After the droning hymns, with the congregation half-hypnotized by staring at the glowing tree in the warm, dark church, Reverend Kallsen pronounced his blessing and drew the sign of the cross in the air to settle out upon them. But every time Vernon made that gesture—his forefinger raised— he thought of Eugene, and now a memory of the Christmas he had been with them—the only Christmas—rose in Vernon's mind and carried him off.

He remembered the difficulties of the weeks before the holiday when he had tried to hold rehearsals of the pageant. No one knew his lines or seemed in the least concerned. The pageant had always been a church ritual of which Vernon was most proud, and he felt, too, that the ceremony came very close to moving the hearts of his congregation. Each family had some child performing, from the smallest three-year-old on up. Some of them were the Magi, in bedsheets, with their little heads crowned with tinsel; others were shepherds, with cardboard staves, watching their flocks by night—or the Virgin Mary and Joseph bending over the doll's cradle. The pageant was much the same each year, since after all, the Christmas story was unchanging; that was its beauty. The whole unfolding seemed to bind the congregation together, and Vernon always felt that for one hour on Christmas Eve, Christianity held them luminous in its grasp. The Savior was born! This was the magic news which gave the lie to a whole year of religious indifference in Stilton. They believed, at least for a moment.

But with Eugene present, the whole program was changed, for although he was not in the pageant itself, but a member of the choir (and Vernon put him in a black choir robe to disguise his presence), The Joker came through the garb. Following Vernon, who led the procession singing, "Oh, Come All Ye Faithful," Eugene's squawky baritone voice was so loud that he almost drowned out the organ. He was not only noticeable but highly ridiculous; he knew this and was amused by it. The old feeling of mastery did not rise in Vernon's throat as the organ music swelled and the congregation leapt to its feet to honor the holy parade. An imp was dancing at his heels, distorting everything.

Vernon saw the whole Christmas Eve service alter subtly before his eyes as Eugene turned into an anti-Christ. He grinned and bobbed his head, nudged his neighbors, whispered all through the pageant, and ogled the congregation. Since the downslope of ridicule is always easier than the uphill task of infusing faith, Eugene ran away with the evening. While reading the precious words of the Gospel of St. Luke, Vernon could not concentrate on the text; he thought, instead, of how his adopted son had chosen the most vulnerable moment of the whole year to wreak his worst damage. This night most precious was being sullied by a basketball star. At any moment, it seemed, Eugene might step out of the choir loft, fling aside his robes, and in his blue-and-white-satin uniform go dribbling down the aisle to shoot a basket in the narthex.

Suddenly the overhead lights in the church were turned on and Vernon was back in Kaleburg, facing farmers and townspeople who could not know the old patterns his mind kept tracing. Before him, the ushers were busily passing out goodies to the children: brown paper bags filled with a disappointingly standard array of candy and nuts, every sack the same, so that no trading or gloating was possible. And each Sunday-school teacher deftly opened all her gifts, pretending delight over the handkerchiefs, hair clips, and painted pencils—no student had been allowed to spend more than ten cents. While this took place, the elders distributed bowls of apples and nuts among the congregation; neighbors murmured greetings to each other as the long restraint of the church service ended. Soon everyone was laughing and talking, completely oblivious to the fact that this was the house of the Lord. They ate apples, snapped nuts, and crackled bags among the holy pews.

Late in the night, while the children slept, Henry left Vida's side to creep into the kitchen, where he placed Santa Claus' presents on the seats of both chairs tucked under the table, as if Santa Claus had come down the black stovepipe, lifting the lids of the iron woodstove, to deliver these gifts. Henry was about to place the gold bracelet wrapped in a small white box upon Vida's chair and draw that up to the table, but he changed his mind. He chided himself for nearly allowing the boys' magical Christmas to intercept his pleasure in giving the present to Vida in person.

She had dozed off, and when he came back to bed he touched her flannel nightgown, surprising her with the gift. She sat up, pushed back her dark hair, her eyes alert and wondering as she undid the parcel. When she held out the glittering bracelet, Henry knew that her awareness of how little they could afford such a luxury actually added to her pleasure. She tried it on, held the gold band far from her eyes, and then up close; she hid it behind Henry's back as she embraced him. He kissed her warm neck, snug under the nightgown, and he felt with pleasure the two pads of warmth where she pressed his back. He began making love to her with an ardor that sprang surprisingly alive. They had not had a time like this for many months—in the middle of the night, alone, with no fear of being overheard through the thin walls.

Before they fell asleep again, the wind sighed as it shifted direction, and new snow scratched icily on the storm windows. In the morning they awoke to another blizzard, with the wind defined and embodied by the currents of snow. The storm broke through the flaying limbs of the bare trees in the grove, streaked in long waves across the orchard, and disappeared in a mist around the barns. "Have you ever seen a storm like this?" he asked Vida, as they dressed in the cold bedroom. "It keeps coming back."

"Maybe it's trying to bury us here," she said casually as she combed her dark hair. At her dressing table, surrounded comfortably by cosmetics, she enjoyed a mood peculiarly private. Moments such as this, with the mirror reflecting her image, stretched back to that young round face of girlhood, and the day she first put on lipstick.

"We're buried, all right," said Henry, lacing his cowhide shoes. "Snowbound since last night, I'll bet, with this wind drifting shut the hole the snowplow made."

"There's nothing we can do about it, I guess," she said, glancing at him in the mirror. "And there really isn't much we *have* to do," she added, with a smile.

"I've got the chores."

"But what else?"

Henry laughed, rubbing his blond, stubbled chin. "What are you getting at?"

"I guess we have a holiday!" With satisfaction, she turned back to her own face in the mirror. At thirty-five, her beauty was superior to the baby prettiness of her plump early twenties. Now her cheeks were smoothly planed, and her face seemed lean and sophisticated; in the right clothes, which she took great pains to sew, she could walk any city street with confidence. Only her coarse, chapped hands betrayed the nature of her work.

The boys knocked on the bedroom door, clamoring for breakfast. "What's the matter? Why ain't you people up?" called Paul.

"Oh, go away," replied his father with a laugh. And later, when they emerged, while Vida mixed the pancake batter, Henry told the boys: "Since you're on vacation from school, you can help me full-time with chores."

He had said it in jest, knowing how much they wanted to exhaust the store of untried imagination hovering over their Christmas toys, but when he began fighting his way through the drifts toward the barn, with his children hugging his heels,

Henry was happy for their help. Normally, during the school year, Paul's farm tasks were light.

Paul shoveled ensilage into the feed bunks for the white-faced Herefords, who crowded close together in the steaming barn, their coats hoary and eyes benevolent. Henry, meanwhile, attended to the milking. Floyd was too small to be good for much except arbitrating disputes among the fourteen cats, although later he helped turn the handle of the cream separator. Both boys assisted Henry in trying to lure the pigs from the warm hog house to eat the corn Henry scooped into bins on the snow-cleared feedlot. A few of the greedier pigs stole out, until the cold overwhelmed them, and they hurried back on their pointed toes to the warm straw within. The chickens in the henhouse breathed little clouds of vapor around their beaks. White and pale-cold as the day, the Leghorns stood high on the straw bedding of their barn; they, like the other live-stock, looked up at Henry and the boys as they entered as if long ago they had given up rescue, and, with beak touching beak in communication, had resigned themselves to a cruel death. Only the dog really seemed to enjoy himself, for he loped through the drifts close behind Floyd, delighting in the bliz-zard for its harassment of everything.

The storm made all normal winter work impossible, excus-ing Henry from repairing machines, sawing logs, or cleaning out the barns. He returned to the house before eleven o'clock and read the *Wallace's Farmer* until the noon market and weather report on the radio. Then, after their meal, Vida read Kipling to them all, while Henry sat with his shoes off, his feet propped against the warming reservoir of the woodstove.

"You know," he smiled at Vida when she finished a chapter, "I'll bet all our neighbors aren't doing a thing, either." It was a comforting notion, for especially in spring, when the Schnei-ders or Joe Clausen started field work before him, Henry would anxiously test the soil to see if the frost were out; and even when he knew that it was still too early to plow or disc, he would be made uneasy by a neighbor's premature start.

"We can sleep as late as we please, without worrying about being caught in bed," Vida said. They recalled the morning when the alarm clock had not rung, and having overslept, Henry was seen in his pajamas by John Hendricks, who knocked on the door at seven thirty. Old John told about it in Meecher's Tap, and for several days people teased Henry when they saw him, for he wasn't the sort of man ordinarily caught that way.

The whole family speculated about when the snowplow would come again, but on New Year's Day it snowed more and they began to lose their expectations. Floyd and Paul could not even walk to country school a mile away, for Vida felt it was much too cold; the boys were not restless, having taken considerable interest in the challenge of the bad weather. Henry told them they were "real hired hands," and thus encouraged, they worked part of one day repairing the blowtorch in order to thaw the watering troughs in the chicken barn. The boys also hollowed out caves in snowbanks, pulled each other on a sled, and played fox-and-goose with imaginary companions. And when the bitter cold numbed their noses and hardened the lobes of their ears, they moved inside to convert one whole room of the house into a vast map of Europe, with armies of marbles marshaled on the frontiers, guarding paper kings and queens on tinfoil thrones.

Since their coal burned rapidly during the sub-zero weather, Henry told Vida he would have to stop being lazy and dig in the grove until he found wood for fuel. He gave the boys shovels to help excavate where he thought a fallen pine tree lay, and then, with Paul and Floyd exchanging turns on the other end of the hand saw, Henry bent to his task, watching the golden sawdust spill from the log and scatter upon the snow. Each noon the hysterical siren from Kaleburg swept across the empty miles to mark the half of day. Loaded with wood, all three would tramp through the drifts toward the house.

It was not hard managing thus by themselves; it was surprisingly easier than Henry had expected. For one thing, Vida always canned more vegetables, fruit, and meat than she ever used in a year. Now they drew upon leftovers still perfectly preserved from other seasons, and as they opened each jar, memories of the strawberries, cherries, tomatoes, or beans of those forever past years came vividly back to dispel the barrenness of winter. Henry knew they could withstand a siege of months, living off these summer earnings from their fertile farm. The thought made him feel enormously proud, rich in his stewardship of the land. What if they didn't make money? They made a living.

When the electricity was cut off, they heard no radio and could not share the news of other isolated communities, although lately the announcers, tired of talking about the weather—the worst winter since 1882—had been mentioning local conditions less frequently. Henry and Vida did not miss the news, for it seemed to matter little what Roosevelt was doing in Washington or Mussolini in Italy. That world was far away and unreal compared to their winter and unbelievable next to the facts of existence on the snowy plains.

The Ketters were also without a telephone, which worried Vida, for if one of the children should fall ill they might need aid desperately. "With the roads blocked, how could help come?" Henry laughed. "Even if you phoned? We're on our own, and if there's any help needed, we'll have to help ourselves."

But Vida could not dismiss the awful possibilities, not like Henry, who perhaps in childhood had experienced this kind of isolation. For her they were snowbound and lost—subject to constant danger. She cautioned the children as they marched with their father to the woodlot: "Don't cut yourselves!" Vida imagined a lacerated hand, bleeding profusely in the stark, white snow. Against the possibility of disease she felt somewhat easier, unless the boys during the Christmas pageant had been exposed to germs which now were incubating. Measles, chicken pox, colds—these she had come to expect, and they did not trouble her. She tried to quiet her fears in Henry's presence, for she noticed his pleasure in the easy days and knew that the relaxation was good for him, before the difficulties of the coming spring—the job hunt in the city and all the dark uncertainties facing them. Let him have this one time of peace, she thought.

The leisure brought them closer together, and Henry came to her like a bridegroom on those long dark nights. Vida gave herself willingly to him, although they had resolved not to have another child, considering their low finances and unsettled future. Now even their casual glances in the kitchen, over the heads of the boys, held a latent sensuality that stirred her deeply. She had thought she was growing older, past the time for this kind of behavior—and Henry, too—but as their daily love-making stretched on she began to think that they had only now come upon their true experience of physical happiness. Everything of love they had known before was a kind of preliminary to this shuddering, new relationship.

Vida was embarrassed for fear the children might wonder about the change that had come over their parents, but Henry did not seem to mind and even kissed her in front of them, which he had never done before, except in the dutiful way of aunts' parting. She was greatly encouraged by his attention and much more at ease about what the future held in store. She had not been uncertain of his love, for Henry was too reliable ever to change the focus of his affection, but she knew he had tried to hide his bitterness about losing the farm. He pretended it meant nothing to him, but Vida knew that the home where he had been born would not pass lightly from his hands. Only a greater loyalty, a higher demand, such as this new, powerful serenity they had found between them in their love, could lessen the loss of the other.

"Do you notice?" Henry pointed out one day. "The boys don't fight between themselves like they used to."

"They have so much to keep them busy, I suppose."

Henry rubbed his hand through his hair in an awkward gesture that always preceded some half-embarrassed disclosure. "This is a good life for them, that's why."

"Yes," she said, catching his full intent. "It's a fine place to raise boys *if* they're going to be farmers."

"Well, there's no use talking," he said, hurrying off to the washroom.

A few minutes later he stepped into the stinging wind; his eyes watered out of focus. Occasionally, the sun shone brilliantly through gaps in the soft, swift-moving clouds, and wind-driven snow needled his face with icy jabs. Just this morning in counting the cattle he had noticed one of them missing, and now, fearing it might have strayed to the frozen fields, he meant to try to find the animal, if it were not already too late. He lunged through the deep drifts until he came to the smooth, wind-swept fields. His numbed face would soon be endangered by frostbite, but even so, this work was worth doing—every bit of it, and that was what Floyd and Paul were coming to realize. If they did not thaw the chicken water, those birds would die. Theirs was a man's responsibility, learned by a couple of boys; a lesson at the very crux of life. It was why man was on this earth: to live and behave in this fashion. Henry bound a scarf over his nose and cheekbones and followed the fence row out, his gloved hand touching the taut wire that stretched ahead over the blurred hill.

Near the bottom-land, where he cut several harvests of hay each year, he found the cow, but she was already a furred, frozen rock half-buried in a snowbank, and as he stood beside her, he wondered what had possessed her to wander like this. What dim reaction drove her on and on to this far end of the field—the memory of waving, dark-green grass, jeweled with the dandelions of early spring? What an unending and wondrous thing was life! Affectionately, he kicked the hard, immovable hide with his boot.

When finally the wind died in the third week of January, when every particle of snow had been swept into place, sculptured along the roadsides and under trees, Henry and Vida began to think their isolation from the outside world was near an end. The county snowplow would be very late clearing their road, however, since it was not a major thoroughfare, and more populous sections would have preference.

The frigid days declined into sunsets of delicate pastels that were the softest, most fragile colors of the year's evening sky. And just when it seemed certain that a warming trend was in the air, several inches of new snow fell without the prelude of lowering clouds or the ominous stillness of the wind before it shifts—the usual ceremony before a storm.

With some pride, Henry announced to his family, "I think I'll make a pair of snowshoes and walk to town tomorrow. The flour bin is about empty, isn't it?"

"I have enough to last three or four more days," said Vida, "but if the weather's decent, you ought to go tomorrow. Then you can pick up the mail in town. We should have a sackful!"

As Henry hammered in the basement at his workbench, he seemed to be knocking the pegs loose from their snowbound world. Floyd and Paul bickered and whined: "If Dad walks to town on snowshoes, we ought to have snowshoes, too, and go to school." They were all eager to break loose. Vida felt in herself a great desire to read new magazines, catch up on the gossip, and eat fresh apples and bananas, instead of canned peaches and plums. Soon she herself would get to Kaleburg and unloose her tongue in the presence of women.

That evening a litter of pigs was born, and Henry brought them to the house, fearing that they would die if left in the chilled hog barn next to the wheezing old sow. The boys scrambled to find cardboard boxes, in which they placed them, one to each shoebox; they slid them under the kitchen range on a cookie tray. Every half hour Paul and Floyd fed the pigs from baby bottles with worn nipples that they themselves had chewed. They stroked the black, silky coats of the animals with fascination as the pigs turned up blue, black-lashed eyes and pink snouts to look in wonder at the world.

In the morning, before he started for Kaleburg, Henry asked Vida if she wanted other provisions, besides groceries. He had asked her before, and on each occasion she had seemed close to speaking—enough of a hint for him to expect what she finally did confide, that she was probably pregnant, and he might buy some yard goods for maternity dresses. He received the news as he had each of the other times, exultantly, and he kissed her cheek but said nothing, since Paul had come into the room and was watching them closely.

Henry set off across the drifts, lifting his platter feet high with each step, until he became used to a more natural gait. The fields passed under him without being recognized, for he skimmed the surface of the snow-covered earth. When he reached the edge of Kaleburg, a group of town boys who had been rabbit hunting stopped to stare at him, snickering at first, and then openly laughing. One of the boys laboriously lifted his feet in mockery of the snowshoes. "What you got on your feet?" They tittered and ran away.

Angered by their insolence, Henry quickly dismissed them as foolish boys with nothing better to do. He was tired and cold, and he dragged along toward the center of town with slow feet. Several housewives on the way ran to their windows.

He saw the white front curtains part like camera shutters. Finally, he stopped by a tree and removed the cumbersome shoes, saying to himself, "In town they have the sidewalks shoveled, even. It's not like the country, that's for sure." Would anyone believe him when he told how he and his family had been marooned for weeks? Never had he felt so foreign in his home town. The snowshoes he carried under his arm drew surprised glances from people he met on Main Street. Henry first stopped at the dry goods store to purchase the cloth, for he didn't know the clerks and would not have to talk about where he had been these past weeks. For some reason, he did not want to discuss the matter with any of them.

In the grocery store where he regularly traded, he expected many friendly questions from Schmidt. But the owner was nowhere around, and the clerk, whom Henry knew less well, only nodded a pleasant hello. Henry placed his order, adding: "And I guess that's all I'll be able to carry home."

"Pretty cold out, ain't it?" said the clerk.

"Yeah, and it's a long way I've got to carry this stuff."

"Guess winter must like it here, he's been staying so long," said the youth, busily making up the order.

"I have to go to the bank," said Henry, suddenly irritated by the young man's blandness. "I'll be back to pick it up."

Henry knew that by now Bill Wolbers could tell him if the bank would allow him another season to make good on the loan. He did not feel hopeful, because he did not believe Wolbers could be counted upon as a real friend, even though they belonged to the same church and had known each other many years. He never felt completely at ease with the man, although Bill had an easy line of talk and mixed well with all kinds of farmers. He was undoubtedly a clever businessman, and some people thought his shrewd managing had kept the Farmers Savings Bank open when other banks failed a few years before. Wolbers did not, however, even look like a banker, for he seldom wore a tie; his talk was full of slang, and he always knew jokes that nobody had heard before. Although involved in agriculture, he was not really under its sway, not vulnerable and committed as farmers were.

Henry turned the shiny brass knob and stepped upon the marble-tile floor. Two girls and the teller glanced at him with friendly smiles, but Henry paused to handle some income-tax folders, just to have time to get a grip upon himself. He felt quite sure that he could expect no aid from this quarter. He cringed at the thought of hearing the final word of doom for his farm, flung into his face on this day, despite all his family had been through out there.

Bill Wolbers strolled by from the drinking fountain and put a friendly hand on Henry's arm. "Oh, golly, I've been meaning to talk to you. Come on into my office. I almost sent you another card, since you didn't show up after the first one. Thought I'd better explain."

"We've been snowed in," said Henry. "Haven't had any mail."

"Is that so?" Wolbers grinned. "For a couple of weeks? I'd heard some folks were really buried, but I didn't know *you* were stuck."

"I came about the loan," Henry began.

Bill Wolber's cheerful, round smile turned suddenly astringent. "I know, and I wanted to tell you personally how sorry I am. But Henry, we've got to earn our living, too, and there are hundreds of farmers like you around the country. Why, if we gave you another extension, we'd be swamped by everybody else. I mean, what's fair to one man has to be fair to the other." He frowned sympathetically and reached out for Henry's sleeve. "And believe me, Henry, I *know* you intend to make the payments. If at all possible, you'd do it."

To Henry his voice sounded rich in false sincerity. He studied the banker's small, dome-like head.

"You expect this year's crops to be good, but what if we have another drought? These are simply *damn* hard times." Wolbers came down hard on the word to show Henry how deeply he felt about all of this. Since Reverend Kallsen often preached against swearing, even "damn" had considerable force —but not to Henry now. He hardly listened and made excuses to get away quickly. "I hope you understand," said Wolbers, rising quickly from his leather chair.

"Sure, I understand," said Henry.

A mealy sickness filled his stomach as he left the bank. He headed blindly across the street to Schmidt's. Mechanically, he gathered his groceries and secured them in the pack on his shoulders; then he stopped at the post office before beginning the trek home. The daily papers were too bulky, and so he threw some of them away, for they only recorded days that he had known more intimately than the writers of the news. There were not many letters; he put them inside the pouch without glancing at them. As he strapped on his snowshoes and tramped down the streets of Kaleburg toward the country, he did not care who saw him. He strode across the bare fields nearly bereft of snow from the impact of the wind, across deceptive, hidden cornstalks, over fences. The trip home was long, and when he reached the forelock of a hill where he could see his farm, he paused, leaning against a fencepost.

Yes, he was returning to his land, by God. And hard work it was, being a farmer, but it was a man's work. It was better than anything else one might do. He would not have that grocer's job for anything, to say foolish things about the weather while dusting canned peas on a musty shelf; nor would he be a clever banker like Wolbers, who walked on marble tile all day. Henry looked across the frozen white stretch to the black grove like an island in an arctic sea. That was his farm, his home: there would be no other, not in all the years that might stretch ahead, for it had been his home for all the years that lay behind. This he knew now, as surely as he knew himself and who he was; and from the reaction of his family and the happiness they had found in the midst of the storm, he knew what was truly best for them, too. Somehow, a way would open; they would find money; they would hang on.

He leaned forward, slipping faster across the snow as he neared the kitchen. Would the boys be at the windows watching for him? At last he unstrapped his snowshoes and tramped upon the back porch. Eagerly he entered the kitchen, and Vida kissed his cold cheek as she undid his strapped mail pouch. The boys, she told him, had gone to school shortly after he had left. "I let them go. They were so determined, and so worried about catching up on the arithmetic and history they'd missed."

Henry felt oddly undermined and quite exhausted. He had expected the whole grateful family to clamor around upon his return, rejoicing in his accomplishment of the journey. He began to tell Vida about the snow-clear sidewalks and streets of Kaleburg and how the whole world seemed to be going by without much attention to the storm at all; but he saw his wife impatiently opening the letters, smiling at him with half her attention, her eyes eagerly scanning the tissue sheets in her hand. Then he stopped talking.

"Oh, listen to this," Vida said, her cheeks coloring from excitement, and she rose quickly to show Henry the actual words on the page. "It's from Irene in Denver—and she says there're quite a few jobs out there, and we could stay in her apartment until we get located. See?" She thrust the letter close to his face, but he did not read; he believed her. "What do you think? Oh, I know we haven't considered going so far—but she's my only sister. The closest family—I mean, next to all of you. And she might even have some connections."

Henry felt the flesh heavy on his face, clinging to his skull with a weight, and only by conscious effort could he feign interest in his eyes. He wearily put his arms around Vida as the two of them sat near the kitchen stove; he imagined her eager thoughts leaping to Denver, and he kissed her brow gently, without passion.

Floyd and Paul rushed in a few minutes later, shaking snow from their boots upon the linoleum floor, where it sparkled in small puddles. The country school had been open following New Year's Day. Bitterly disappointed because they had not struggled through the snowbanks earlier, the boys complained that they would be denied their gold stars for attendance. Henry scoffed at their concern until he saw the look in Paul's eyes and the angry way he clutched the arithmetic book to his chest. Both boys were good students, he and Vida had always known, but not until this moment did Henry realize how much they really cared. In high school they would win honors, followed by scholarships to college, and the farm would be quickly abandoned in their expanding lives. They were reaching for city life right now, and Vida, too, although in a different fashion. Henry left his chair near the stove and stepped into the washroom. He would not force the farm on any of them, aware as he was now of their farther dreams.

As Henry pulled on his wool mittens and left the house he noticed that dusk was already creeping through the grove. He thought of the unborn child, heir of the winter; perhaps, although born in some strange city, it would always sense a dim connection to a farm never seen. Slowly he inhaled the moist air of the south wind. Tomorrow the sun would shine more warmly as the January thaw set in, and all this snow would sag, melt away, and sparkle with the false promise of spring. But he knew also that the snow never stops: flake follows flake and drift succeeds drift until the unending whiteness covers all.

 When Vernon Kallsen finished counting the collection-plate money after Sunday service, he joined the throng on the lawn and sidewalk in front of the church. He wore a dark silk summer suit, was hatless, and the flesh of his forehead and cheeks had a slightly grayish tinge, quite strongly in contrast to the late summer flush on the faces of his parishioners. Vernon's somber clothes gave the impression of a gloomy shadow moving among the bright pastel summer dresses. Conversations stopped as he passed. Everyone smiled and nodded dutifully, and in his wake, resumed their talk and tried to forget him.

Hans Albrecht on this particular Sunday in late August was unusually friendly—and quite embarrassed. "I—I suppose you heard about my boy Chuck—getting married to Shirley Maxwell?"

"Yes—yes, I did," Vernon said, recalling Letty's dramatic reading of the item in the *Kaleburg News.* A shotgun affair, she supposed, else why did they rush off to South Dakota? But Vernon had not allowed her to speculate further, for he hated the voracious look on her withered face as she began gossiping.

Hans Albrecht, one of the church's most reliable elders,

nervously stroked his reddish beard. "Now I can explain all this, Reverend," he said, moisture glistening his brown forehead. He looked around hesitantly at the people who seemed to be engaged in desultory conversation but who were really trying to eavesdrop. "Would you mind—could we go inside—in the parsonage?"

"Why, yes," Vernon replied uneasily. The last thing in the world he wanted was a complete account of the business. He also had a vague fear that if Hans Albrecht really got personal and revealed his secrets and then asked for advice, would he be able to give counsel?

At the parsonage door there was an awkward moment about who should enter first. "Please," said Vernon extending his hand. "We'll go into the study." The shades were drawn in the room, and it was delightfully cool and dark—not so dark, however, that Vernon could not see the bewildered, guilty look in Hans Albrecht's eyes. Hastily, Vernon turned away. At least they could avoid glances. "Sit down. Make yourself comfortable."

Hans Albrecht continued to pace about. Frequently, he stopped at the window and looked through the opening at the edge of the blind. "What I wanted to say, Reverend, is about the church bulletin."

"The bulletin?"

"Mrs. Kallsen said you wanted to put Chuck's address in the bulletin, so people could write him. She told me twice."

"Oh, yes, yes."

"Well, I'd rather just now—if you don't mind—I mean, he won't be where he is right now for very long." He was beginning to perspire heavily.

"I see."

"He's in the Navy, you know."

"Yes, I'd heard that," said Vernon quietly, feeling more and more apprehensive about what would come next. If only people could learn to keep their troubles to themselves, since ultimately, all afflictions are personal and cannot be shared. Didn't this man realize that the whole basis of Protestantism was the individual's direct confrontation with God no matter what the sin, no matter how weighty the guilt?

"I know what you're thinking," said Hans. "Chuck's just a kid, and he didn't plan it out very well—getting married and then joining the Navy. You must be puzzled about it."

"No, of course not. I haven't given it any thought."

An odd look of wonder and half-disbelief crossed Hans' face. He stroked his beard reflectively and looked at his shoes. "I figured you might—"

"Whatever it is, it doesn't matter," said Vernon quickly.

And in that moment there passed away the danger of a confidence shared. Hans' words came glib and fast, and he smiled with relief. "Kids, you know—restless when they're young. They graduate from high school, and then what should they do? Naturally I want him on the farm to help me—and he'll be back. It's hard to know what to do. And there's Hitler over in Germany. Maybe President Roosevelt is right when he says we've got to get ready for trouble. Honestly, sometimes—"

"In any case, I'm sure you'll do the best you can," said Vernon, and silence fell soothingly between them. Before parting they shook hands—there was almost a recognition of complicity in Hans' glance. And yet, Vernon thought afterwards, their bond was not one of shared secrets, but of mysteries left alone.

It began with daydreams in the spring, smug, self-satisfied daydreams—as Hans Albrecht again thought of the Ketters, who just two years ago had left Kaleburg forever. Hans had always been a good neighbor to the Ketters, but he could not help smiling over the fact that ironically it was honest, upright Henry Ketter who folded in the depression. Who would have imagined it? And if, years ago, Vida had envisioned this outcome of Henry's career, would she have married him at all, in preference to Hans' long-standing suit? Of course, those past days should be forgotten; events had taken their inevitable course, but he suspected that Vida must sometimes indulge in fantasies about what might have happened, had she done this or that instead of what in fact had actually taken place: her sudden marriage to Henry. In recent years Hans, Vida, and Henry had even laughed together about the early times, when there had been a romantic mix-up between them. And yet for Hans, what had happened then remained valid; her decision to marry Henry and his marriage to Emma in no way vitiated the fact that he had been in love with her.

Vida had been a giddy seventeen, he an older man in his late twenties. Hans suspected later that she had never really loved him; she had probably been flattered at having an older man so smitten by her; perhaps, too, he had been the first to ask for her hand in marriage. He remembered her surprise— her delight that people did these things, said such words! He never forgot her fresh, dark-haired beauty and how she loved to dance until dawn. She had been only amused by his re- minder that since he was a farmer he would have to milk cows after taking her home, whereas she could lie in bed until noon. Vida as a result had not been much interested in marry- ing a farmer—even if he had had a farm to offer her.

During those months when he was courting Vida, Hans had repeatedly urged his father to retire, or at least relinquish eighty acres of the land for Hans to start farming on his own. Old Peter Albrecht had thought Hans too hasty: he did not be- lieve it would be wise to simply give up the fruits of a lifetime's work to his son, who might fritter away the inheritance. And so, while Hans remained an apprentice, working for his father as a hired hand, Vida slipped from him, first by dating a sales- man, then a bank clerk, and finally Henry Ketter. All of this had happened without Hans' being able to stop her and say, "Marry me, marry me now."

The elder Ketters retired to town and gave their blessings to Henry and his new bride. The Ketter farm lay only a mile and a half from the Albrechts'. Although Hans finally got control of the ancestral property and married Emma, had children, and grew prosperous, he often wondered what his life would have been like had he married Vida. At least, he wished that they had given in to their passion and enjoyed a consummation of their love, if only to exorcise from his mind the hot wondering that plagued him all these years. Most likely, Vida would have been amazed to learn of his persistent longings. Hans knew he was supposed to be middle-aged, but the lusts of his body were as strong as ever. He was lean and vigorous; his reddish, neatly trimmed beard was thick and scarcely streaked with gray.

He remembered how Vida Ketter had laughed and joked about his beard when he first started growing it a few years ago. His wife, Emma, hated the beard, not because it pricked her when they embraced, for they rarely did embrace, but because she didn't want Hans to appear different from other Kaleburg farmers. Sitting in a church pew that was too greasy with furniture polish, Emma was constantly aware of his appearance, made striking by his red and black beard. Beside him, she was dressed in muted browns, drab as a cowbird and as songless and awkward; she told Hans that it was sinful vanity to call attention to oneself. But Hans knew, and she did, too, that his sexual longings were more sinful, if one reckoned in those terms at all. He had in fact chosen Emma for his bride because he hoped she might cool his carnal nature and draw him with her into the company of the righteous, where there seemed to be peace.

But for all of Hans' wicked and lewd thoughts, the Lord did not plague his luck, and while admirable Henry Ketter went broke, Hans slowly prospered. In the late thirties prices became better, so that by 1939 when his son Chuck was a senior in high school, prospects for the future looked very favorable. Hans had even acquired more land, and soon Chuck would join him permanently; together they would nurse the earth to green abundance. His life was outwardly good and filled with riches, and in fact, not in many years had he felt greater anticipation about the future than that spring of Chuck's senior year.

Kneeling beside his corn planter in May, Hans crushed the moist loam in his hand and slowly opened his fist to see the dark fetus-shaped clod, imprinted with his fingers. It was such good land! He threw the molded earth into the pale sky, as he stood up and remounted the tractor. He crossed the field with the planter behind him and listened over the motor hum to the steady click-clack of the planter-box discs as they regulated the drop of each kernel flung into the black furrow.

When he neared the other end of the field, he glanced across the road at the hired man's house, vacant now until Chuck and his bride moved in. The wedding date had not been set, but Hans was sure that since both Chuck and Shirley were seniors, they would get together quickly and settle down to raising a family. To become a grandfather would seem strange. He smiled at the thought, taking a lusty satisfaction in the fertility of his stock. He himself had produced only two sons (one now dead), but not through any fault of his—Emma had turned him away. Shirley would be another kind of wife for his son, of that Hans was sure. She was obviously very much in love with Chuck, and she would make a home of that empty hired man's house; she would greet her young husband with love as he trudged to the doorway from the fields.

Hans paused and looked again at the white clapboard house, which was plainly visible through the grove around it, for the trees always flowered later there. Then he picked up several white seed bags nestled along the fence, and as he carried them to the corn planter, he kneaded them gently. After lifting all the lids, he pulled the sack cord above the first box, and a torrent of flashing kernels poured with fertile profusion into the dark cavity. Hans felt elated by the warm day and the pleasant work.

Then he started off across the field again. He remembered how surprised Emma had been when, earlier this year, he had suddenly painted the rooms of the empty house and told her that he expected Chuck and Shirley to marry soon. "He's just a boy and you talk like that—before even Chuck comes around." Mothers were always that way about their sons, but Hans recognized the itch in Chuck and sympathized, knowing the sleepless nights it caused. After all, the young couple had been going steady for two and a half years. Chuck had been not quite sixteen and Shirley about the same age when it had started.

"Shirley's a fine girl," he had told Emma as he washed his paint brushes in kerosene. "You can be sure Carrie Maxwell's daughter has been brought up properly." Everyone knew that if there was a glimmer of a chance that good works could get one into heaven, Carrie Maxwell would be there. Of course, old Charlie Maxwell was a drunkard—that marriage hadn't turned out so well—but nobody thought it was Carrie's fault, and as the years passed, people hardly remembered that Charlie and Carrie Maxwell were connected in any way.

"The important and obvious thing," Hans had told Emma, "is that Chuck's infatuated with the girl. His mind is on her so much he doesn't know what he's doing. Why, last week he nearly lost his hand in the saw mill, he was dreaming about her so much." And as for Hans, he knew how spring exhilarated a man. You couldn't even look at the trees without seeing birds copulating. In spring the boy's passion would mount higher, and what better graduation present could Hans and Emma give their son than permission to marry and make a home?

Emma kept murmuring that she doubted if the romance were

serious, but Hans knew that she simply hated the idea of Chuck's mating. One would hardly believe Emma had lived on farms all her life, the way she would shout and run after roosters in the yard if they trod hens right in front of her. The religion was partly responsible, Hans believed, for once Emma had decided there would be no more babies, that was the end, unless you wanted to wind up in hell and pay for your pleasure that way. Reverend Kallsen every once in a while slipped the reminder into his sermons that the Bible teaches that it is wrong to cast your seed upon the ground. When Bobby and Chuck had been young—before Reverend Kallsen had arrived in Kaleburg—Emma had felt differently, and they'd had some good times. But Emma took the older boy's death as a curse and wouldn't try for more children, not when God had shown His feelings so clearly. Hans during this period had had secret worries, for in some ways, perhaps he was the Jonah who had brought about the misfortune. Should he subscribe to any of the church's beliefs, that would have to be his conclusion, for his sexual appetite was far beyond the minimum required for procreation—that ideal which Emma seemed to have in mind.

After the boy's death Hans had lain monk-like beside her wooden body, and he had tried to share her ascetic pleasure in their abstinence. But desire enveloped him while he slept, and Emma suspected his defection when she saw the lazy smile on his pink, sleeping lips. They moved to separate beds. On the cultivator during the hot monotonous hours he swayed over the broken ground, each lurch of the tractor awakening new desires. He decided to court Emma, to pursue her with affection as if they'd just met.

On the way home from the fields at noon he stopped to gather daisies along the lane and mixed them with wild blue flax from the vacant woodlot. His bouquet astonished her so much that Hans had to press the flowers rudely into her hands; then Emma smiled. All afternoon as the thin, glittering shovels of his cultivator turned over the earth Hans plotted his evening strategy. And at the supper table, after setting down his coffee cup with an appreciative sigh, he lavishly praised the chocolate cake. "For such good cooking I'd better buy you a new dress," he said. She was softening under his flattery, Hans knew, though she said little. That night as he sat down on her bed to kiss her good night he rubbed his hand across her shoulder blades.

Her small eyes filled with dark alarm. "Get away!" she said menacingly. Her voice rose, so that even Chuck in the next room could hear. "Get away! So that's what you're up to!"

After that evening, Hans did not try again. They were outwardly dutiful parents, but they renounced each other physically and the pattern of the years set in. Now with Chuck's impending marriage the old failure was recalled. "We must think of the boy," Hans kept insisting. "What's best for him? What does he want, and how can we help bring it about?"

The first May evening Chuck was home from school early enough to assist with milking, Hans questioned him about his plans. "Been looking to the future, Chuck? Now that you're graduating?"

"Yeah, I've been doing some thinking." But Chuck did not want to talk about it now, and the barn was quiet except for the rhythmical singing squirts into the milk pails, a wailing cat, and an occasional stomp from a cow imagining flies, though it was too early.

But at the supper table Chuck said: "There's something I ought to tell you. I've got a football scholarship to the University, and I figure I can go right through college on it and not cost you a cent."

"But you don't have to go to college to learn how to farm," Hans said, smiling, for he could hardly take this seriously.

"I know. Lately, though, I've been thinking of engineering."

To himself his voice sounded miserably indeterminate. Chuck despaired of convincing them that the great world's opportunities were infinitely more attractive than dull farm chores. But of course, there was Shirley to think of.

Hans seemed almost to have read his mind. "And just what about Shirley? I thought you considered yourselves engaged."

"We've only been going steady—not engaged," he said, his voice drained of masculinity. He felt like a fourteen-year-old.

"The boy's got plenty of time to decide about things like that," said Emma with serene relief. She smiled warmly across the table; that Chuck meant to leave the farm came to her with surprising pleasure. Now she imagined him directing corporations and being consulted by governments.

"I suppose you could make a lot of money as an engineer," said Hans, looking down at his plate, "but what will happen to the farm? Did you think of that? I won't be able to work forever, and somebody's got to take over."

"Oh, you could find plenty of renters, I suppose." Chuck saw a spark of shock in his father's eyes and guessed his thoughts. To suggest strangers walking these floors, sleeping in the beds, tilling the soil that had been broken by Hans' grandfather made Chuck seem an unnatural offspring. Chuck pushed back his chair and left the house; already he felt estranged, no longer securely enfolded by the tall cottonwoods that surrounded the farm buildings, no more a sentient part of this land or these people. He was saddened and lonely, for he had not expected renunciation to strip him so completely or so soon.

Hans guessed where Chuck would go—to Shirley for comfort and reassurance. But Hans knew with secret pleasure that his son would discover only further involvement. Shirley's arms would encircle him tightly, once there seemed danger that he might slip from her grasp. Hans reflected on all the jokes about girls trapping boys, and he wondered, by God, what was so bad about that? You find a girl who wants you, and you desire her

—what could be sweeter? No, he did not worry as he saw his son storm off to Kaleburg without further word.

Shirley recognized Chuck's step on the porch and opened the door of the Maxwell bungalow before he had a chance to knock. "We're in luck," she said. "Mother's at the church, giving a talk on the missions of New Guinea." She moved familiarly into his arms.

For a moment he simply absorbed the physical pleasure of her soft, rounded body tight against him. "You're—you're not sore, are you, Shirley? About that college deal?"

"Of course not." She burrowed her head playfully against his chest.

"It's an awful long time to ask you to wait, I know."

Shirley, her eyes closed and head tilted back, knew Chuck's anxious gaze roamed her face. Her blonde hair fell luxuriantly down her back and covered his hands. "But I will wait, Chuck." During their first talk about this matter she had suggested working at the local attorney's office during the four years he would be away at school; she would save money for their future home. But his ready acceptance of her sacrificial role surprised her, and she didn't intend to mention it again. If he really meant to leave her for long months, she planned to date at least— though not seriously, of course.

Now here was Chuck hungry for her love. She plucked the antimacassars off the mohair davenport so that they wouldn't wrinkle, and Chuck eagerly reached for the floor lamp switch. Their necking began at once; they had at least two and a half hours before there was any danger of Carrie Maxwell's re- appearing. There was no chance that Charlie Maxwell would show up because he lived in a rooming area for derelicts above a barbershop downtown. Carrie was unhappy about this, but she had long ago given up on Charlie; he was too weak and degenerate for anything to be done. Carrie approved of Shirley's romance with Chuck, but she did not dream that they petted this way on her living-room couch. Throughout the long, languishing hours neither Chuck nor Shirley spoke; they kept arousing each other to a certain level of desire, then allowed the fervor to die, only to be rekindled a minute later. Neither had any uncertainty about the limits of this petting; only in the dim, far-distant marriage bed would this exhausting stimulation reach an end.

After high school recessed and before the University spring term ended, Chuck visited the campus to make room reservations and talk with the coaches. On the day he left, Shirley drove her mother's car to the farm during the noon hour to deliver a copy of the high-school yearbook, which had just belatedly arrived. Emma lurked in the kitchen, complaining of a dirty apron, but Hans very happily greeted her at the gate. He did not take the bright-red yearbook from her hands immediately, for to dismiss her so abruptly would seem ungracious, and he particularly wanted her to understand that Chuck's college plans were none of their making. The dog sniffed Shirley's small round toe that peeked suggestively from her cut-out shoe. "Go away, Duke!" Hans said. "The dog, you know, misses Chuck already."

"He's not the only one," she smiled.

"I just don't know what's gotten into Chuck." Hans paused absently, then turned away with a blush, for she had caught him looking intently at her dress—a simple, close-fitting cotton print—and he had been thinking that she had the plump, full type of body that would get fat as soon as babies began coming. But he did not think Chuck would mind. "We expected you and Chuck to marry this summer, perhaps—and move into that hired man's house across the road."

"Oh, Hans, I think that's wonderful of you." She had always called him by his first name, as did all the young people. She admitted that she was unhappy about the scholarship.

Hans plunged his hands deeply into his pockets, shrugged his shoulders with a knowing smile, and predicted that Chuck would change his mind. He squinted at the sun, as if he could tell the exact hour of the day. "We've got time to look at that hired man's house. Wouldn't you like to see it?"

She did not even glance at her watch to see if her lunch period had expired but followed a little behind him as he took a short cut through the orchard. Once he stopped to hold a thorny plum bough until she had passed; he was thinking that if she saw what might be her future home, she would be more persuasive with Chuck. How could the boy resist, when a girl like this really put her mind to it? Hans remembered the two of them walking together, early in their romance, and how Chuck couldn't keep his hands from caressing her. Through all these months of courtship it was hard to believe they had remained innocent, although he knew they had, and that Chuck was as much a Puritan as Emma.

After Hans unlocked the door of the house and bowed her in with a mock sweep of his arm, Shirley eagerly explored the first-floor rooms. Then she found the stairs, looked questioningly at Hans, and he said, "Yes, go on up," and followed quickly behind her. They paused together at the bedroom windows as Hans pointed out the view. "Pretty nice for a couple of honeymooners, huh?"

She turned to him with a frown of self-pity. "You know his plans. And nobody can argue with Chuck when his mind's made up."

"A cute girl like you don't have to argue, you know," said Hans lightly. "I mean, some things work better than talk." He scratched his beard reflectively. "Don't all women know that?"

"Just what—"

He interrupted quickly, afraid that she had taken offense. "A good-looking woman can have her way. And we both know yours will be the right way. Remember, Chuck's a man, and all men are weak when it comes to that. So what are you waiting for?" He spoke rapidly without looking at her. "It's not so wrong, when you'll be marrying soon anyhow. How do you think most marriages are made?" He glanced at her with a wry smile. "Oh no, not mine." She was not as shocked as he had expected. He had wondered if a strong religious streak didn't underlie that lovely exterior, but knew now such was not the case. She was openly astonished by his remarks, but her eyes seemed awakened with a new knowledge. A bond of frankness had been established between them—more, Hans knew, than had ever existed between this girl and Chuck. "Come on, now. Let's go back to the house." Hans had not intended to say any of this, but he was not sorry.

As Shirley fled the farm she was angry with herself for being attracted to the idea but turned this quickly into imprecation against Hans. And all these years her mother had held up this family as exemplary—with Hans a shining contrast to her drunken father. But Shirley could not quite forget Hans' suggestion, either, and it flowered in her mind like a many-hued tropical plant which her cold reason tried to snuff and kill before new formations grew. She did not think it would be easy to seduce Chuck, but countless schemes of approach entered her thoughts. Shirley knew the quality of Chuck's honor—he would not take her virtue irresponsibly; it was, as Hans suggested, absolutely safe.

When Chuck returned from the University, glowing with accounts of a starlit dance on the rooftop of the Union and how he had worn a tuxedo lent by one of the men in the fraternity house where he had stayed, Shirley felt jealously possessive. She wanted him, but she hesitated risking her self-respect and his.

The following morning while she was drinking coffee in the Kaleburg Kafe next to her office, Hans walked in and sat down. "Shirley, what do you think?" He paused before telling her the news to snatch a fly in mid-air with his deft fist. "The Mrs. and I are finally going fishing for a week." The waitress set a glass of water in front of him and listened attentively. "Chuck told me he would keep things running on the farm. I expect he'll be so busy now you won't have much time to see him."

The mischievous glee in his eyes alarmed Shirley. "Where're you going?" she asked, trying to sound natural.

"To Leech Lake in Minnesota, I guess. Since we got a whole week, that's plenty of time." He smiled very broadly, even at the waitress, as if only his anticipation of the trip caused him cheer.

Shirley glanced apprehensively across the counter, saw the waitress' suspicious eyes move back and forth between them, and said quickly to Hans: "I hope you catch some big ones."

"If we do, we'll let you know," he said grinning. "And you do the same."

Shirley swung off the counter stool murmuring, "I've got to get back to work. It's awfully late." But in her hurry she forgot to pay for her coffee.

Just as the waitress was about to call after her, Hans pushed another nickel forward on the counter. "I'll take care of it."

Upon leaving the restaurant Hans asked himself why he had immensely enjoyed teasing her? It was as if the devil held his heart and delighted in corrupting the innocent—that, at least, would be Emma's interpretation, but Hans knew better. For his son to take a wife and settle on the farm would be no sin. Yes, he was amused by Shirley, but all brides and grooms were comic —naïvely frightened about what would soon be compellingly delightful.

For the next twenty-four hours Shirley struggled to decide how she would meet this open temptation. She knew, next morning, that surely Hans and Emma had already departed. But she could not brazenly set a snare for Chuck, for it would be both disreputable and wicked. She felt suddenly strong in high, moral resolves and had an impulse to visit Chuck during the noon hour and fix his lunch. Together they would be aware of their opportunity to sin, and their vigorous shunning of desire would bind them closer in love.

Since Chuck hadn't expected her, he had taken sandwiches and a Thermos to the fields in the morning and didn't return home at noon. Shirley waited on the front steps for half an hour, with the dog looking at her expectantly and the whole farm brooding and silent in the warm air. Finally, somewhat irritated and disappointed, she drove back to town. But all afternoon she felt suspended and oddly uncertain of herself. She must see Chuck at once, she knew.

After telephoning her mother that she would not be home for supper, Shirley drove again to the farm at five o'clock. Chuck had just returned from cultivating corn, and he waved to her from his tractor-mount. He began to run toward her across the length of the yard, his legs stiff at first from sitting so long, but then he hit the full stride of his track-season form and could scarcely stop short of her. She was flattered by his greeting, yet could think of nothing to say. He put his arms around her waist, asking, "Are you going to fix supper for me tonight? Come on, be a good wife," and he playfully pushed her from him. Shirley had taken only one step when he suddenly turned her around and kissed her. "I'll be up to the house in a little while."

He finished chores, showered in the basement, and after supper they sat together on the creaking porch swing. They began to make love slowly, as if approaching from far off. Several times Chuck broke away and said agonizingly, "We'd better stop or we'll be sorry," but Shirley made no reply. Rather, succumbing to a feeling of relief and irresponsibility, she pulled his head down to her breast. He caressed her with his lips, then tore himself away and dashed into the front yard. She heard his bare feet move through the dewy grass. "We ought to go for a walk," he said in a strained, suppressed voice. She opened her eyes and saw him shadowy on the lawn, his head lost in the dim blur of the cottonwood trees in the background. Then he came forward to the edge of the porch, threw his arm around a sturdy wooden pillar, and said, "Shirley, I'm telling you—" But at that moment he realized that he was telling her nothing. He walked quickly forward, and, taking her hand, drew her from the swing and guided her inside to his bed.

At midnight when they finally parted they made plans to spend the rest of the evenings of the week together, provided she continue her job and sleep part of each night in her own bed, so as not to alarm her mother. Shirley waited for remorse to consume her, for the fires of repentance to sear her bones, but nothing happened. She felt more in love than ever and re-assured about the future, for Chuck talked of an early marriage. The next night they decided Chuck's bed was too narrow, and they moved into Hans' double bed. Once at noon when Shirley had driven out for a brief interlude of love-making, they were interrupted by a Watkins man whom they hadn't heard knocking. He was halfway into the kitchen before Chuck confronted him, shouting that his mother wanted nothing today. On Friday they received a postcard from Hans saying that he and Emma would be home Saturday evening. "Would Shirley mind fixing a snack for us, so we won't have to stop for supper on the way?"

Chuck wondered uneasily if their guilt would show when his parents arrived, and what if, later, there were issue from all this love-making? Several times during the week he had been concerned about taking precautions. Shirley had assured him that it wasn't a dangerous time of the month for her, but she admitted not being sure. She told him that it cheapened their love to think of this.

The supper dishes had just been stacked in the cupboard when Hans and Emma drove into the yard. Shirley turned up the fire under the coffeepot while Chuck walked slowly out to greet them. "How's the boy?" Hans called cheerfully, then slapped his son on the back. "Cultivating been going all right?"

"Yeah, I guess so," Chuck murmured. "Though I fell a little behind schedule."

So it has come to pass, thought Hans, looking with amusement at Chuck's handsome, nervous-eyed face. "Don't you worry about that," he said. "We've got plenty of time to catch up."

When Shirley told Chuck of the coming baby, he accepted the news fatalistically; the summer was not yet over, but he was already reaping the harvest of their love-making. He had tried to use reason to stop their intimacy, but they were too weakened by pleasure. "It is stronger than we are," he told Shirley with regret, half-believing the popular songs whose whining insincerity had previously sickened him. "I'll go to work on the farm for Dad," he said, not even mentioning college, which now seemed a passing dream of youth.

He was frightened that evening at the supper table when he told his parents that he and Shirley would marry immediately. "Not going to college?" Emma asked, but Chuck couldn't lift his eyes. His father, all the while, spoke with easy reassurance. He even gripped Chuck's arm affectionately and said it was a wise decision. Chuck drew back, feeling loathsomely dishonest, for he knew they didn't understand the situation entirely. "What I mean is, we've *got* to get married."

"Well now, Chuck," said Hans hurriedly, "what's your business is your business."

But Emma scraped back her chair, and in a wavering, anxious voice insisted that Chuck explain further.

"The sooner we marry, the less people will talk." Suddenly he did not feel old enough to be a father; all of those masterful moments of love shriveled in his memory. And surely his mother was the most difficult of all to face, despite the fact that, having had children herself, she might have been the first to understand.

"We'll be proud to welcome Shirley into the family," said Hans. "And proud to have a grandchild, too." He said it loudly, overriding Emma's inarticulate protests. "And let's have no more discussion." Taking a firm grip on Chuck's arm, he drew his son from the room.

But Emma found her words. "So you've been at the nasty business, too."

Chuck saw his mother's pained, taut face and the glistening eyes too stung with tears for one to drop. He clenched his fists to hold back his grief, but began to weep anyhow—not just for her or even for himself, but for all the disappointments they shared.

"Come, Chuck—outside," said Hans softly, tugging nervously at his beard. Chuck allowed his father to lead him from the house. "She'll get over it, Chuck. Don't you think too much about her."

"I guess I never thought *enough* about her," he answered, still staring at the lighted kitchen windows. Never before had he loved her so much.

Dusk had fallen, a welcome mask for both their faces, and Hans pumped a cool cup of water and offered it to his son, then took one himself. "Ah, that's good!" He smacked his lips. "Want another?" In the pause before Chuck answered they heard Emma blowing her nose. "Now let me tell you, boy, women get some funny ideas. And your mother, too. They like to pretend they don't know a thing about what boys and girls do together."

"Please, Dad, I'd rather—"

"Now, Chuck, I want you to know I don't feel that way about it. After all, I'm not that old. I remember before I ever had any experience of that kind I just couldn't help thinking about it and—"

"Dad, can't we talk about something else?"

"But this is nature, Chuck. It's not something to be ashamed about. We have every reason to talk now and have it out, right from the start. I don't blame you one bit. You kids were alone together and seeing each other every day for two years. A fellow can only stand for a girl to give him a loving-up just so long, and he's liable—"

"Dad! Dad! Will you shut up?" Chuck's voice broke like an adolescent's.

Hans wondered, how can I reassure him? It would seem a simple thing to let your son know he has your blessing.

Chuck hated his father with a loathing he had felt for no one before. He snapped open the yard gate and ran for his car. As he drove off hastily, insects attracted by the headlights swooped down from the darkness and smashed against his windshield. He could not erase the awful memory of his father plucking on his sleeve. He tried to think of the future, of this land he would not farm and that house into which he and Shirley would never move. The very notion of living with Shirley repulsed him, and he wondered how he had ever gotten involved. There had been that day she came to the farm, knowing he was alone; it was almost as if she had purposely tempted him. His lips hardened, thinning tightly across his teeth, and he hunched closer over the wheel to see the gravel road more clearly.

By the time he rang the doorbell, knowing Shirley would be home alone, for it was Carrie Maxwell's night for town council, Chuck had attained a cool and detached view of himself and their situation. Obviously, he did not love her—they had been merely sexually attracted. He felt no ties at all to the embryo growing within her. And yet, he almost hoped that the first sight of Shirley—her blonde softness—would win him back. But it did not. Nothing warmed within him when he saw her standing before him, her full breasts under the nylon blouse moving slightly with her breath. He walked in, sat down, and briefly informed her that he had decided not to live on the farm. He knew he had to support her and the child, but he preferred to get some sort of job in Kaleburg. He was tense and refused to let his body sink into the sofa cushions; his fingers picked at the white antimacassars, and when he had finished his remarks, he withdrew the pin that held the doily in place and then plunged it more deeply into the mohair.

But Shirley had changed, too, since she had become certain of pregnancy. She sought security for herself and the child and did not frivolously think of trying to win him back by romantic maneuvers. She sensed the cold curtain of his logical mind drawn across the present scene, and she addressed that, mentioning Hans and his certain help, the attractive hired man's house, and Chuck's probable farm income. Her calculating, even little voice shocked Chuck so greatly that he hardly heard what she said. He had not completely dismissed his suspicions that Shirley had set a snare for him, and he stirred to ask her, "How does it happen you know so much about that hired man's house? Who let you in? I don't have the key and never showed it to you." As she hesitated, he heaped up further queries until she admitted that Hans had taken her through the house.

"Yes, I know now." She gestured limply with her hand but did not smile. "It was when you went to the University— remember, I brought out the yearbook?"

"You drive to the farm every time people are away. Is that it?" The alarm he saw in her eyes only drove him on, to hurt her if he could, as she had wounded him. "What were you doing? Talking over marriage with Dad? Is that it? Oh, don't pretend I don't know. What do you think I am, stupid? I know what you've been up to, and now that you're good and pregnant you figure you've got me where you want me. I may be trapped, but I know who sprang it."

Shirley paled as if slapped. She had not dreamed that Hans

would reveal what had been discussed so elusively between them. Chuck sat now so stiffly, so smugly; there was nothing to do but fall upon his mercy and explain. "Oh, please listen to me, Chuck." She knelt on the carpet and flung her hand across his thigh. "It wasn't *my* idea. It was *his*. He said he'd back us up—but I wouldn't have anything to do with it. I never imagined things would turn out like this. You've *got* to believe me." Their whole life together was suspended in the balance of this moment. She felt his muscles harden under her hand and knew that she had lost.

"You mean you *did* talk to Dad about us?" Chuck leapt to his feet, almost stepping upon her. "Did you?"

She did not know how to answer, except with the truth. "But I didn't agree to anything. I didn't plan for what happened."

"Christ! What have you two done to me?" He could not stop protesting tears of rage and self-pity, though he wiped them away savagely before they fell. "I'll let *him* take care of this business, since he brought it on so nicely." His voice came queerly from his throat, as if another person were speaking. Chuck remembered the postcard and Hans' request for Shirley to fix sandwiches—he had known she was there all week. "Some fishing trip," he said, trying to sound sarcastic, but he gasped on the phrase and it came out like a sob. He left the house hurriedly.

In the dark car the dashboard lights swam before his tear-filled eyes. He wanted to drive and drive without stopping, but he would need money, and where could he find a job? He thought of the armed services—the Navy needed recruits, for President Roosevelt said the country must arm. He had seen a new Navy placard in the post office; they might take him in at once, without the usual waiting period.

When he arrived at the farm, his mother was cloistered in her bedroom, and Hans had not yet come in from the barn.

Chuck dumped toilet articles into a bag, rifled through drawers looking for his hidden money, and then sat down to write a brief note telling where they might pick up the car. The dog followed behind as Chuck left the house, and he turned around to stroke Duke's hard, familiar head. Then he set off for Missouriville, where he would spend the night in the Y.M.C.A.

This flight was for good, Chuck knew. He would never be able to look his mother in the face; he never wanted to touch his father; and Shirley was already far behind him. He imagined that eventually none of them would enter the slim end of a thought for months at a time. Even in the distant future, he would not marry and be reminded once again of all this. Although his mother might never know, he would measure up to her idea of him—her previous image, the one now shattered —by henceforth remaining pure. The masculine sanctuary of the Y.M.C.A. was a promising beginning. In the morning he signed up at the recruiting office without difficulty.

Hans met Shirley at the gate, just as he had that first day in spring when she arrived with the yearbook; but Emma hung back, squinting at the girl through the veil of the dining-room curtains, despising what she thought was the first rounded sign of pregnancy. Chuck had now been gone a week, and there was still no word from him. Hans, however, smiled cheerfully at Shirley; his pink lips were more exposed, for in the summer's heat he had clipped his reddish beard shorter. Shirley did not seem as bewildered as he had expected. He took her hand to lead her toward the house and solicitously guided her up the steps, so that she would know, if she did not already, that he was aware of her condition.

Such subtleties, however, were unnecessary, for Shirley was in no mood for anything but frankness. "Just what do you plan to do about this?" she asked. "He's a minor and you're responsible."

Her legal talk suggested to Hans that she may have already consulted her employer, Mr. Nemmers, the town's attorney. "Now, Shirley, don't worry. He'll be back."

"But when? Two years—four years from now?" Emma stood far across the kitchen, staring, unable to sit down. "Small comfort for me, carrying his child," Shirley said, looking directly at Emma. It pleased her to see the proud woman wince. "And I won't have an abortion. I'll have the baby, and everyone in Kaleburg will know who's the father." She gazed defiantly at Hans and watched the effect of her bluntness.

He was moved in an unexpected way by her ferocity. She was putting up a magnificent fight—it was the old maternal lashing, the beating of a quail's wings to protect the young. She inspired Hans to a command of the situation he had not known he possessed. Speaking boldly and firmly, he told her that there was no question but what they would take care of her, "just as Chuck will certainly marry you and make his child legitimate. But we shall have to be patient and sit out this storm." And so he proposed that she set up housekeeping across the road, for no one need know that Chuck hadn't actually married her before he left. "We'll call you his wife, and I'll buy you all the furniture you need." They discussed finances item by item, from hospital bills to grocery money, and Hans assured her of support throughout, especially when he learned she had kept quiet these seven days. "You're one of the family now. We'll put a regular announcement in the paper saying you were married in South Dakota in June. Since you're both so young, people will understand why we're going easy on the news. Of course, Chuck won't be around to hear the story or deny it, and when he finally returns—and finds everyone thinks he's married, and you with his child, he'll come around. I know my son. There's a lot of honor in him."

Emma sucked in her breath, sighing deeply, but she hardly seemed aware of what they were saying until Shirley mentioned her own mother, who as yet knew nothing. "Oh, poor Carrie. What has she done to deserve this?" Emma shook her head. "But we'd better tell Carrie everything. With all this lying, at least in the family we've got to tell the truth." She coughed and blew her nose. "I'll tell her myself."

And later, when Emma did see Carrie Maxwell alone, she stayed nearly two hours, finding a common bond of suffering that drew forth prayers. From that afternoon the attitude of both women toward this family trouble shifted to the spiritual plane, where they sought atonement for the interwoven net of worldly wrongs. While Hans took Shirley to the furniture and hardware stores and they selected, priced, and chose house furnishings, Emma spent the time on Carrie Maxwell's sofa, reading aloud from devotional pamphlets.

Shirley bought an expensive walnut dining-room suite, a fifty-five-dollar floor lamp that lit up in blue, green, and yellow, and a coffee table of glass and plastic in four sections, mirrored at every corner. Though Hans thought her taste rather wild, he did not stop Shirley from selecting a fuchsia sofa and brilliant blue chair, but he cautioned that she might soon tire of the leopard throw rugs she planned to scatter throughout the house. She seemed to be indulging a dream, rather than furnishing a house, but Hans went along laughingly with her purchases; he wrote out checks, one after another, and explained to the curious store managers that Chuck had gone into the service— hated to leave Shirley, "since they were married in June, though we tried to keep it secret."

After church each Sunday Hans very deliberately circulated among the gossiping congregation, and when they asked about Chuck, he smiled and said some phrase such as, "The boy sure surprised us," or "Young people's lives move awful quick, don't they? Us old folks can hardly keep up." His laugh was rich and easy, but he did wish Emma hadn't such a nervous, worried look in her eyes. Anyone seeing her face could tell that something was awfully wrong.

Then there was the matter of Chuck's address, which Letty Kallsen wanted for the church bulletin—no doubt the curious minister was behind that. Hans suspected this little ruse was merely to find out more information. He was afraid that Reverend Kallsen might unwittingly—or deliberately—keep the whole issue alive and in everyone's thoughts, and so, on a Sunday late in August, he asked to speak with the minister alone, and they went off to the parsonage together. But once they were closeted in the study, Hans' fears vanished. After all, no one need know anything about it, now or at any time, and henceforth he would be careful lest in his anxiety he overexplained himself.

After a few weeks it was apparent to Hans that he had maneuvered his way through with the deception. He also admitted to himself that he had rather enjoyed it—and Shirley proved herself to be a fine actress. Shopping with her was time-consuming but fun, and half-jokingly he lamented to her that he was going to financial ruin fast. Shirley insisted that he drive her to Missouriville, where, in the larger shops, she had a wide selection of table linens, drapes, and kitchenware. Emma did not go along, for each shopping excursion lasted a whole day. In addition to Shirley's purchases, Hans bought her a radio and a young Irish setter. He hoped she would be kept amused in her new house and not suffer too greatly from loneliness.

As Shirley's life across the road began, Hans realized that she did not intend to be bored. She invited envious girl friends from town to help her decorate, and in early October, when she was already showing her pregnancy slightly, she threw several gay parties in which her young friends danced in darkened rooms. Hearing the noise, Hans crossed the road and looked casually through the windows, but it was hard to tell what was

going on. Knowing that everything depended on Shirley's remaining content, Hans kept a close watch to test her feelings
and attitudes, and he suspected that she was aware of the power
her slightest inclinations had upon him. Although she had taken
his purse for a scandalous amount, he did not resent it. She was
very much the lady of the house when he stopped for coffee in
the mornings or at four o'clock, and if he missed a day without
seeing her she scolded him or feigned unhappiness, obviously
expecting him to jump quickly and find some way to amuse
her, like a spoiled child.

As a result, Hans became more restless and disturbed, and
in an absent moment during corn picking, nearly severed his
finger in a moving gear. He found it difficult to keep his mind
on his work. Two farm hands who were helping with the
harvest talked about the fun they had had in the Lake Hotel
in Missouriville, where girls were on call if you tipped the bellhop. They mentioned the hotel laughingly several times, and
Hans joined eagerly in the joking, pretending casual familiarity
with such matters, but he secretly hoped they would say more.

At last one afternoon he drove to the city and entered the
lobby of the dim, towering hotel across from the railroad tracks.
His breath came in short gasps, and he was so unsure of his
voice that he sat down in a lobby chair. This was a shoddy but
compelling place, with huge, slowly gyrating fans, like the
wings of lustful moths, hovering in the air above. The bellhop
stood by the desk, his hands jingling coins in his pockets, and
Hans was relieved to see that he was a man at least as old as
himself, though more wise and experienced—no young pimp
to contend with over the vice of the world. This man came
from the spiced chambers upstairs with all the serenity of a
knowing intelligence: trusted, functional, and discreet. From
such a man, Hans could have no secrets. As their eyes met,
Hans felt a current of recognition clasp them irrevocably together, and he sank back into his chair with relief. How very

long he had been coming to this, how many straining, troubled years. He reveled in the release of his half-known guilt, savoring the moments before he would step up to the desk, register, and then hand the bellhop ten dollars, so that later the door would open, close softly, and *she* would come dutifully toward his bed.

He stirred from his reverie to see one of the girls descend the stairs, visible first from the ankles. Hans watched the whole body, dressed in a clinging green crepe, slowly appear from above—and at last her face. The girl's shockingly empty eyes met Hans' anguished gaze with the numbed impersonality of an unpainted barn door. Nothing, nothing at all of comfort, nothing of understanding or love. Hans looked at the bellhop questioningly, and the man looked back wisely at him as if to say, "This is one—yes, what did you expect?"

But Hans felt leaden and unwholesome; he was aware now of the stale cigar smoke that clung to the fabric of the soiled, overstuffed chair, and the faint odor of vomit that emanated from the brown-stained spittoons. He did not know where to go, but he decided to leave this place. In the street he hesitated, still unwilling to return home, for a vague, irrational impulse made him feel that if he could but stay overnight in this hotel, there would be an ease and straightening of his life. And so, when he telephoned Emma, he told her he would not return tonight, that she should milk the cows and not worry about the other livestock, for they had plenty of feed. He emerged from the phone booth perspiring and considered heading for the park, where he might meet someone who would not look like that girl on the stairs.

He walked block after block but came to no park, and gradually the Lake Hotel seemed attractive again. He stopped at a dime store and purchased a small suitcase and decided to pick up pajamas and toilet articles for overnight. He would not enter the hotel until after dark, and then, when he got to his room, he would keep all the lights off, all night. He hurried from store to store, dropping items into the suitcase, like a man packing hurriedly for an unexpected trip. Then, just as he approached the Lake Hotel, luggage in hand, he was stopped by a shout. "Hey, Hans! Where're you going so fast?" It was Herman Johns, long-time neighbor, who was now retired and living in Kaleburg.

"Oh, Herman! How are you?" Hans grasped the man's hand and laughed nervously. This was the worst sort of luck! How could he get rid of Herman without seeming rude?

"Where're you bound for?"

"Oh, no place at all. Just carrying this." He looked at the suitcase critically.

"You seem all set to go somewhere. Thought maybe you're taking the train to see your boy."

"Chuck—why, Chuck's in the Navy, you know. I'm just now on my way to the post office to send him this bag."

"I'm going that way. I'll take it for you." Herman Johns shifted the parcel he was carrying.

"Oh, no, no," Hans began, moving backwards. "Have to— have to go right now." He did not even hear what Herman Johns said in reply, for he broke into a run. After turning a corner he stopped, panting. He regretted having behaved so peculiarly, and now, ill-composed, he entered a restaurant for supper and a chance to think. After a long, brooding meal he returned to the Lake Hotel, where he sat indecisively in the lobby and watched girls flounce by who did not interest him. Finally, at eight-thirty he suddenly jumped to his feet with the decision to return home.

Hans saw no light through the thick grove surrounding his place, but the windows glowed warmly in the hired man's house. He had missed his four o'clock coffee-break. The thought of Shirley and coffee on the stove made him swing into the driveway, and he returned to his real life with joyous anticipation. Dousing his headlights, he traveled the last twenty yards with even the motor dead. The dog began barking in the house, and Shirley snapped on the porch light from inside, just as Hans stepped up to knock. He blinked under the glare, but already his knuckles had pounded out the urgency. "Who is it?" Shirley called, then pulled aside the café curtains. "Hans!" She smiled delightedly and unlatched the door. "I missed you today." She took his corduroy cap.

"I missed you, too, Shirley. I've been a long time coming here."

"Just a minute, I'll heat the coffee. Tell me, where've you been?" As she began to leave for the kitchen, he stopped her, reaching for her hands. She looked at him closely, more interested than alarmed. "There isn't anything the matter?"

After locking the door he turned toward her, almost with a smile of apology. "Yes, yes, there is." He ran his fingers up her soft arms, lifting them gently so that her hands touched his shoulders. "But it's too late now to stop it."

IX

 Herman Johns certainly hoped that his old friend Hans had not suspected something strange— finding Herman in this district of Missouriville, at this hour of the day, and then so shamefacedly greeting him, as if trying to hide behind words. Whether Hans had noticed the brown parcel in Herman's hand was another matter. Whatever had possessed him to offer to mail Hans' suitcase?

He found his car in the all-night lot, unlocked the door, and climbed in behind the wheel, just as the street lights were turned on. This would be his room for the night. Nobody would disturb him, since he had paid the attendant for a twelve-hour stay. Quickly, he ripped the brown paper from the bottles, snapped the wrapper off the cap, and opened a fifth of brandy. After a long drink he settled back, more relaxed, and wondered uneasily again about the misfortune of running into Hans Albrecht. Something like this was bound to happen sooner or later. But after all, Hans had asked him no questions. Their meeting had been brief, and not only that, in what way had Herman given himself away? Only if Hans had actually noticed the brown-paper parcel and guessed it was liquor by its shape would Herman be in any danger of word getting back to Kaleburg. His wife, Christine, thought he was in Missouriville with a friend who was buying cattle. On another occasion he had made the excuse that he had to go to Missouriville to clear up a controversy about his insurance policy. He always managed to think of something that sounded reasonable—so far, at least; and Christine did not question him. She trusted him completely, and Herman for all the world would not have her know that he had become a rummy, a sot, a slave to liquor—that he had indeed fallen prey to this vice as thoroughly as Charlie Maxwell or any other drunk who inhabited the taverns of Kaleburg.

Herman took another swig of brandy. Across the lot was a blank brick wall of a candy factory, but he did not see it. In his mind's eye he traced again the strange course which had brought him here; as little as a year ago, if someone had predicted this blowsy fate for him, he would have said, "Impossible!" Though he viewed with irony the events which had taken place, he knew he would not change his ways. "Nothing can save me now," he said aloud. Of course Christine and Verna both knew he still drank some wine before meals—that was a carry-over from the grape-cure experiment they had all tried, hoping to save Lola's life. But the women certainly didn't know about these periodic binges.

It had all started with Lola's sickness—Lola, who still lingered, half alive and half dead, in her bedroom upstairs. The three Paff sisters had always enjoyed boundless health, and they had not expected illness, even with encroaching old age. Herman used to remind Christine, who was the youngest of the sisters and the only married one, that the Paff girls were human, too, like everyone else. To hear those three talk one would suppose that the Paff family was the most extraordinary that had ever lived. In the thirty-four years of Herman's marriage to Christine, he had managed to wean her away somewhat from that strident sisterhood. On the farm, Christine had developed interests apart from her spinster sisters, what with the arrival of children, a field garden to look after, and a flock of laying hens. But when Herman and Christine retired to the Paff house in town, the three women took up their old close ways again.

Christine had always been rather humble toward Lola and Verna, especially on matters of learning, for she had never gotten beyond high school, while Verna and Lola had been to the state teachers' college. Herman knew that his wife really felt that Verna and Lola didn't realize sometimes how ridiculous they were—for they had no one like Herman to keep them sensible, or children to question them. They did some outlandish things, such as traveling farther each summer on sightseeing trips, outdoing themselves year after year, as if they were in some kind of contest. Christine, busy on the farm in summer, envied neither their endless hours through the hot desert toward Mexico nor the frightening journeys high in the Rocky Mountains. It made her nervous just to see the colored slides, proof of their adventures, which they projected against the living-room wall for the farm stay-at-homes to witness. Verna and Lola insisted that Christine continue fully informed of their lives, participating, though absent, in every aspect, just as all three had shared when little girls, so that all through the years there would be no slipping away among them.

The illness began so gradually during the last year of Lola's teaching that she was hardly aware of it. From time to time she suffered considerable pain in her abdomen, and Christine kept observing, "You're getting so thin, Lola. And you're not eating." She and Herman had been eating too well, for since they retired to the old Paff home two years ago, leaving their son to manage the farm, they had both put on weight.

Verna was inclined to make light of Lola's little "upset," and Lola was determined to finish her term before seeing a doctor. Actually, she could have stopped teaching the previous year and retired on a pension, but she had stayed on, enticed by the knowledge that the pension would be larger. At last, in late

May, when Verna drove Lola to the Mayo Clinic in Rochester, Minnesota, the medical examination revealed that cancer had been advancing for some time. Lola was not told this, for Verna and Christine tried to keep it from her; but after the brief, exploratory operation, when nothing more was said or done and the nurses looked at her strangely, Lola knew.

Back in Kaleburg amid a great deal of forced gaiety, Lola was put in the many-windowed sunroom on the second floor to convalesce, and there she sat, a dark shadow in the golden sunlight, while downstairs her family huddled around the kitchen table and tried to decide what should be done next. "Do you think she suspects what it is?" asked Christine.

Herman thought so. "Even a little child with a fever you can't fool. The sick seem to know."

"Why do you say that?" Verna snapped, irritated by Herman's stubborn, slow manner and by his clothes—farm overalls that he continued to wear in the house and on the streets, as if he could not get it through his head that he had retired from the farm and was now a city man.

"You three sisters," he said slowly, his face still red from years of windburn, "you're just like this," and he locked his fingers. "What one is doing the others know. Do you think you fool her on a big thing like this?"

"Shhhhh," said Christine, trying to soothe the conversation in a motherly fashion, as she had done so often on the farm when her children bickered. "She might hear you up the stairs."

"Maybe that would be a good thing," said Herman stubbornly.

Verna frowned, and she drank her coffee with studied lifts of the cup to her lips. She did not want Lola to lose hope by learning what the doctors had discovered, for a sick person is easily depressed. All through the meal she thought of inspiring things to say, and then, pressing her napkin into creases, she stood up. "Let's have a cheerful talk with Lola." Leading the

way, wearing her old yellow rayon house robe, which accentu-
ated her thinness, Verna mounted each step with a straight
body, her thigh and calf muscles lifting her, while behind her,
Christine and Herman, their backs as round as potato sacks,
clutched the railing for support as they climbed.

The upstairs hall led directly to the sunporch, where Lola
sat wrapped in blankets. She watched them coming down the
hall toward her, make-believe smiles on their uneasy faces. She
was large-framed like Christine, but nearly as thin as Verna,
and somehow the combination made her seem more delicate
than either of them, for the bones of her face were painfully
prominent, as if the flesh were sinking away, and when she
brushed an arm against her hip bone, she almost bruised herself. "I've got hip bones like a Guernsey cow," she once told
Verna, but what she really meant was that the angular back
of a milch cow always made her uneasy, for she imagined that
the bones would pierce the hide some day, honing themselves
sharp when the cow ambled across barren pastures in search
of a tuft of grass; and that would be the end of her.

"It's cancer, isn't it?" Lola asked when the sisters came toward
her.

Christine gasped and turned away, for she was never good at
concealment. Verna massaged Lola's shoulders. "We've got a
fight on our hands. But we'll put our heads together and figure
out what to do."

"Those doctors don't know everything," said Christine.

Herman hung back in the hall, listening to the three women
speaking all at once, their indignation at the medical world
mounting. There were cures for cancer—boxes to sit in, special-
ists with clinics in Texas, and certain diets to try. Doctors were
always so quick to say no, just because someone comes up with
a new idea that they themselves hadn't been smart enough to
think of. The women seemed to gather strength from the united
gabble of their talk, and at last they all agreed—Herman

nodded, too—that the final word was not yet in. Something could be done, and Verna would begin research on cancer at once.

She started her investigations in secret, traveling to nearby Huntford, where neither of the librarians knew her. She devoted herself to becoming a cancer specialist, without a doubt but that somewhere among the mass of material collected she would find a cure. All her life Verna had paid attention to little details, as a public accountant must, and she had never yet failed to find the missing account that threw the balance off, and once she had even detected the clever "error" that sent a bank embezzler to jail for fifteen years. Verna had gone to the trial every day, enjoying the publicity and posing for newspaper pictures.

Each day the notebooks, magazines, and books piled higher on Verna's desk, and once in a while Lola hovered uncertainly over the mound of information, leafing through folders, glancing at hideous colored pictures, until Verna sent her away by saying, "Now you let *us* take care of this. Your part is just to get well, and we'll do the work."

Verna dispatched airmail letters in hasty succession, for she was a very fast typist, and soon replies filled their brass mailbox. When the packet from California describing the grape cure arrived, Verna assembled the family around the kitchen table, where Lola had been seated since noon, not feeling strong enough to go upstairs and come down again at suppertime. "I think the sap's all run out of me," she explained to Verna with a wan smile.

"Nonsense," replied Verna, "you're just about to start getting better." She fingered the California leaflets with barely suppressed excitement. Then, after supper, she began to tell her news, speaking slowly and precisely as if she were addressing the board of directors of the Farmers' Elevator. "All right, this is the material!" She spread her long, agile fingers, maidenly well-kept, across a packet of brown Manila envelopes and illus-

trated pamphlets. "I have consulted the United States Government, the American Medical Association, and a special agency
of the League of Nations. That's where I began, and you'd be
surprised to know where it all led me." She smiled triumphantly
at them, and Herman lowered his eyes, his lips in a pout, for
although he knew these women would decide what they wanted
to decide, he felt a man's opinion was still worth consulting.

Christine sank back upon the hard rungs of the kitchen chair,
basking in the good news forthcoming; her fingers, rough as
parsnips, lay folded quietly in her wide lap, and glancing at
Lola, she noticed the color of life coming back into her sick
sister's cheeks as she, too, caught the heartening intimations of
Verna's deliberate, unnecessarily loud introductory remarks.
When you had a family behind you, there was nothing in the
world to stop you; hadn't all of them found that out?

Verna explained in considerable detail the marvelous grape
cure discovered in California, adding: "Although it sounds
promising, it's still unproven, of course. There are doctors all
over the country who charge there's nothing in it. But listen
to this." She picked up a testimonial from a California doctor
and began to read. "And what about this from a patient who
was cured?" After reading several statements, almost breath-
lessly she concluded: "I suggest we all go on a grape diet, Lola,
until you are well and have your strength back."

"Oh, no," Lola said at once. Herman's downcast face was
enough to convince her that he would be reluctant. "There's no
reason for all of you to go on the diet."

"Lola, dear," said Verna, reaching out to touch her sister's
thin wrist, "this diet is *all* grape."

"Yes, yes—and I think it would be too much for you. I
would feel guilty."

"You just let us help you, Lola," said Christine loudly.
"Herman is willing, too."

He nodded slowly, after Christine turned to him. "I always did go for grapes, pretty much."

"There's no reason why we couldn't buy grapes and start today," Verna said, smiling; she hoped the immediacy of her proposal would not alarm Lola.

"Did you find out that grapes were especially good for people?" Lola asked, somewhat bewildered. Perhaps she had missed that part. "All of you keep eating regular meals," she insisted again, "and I'll just eat the grapes."

Verna shook her head stubbornly. "After a few days, Lola, when you think you can't take another grape, if we were frying potatoes they would seem the best thing you ever smelled. You and I have gone on many a diet together. If everybody does it, then nobody feels deprived."

How odd that it should be grapes, thought Lola, remembering the day she had noticed on Verna's desk a vivid drawing of a cancer growth and how much the deadly disease resembled a cluster of grapes. There was a country adage that the antidote for a poisonous weed could always be found growing right next to the offending plant. Now, Lola mused, perhaps in the mysterious ways of nature, the cure for cancer could be found in the fruit most resembling it.

Herman volunteered to walk to the grocery store for grapes, for he was happy to feel himself useful and occupied. He put on his familiar blue and white striped cap that Verna scoffingly said made him look like a train engineer. But his clothes, like his habits, were too patterned to be changed now, just because he had retired to Kaleburg. He itched a little against Verna's blatant successes—financial achievements in business, and her ability to make people act the way she wanted them to. He had spent his life with plants, animals, and machines, and he knew how to handle them—an equal accomplishment, Herman felt, but he knew he would never convince Verna. He would not trade the life he had spent with Christine for all the vaunted freedom of Verna and Lola. Here was Lola now, perhaps near the end, and what did she have to show for it? The sisters were dear to her, and her teaching had been successful, but Herman knew that on *his* last day he could think of his children, the grandchildren, and the neat, fertile farm.

Leaving by the back door, Herman undid the night latch, which the women kept secure during the day, though no Kaleburg house had been burglarized in twenty years. Herman hated to fuss with the lock; he knew that simple old-maidishness had inaugurated this little custom. It only reminded him of what a masculine clod he was in that maidenly house—next to the fancy linen hand towels in the bathroom, the doilies on chairs, and the pictures of laurel-crowned nymphs on the walls. Odd scents met him in halls and when he sharply turned the corner of a room—odors he couldn't quite identify and didn't even know if he should try. Herman loved his cigars, refusing to give them up when he and Christine moved in with her sisters, and they had decided he should have a smoker. After each meal he retired alone to his upstairs den and filled the place with a blue cloud; yet try as he would—and he had been in the house two years now—his tobacco smells could not penetrate that sweet floor-wax smell, or whatever it was, that continued to make the room Verna and Lola's, not his.

Christine sensed that he felt unwelcome, and soon after moving into the house, of which she owned one-third, she had said to him: "We've got a perfect right to be here, Herman. Don't you feel put out by some of the little things the girls say. They're so used to having everything to themselves. But even that chair you're sitting on is one-third mine. That's the law, and it was Pa and Ma's wish, too."

"We've got the money to build a house of our own," he said. "We should maybe do it yet." Herman knew her real reason for insisting on living in the old family home was to save their money, so that when they died there would be more inheritance for the children. Herman didn't think the children particularly needed extra money, though. Perhaps they should think of their own lives for a change, before they suddenly found themselves near the end—like Lola.

As Herman walked toward the grocery down gentle, shaded streets, he admitted having no faith in the grape cure; yet it was something to do, and who knew but that it might not help? Herman was eager to lend his time to something useful like this. Finding extra hours on his hands, he had tried playing cards in the saloon uptown, but he always felt a little ashamed when he came home for dinner at noon, knowing he had not really earned a meal. He looked forward to shopping trips or picking up the mail at the post office, for these were useful moments in his day. His people had never played cards, drunk liquor, or wasted time gossiping; there were certainly more important things to do. But Herman realized, as a retired farmer, that it was harder and harder to find these more important things.

Downtown, Herman greeted the fat German grocer, who looked guilty, as if he ate his own wares without stint. "Ah, Schmidt, what do you have in the line of grapes today?"

Schmidt ambled over to the fruit racks and swiped the air furiously at gnats hovering around the bananas. "Nice Thompson seedless here, good for eating."

"That's what we want. Give me the whole bunch. And how about those?" Herman pointed to a mound of reddish Tokays. They were somewhat flattened—long and pressed into odd shapes from the crated journey from California. "Yes, give me plenty of them." He suddenly realized that he did not know any other kind of grape, except the Concords on his farm, which ripened in September. The prospect of the grape diet stretching day after day came upon him with full force. "Are you—are you getting any others in?"

Schmidt looked at him rather strangely. "What others do you want?"

"Will there be other kinds, later on?" Herman asked.

"What's wrong with these?" asked Schmidt, lifting the Tokays gently, as if the grapes had faces. "And these seedless, they're the best you can buy."

"All right, we'll see how it goes," said Herman.

Schmidt wiped his fingers on his butcher's apron and accompanied Herman to the door. "No hamburger today? What about bread?"

Herman finally raised his hand in protest, for fear Schmidt might follow him all the way to the street. "That's all. But don't be surprised if I come back tomorrow for more grapes."

Schmidt's mouth gaped open. Then he turned back into his store as if Herman had insulted him. Herman chided himself for not keeping quiet and allowing tomorrow to take care of tomorrow. Walking slowly, he thought of devious excuses for buying more grapes, but none of them sounded sensible.

Christine met him in the kitchen when he came home with the sack. She wore an old violet house dress of their farm days and a bandana tucked like a cap over her hair. Now that Lola was ill and Verna was busy with research and her job, Christine did all the cooking and housework. She preferred to keep busy this way, so that at night she could feel tired to the very edge of ache and pull her limbs wearily into bed after her. Nursing a sick person was a full-time job, like raising a family or anything else. "Well, what did you get?" The bag crackled as she peered in. "You didn't remember juice?"

"No, never thought of it. Does grape juice have the same stuff in it?"

"Sure," she laughed, "what did you think? Everything grape, that's the important thing. But I've got some canned Welch's in the cupboard. It'll be fine for now."

The table that evening was laid in the dining room—and

more festively arrayed than usual, with linen, sterling silver, and a candelabra centerpiece on a mirrored base. As a starter, the dark Welch's grape juice was served in goblets with a tiny vine pattern; all of them were surprised by how really good it tasted. Somehow, they had never concentrated on grape flavor with such intensity as now, when it had become their vital juice. "You feel that dry quality on the tongue, after you've swallowed?" asked Verna, who was dressed rather conspicuously in dark purple with a choker of grape beads. "That's what I read about—that's the astringent element peculiar to grapes, and it's working away in your innards right now, Lola. Tannic acid. Cleaning everything out. You'll be as good as new before you know it."

Lola's face, sharply shadowed in candlelight, looked palely ethereal, for since her illness she had become strikingly more attractive. In former years, with her face filled out between the prominent cheekbones, strong jaw, and large nose, there had been no suggestion of this pensive, frail beauty. Her eyes were darkly alive in the blue evening shadows under her brows, and now that she no longer dyed her hair, dramatic streaks of white swirled across her head—the lavish brush strokes of age.

The second course was Herman's specialty, for he had labored nearly an hour to pit the Tokays, split them in half, and chill them in the refrigerator in frosted tumblers. He was disappointed, for they were not as good as they should have been after all that labor. Having been picked green, they had little flavor, and the flesh was pulpy, not full of juice. "I don't taste any of that acid in these," said Herman, glancing at his sister-in-law.

Verna bowed her head to concentrate, her jaw rolling gently as she gave the tastebuds a full chance. "No, I'm afraid these aren't much. I'm going to send off some special orders by night letter to New York and California. If we're going into this thing, we're going all the way." She looked around the table, connecting their glances, and as if a circuit had been suddenly opened, each felt the strength of their united determination. Herman, glimpsing the possibilities of this power, wondered if after all the grape cure might not work.

They ate on, day after day plucking grapes from dry brown stems, and all the while the diet was kept strictly a household secret, for Verna wished to astonish the town by literally bringing back Lola from the dead. She imagined with delight how heads in church would turn, and she could hear surprised questions from friends and saw them touching Lola, wondering if, like Lazarus, she could be real. Furthermore, Verna realized that if it were generally known what they were up to with the grape cure, the objections and doubts from many people would only make the fight more difficult. The doctor was notified to stop his weekly visits, and no explanation was given. Even the minister was barred for fear he might raise some theological question about the proceedings.

On the fifth day during a noon meal of Thompson seedless grapes, Herman and Christine's son barged into the kitchen with produce from the farm. Although the faces around the table looked up from their plates with embarrassment and Lola even cupped her hand over the cluster before her, Irving Johns did not notice anything extraordinary. He carried a basket of three dozen eggs in one hand, and in the other, a box of lettuce and radishes which his wife had gathered and washed.

"Oh, we got plenty in our garden right here in town," Herman told his son, waving the vegetables away, but he did not dare look into Irving's face as he refused the eggs.

"You people ought to eat more eggs," said Irving belligerently. "Eggs are good for you."

"The store's got 'em, too, you know," said Herman. "I picked some up there," he lied, "and they're just fine."

Now Irving was really astonished, for the family strongly

believed in the superiority of all home-raised produce to what could be bought in grocery stores. "You don't need anything, then?" he asked, rubbing his sunburned neck awkwardly, shuffling backwards toward the door.

"Nothing," said Herman, glancing at Christine. Head bowed, she nervously wound a handkerchief around her finger so tightly that it glowed as red as a sausage. He knew that if he did not immediately dismiss the boy, Christine would spill the whole story about the grapes.

After ten days of the diet, Herman was thankful that the air express boxes of grapes were arriving at the house, for he barely felt strong enough to go to the grocery store. He only picked up mail every other day, summoning all the strength he had. On that tenth day at noon as he passed a restaurant, the exhaust fan blew odors of French fried potatoes into his face. For a moment he staggered and wiped his brow. It was a hot, brilliantly sunny day, and he felt faint. He stumbled into the restaurant for a moment's rest, collapsing gratefully on the first counter stool. The waitress slipped him a glass of water and asked, "What'll it be, roast beef, meat loaf, or ham?" He gave in, and in a few minutes he was devouring a thick slice of beef, mashed potatoes and gravy, and peach pie à la mode.

But he ate too much and too quickly, and he had a sudden sickening realization that he would lose it. Hurrying to the lavatory in back, he made it just in time, and then slowly he walked out to the counter stool again. He self-consciously sipped water each time the waitress glanced up. She was obviously wondering why he still hung around. After several minutes he asked her for a whole new meal, although it was difficult to make her take him seriously. She kidded him about getting fat as a hog, and didn't an old man know enough not to eat like a boy of sixteen? "When was the last time you ate?" she asked, laughing. "You're the hungriest man I ever seen."

He didn't respond, except to murmur, "Yeah, I'm hungry all right."

Although physically more comfortable after the meal, Herman was mightily depressed. He had been the first to weaken, the one to give in, the one not strong enough to sacrifice. Neither Christine nor Verna, nor, of course, Lola, must ever learn of this defection. He walked slowly, defeated, to the post office. His eyes were on the tips of his work shoes, which were scuffed shiny from long wear. He felt wiser now; and he had a certain humility about himself which he realized had been absent ever since the grape diet began. Strong might be one's muscles and strong one's resolves, but what did it all come to? The flesh was weak. Sooner or later even Verna would meet her match, Herman knew.

In the post office, Reverend Kallsen turned from the stamp window and almost ran into Herman. Instead of stepping aside, Herman grasped the minister's smooth hand, welcoming the benevolence of the church, embracing again the old doctrines learned long ago: all are sinners, each and all, and only by grace are the fallen saved.

Vernon Kallsen was rather startled by Herman's affectionate behavior. He uneasily moved away, blinking his eyes; he wiped the film of perspiration from his wide brow. "Why . . . a . . . Herman—how are you? And tell me, how's Lola?" He remembered Letty having said that everyone thought it was cancer, the way the family was trying to keep it secret. As Herman stood before him, shifty-eyed and haunted by guilt, Vernon was momentarily tempted to probe the mystery; but it was a principle with him, remembering his own shrouded past, never to violate the sanctity of a secret well kept.

"Why, Lola's coming along pretty good, I think," said Herman slowly, his face red.

"I really should pay her a visit," Vernon said dutifully. "Do you think she wants to see me?"

"Oh, no, Reverend—I mean," he began hastily, "she really isn't seeing *anyone* just now. Maybe after a while, but not just now."

"Well, then," said Vernon, extending his hand, "goodbye, and may God be with you."

Herman hoped that he had not lifted the lid of suspicion, speaking evasively as he had. He hurried along the street, taking the long way home in order not to walk with Reverend Kallsen. As he passed the grocery, Schmidt called from the door at his heels, "Hey, you want some grapes?"

Herman wheeled around in sudden concern at the word noised so loosely about the streets. "What is it?" he said, turning back.

"Got a nice shipment of Thompson seedless this morning, Herman. You folks had me bought out for three days running."

"I—I don't think we'll need any right now," said Herman, and he continued on his way. The express truck had delivered a crate this morning—it still lay unopened in the basement.

The women were all resting in bed when Herman arrived home. It seemed they rested most of the time now since the grape cure started. Christine even made excuses about not bothering to clean house, for they had no visitors. She looked tired, and Herman was beginning to worry about her health. Still, he did not dare speak to her concerning the diet, because they were doing this for Lola, and it was a matter of life or death.

Excelsior shavings littered the blue and yellow kitchen linoleum, and Herman saw a large cardboard box stuffed into the waste basket. "Oh, more grapes," he mused, opening the refrigerator. But he was startled by what he saw. There, under the glare of the bare light bulb, were the most fantastic grapes he had ever seen. One bunch of dark Malagas hung over the side of a refrigerator ledge, and he touched the tight skins with his fingers, rubbing the smoky surface of one grape until the rich sheen of purple marble came through. He picked it from the stem and crushed it succulently on his tongue. These were grapes pictured in Biblical books as having come from the Lord's vineyards in the Holy Land.

On another level he found clusters of large amber grapes, each with a blush of red like the tint of a pear. They were juicy, with a sweet muscat flavor, and he ate several to keep the fine taste on his tongue. Then he closed the refrigerator door and prowled in the trash until he found the sheet which had come with the grapes—they had been imported and flown from New York. He read off the list: Ohanez from Spain, red Malagas and Ribier grapes from the Mediterranean, table Rieslings from Germany, and several varieties from Afghanistan with names he could not pronounce. "And still in the basement there's an unopened crate!" he said aloud.

He hurried downstairs to inspect the large box that had arrived that morning and found that they had been shipped from a university experiment station in California. Almost with fear he ripped the thin wood away, wondering what strange new marvels of the grape world would be revealed. He drew the bunches from their tissue paper nests and tried each one. A very red bunch had such tough skins that he could scarcely pierce them with his teeth. They were like balls of plastic in his mouth, and the juice that finally squirted from them was bitter, like the grape juice concentrate that the Watkins man sold in bottles. Herman found tiny grapes that looked like deep purple currants, and pale, anemic grapes that seemed to have scarcely seen the sun. He hunted in the box but found no sheet with the names that would give identity to these queer distant cousins of the grape family. Then he found a printed folder which read: "You are cordially invited to send your opinions concerning these ten new grape varieties which could be grown in California on a widespread basis." Herman looked down the code list of numbers, realizing that the grapes had no other names. They were hothouse products of cross breeding, and they had hardly any existence as yet. Ah, he thought, Verna's call for grapes has reached far-distant ears.

He washed samples from all ten varieties and brought them upstairs, just as the doorbell rang. The expressman with another airmail box looked at Herman rather wildly and said, "The third package today! By rail, truck, and bus you're getting this perishable stuff. What's going on?"

Herman signed for the package. "This is a busy place," he said and sent the man on his way without satisfying his curiosity.

Herman was unable to imagine what more could arrive, so overwhelmed were they now. If only Schmidt could see these grapes. That man didn't realize that there were more grapes in the world than he had ever dreamed of. Thompson seedless and Tokays, indeed! Herman would never be satisfied with those common grapes again. He ripped open the parcel, but to his surprise found not grapes, but raisins—huge, dry, wafer-shaped raisins—all still clinging to one another like smashed grapes in a bunch. In a separate package farther in the box were loose white raisins; Herman felt more dry skins underneath, but he did not pull them out. He stood for a moment in the kitchen of the quiet house; a surge of grapes had found its way to this Iowa town, and a delicious excitement filled him—the kind of inebriation Verna felt when she and her sisters started some project. He realized that he knew now what moved through the veins of the Paff sisters. His afternoon indiscretion—eating roast beef—loomed shamefully, and he resolved not to slip again but do what he could to keep the battle waging.

In the evening they enjoyed a splendid banquet, sampling, describing, and arguing the merits of all the varieties, and Lola was more gay than any of them. Her thin wrists were deli-

cately veined, her complexion like paraffin, and she laughed
ecstatically when Christine retold old family tales. "Oh, I feel
wonderful—never better! And now we have some new grapes."
She nodded her head affectionately at Herman. "You certainly
tried to vary the program, but none of your efforts were as good
as this."

Herman, indeed, had peeled grapes, diced and pureed them,
and he had served them half-frozen, partly fermented, and
slightly warm. But tonight he had an idea that surely promised the most variety of all. "Say, Verna, how about wine? Is
that on the diet list?"

Christine scoffed at his suggestion. "Oh, no, surely not." No
members of their family had ever been tipplers. They only
drank wine which Reverend Kallsen served at the communion
rail, and Christine felt a little devilish after each of these holy
draughts and wiped her lips nervously. She always thought
people talked more volubly after church on Communion Sundays and admitted feeling a little giddy herself.

Verna left the table to check through her grape-cure material, but she found no reference to wine. "Isn't that odd?
Surely wine is made entirely of grapes, isn't it?"

Herman was certain. Although none of them enjoyed the
taste of wine any more than a medicine, they agreed to drink
it for variety as part of the diet. "And there's lots of kinds of
wines," Herman said.

He did not want to buy the wine in the local liquor store
because of the talk it would cause, but the next day he drove to
Huntford. He left around noon, and soon after he arrived,
found himself in a restaurant, eating a large meal. This time
less remorse overcame him, and he picked his teeth with considerable satisfaction.

On succeeding days as he slipped off to a café, he did not
bother to reprove himself; he knew he did not have a martyr's
fortitude and never had had. The wine piqued his appetite, and

he would usually stay for the noonday drinking before taking his trip uptown. At first he brought home only the wines which were red and had a distinct grape flavor, but he was soon buying sherries and brandies and comparing their various qualities. Dubonnet and Mogen David were out-and-out favorites, but after a steady week of sampling, Herman and the women found themselves quite comfortable with a number of wines. Verna and Lola were partial to Mogen David for every meal but breakfast, when they preferred white wines. Verna often picked up the Mogen David bottle and examined the Hebrew writing on the label—as if it were some mysterious treasure floated to her from across the ocean, with only this message on the side. "Those Jews have something good there," she would say approvingly.

Although Herman was quite aware of their increased wine consumption, he was surprised one night when the women utterly refused to eat another grape. They stuck to their wines and glanced at Lola with rising spirits. "You're looking better every day," said Christine.

"Getting stronger by the hour," said Verna.

"Yes, I'm fine—really fine." Lola closed her eyes in a slow blink, her purplish lids lowered dreamily. Then she caught her head sharply from swaying. "I'll bet I could even dance—see if I can't!" Lola pushed back from the table by grasping the tablecloth edge. Her hands were as thin as claws, and the dress, as she stood up, fluttered as if wind from some dark corner had passed over her; it was several sizes too large, an old rose silk dress that she had always been fond of, with a low waist and folds of cloth around the bosom, like layers of petals. Her silk stockings hung on her bony legs in loose rivulets, as if she were melting away.

Verna began to clap hands in two-four time and to sing, her head bobbing as she watched Lola gyrate slowly around the ottoman in the living room, wheel to the left to avoid a coffee table, and dance back into the dining room, turning deliciously, as if to a ghostly partner.

"Go on, dance with her!" Christine urged Herman, and he stumbled to his feet. Just in time, he caught Lola's wildly waving arm before she careened against a doorpost.

But Herman had seldom danced and certainly never in this European, formal way, with Lola's arms stretching out to his shoulders like cables on a suspension bridge, and between them enough space for a third party. Herman kept glancing over his shoulders, wondering what they might hit, for he did not feel steady on his feet. When at last Lola sagged, he caught her just before she crumpled to the floor. "Hey, watch out," he said, holding her up. The scent of her lily-of-the-valley perfume was strong in his nostrils. "I guess we've had enough dancing!"

Lola anchored her right hand on the back of the mohair davenport and sank down slowly, her head lowered in dizziness. Christine hurried to the couch and flicked water from a tumbler into Lola's face. "I'm all right. Really, all right," said Lola, pushing them away. "Maybe we should have a little more wine."

That sent everyone back to the table, and as Lola settled in her chair, her face flushed and eyes limpid, Christine began to weep, suddenly overcome with joy. Turning to Verna, she said: "Lola's getting well!"

Lola, hearing the pronouncement of victory, smiled at them all.

"I haven't seen you move around like that for half a year," said Verna.

"You must write to those grape-cure people," said Christine to Verna, "and tell them it works. Give a testimonial."

Verna found some stationery and began to write a few opening sentences; soon they were all dictating.

"The grape cure works like a miracle!" said Christine.

"You eat grapes every day, and you'll keep the doctor away," Lola laughed.

"We, the undersigned, swear," said Verna solemnly, writing furiously, "that we have undergone the grape diet."

"Day after day," said Herman.

"And night after night," added Christine.

"With the result," continued Verna on a new sheet, "that never have we enjoyed such good health, fine spirits, and general well-being."

"Try the grape cure and you'll live forever!" Herman said, throwing his hands in the air. Then he grabbed for Verna's sheets of paper, though she tried to pull them away. He began making flying paper darts, and soon they were all sailing them about the room.

No one got up to wash the dishes or even clear the table. It seemed as if every word spoken were enthrallingly funny, and Lola said, with an air of finality, "I've laughed so much I hurt all over." Her white, skeletal hand stole across her bosom.

Immediately, a doubt settled over them, for they wondered if the hurt might be the old trouble. Herman announced that it was eleven o'clock, and the women, protesting that it could not be so late, retired to their bedrooms upstairs. As Herman climbed into bed beside Christine, he felt a gentle undulation under him, as if he were on a raft in a river; he had drunk too much. Every bottle in the house was empty, and tomorrow he would lay in a whole new supply. On that thought, he dropped heavily to sleep.

Sometime in the night he awoke with a start, feeling violently thirsty, and his tongue was thick, as if too large for his mouth. Also, something was wrong. Christine was not next to him. He leapt up and swung his feet to the floor—much too quickly, for his head throbbed in heavy pain. He noticed then that he had forgotten to shut off the closet light, and he padded across the room to the yellow wedge showing thinly under the door. But to his astonishment, when he pulled open the door, there sat Christine. She gave a little gasp of surprise and tried to hide her ham sandwich in the folds of her gown.

Herman staggered back, blinking; they both looked at each other, measuring the moment's guilt, and then Herman started to laugh. It pained his head, but he could not help it, for Christine was sitting on that little stool, caught in the act of eating, and he found this discovery quite ridiculous. "Oh, stop laughing, you fool," she said in a whisper, coming out of the closet. She continued devouring her sandwich in large, hungry bites. "You wouldn't want me to get sick, would you? I'll bet you've been snitching on the side yourself."

"Oh, yes, Christine, I have," he admitted. "How long have you been at it?"

"I figure the Lord meant us to eat food, otherwise He would have made us some other kind of body."

"Well, why didn't you say something to me? Instead of sneaking into that closet."

"Oh, I don't know. I haven't known what to think."

"Because this was all Verna's idea, that's why," said Herman wryly.

"Don't you think Verna's not taking care of herself, too. That's why I started. I woke up one night smelling pork chops. It came up the air register from the basement, and I knew she was down there using the old oil stove."

"What?" Herman laughed and sat down on the bed. "Wouldn't it be fun to sneak down and catch her some night?"

"It would not!" said Christine wearily. "No, not at all. I don't know what's happening to us—skulking around like this. It would be better if everything was out in the open, sometimes I think."

"But maybe Lola *is* getting better."

"Nonsense," said Christine. "Tonight we were all drunk like bums in the taverns uptown. I ask myself now, just why are we doing this? I mean, it won't help. If it did, why doesn't everybody else who's got cancer do it? Why do they just wither away to nothing?"

"Verna did all that reading," said Herman.

"But is she a doctor? Does she know more than anybody else in the world? Well, none of it fools me, and I'll bet it doesn't fool Lola."

Herman walked across the room and turned on the overhead light. "Yeah, I think you're right." And he knew, too, that it was time for him to step in. Women could go only so far, and then it took a man to settle things. He pulled on his robe and in his bare feet tiptoed to Lola's door and knocked softly. "Do you want some food, Lola?"

He opened the door. All he could see was the dark shape of the big bed. "Yes, Herman, that would be fine. And maybe a little coffee." Her voice was far away.

As Christine moved past him, the floorboards in evening rest creaked heavily. She lit the red-shaded lamp of Lola's dressing table, which turned the china hair tray and vanity set the color of flesh. Herman started for the kitchen, pressing light switches along the way until the whole downstairs blazed fiercely. While water was heating on the stove, he rummaged through the refrigerator for hidden food. Finding none, he opened the cupboards and finally reached down a box of wafers. Later, he carried them upstairs with the coffee.

Christine was fluffing pillows behind Lola as Herman crossed the threshold. Lola smiled at him, an incredibly wide grin that seemed to bare all of her teeth. He settled the plate across the hard ridges of her lap and stepped back. When she took the first wafer, she thanked him, and at that moment Verna marched in. The yellow rayon housecoat fluttered out behind her like a saffron shadow. Her eyes had a staggered, innocent look, having just been aroused from sleep, and she glanced from face to face to get her bearings. "What are you doing?

What's the matter?" Her gaze fell upon the plate. "Oh, Lola, no, you're not—" She pulled the housecoat around her tightly. "Why didn't you tell me you were about to break the diet?" she asked softly, in a betrayed voice. "You seemed so happy tonight. Why, we could all have gotten together and helped you over temptation."

Lola munched slowly, her fingertips barely ahead of her mouth as she consumed the wafer. "You couldn't help me over this," she said, shaking her head slowly in the socket of the pillow. No one moved and there was no sound but the muffled crackling of the wafers in Lola's mouth. When she finished, she set the plate aside and leaned over to the night stand. "Look here under the stationery," she told Christine, pointing to the top drawer. With mounting surprise, Christine pulled into the light a wedge of cheese, a package of Rye Krisp, and loose balls of cinnamon candy. "See?" Lola glanced without guilt at all of them. "I haven't been a very good girl."

Verna carefully inspected the items which Christine had placed like exhibits on top of the night stand. "How long have you had this food?" she asked.

"I've kept some in there since the very beginning."

Verna rubbed her forehead until a metal hair curler bobbed forward and swung lazily over one brow. "Oh, Lola, why didn't you at least try? Why didn't you give the grape cure a chance?"

A mischievous smile crossed Lola's face. "After all, I did just like the rest of you." She struggled to sit up straight against the pillows, tilting her head back to rest against the carved walnut headboard. "I thought if I went along and ate my grapes, it would be easier for all of you. I was willing—if it would help you people over this."

"Help *us?*" asked Christine incredulously. "You don't bother thinking about us—not at such a time!"

Lola shook her head. "Especially now, I want to think of

you." She said no more but looked affectionately at each of them, then turned away as Verna's eyes glistened with tears.

"Oh, Lola, forgive us," said Verna, barely able to speak.

Lola smiled and murmured quickly. "We had some fine times, didn't we?"

Verna began to weep; she averted her head and came toward the bed. Christine sat down on the other side, and both sisters bowed their heads silently, as the petals of a poppy close at night; Lola reached out for their hands.

Embarrassed by this sudden intimacy, Herman felt warm, and he moved briskly to open the window. The dark south wind snuffled across his fingers with a dry breath. He glanced out into the night—but saw only his reflection in the glass.

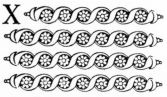X Lola Paff lingered on, her life seeping away, long after the meaning of her illness had overcome the household. Each Sunday at church townspeople greeted Herman, Christine, or Verna—depending on which of them left the sickbed—with phrases of commiseration, so that even when they were out of the house, they could not forget Lola for an instant.

But grief finally wore out. The mechanics of caring for Lola gradually became more absorbing than their sorrow and despair that they would soon lose her. Christine never was as automatically crisp, as nurse-like and professional in her attitude as Verna, but Herman realized, in candid moments, that his wife had seldom seemed as healthy and full of purpose as now, under the challenge of this awful and increasingly victorious disease. He himself found comfort in brandy, and he spent as much time away from the house as he decently could—taking trips to Missouriville to drink by himself in a parked car.

With no possibility of overcoming the cancer, for the sisters who fought to help Lola, for the living who would survive, there came a soul-swelling sense of nobility. Friends called Christine and Verna gallant, and indeed, their lives seemed

dramatic to themselves; they were oddly uplifted. Lola in her
pain turned inward, became at times as petulant as a child;
she did not notice the loss of close concern on the part of her
sisters. The living and the dead were already parting. As summer ended, Herman spent more and more time outdoors. He
took long walks under the trees of the town, shuffling through
bright dead leaves and watching the work of autumn.

Lola lasted all winter, and though she kept predicting that
she would not see the crocuses bloom again, she was still alive
to look at the rose garden in June. Vernon Kallsen visited her
twice a week now and read passages from the Bible—those
alarming, sweet verses about the many mansions and this life
being but a vale of tears. Vernon felt, as he read, that Lola
gratefully took the Christian comfort; not from her would he
hear an off-guard remark, an anguished "Why? Why?"

Herman spent more and more useless hours in Meecher's
Taproom drinking brandy, and he gave up trying to conceal his
liking for liquor. There were no more phony trips to Missouriville for secret binges, no lies to Christine and Verna. At
times he returned home quite drunk, and Christine would turn
upon him bitterly. "What's the matter with you? Don't we
have enough trouble as it is? Are you losing your grip or
something?" He could not answer, for he did not know why
he was drowning himself in liquor, and he did not particularly
care to find out.

Lola finally died quietly in late October—"in her sleep," was
the phrase passed around town. Christine and Verna had
thought so long about funeral preparations that the usual
arrangements were easily made; even the marble tombstone
had already been cut. Now at last neighbors could bring pies,
cakes, and casseroles; at last the flowers could descend upon the
household; at last it was all over. Herman went through the
wake, funeral sermon, and cemetery graveside service without

feeling much emotion. He kept brandy in his room now, and he had fortified himself unusually well for this ordeal.

Christine hoped that Herman would stop drinking, since the terrible crisis was over and they could all settle down once again to their normal lives. But Herman was content with his routine, and he enjoyed his companionship with deaf old John Leech, night clerk at the Kaleburg Hotel, and the mayor, Dan Beers, and other cronies in Meecher's Tap. Herman, in fact, not only began to share the laughter over tales of shrewish wives and flying rolling pins, but he told a few himself; he was emancipated at last, free in the world of men, where he hoped to stay the rest of his life. Christine set up a cot in the smoker for him, because she could not stand his alcoholic breath. She grumbled whenever he was around, and to keep herself from sinking into despair, turned to church duties, and then, after Pearl Harbor, began working part-time for the Red Cross.

Verna was highly aroused by the treacherous Japanese attack. The country was in danger, and she intended to be a stalwart defender. She was proud when she received word of her appointment as county chairman of the Office of Price Administration. Each day she drove her car to the county courthouse at Huntford, where she directed a large staff of part-time people whose duty it was to mail sugar and gasoline ration books. Most of the volunteer workers were high-school students who got credit for their time spent this way, for it was considered on-the-job training in office work. They also earned points toward acquiring a red felt V, which they could sew on their grey gabardine Victory Club caps.

The Victory Club idea swept through Huntford high school, and soon most of the students were wearing caps with V's to school; "like an army of the young," said the principal proudly, "you're fighting this war, too." The students at the local O.P.A. office looked upon Verna as something of a four-star general. There was not a farmer who got gasoline coupons he didn't deserve, and she was ruthless with those innocents who tried to corrupt her by offering baby beeves for her frozen-food locker or new tires for her car. She was staunchly for the United States Government and never gave an inch from her hard, austere principles. She felt that now was the time for "taking in that extra notch on the belt," and she was contemptuous of the flabby people who whined that they needed extra gasoline, more sugar, or complained of the hardships of war.

Then, quite suddenly, Verna became the first war casualty in the whole county. Apparently while driving home to Kaleburg late one evening after a meeting with the supervisors, she fell asleep at the wheel and crashed into a bridge abutment. The shock of Verna's death was staggering to Herman, but it temporarily unhinged Christine's mind altogether. The doctor prescribed drugs and confined her to bed, even on the afternoon of the funeral.

Herman found Reverend Kallsen no help, for he kept poking around the house, Bible in hand, ready to comfort if he could. But Christine refused to let him in the bedroom, as if she suspected the minister were bewitched and his bedside touch, the kiss of death. "I didn't send for you," she shouted from her bed as Vernon Kallsen stood bewildered in the hall. "Herman! Herman! Is it as bad as that? Did you send for the minister? Oh, God!" and she turned her face away. At least this is what Herman thought his wife said; he was rather drunk at the time.

Even in his sober moments Herman could not believe what was happening to Christine, for of all the sisters she was the most levelheaded. Perhaps the strangers in the house upset her, but Herman couldn't keep them out. Carrie Maxwell and her Sympathy Committee of the Ladies Aid did all the cooking, shopping, and housecleaning. They brought cookies and made coffee for the wake. They washed every sheet and curtain in sight and scrubbed the basement rooms—even the potato cellar, which hadn't been mopped in all the years since the house had been built. Herman felt powerless to stop these women—they were everywhere. The only place he could be by himself was the bathroom, and even then he couldn't insure privacy unless he bolted the door. One of his favorite socks was ripped in the washing-machine wringer, and his striped cap was scorched by some woman who thought it should be ironed.

Again for Herman it was Meecher's Tap that seemed home, and he didn't care that some busybodies said he was showing disrespect to the dead by drinking himself into a stupor. His brandy drinking gave him too much comfort—he was allowing himself too easy a time in facing grief: he could stumble through this bitter moment in a haze, his perceptions and feelings dulled, while at such times decent people had to take straight what life dished out. He was not morally strong, as Verna had been—these things, he knew, people were saying behind his back. But he didn't care.

Of course the church was packed for the funeral, and Vernon was ready to meet the dramatic test of this moment. He chose for his text a passage from John: "Love not the world, neither the things that are in the world. If any man love the world, the love of the Father is not in him. For all that is in the world, the lust of the flesh, and the lust of the eyes, and the pride of life, is not of the Father, but is of the world. And the world passeth away. . . ." He meant to prove by this that death was nothing but a losing of this dreary mortal life. Hadn't every funeral oration tried to make that point? And yet to say that this loss meant nothing, that everyone should actually rejoice that for Verna, at least, the toil and afflictions were over, was especially difficult, for who had taken more pride in life than she? Thus, even as he spoke with mellow certain words, he was arguing with himself. He was relieved to come at last to the sentimental section of his message: the two sisters departing this world together as they had spent their lives together. Could we not imagine them arm in arm in heaven, Vernon asked? And as he expanded the image, a sweet note of joy crept into his voice, hastened on by the sight of so many wet faces below him. A funeral was after all for weeping, not for comfort.

The bugler of the American Legion post blew taps behind the pine trees in the cemetery at the close of the graveside rites; a flag was on her coffin, for she had died in the service of her country. This was 1942, and there was still a novelty in such patriotic sacrifices. Vernon Kallsen drew Herman away from the heaped-up fresh earth, for the diggers were already starting their careless shoveling. "Let's go home and see how Christine is," he said gently, calling her by her first name, which he had never done before. "These are the most difficult times of life," he added softly.

The liquor was wearing off, and it seemed to have cleared abruptly when the minister spoke. Herman looked at his pastor with a feeling of astonishment. "What do you know about it?" he asked bluntly, without thinking. He had had about enough of all these people.

Vernon was shocked, but he could not say—he could not admit that he and death were old familiars, that long ago a terrible thing had happened: his son had died as suddenly as Verna. "Believe me—I, too, know of grief." But he said no more and they walked all the way in silence.

When they arrived at the Paff home, Herman finally spoke. "You see, Reverend, here it turns out that Christine and I are left alone. Isn't that strange?"

"We must accept what the Lord gives us."

But Herman was wondering about the hidden meaning behind all of this. There was a faint suggestion of some purpose, some progression in his life, and he would like to understand it. "You see, there we were on the farm—Christine and me—and we had children. And these children—I mean Irving, not so much the daughter—came at last to push the old folks out."

"You retired from the farm, wasn't that it?" asked Vernon.

They moved inside and sat down in the living room. "Well, yes, it was all agreed that Irving should have the farm. That's the natural thing, after all. But the fact is still there—when the time came for Irving and his family to enjoy the full strength of their lives, me and Christine had to go. And so we moved back here to the Paff home where Verna and Lola were firmly settled—they hadn't changed in their lives at all—*as you know very well, Reverend.*" He shook his finger in the air.

Vernon nodded. Herman's excited talk, he concluded, could only come from an overdose of liquor. It was pathetic to see a man fall apart as completely as this.

"Now Verna and Lola were here, and what did we do? We muscled in. We said this was our home, too. Of course, it was all done in a nice way, and they said: sure, come on. But the truth is, Reverend, me and Christine—we just put our feet in the door and pushed our way in. Now isn't that about the size of it? And what happens? After a few years, here we are, own-ing it all—having everything to ourselves, from the silverware in the dining room to the trunks in the attic." He lifted his arms, then collapsed them. "But why? That's that I want to know from you, Reverend. Why has all this happened, without anyone being able to do anything about it? Can you tell me that?"

Nervously, Vernon bit his lip. He was about to say the only automatic thing that came to mind: that God's ways to man are mysterious, but this seemed to be exactly what Herman was telling him.

"A man keeps moving through the years," Herman con-tinued, "never stopping to think of his life until it's too late to do much. Unless—unless this is what we're supposed to do. If you try to hold anything too hard, it melts away, slips from your grasp—your farm, your loved ones—wife, children, friends, money—all the same. You know that, Reverend."

"Now there's no reason to get so depressed. Remember the words of Jesus—"

"I know those words. We all know them. You needn't say them as if it was the first time they struck our ears. What I'm saying is entirely different. I mean, it's terrible, the way things happen. Now I'm old and useless—but I never wanted so much to keep on living. *That's* what I can't understand."

And neither could Vernon Kallsen, so he said nothing.

In the aftermath, Christine sought recovery by throwing herself into work, an age-old German remedy for anything that ailed you. She kept saying, "There's a war on, and we won't be the last to lose somebody." She sent boxes of food overseas to every boy on Reverend Kallsen's list, whether she knew him very well or not. For everyone, the church became a center that it had not been before. There were special prayers requested on Sundays, and the congregation listened carefully to the names Reverend Kallsen mentioned, learning thereby which families were most worried. The minister made a large beaverboard sign which covered the whole wall of the narthex, and whenever a member of the parish was drafted, Vernon wrote the name in his clear script and affixed a shiny blue star at the end—each star a candidate for the honor of being replaced by a gold one. Churchgoers saw the board as they entered on Sunday mornings, and it never failed to fill their hearts with anxiety; they were put into a receptive frame of mind for the sermon. Church attendance jumped, for no one wished to risk a careless Sunday and then during the week have a telegram arrive from the War Department. People were willing to try almost anything, if it would save their men in uniform. Communion Sundays seemed especially important: the high ceremony of the wine and wafer—the old and the young of the congregation standing up to be counted; trooping to the communion rail in front; falling on their knees before God, Reverend Kallsen, and man; partaking of the Lord. And if the old magic of surrender and prayer did not help either themselves or their soldiers in North Africa, Italy, and the Pacific, then at least they had done all that was humanly possible; they had followed the spiritual laws devotedly, as they were supposed to do. Their consciences could rest; what would happen would happen, and no blame could be placed anywhere, by themselves or other people. During those dark months, never had the Protestants and Catholics been closer in their faiths, had they but known it.

There was a period in 1944 when Kaleburg fatalities reached one a week, and memorial services were just about the only kind of funeral ceremony. It seemed that death was an occurrence which happened in some distant place, the news relayed by telegram; and so, when old people reached their last gasp or infants died, when any of the ordinary local people succumbed, it caused a certain surprise, as if the prevailing thought was (addressing the corpse): "What? You, too? What's the very idea, taking over in this area, where honor and glory should be heaped upon the dead and their bereaved?" It was almost as if lesser deaths were presumptuous, demanding mourners under false pretenses. It was not patriotic to die.

And then one morning when Christine went to the basement storeroom where farm eggs were kept, Herman in the kitchen heard a great clatter. He feared she had slipped on the stairs, and indeed, when he reached the basement staircase he saw her in a heap at the bottom, with the mire of broken eggs on the steps, on the cement floor, and most awful of all, in her hair. He rushed down, gripping the railing, careful not to slip on the egg slime and himself tumble forward. He called to her. He lifted her to a sitting position, thinking she had fainted, but with dread he also put his hand under her breast, searching for the telltale sign of life. His hands were too thick to feel a beat and his fingertips too insensitive to detect a pulse at her wrist. He put his cheek against her mouth, and then in panic put his lips to her nostrils, as if he were God breathing life into the first woman. But still, he felt no breath at all; he knew then for certain that she had been whisked into death. He left her where he had found her and went upstairs to phone the doctor. Beyond that, he was too dazed to think what should be done; he knew well enough that friends would come to his aid. With a bottle of brandy and cigars, he retreated to his smoker upstairs. The doctor told him later that Christine had suffered a cerebral hemorrhage.

Neighbors and friends entered the house through every door. The women took over the kitchen and sent their men for groceries. Irving Johns and his wife made the funeral arrangements and telephoned Herman's daughter in California. With the household filled—every bedroom taken—Herman was mercifully left to himself to get quietly drunk.

Reverend Kallsen did not think this was right, for he remembered Herman's restless probing of a few months ago and had felt then that he was veering close to the edge and might lose control altogether. Vernon therefore took it upon himself to try to comfort Herman, and he knocked on the smoker door where Herman was closeted. At first Vernon was scarcely able to breathe, for the smoke and odors of liquor were offensively strong. "You know why I've come," he began.

"Yes," said Herman sullenly, slouched in his leather chair. "But I want to be alone."

"Sometimes it does a person good to talk," said Vernon, though he himself had never followed this advice.

"Yeah, maybe," said Herman, rubbing the tip of his cigar against the ash tray on the table beside him.

While he waited, a sudden disturbing thought occurred to

Vernon. He understood why he had come, and it was not at all
the reason he liked to believe. He was not here to dispatch
comfort, but out of curiosity to see what Herman would do and
say now. Vernon was ashamed of himself. "I know this has all
been quite a shock," he began, "and I just wanted you to
know—"

"It's as though," Herman interrupted, "it's as though Lola
was calling and calling from the other side. Those three sisters
—they always did everything together."

A chill ran up Vernon's spine, and he gripped the arms of
the chair where he was sitting. Such a startling, primitive suggestion seemed to have been wrenched out of the dark,
unknowable night itself. He got to his feet. This sort of super-
stition would get neither of them anywhere. "You shouldn't stay
here alone, Herman. You shouldn't—shouldn't think too much.
Perhaps, after the funeral, you could go and live on the farm
again. I'll speak to your son, if you like."

Herman shook his head. "No, no. You needn't think I'll do
away with myself."

"I didn't say that," he began. But of course, this was exactly
what Vernon had been thinking, for there were moments when
a man pushed himself too far—and then took the leap into
oblivion rather than struggle farther. And it always happened,
Vernon suspected, not in moments of confusion, but when the
mind was so clear that it cut through the fabric of life itself.
Here in this room he felt that death had come ominously alive.
He was very much relieved to say goodbye.

Living a rural life all these years, Vernon knew that there
was a time each spring—usually in March—when aged farmers could not stand to witness another growing season in which
they would have no part. Just when lawns began to turn green
again and there was a stir of life and activity, suggestive of all
that was to come, despairing old timers threw ropes around

their necks. To a city person the bleakest time of the year is dead winter, but to these country people there was no period more terrible than the surge of life at the beginning of spring. No season more clearly foretold the end, and all of the years of green earth to come after each man's time.

XI 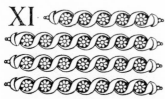 The mayor of Kaleburg—a card-playing, gossipy member of that fraternity of men who spent their time in Meecher's Tap—was a particular friend of Herman Johns. It happened that, having quarreled with his girl, with whom he had been living flagrantly, Dan Beers was looking around for new lodgings. Herman invited him to the Paff house the week after Christine's funeral, and Dan arrived with his belongings, ready for a permanent stay.

Beers was a raw-boned, handsome man not yet forty, but he hadn't gone off to fight in the war. He allied himself with the retired farmers in Meecher's, complained of stiff joints, and constantly made allusions to his advanced age. The trouble was, of course, that he felt guilty about not fighting for his country, and no one really knew what had happened when he took his physical examination for the draft board. Just before entering the examining room, he had swallowed five aspirins, and since his papers indicated a heart murmur from a childhood bout with rheumatic fever, the doctor was highly disturbed by the palpitating heart after Dan hopped up and down on one foot. "I guess we'll have to throw you back. Let the younger boys take over."

Around Kaleburg there were many young men who did not go to war, for they were deferred because of their work in the vital industry of agriculture. This was a laugh to townspeople, who had never thought of farming as anything but simply farming. It made them angry to see farmers having special favors of gasoline and tires and getting their sons deferred. There were frequent brawls in the alley behind the Cornflower Ballroom, as taunts of cowardice were tossed about. Some young farmers, during the time of heavy casualties following D Day in Europe, did not want to show up in town at all, even for a movie.

Dan himself felt more comfortable in the country, where, despite the war, things continued very much as always, with plenty of tractor gas for automobiles, bountiful food from gardens, and usually enough sugar for pies, cakes, and cookies. Threshing rings were shorthanded during the oats harvest, and the summer Dan was living with Herman Johns, the two of them went out to join the old crew with which Herman had been associated all his life. Thus Dan got to know Irving Johns, Hans Albrecht, Tony Nisson, Joe Clausen, Robert Schneider, and the others. Threshing began at the old Ketter farm, now owned by Robert Schneider. Although Henry and Vida had been gone from the community all these years, the farm was still known as the Ketter place, to distinguish it from the other Schneider holdings, which were considerable.

Herman Johns was too slow and old to do much except "tend the water jug," but he enjoyed getting dirty from flying chaff, sweating under the sun, and having his ears buzz from the interminable noise of the tractor and the big, rattling threshing machine. He also kept a careful watch on the oats wagons, which stood close beside the machine. When one wagon got full, he transferred the spout to an empty wagon behind it. He followed the yields of various fields with great interest, remembering from year to year not only what his own land had produced, but also the history of his neighbors' fields. Meanwhile, Dan volunteered for work in the burnt stubble fields. He spike-pitched for Irving Johns awhile, then Hans Albrecht, and finally Joe Clausen.

The most cheerful man in the whole crew was Joe Clausen, and Dan enjoyed teasing him about his devoted dog, Betsy, who followed him everywhere. There had always been a Betsy on the Clausen farm; when one died, Joe simply got another. He claimed that the children loved dogs, but Dan knew it was simply to cover up his own liking for the animals. Joe had seven daughters, all of them with pale blonde hair, rather rectangular faces and slightly protruding teeth—amazing little replicas of Joe himself. Clausen was often teased about his daughters, since a farmer with so many children and not one son had had a rather amusing turn of bad luck. Joe didn't seem to mind. He boasted that his girls would be great beauties, good-looking enough to marry the best young farmers around, and any of them could take over the land in the future, if things worked out that way.

Even though Dan teased Joe, he envied him. He tried to imagine what it would be like to head a household as large as Joe's. Surely this would give you a great sense of dignity and importance, not only to rule one hundred and eighty acres, but to have a whole army of people under you, including a wife like Marygold, who would take directions willingly because she loved you. How had all this happened to Joe, and in what way did he deserve it? Inevitably, Dan lined up his own life in comparison, for despite the advantages of his bachelor freedom and having cut himself away from Dorene when that seemed imperiled, already he hungered for a new attachment. There had been many fine girls before Dorene—all in good fun. But the forming of relationships and the tearing away wore him down; he knew, too, that each time he took up with a girl, the quality of love he had to give was thinner; the words sounded hollow more quickly.

It was a relief simply to pretend that he was a farmer in the threshing crew, and he went along with the men in overalls to the country houses at noon. In a shaded dining room, he would eat heavy meals which had been fixed by five or six women in the overheated kitchen; here the neighbors were all together: the men with the men, the women with the women. And in the afternoons, when Dan tired of work, he would sit by the water jug in the shade of the bundle racks and tell his stories. Each farmer, as he drove up with his team and wagon, was rather self-conscious about how skillfully he had rounded off the bundles on top, the way a barber shapes and cuts hair. You could always tell a braggart by the preposterous size of the load, and a sloppy farmer by the ragged sides—the whole load looked as if it would fall apart before reaching the feeder-belt. The country was a good place to take the measure of a man: things were easier to understand; less chance for important factors to hide behind complexity, as they seemed to do in the city. With these farmers Dan relaxed over every new anecdote; along with the other men, he made fun of the community fools, jibed at the misers, and gave new twists to the latest strands of gossip.

But Dan Beers was not a farmer, and inevitably, he was forced to return to the realities of Kaleburg. During winter, Dan and Herman's life together in the big Paff home seemed too depressing to stand for long. Both of them purposely created as much of a mess as they could; they were defiantly bachelors, men without women—and the kitchen was littered with coffee grounds, eggshells, orange peels, empty bottles, torn newspapers, mud, and cigar ashes. Herman rather enjoyed being scolded by the cleaning woman who came each week, for he was reminded of Christine's grumblings. But Dan realized that he was messy because he was revolted with himself and his life. Much of the trouble, too, was sad-eyed, puffy-skinned old Herman, and his familiar, slightly dazed walk. This was too strong an image for Dan to have constantly before him. I'm not old yet, he told himself, so why get into low spirits, just because I'm quartered with an old man? I don't have to reckon with that business yet.

One night he enticed an eighteen-year-old girl home to his bed—she had already wearied of playing around with boys her own age—and Dan found her remarkably adept at giving a man pleasure. Meanwhile, Herman was getting drunk in Meecher's Tap. Dan realized that it would be perfectly possible for him to carry on an affair with this girl which would last for months, but he shuddered to think of how the ghosts of those three sisters would walk. The next morning, disgusted with himself, he decided to move from the Paff house and live by himself again. There was one room in town which he thought he deserved: the lodgings above the Gambles store—the place where homeless, unconnected men often spent their last years, and where old John Hendricks had died.

In 1946 Kaleburg was a century old, and at first Dan had been enthusiastic about the celebration planned for August; but, by the end of June, when his thick dark beard, which he was growing for the beard-judging contest, was down to his second shirt button, he was becoming weary of the whole business. He settled a scrap between the Legion Auxiliary and the wives of the Veterans of Foreign Wars by flipping a coin, since both groups wanted the lucrative hot-dog concession in front of the Farmers Savings Bank. Carrie Maxwell gave him trouble by trying to cancel the carnival free entertainment, claiming that crowds would be drawn away from her pageant of the town's history—an event scheduled for the same hour each night of the Jubilee. A town council vote decided the issue against her, partly because of the interest in the contest for queen.

The Queen of Kaleburg would reign each night during the

Free Acts. All through late spring and continuing into summer, merchants gave out ballots with each five dollars of goods sold, and the ten queen candidates were actively soliciting support among their friends. At a Commercial Club meeting it was estimated that business had increased 15 per cent because of the balloting. Jake Orley's oldest daughter was among the contestants, and when he phoned, asking to see Dan in the mayor's office as soon as possible, Dan was afraid that Jake's fatherly interest in the race might prompt him to try to stuff the ballot boxes—with Dan's aid.

Orley shuffled into the mayor's office wearing orange trousers with black stitching up the sides. He was one of the few beardless men of Kaleburg, and his pink, rather babyish cheeks were flushed. "Listen, Dan," he began at once, slumping into a chair, "we need the Sale Barn for our cock fights, but here I find you've promised it to the 4-H Clubs. What kind of mix-up is this? Don't you remember, I told you about that guy from Florida—the one who got the world's championship? He's going to enter his birds here. Christ, Dan, we'll have to have a big place to take care of the people. The Tony Nisson barn will never do."

"The kids have to have some place, too, you know."

Orley laughed. "Who the hell cares about 4-H baby beeves and patchwork quilts? Come on, come on, Dan. Be reasonable. You want a crowd for this Centennial, and you know what they'll come for. Let me tell you, Dan, when that guy from Florida puts his cocks against ours, he's not going to win. I don't care what kind of bird he has. I've got Lucifer—a fighting cock like none you've ever seen! Remember Flame, that fiery red rooster? You thought he was something! Well, Lucifer comes from the same stock. I'm putting a couple thousand on him myself, and you'd better scrape up all the cash you can. Why, Dan, they've taught this little Lucifer to give a death rattle and lay down. The other cock will strut around and think he's won, but Lucifer ain't dying. He's just playing possum. He waits till that other rooster is off guard, and then he rakes in for the kill. One, two, three! He leaps into the air and digs in his spurs. It's all over." Jake spread his hands and blinked. "I've seen one of these birds fight, Dan—Lucifer's brother. The crowd yelled 'My God, he's risen from the dead!' "

"Nevertheless, the kids get the barn," Dan said slowly, "because I promised it to them."

Orley frowned and stood up. "You want people to come to town for this celebration, don't you?" he asked angrily. "Isn't that the point? Well, I'm telling you they'll come for a cock fight. Anybody would!"

Dan smiled to cover his uneasiness. "Suppose, just for a minute—suppose we decided to have a corn-on-the-cob eating contest, and I was able to down twenty-four ears in one setting, like I did at the Catholic bazaar a couple of years ago. Do you think that would draw a crowd?"

"Sure! You God-damned right it would. They'll come to see that!"

"Well, I wouldn't," said Dan.

Orley frowned. "What's the matter with you these days, anyhow?"

"Look, Jake. Don't you get the point? We've made certain plans about everything, and I'm not going to change them just because you want what somebody else's got. This is a celebration involving the whole town, and it's got to be done decently."

"But they're just kids!" Orley said, his voice growing louder. "It's nothin'. They're going to use the barn for nothin'—what I'm saying is that in the interest of the town we should hold a cock fight there and draw hundreds of people. Big attraction!"

"What's wrong with the Tony Nisson barn?"

"It can only take a hundred—standing room for a few more. Tony's willing to knock out some walls and make alterations, but his landlord—Junior Hendricks out in Seattle—won't say yes or no. He just don't bother to answer letters."

"Figure something out, Jake. The Sale Barn is taken."

Jake sighed, disgusted. "I'll talk to you later, Dan. You don't make sense now."

"I mean it," Dan said, without looking up.

"See you tonight, maybe—or tomorrow," Orley said. "You're all excited about this Jubilee business."

Instead of going to the Kaleburg Kafe for supper Dan Beers ate in another restaurant where he was sure to see nobody he knew. He told himself that he wanted to digest his meal in peace, and he chose a table in the dim rear of the Highway Café, occasionally frequented by motorists.

The front screendoor slammed, and Dan was surprised to see Reverend Vernon Kallsen. He was dressed in his usual black summer suit, and after glancing around nervously, he sat down on a counter stool. Not having noticed Dan, he obviously felt safe and anonymous, for only strangers surrounded him, and not many of them. Dan studied the minister's pale, worried face and noticed his shyness as he gave the waitress his order. With quick, darting glances over his shoulders at the few people eating hamburgers and drinking soda pop, Vernon Kallsen was an oddity that quickly drew attention—surely the opposite of what he wished. Or did he? Dan seized upon speculation as a fine alternative to his own problems. He also breathed a silent, grateful prayer that the clutches of guilt and the distant rattlings of a wrathful god no longer had power over him. Sanctimoniously, Vernon poured out his Coca Cola and lifted the glass to his lips as if he were partaking of a private communion with the world. Safe this way, for no one would see him. To the minister this late-afternoon imbibing was probably a secret adventure, a necessary addition to his punctual daily walk to the post office. Vernon finished his Coke just as Dan wiped up the last gravy on his plate with a wedge of cottony bread. When the waitress brought pie, Dan asked her, "Does the parson come here often?"

She turned around, and they both looked at Vernon, whose feet dangled slightly from the high stool. "Every day or so; it depends. I guess he ain't got much to do," she laughed.

A minute later, with a cheery good-night to the waitress, Reverend Kallsen left; Dan, watching, suddenly realized that Vernon came here to get "out," whereas he came here to get away. "We're about as different as two people can be," he said to himself. And his renewed pleasure in who he was and the way he was sent Dan out of the Highway Café with a whistle on his lips and a swagger in his stroll.

He began his night watch, and since this was Saturday, by seven o'clock the neon lights were glaring above the taverns and visitors were parking their cars along Main Street. Dan changed to a dark blue cop's uniform and felt his mayor troubles far away. He was on duty now, and he made the usual rounds. When he strolled through the basement gambling rooms of the Kaleburg Klub, he stopped at the bar for his customary one beer on the house. In a dim corner glowing with flamingo lamps, several blackjack and poker games were already underway, and Dan leaned against a wall nearby and watched the players.

Shortly after eight-thirty, Reverend Kallsen's young choir members, dismissed after rehearsal, entered the bar and looked uneasily around. They ordered 7-Up Highs and giggled with excitement, wondering who might betray them to their parents. Dan fingered his whiskers and moved on, nodding and smiling to all who greeted him. He left in his wake an aura of well-being, for he was the law, both cop and mayor, and he felt like some great pacifying barge cruising among the islands of pleasure.

The last room in the basement was small and crowded with couples; a back stairs led up to the alley which adjoined the

Cornflower Ballroom, and here dancers congregated between numbers; they drank spiked Cokes and snuggled in leatherette booths. The only lights were a border of rainbow colors around the edge of the ceiling, shining dimly from inside glass bricks, as if a string of Christmas trees bulbs had been frozen in blocks of ice. People noticed him as he entered, and though he knew most of them, he suddenly felt awkward. What was the fun in standing around and watching them? Tonight he took no pleasure from the noisy music, the laughter and shouts.

He walked up the back stairs and stood for a moment in the dim alley. He noticed a young couple approaching from the rear of the ballroom, and he hastily slipped into the shadow of the next building. Then he walked away, toward the town jail.

It was an old brick building with four cells, and sometimes on dance nights Dan had a full house, although tonight thus far it was empty. Without turning on his flashlight he unlocked the door, closed and bolted it behind him, and sat down on a chair inside one of the cells. He could see a few stars through the solid bars of the high, narrow window. The muffled rhythm of the dance band pulsed through the still, sultry night; he heard the shuffling of the dancers' feet. But everyone was far away. He sighed, stretched out his legs, and thought of nothing except that no one knew where he was, and if wanted, he could not be found.

On Wednesday, just before the Jubilee, a reporter from the *Tribune* was expected in town for a feature story, and to make a startling impression upon him, Carrie Maxwell wanted a group of horsemen to stage a simulated raid. She called upon Jake Orley to pitch in and find horses and men to pose as Jesse James' gang, which in the early days had robbed a Kaleburg bank.

Shortly after noon on Wednesday, Dan met the young reporter as he stepped off the train. Without saying a word about the mock raid about to take place, Dan walked with the newspaperman to the Kaleburg Kafe for lunch. But they did not reach the door, for as soon as the train pulled out, six masked men riding heavy plow horses came galloping down the street from behind the Farmer's Elevator. They fired blank cartridges, and Kendrick, the reporter, immediately began grinning. "Hey, what's this?"

"Jesse James, boy—we'd better run."

There was not much of a crowd to watch the demonstration, for it was too early in the afternoon. Kendrick readied his camera and took a few pictures. Several businessmen came out of their stores, and by their grins and hoots, Dan could tell how ridiculous they thought the whole stunt was. He felt a little ashamed because it seemed childish. Whooping it up, the men circled and finally stopped in front of the Kaleburg Klub. They dismounted, tied their horses to a fireplug, and went inside for a round of whiskey. "Let's go over and join them," said Dan.

Kendrick was surprised to find a fully equipped bar with liquor bottles lined up in plain sight before the mirror along the wall. "I thought this state was dry," he said. "But if this is the way it is, I'll take Scotch." He signaled the bartender. "Black and White."

"This is Jake Orley's private club. Isn't that right, Vern?" Dan asked.

"You bet," said the bartender.

"People around here figure the law ought to follow a man's inclinations," said Dan. He enjoyed astonishing this young city fellow. He was sorry the gaming tables were dark, the roulette wheel still, and the slot machines covered.

"But tell me, what's it like to be mayor and marshal of a wide-open town like this?"

"Easy." Dan shrugged his shoulders, but he did not quite like the measuring look in Kendrick's eyes. "I mean, what do *I* care, if this is what the people want? What's the harm?"

Kendrick laughed. "Sure." He paused, sipping his drink. "But who's this guy Orley? I want to see the man who runs this town."

"I run this town," said Dan, with just the right mixture of humor, so that the comment seemed neither boastful nor earnest.

"Oh, sure, I forgot," said Kendrick with a smile (or was it a snicker? Dan wondered). "Well, Mr. Mayor, what's next?"

"Come, I'll show you the Sale Barn, where we're having the farm fair."

They walked down the street together, crossed the railroad tracks, and entered the Sale Barn on the edge of the city limits. It echoed hollowly; there was no one around. Rows of empty planks for spectators and bidders ran like a continuous stairs to the open ceiling beams. "Now what the hell," muttered Dan, more puzzled than irritated. "Where're the kids? This thing is supposed to be all set up for tomorrow. I'd better get on the phone."

"Well, I want to find the hotel. Didn't get much sleep last night."

They stopped in the newspaper office on the way and picked up a fat Centennial edition before checking in with John Leech, the hotel clerk. In the lobby were lumpy old easy chairs and several stained spittoons; they walked with Leech up the creaking stairs. All of the six rooms in the upper hall were alike, with chipped white-painted metal beds, no running water, and blankets that smelled like a tramp's overcoat. "Now, during the middle of the week, it should be quiet up here," said Dan. "Weekends, this place does a lot of business. Couples in and out, you know."

Downstairs, Dan phoned the president of the boys' 4-H Club, who explained why they were not setting up exhibits in the

Sale Barn. "Jake Orley said we'd get in the way of his roosters. He said *he* was supposed to have the barn—there'd been a mistake."

"Now listen, there was no mistake—except Jake's. You move into that barn, do you hear?"

After a long pause the boy replied: "But it's too late now. We're going to have our exhibit at the county fair in September."

Dan felt his face grow hot. "Why didn't you tell me?"

"I told Jake. I thought he'd tell you."

"No, nobody tells me anything," said Dan. He set the receiver down; his hand was moist. This was too much—Orley had gone too far. A mistake! Not after an issue had been made of it. Jake knew perfectly well what he was doing. Sooner or later Orley had to be put in his place, and now was as good a time as any—in fact, it *had* to be done now, for Dan knew that if he knuckled under to Jake on this affair, he would never be able to look himself in the mirror.

Dan marched past the secretary, threw open the door marked "Jake Orley, Farm and Property Manager," and caught Jake by surprise. He whirled around from a filing cabinet, as if to defend himself. Then Jake relaxed, smiled, and tapped shut the drawer; the sliding sound was as companionable as a closing door, allowing privacy to two friends. "Have a chair, Dan. Your face is as red as a summer sausage."

"You know what I just found out?"

"How about a drink? I've got this little refrigerator here."

"You screwed those kids out of their barn! I warned you, Jake."

Orley smiled, his face relaxed and innocent. "It was such a little thing, Dan. They didn't mind—and I know we've got to have that cockfight in a good place, to take care of the crowds."

"You knew damn well how I felt."

"The thing is settled. The cockfight's tomorrow night. Relax,

Dan. You're all excited about this Jubilee. You're as bad as Carrie."

"I've worked hard on it. I want it to go right. But bastards like you gum up the works. That's what I'm trying to say, Jake. This time I'm not going to let you get away with it. Remember, *I'm* the marshal, as long as I wear this badge." He pressed his fingers against the sharp edge of the star.

"Dan, for Christ's sake, what's the matter with you?"

"I'm fed up, that's all. I've had enough of the way you operate." He turned on his heels and left the office.

Outside he walked slowly along the sidewalk. He wanted to *do* something—anything to keep himself going steadily ahead with purpose. He noticed the moving vans of the carnival company and the ferris wheel, partially assembled. The gala scene was a sickening contrast to his own inner state. If a man can be a man for at least one moment of his life, he has something to go by for the rest of the time, he thought. Dan felt strong and clear-headed, capable of delivering crushing blows to all who dared tamper with his honor.

But he told himself to be calm, to think and plan what must be done. Where was Jake most vulnerable? Obviously, at every point he broke the law: cockfighting, selling liquor, all the forms of gambling. What if a lot of people knew about this—influential people outside Kaleburg? What would happen if Kendrick wrote a full exposé and it were printed in the *Tribune*, with its circulation of half a million? Dan imagined the bold black headlines, perhaps even pictures across the front page. The real inside dirt on a little out-of-the-way town. Of course, this scheme might flop if Kendrick wasn't interested. The paper might not run the article; or the state's attorney general might do nothing about it—perhaps he already knew about Jake and was handsomely paid off. But this was a time to act, to take risks, for if he did not, what was there to him? He urged himself on; he knew the stuff of which he was made.

Kendrick was to have supper with Carrie Maxwell, and afterwards, the two of them would be in the audience as Dan, master of ceremonies, crowned the Queen of Kaleburg. But later tonight, Dan knew, when the town slept, he could sneak over to the hotel, walk past deaf old John Leech, and go upstairs to have a long talk with Kendrick. "Yes, you can quote me on that," he would say to the reporter. "Put it down: 'Dan Beers says. . . .'"

That evening in the Community Building Dan placed the tinfoil crown on Gloria Wolbers, Queen of Kaleburg. Bill Wolbers' only child had grown into an astonishing beauty, with golden hair as soft as cornsilk, deep blue eyes, and a fine figure, although she was not quite fifteen, a high-school freshman. With great poise she made a pretty speech, promising to faithfully undertake the duties of queen. Dan heard some people grumbling later that the honor should have gone to an older girl, for Gloria Wolbers seemed destined to win many beauty contests in the years ahead. Dan, listening, thought how frivolous these concerns, compared to the big things on his mind.

At last he was left alone; the janitor turned out all the lights, and Dan sat in the dark behind the mayor's desk. In his mind he reeled off the facts he would tell Kendrick later. He got up, turned on a light, and paced up and down the room in his pioneer regalia. Glancing at himself in the mirror on the back of the door, he adjusted the loop in his string tie, then briefly shined his boots on the back of his pants legs. He strapped the holster around his waist and once again looked at the image in the mirror, sharing with himself the excitement of the moment. He looked at his watch. It was still too early. He again shut off the light.

The usual rounds to check the safety of Kaleburg would not be made tonight: the door of the Farmer's Elevator would not be tried, nor would he flash his searchlight into the bushes of the shadowy park. All of that was sham. He had been cutting the figure of a cardboard marshal, but tonight he was the real thing. He sat in revery until the moon came up, and at midnight the street lamps dimmed. At last he stirred himself to leave. Surely by now he had thought of everything—all the repercussions of hate, as well as the glory.

He slipped out into the night, watching his ink-blot shadow dip and move along the grass. On upper Main Street where the carnival lay sprawled, the tawny canvas tents and covered booths were Arab-looking, a safari camped for the night, a caravan en route, pausing briefly in this deserted town. Hardly a light anywhere—a dim glow in the Kaleburg Hotel, a few night lamps in stores along Main Street, but that was all. Red, white, and blue bunting was draped in heavy folds around the light posts and arched over the street in long ropes, like Christmas-tree tinsel. Signs and banners decorated the storefronts, but it was too dark now to make out the lettering, and they appeared like black bands or mourning shrouds, heavy in the night.

Dan circled the edges of the loop-the-loop, which looked like a giant hammer up-ended; he passed the fluted platform of the tilt-a-whirl. The ferris wheel was silent as a windmill on a calm night; the carousel was motionless, all of the fiercely galloping horses arrested in mid-air. He stroked the slick enameled flanks of a chestnut charger, and then, on an impulse, swung into the saddle of a black stallion which had its mouth open, the teeth painfully white, the red tongue lolling. He hung onto the pole with one hand and with the other clutched the wooden horn of the Western saddle. The horse sank under his weight, and he felt the whole carousel move slightly. Three wheezy notes sounded celestially in the air from the merry-go-round organ. It was only the briefest tag end of an hypnotic, calliope song, and the moment passed so quickly that he wondered if he had really heard the music at all. Then he saw a flashlight beam splash on a tent canvas nearby, and he quickly swung off the black stallion and slipped behind the rifle-shoot booth. "Who's there?" the night watchman of the carnival called. Dan, in heavy shadow, made no noise.

When all was quiet again, he slipped out and moved down Main Street away from the carnival, feeling strangely exhilarated. He strutted in his Western pioneer costume, stretching out his legs in long strides as each click-tap of his metal-edged boots echoed up and down along the buildings. He felt like some hero in a Western movie of courage and danger, as if from one of these dark façades, secret eyes and a loaded six-shooter were trained upon him. The vision became so frighteningly real that he swerved suddenly, as if dodging bullets. He melted into the dark shadows and moved close along the windows of Schmidt's grocery; every nerve seemed exposed; he was listening; he was aware of everything around him.

Upon reaching the park he haunted the shadows of the Square House, then stepped to the porch and peered into the windows at the barely discernible, calm scene within: it was a room too full of furniture, antiques everywhere and not a living person about—all killed by Indians, dead on the floor, with the grandfather clock ticking on and on, measuring time unnoticed. Then he wheeled around and saw the black buggy drawn up on the grass ten yards away. The tongue lay flopped down in front, as if the carriage had been left by abandoning horses. Dan reached out to finger the cool gas lamp, to rub his thumb across the polished brass; but suddenly he saw his reflection in the celluloid circles of the drawn curtains, as if, inside that black, closed hearse, someone were looking at him. The image wavered when he turned away and walked back toward the business district. Now he saw Kaleburg in its real perspective; the false-front wooden stores looked as old-fashioned as a Western ghost town, for the neon signs were not visible, and there were no automobiles on the street—only the dim paraphernalia of the carnival.

As he tapped in his Western boots up the moonlit side of the street, he caught his reflection in several store windowpanes; and yet it seemed not himself but some legendary figure in pioneer garb with a full beard and a wide hat. He saw a powerful, broad-shouldered, indomitable man of the frontier looking back knowingly at him. Dan lifted a hand to stroke his beard; the watching man did likewise, making the gesture a kind of salute. They eyed each other silently with an animal respect and alertness, for Dan knew it was himself he thus encountered.

Boldly, he turned around and continued his tour of Kaleburg. The supple shadow followed from windowpane to windowpane until Dan came to a street crossing, and then the two were one and strode the moonlit town together. Up and down the neat blocks of tree-shrouded houses, the mayor of Kaleburg marched.

Dan paused outside the hotel to wipe his brow against his sleeve. He thought of Kendrick asleep upstairs and knew that he must now hurry to rouse him. Sleepy, drunk old John Leech sat behind the desk, his head in his hands, and a lightbulb with a green celluloid shade hung over him. The screen door accidentally slammed behind Dan as he walked in. His walk was still a strut; with his hands looped over his holster, he marched to the desk.

But as he entered the pool of light, he paused, and at that moment John slowly opened his bloodshot eyes, dawning terror in his face. "What—what do you want?" He did not seem to recognize Dan.

"I—I just—"

"What is it?" John shouted, his voice loud in the still night. "I didn't hear you. What did you say?"

"This man Kendrick," Dan began, but he shaded his eyes from the glare of the light, and his mind was spinning. "I wanted to see this Kendrick," he repeated lamely, now suddenly not at all sure that he wanted to go through with it.

"I can see you plain enough, Dan Beers. But what's this? Eh?" Leech fluted his hand behind his ear. "Speak up. Speak up. It's no secret I'm deaf as a stone."

"I didn't mean to—" Dan began, then stopped.

"Something wrong? Something the matter?" Leech shouted.

"No, no. It's nothing—I—I was just making the rounds." Dan turned and shuffled slowly through the lobby toward the dark street. Weariness dropped upon him so heavily that it was as if he had not been in bed for days. Sleep was all he wanted; he had been working too hard, too long—cared too much. He was a fool.

He climbed the stairs to his room above the Gambles store; he hesitated to turn on the light but finally did. Then slowly he moved toward the dresser to look at himself in the mirror. The bare lightbulb swung gently behind his left ear. He awaited the crushing indictment of himself in that moment when he saw his image. He blinked once, turned away, then looked back again. There was the saddened, defeated, familiar face—bearded and strange though it was, it was no longer a mask to himself. He had reached the depths, and he stood there, ready for self-loathing and hate to consume him.

But all was peaceful and quiet in the room and, oddly enough, within himself. He felt spent and almost happy. He did not move. Gradually, in the mirror, he saw a slow smile working out into his cheeks, widening the beard. Ah, he thought, how strange! The little game was over—not so different, after all, from all the other diversions of his life—but there was nothing he could do, except what he had been doing all along: he nodded his head, and looking deeply into his eyes, accepted his own forgiveness.

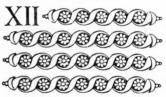

XII Vernon Kallsen loosened his white collarband and slowed his pace as he walked home from the post office. It was unseasonably hot for June, and the foliage had lost all traces of spring-like green. He moved from one island of shade to the next, grateful for the big trees along Main Street. The sky was cloudless and seared with heat, and very few people seemed around. Summer possessed this town, and those who did not have gardens attended to pots on window ledges or drowsed in rockers on screened-in porches. The farmers were all busy in the country. Only a rainy day would bring them to Kaleburg for provisions, repairs, and gossip—the three essentials of their lives.

Vernon fingered his mail impatiently. One letter among the small packet of second- and third-class material was too strange to be left until he got home to his study. He ripped open the flap and drew out a form letter dated simply "June, 1948." Above a golden embossed ear of corn was the firm name, National Seed Corn Company, of Chicago, Illinois.

HELP! HELP! HELP!

Attention all school teachers, school administrators, ministers, and housewives. The biggest seed-corn crop in the history of

America is upon us, and we need responsible people to help us with detasseling. Oh, no—we'll let the kids pull the tassels. We want you to inspect their work, either by the hour or by the acre. In our carefully controlled fields we need responsible adults to insure that only quality seed corn is produced. NATIONAL has a reputation to maintain, and you can be a part of this great company.

You are receiving this letter through our local representative, and he can supply you with all the details. The work is not difficult—and think of the fun of joining your children, your students, your neighbors in this vital seasonal work! Earnings can come to as high as $300.00, depending upon the length of the detasseling period. But WE NEED YOUR NAME NOW!

There is no training period. Just a day of instruction at the local plant, and then you're off to the country! Once you have tried this fascinating work you'll be writing us every year to join our detasseling operation.

BUT WE NEED YOUR NAME NOW. Write it here, giving address, age, and profession, and we'll hop to it! Detasseling starts in July. There's no time to waste.

Sincerely yours,

J. Kossworth

At the bottom of the letter Bill Wolbers had scribbled a note in ink. "Dear Reverend: We're sending this to everybody and didn't want you to feel left out."

A definite sadness touched Vernon. No, he would not feel "left out"—how could he? He had always been out of the general picture, except for that brief time in Stilton when people pitied and tried to help him because he had such a wicked son. Of course, Vernon wouldn't even consider this detasseling business—not at his age—though he knew that he would watch the young people set out for the cornfields this summer with a kind of personal interest. He stuffed the letter into his coat pocket and fought down a rising sense of self-pity.

When he reached the back door, Letty shouted from the kitchen, "Any mail? Any letters?" She came out expectantly, as she always did, though the day's gleaning was seldom more exciting than a grocer's advertisement, Procter and Gamble coupons, or the endless printed matter from synod headquarters.

"Nothing much—the usual," he said, hardly glancing at her as he walked past and into the kitchen.

"Well, let me see!" she said crossly.

"It's all for me," he replied and closed the study door. Once alone, he carefully took out the seed-corn letter, smoothed it with his fingers, and began reading it all over again.

The girls waiting in front of the Farmers Savings Bank wore striped overalls, old T shirts, and high-crowned straw hats. Gloria Wolbers felt overdressed in her new orange sunsuit, and she self-consciously pushed the tube of suntan cream into her beaded purse. She had never been detasseling before, and today she would be setting forth without a single friend for company. Jane Orley and June Schmidt had gone to the cornfields with early foot crews last week, as soon as the season had begun. This motley collection of girls—some only fifteen years old, and others, like Velma Nisson, married and holding jobs from which they had taken temporary leave—had been called together by the seed-corn company because a heat wave was rapidly maturing the corn.

Although Bill Wolbers had started the A-Maizing Seed Corn firm four years ago, and each summer Gloria had begged to go detasseling with the other teen-agers of Kaleburg, her father thought the work too strenuous, and her mother considered detasseling unladylike. This year, thanks to Ronald Koch's prodding, Gloria had rebelled, and now in the heat of early afternoon she waited for the company truck. "Do you know where we're going?" she asked Velma Nisson.

Velma pushed back her straw hat and planted her feet wide,

as if she were a hired man on a farm. "Out to my old neighbor-hood." She scrutinized Gloria indifferently. "Never been detas-seling before, huh?"

"No—no, I haven't." She was made uneasy by Velma's swag-gering manner, even though she guessed it was merely a cover-up. Velma looked hardly old enough to be the mother of two children, nor would one guess her history of beatings by a brutal husband who had since left her. She supported herself by work-ing as a barmaid in the Kaleburg Klub.

"I heard we're going out to the old Ketter farm," said Velma. "Know where that is?"

Gloria shook her head.

"The Ketters used to be our neighbors when I was a kid, we went to the same country school. They lost their farm in the depression. But I suppose you know all about it."

"No, no I don't."

"They went to your church," said Velma, accusingly.

"I've never heard of them."

"Oh, I guess your dad don't tell you about *some* things," she said ominously, her eyes widening. "But you just ask him." She turned around and glanced at the cement bas-relief pillars be-hind her. "Don't he own this bank? How do you suppose he got all his money?"

"He's never done anything he shouldn't," said Gloria firmly. "I know my own father!" Why listen to a tramp like Velma, who was notorious for her tricks behind the bar in the Kaleburg Klub? Ronald Koch said she could set a stein on each breast, pour the glasses full of beer, and by a stripteaser's roll of the body make the foam pile high; she never let a glass fall nor spilled a drop, and even the foam seemed under control.

When the converted cattle truck pulled up to the curb, the driver opened the endgate and told the girls to climb in. They rushed forward, clogging the narrow entrance to the truck box. "Stand back," he said. "One at a time."

Each girl took her turn and leapt up, catching her elbows on the floor and hoisting herself in. Gloria was one of the last, and by then most of the spaces along the sides of the truckbox were taken. The middle was empty, but who would want to sit there and be stared at by everyone?

The driver locked the endgate into place and started the truck. Gloria leaned back against the closed panel and tipped her hat over her eyes. She noticed yellow strands of manure between the floorboards and imagined a herd of heifers being carried to market in this truck. The vehicle ground through gearshifts and then settled down to a highway whine. Velma Nisson, with her hair streaming out in the wind, leaned forward over the cab of the truck, as if she were the bowsprit of a vessel.

It was not a long trip, and when they entered the Ketter farm, Gloria stood up, too. They rode through a rutted yard and halted in front of a gate leading to a feedlot, which was empty except for a few enormous hogs loitering in the shade of a satiny-white feed bunk. Since the driver had to climb in and out of the cab to open and shut gates, he made slow progress, but at last he proceeded down a long lane and stopped at the end. "Here we are," he called.

Almost at once the endgate fell away, and the girls saw an earthy face looking up at them. It belonged to a middle-aged woman with skin as weathered as a used saddle; her straight gray hair, as unmanageable as raw wool, was tucked under her hat, and with intense brown eyes, she surveyed them all. "Well, what a pretty bunch we got here!" she called heartily. A dark mole on the side of her mouth moved like a button when she smiled, then fell back into place. "You girls feel like workin'? You just better! If I catch one lazy look in you, that's the end. I won't fool with you, no sir! I can get plenty more girls, and I intend to hold my reputation as the best crew foreman in this whole area. Nobody's going to stop me from keeping my record and getting my bonus. I'm just warning you, that's all.

You've got to work hard, 'cause I'll see that you do." She studied Gloria carefully, as if she had discovered a suspiciously tender leaf in a pouch of strong tobacco. "Anybody thinks she's too delicate for this work, she can go right back to town with the driver. Now come on, girls. Up and off 'em! We've got a job to do. Think we can stand around here and jaw all day?"

Sheep-like, they leapt from the box to the hard pasture ground, and then in single file climbed over a wooden gate into the cornfield. "Now, girls, gather round so you can hear. I ain't going to shout against the wind. My name's Myrtle Koch— Mrs. Koch to you girls—and I want you to sing out when I call your name."

Gloria wondered for a foolish instant if this could be Ronald's mother in a farm disguise, but then she remembered that the Kochs were a numerous clan and one whole branch lived in the country. Mrs. Koch pronounced the girls' surnames with a military impatience, and when at last she came to "Wolbers," she spat it out as if she had no idea that this girl was the boss' daughter. "All right now, let's get ready. Follow me through the endrows."

As they walked along she told them that the endrows protected the field from unwanted pollen and were not to be detasseled, since they were all males. Then she stopped and turned around. "All right, girls, can you all hear me? I want you to understand what you're doing. Some of you have been out here before, but it won't hurt you to listen to me go over this business again. What we're involved in here is fertilization. All of you girls know by this time how things get fertilized. Well, it's the same with corn—the same everywhere with living things—only this is the seed-corn business, and we try to have a hand in the process. The female plants get fertilized only by the male pollen we want to have doing the job. You see these six rows? They're the females, only they've each got a male tassel in 'em, too—but they shouldn't have—we don't want self-pollination, so you girls will pull the tassels out of the females. These six rows," she spread her hand. "They're the females. Then we come to these two rows marked on the ends with red paint. They're the males, and we'll let their tassels pollinate, because they're the ones the company wants to make the cross, which gives us hybrid corn. You understand?"

Gloria didn't, but she nodded.

Mrs. Koch pointed again to the two rows marked with red paint. "These are the bulls, and they're the ones that do it. You leave them alone. You only pull tassels from the females, so the males can fertilize them properly. Pull every tassel. Don't miss a one if you can help it. Otherwise, we'll end up with a red-flag field."

Gloria was startled to hear the expression, for "red-flag time" was a common locker room term for the menstrual period.

"If we get a red-flag field that means it's condemned. A little red flag goes up on the company map." Mrs. Koch shook her head grimly. "And I've never had a red-flag field in all my life." She spoke slowly, as if she were saying that she had never been caught lying, never cheated a soul, and was as honest as the day was long.

The girls during their red-flag days were always so self-conscious and embarrassed, too, thought Gloria. Some would not admit it, although she always did, in order to get out of gym class, which she hated anyhow. None of her friends ever wanted the boys to know; that was the important thing. One dreadful day last spring June Schmidt tattled on Jane Orley, and word spread throughout the high school within minutes. Gloria remembered how Jane had cowered in the girls' toilet and wouldn't come out, until the English teacher went in and lectured Jane, telling her to "stop this nonsense at once"—as if the teacher herself had never had a red-flag time in her whole life. Or maybe she was too old for it now; the girls speculated on that point but couldn't make up their minds. Some said it stopped at forty, others claimed fifty.

Mrs. Koch's raspy hand clutched Gloria's arm. "You take this row and follow it straight across the field. Stay on one side —don't move to the left if you start on the right—or you'll get mixed up. You might think there's no danger of that, but let me tell you, when you're in the middle of a field you've got nothing to hang onto but this here row in front of you. Now don't start till I say so."

Gloria stood stiffly at attention before the first stalk, which was five feet tall, in front of her. She spotted the tassel, as secretive as the stamen of a jack-in-the-pulpit.

At last Mrs. Koch shouted "Let's go!" her voice high and excited, and the girls attacked the field. Gloria found that the tassels came out of the cornplant tops with an odd little suction noise. Many of them were the size of fat pencils—the enormous kind that the local implement dealer handed out at Christmas. Near the base, the tassels were pale-green and yellowish white; at the tip, which was in the open air, they resembled miniature pine cones, for pollen buds were beginning to form. With each tassel pulled, a leaf or two came along—the fewer the better, as Mrs. Koch explained, because a company inspector would take a sample leaf-count to see that excess damage had not been done to the plants. As the girls worked along, Mrs. Koch moved from row to row behind them, like a belligerent farm dog snapping at the heels of a herd of cows. When they reached the crest of a hill, she called a halt and told her crew to look behind into the valley. "You notice those male plants have deeper green, broader leaves? Now there's no excuse if you can't recognize a male plant when you come face to face with one." Given the slight advantage of a rise of land, Gloria could clearly distinguish the darker color of the male rows; they were like stripes running among the lighter-green, meeker-seeming female rows, which were now deflowered and ready. "Okay, back to work," said Mrs. Koch.

Each girl was perspiring heavily, for there was no breeze below the tops of the corn and the sun shone down relentlessly. Between the rows after the girls had passed the tassels lay littered like fronds behind some magnificent procession. There was an odor of crushed foliage in the air—a fresh, buoyant smell, Gloria thought—as if the destruction going on were actually beneficial, a pruning which for corn as well as other plants would result in more vigorous growth.

Every cornstalk on which Gloria performed the operation seemed to have a nebulous personality. She even remembered for a short time afterward the peculiar differences from plant to plant: the greater number of leaves, rust spots of disease, holes where grasshoppers had eaten, and occasionally, the monstrous, surprising nest of smut. The first time she encountered smut, the fungus seemed almost beautiful in its hideous profusion: a black, creamy growth thriving wonderfully in place of a tender ear of corn; it was evil itself. She gingerly reached around it to snatch the tassel from the top and pass on.

Mrs. Koch noticed her hesitation and came over quickly. "Knock off that smut with your hand. Maybe it'll grow back— it often does—but you can't just walk by. You've got to help the plant, if you can." Gloria doubled up her hand, and half-closing her eyes, quickly struck the soft, mushroom-like growth and destroyed it. Mrs. Koch laughed approvingly. "There! Good work, Gloria. Now hurry up, the others are way ahead of you."

As the novelty wore off, detasseling began to seem a dull process, with an endless assembly line of corn plants. Less and less was Gloria able to concentrate on each plant or even think about what she was doing. Her aching arms went up and pulled, dropped to her sides, rose to pull, and fell away again. They almost seemed to be not a part of her—except for the connection of pain and fatigue, which was becoming increas-

ingly real. The jagged edges of the corn leaves scraped her
tender arms and legs, making dozens of red criss-crossed lines.
Even her face was streaked by the lacerations of those micro-
scopic teeth on the lip of each leaf. Sweat stung her wounds;
it was as if she were being lashed by a thousand tiny whips.
This was how the corn got even with her, how she was paid
back for the brutal, abrupt dismemberment she continued to
perform with increasing dispassion. Some of the girls talked
back and forth between the rows, others sang, but Gloria found
it took all her energy simply to keep going, to force her feet
through the loose turf of the cornfield, to push her arms up and
clutch the tassels.

She imagined herself between the cool sheets of her bed at
home; she felt the lap of water in the swimming pool and
could almost taste the rich cold comfort of a chocolate soda.
There she was, sitting on the center stool in front of the ala-
baster soda fountain, and Ronald was watching her, although
he pretended he was not in the least concerned about her. He
was older, after all, a recent graduate of the school of pharmacy,
and Gloria wondered how she compared in his eyes with the
co-eds at the state university. Perhaps his knowledge of women
was not extensive, for he was hardly handsome, with his round
face, thick glasses, and overly high forehead. At first she did
not think of Ronald as a possible date because of the difference
in their ages, and that made the friendship grow more naturally. All of the high-school boys by this time had had their
dates with her, and she had had to turn them away for becoming too eager. She did not intend to marry for some time, and
her mother warned of the danger in playing around.

Ronald's attention had taken quite a different course, for he
deliberately tried to annoy her by persistent teasing. He would
wink maliciously when he caught her gazing at herself in the
soda-fountain mirror. And when she sauntered into Koch's in
the afternoon, he would ask if she had just gotten up. "Ready

for another busy day, huh, Gloria?" He smiled as he said it, or she might have thought he hated her. When she bought toothpaste, a magazine, or paid for her Coke, he would take her money and say: "Now give me papa's nickels and one of papa's pennies."

"This money is my allowance," she finally replied angrily. "I can spend it for what I want."

"An allowance!" he said mockingly. "I didn't realize you had an *allowance*. The rest of us commoners work for our money. There ain't nothing coming as an allowance."

He purposely used "ain't" to annoy her, just as her father pretended to be a hayseed in order to annoy her mother. Why do men behave this way, she wondered? Although he tried to make her angry, when they were alone in the store together Ronald could do little but hover around her. She would sit in the rear at a filigreed iron table with a marble top and read magazines from the rack. Sometimes he sat down next to her and simply looked at her while she turned the pages. But one day as she sat reading *Screenland*, he ran his hand across her partially bare back; before she could rebuff him he said: "What's the matter? Isn't your life dreamy enough? You have to look at movie magazines, too?"

Despite the cover-up, Gloria was annoyed by his sneaky move —stroking her as if she were a cat on a stoop! "Listen, here's my quarter. I'll take the magazine home."

"You want to be a movie star someday, I suppose. You probably imagine you're good-looking enough."

"Don't you think I get tired of being bothered by you?"

"My dear Gloria, you don't know what it is to be bothered." He pushed his glasses more firmly against his face.

"Oh, yes—you *suffer*!"

"Damn it, I do. You don't have the least idea about anything."

"You'd be surprised how much I know, Ronald Koch," she

said slowly, lifting her eyebrows and fixing him with a smoldering gaze. This aloof, mysterious glance, when turned upon other boys, had always sent them reeling into awkward awareness of their own gaucherie.

Ronald only laughed, snorting through his nose, as if this were all too droll for words. "There's a lot of growing up you've got to do."

"Oh, shut up!" Nothing irritated her more than a reference to her actual age, for she didn't look seventeen, but twenty, at least.

"It's time somebody told you what a worthless piece of baggage you really are. Especially when you're snotty to the working people. Who do you think you are, anyway? Still the Queen of Kaleburg's Jubilee? You flit around here like a butterfly in a barnyard. I'm only saying that sooner or later, my dear, you're going to come up with the facts of life."

"I *know* the facts of life!" she interrupted scornfully. Her mother had told her the whole thing when she was twelve.

"Listen to me a minute, you spoiled brat. What're you going to be like when you're on your own? What's going to happen when you start fending for yourself?"

"Oh, stop it!" she shouted, jumping up. "You're—you're homely! I don't want to see you again." She fled the store.

The heat reflecting from the pavement struck her in the face, and she suddenly felt dizzy. She closed her eyes and leaned for a moment against the brick building, although it was hot as a kiln.

"Anything the matter, Gloria?"

She opened her eyes and saw Reverend Kallsen before her. He wore a hard straw hat on his gray head, and his black silk summer suit shimmered in the sun, like heat devils dancing. He had just made his daily trip to the post office, for he held a newspaper and letters in his hand. "Oh, it's the heat," she said slowly. She did not want to bother being respectful to him, or smile and pretend to be good. She hated him along with all men. "I'm going home." Without another word she turned down the street, knowing that her mother would comfort her. But Gloria also realized that Ronald had been right, and she did not want to be soothed by her mother. Instead, she walked out to the A-Maizing Seed Corn plant to see her father, and on the way, decided to go detasseling.

Gloria had not finished her first row, and yet it seemed as if surely half the afternoon had passed. At the end would there be a tree, a meadow, and a stream? Never before had she been so thirsty, but each step took her farther and farther from the jugs of cool water that the truck driver had slung over the fence and tucked under blankets. Finally she asked Mrs. Koch the time. It was only two-thirty. They had been in the field scarcely an hour, and this shift would last for six more.

Rapidly, the last of her strength and moral resolve slipped away; this cornfield agony was simply senseless, for what if Ronald's pronouncement were true—that she didn't deserve her soft life? Some people were born luckier than others, and why not accept her good fortune? She felt weepy and wondered if a sudden fainting spell might not save her from this hell, even now. The girls would surely carry her back, and they'd love the excitement. If she kept her eyes closed tightly, would Mrs. Koch be able to tell she was feigning? After all, the boss' daughter could not be left lying in the cornfield.

Green cornstalks kept passing in front of her; she tried to concentrate anew on meeting each one, jerking the tassel, and passing on. Somewhere up ahead the plant was already waiting which would be too much for her. She plodded from stalk to stalk, and just when all strength within her seemed dissipated, when she was certain that instead of pulling a tassel the plant would pull her away, she felt the awakening of inner reserves.

Wouldn't it be wonderful if she could keep going? Here she was, working as hard as any man had ever done—and she would not give up easily. The other girls might complain and poop out, but Gloria decided that none of them would hear a whining word from her. Nothing could stop her now, and down the row she marched, doing her job with efficiency. She snatched one tassel with her right hand, while her left came up to clutch the next. Steadily onward she walked in a kind of rhythm, her legs swinging to a certain beat, her arms synchronized. The sound of snapping tassels—the suction pop—was like the beat of a tune, and even the leaves brushing her cheek seemed half-caressing, or like the regular movements of a partner with whom she was dancing.

"Hey, Gloria! Stop!" called Mrs. Koch. "You're in the endrows!"

Dazed, caught by the hypnotic movement, she had gone far ahead of the others. She turned around numbly, and fatigue engulfed her. She slumped to her knees and leaned her back against a stalk, which bent beneath her weight, as it did in the high winds of summer storms. She wondered if she would ever be able to rise again; she hoped the slow-moving crew would take forever getting through. A glistening drop of dew nestled between a leaf and stalk, and she wished that she had the tongue of a frog to dart out for it.

"All right girls, take a break," said Mrs. Koch. "It's a long way back." Her face was very red, and she removed her hat to fan herself.

Rustling the corn, the crew moved wearily through endrows to a strip of grass along the fence. Here, where the cattle had reached through from the pasture, the bluegrass was clipped short. Gloria got up slowly and found a weed-free spot of matted grass that had been beyond the range of the cattle. Green with long blades on top, underneath the dead grass of last season made a mattress, and she sank to the earth. She pushed her hat over her eyes and smelled the curiously pleasant odor of moist straw. Her arms lay beside her where they had fallen, and her knees were rolled out. Dimly, she sensed the irritation of pollen or dust on her bare skin, but she did not relieve the itch by scratching; she did not move. Insects made their prickly, self-determined way across her arms and traveled her legs.

The sun's hovering heat seemed almost welcome, for it was as if that fierce star had finally won the world from its everlasting tendency to chill and death. Her body no longer tried to keep cool by perspiring, for such puny efforts in the midst of this blaze seemed impertinent; she was siding with the sun, and she was bathed in the canicular glow. The sun was a power that no longer enervated her, for, once her capitulation was complete, her interests seemed joined with it, as if she had come to life for the first time.

Gloria detasseled in a semi-private world, for corn rows screened her from all but her closest neighbors. Halfway through the afternoon she happened to catch sight of Velma Nisson, bare-breasted, in the next row. Gloria took a second look to make sure. Indeed, Velma wore only her shorts, and the cloth brassière hung from her belt like the scalp of an Indian.

"What're *you* looking at?" Velma called with a brazen smile. "All the girls out here take 'em off. Who's going to see you? And it's kind of fun." She continued down the row as if she were heading for the showers.

Gloria could not resist checking the girl on her right; immediately she saw, without having to stop and talk, that she, too, was bare-breasted. And what about Mrs. Koch, Gloria wondered? Were all the girls expected to do this, even if they didn't feel like it—as Gloria most certainly didn't? In roaming back and forth, she lost her place. Although the virgin row before her looked familiar, perhaps it belonged to some girl who had fallen behind. She stepped over to a fully detasseled row.

Had she come this far? She could not even tell the bull rows, and each time she counted off six females, she got confused. Sweat broke out all over her; she paused and listened but could not hear the familiar crackling noises of the crew. Only the wind shook the leaves, a sound like the rustle of crinolines.

"Mrs. Koch!" she called, softly at first, then much louder as panic swept through her. "Mrs. Koch! MRS. KOCH!"

Noisily, Mrs. Koch strode through the ranks of cornplants, fully clothed. "What's the matter, Gloria? What are you doing? How come you're way over here on a male row? Have to go to the toilet, or something?"

Gloria fumbled through an explanation, and although Mrs. Koch scolded and complained, she set Gloria on the right row again. "What ever got you off?" she kept asking, but Gloria was too embarrassed to reply that it had been the sight of bare breasts.

After making a complete round the girls emerged near the spot where they had started. With most of them naked to the waist, they looked like South Sea island natives pictured in the *National Geographic*. Velma, whose bosom was most impressive, was the center of a whole group of girls, but Gloria refused to join them. "Did you hear the one about the little boy who was circumcised?" Velma began lustily. "Well, when he went back to school the teacher asked, 'Hey, Johnny, what's the matter? Why are you holding yourself there?' And Johnny, he—"

Gloria, always repulsed by smutty stories, turned away deliberately, and the wind rushed in her ears. Soon there was a burst of laughter behind her.

Mrs. Koch suddenly shouted: "Happy birthday, girls! Happy birthday!"

The cluster dispersed, and everyone frantically reached for her halter. "Happy birthday! Happy birthday!" They echoed the cry.

"What is it? What does it mean?" Gloria asked Velma, who was busily tying the strings of her brassière behind her back. "Whose birthday?"

"Oh, you'll see. It's probably the inspector coming."

A moment later a man approached, as if he were making his way through a jungle of cane brush. "Yeah, he's the inspector," said Velma. "See that little metal counter in his hand? He's been checking up on us already. With a new crew they like to do it right away. Come on, let's get a drink."

Gloria followed behind her to the blankets along the fence row, where several girls were already seated with jugs between their legs. "Now don't drink too much at once," Velma warned, "or you'll get sick."

Gloria drank from the crock lip; the dark, cool interior smelled like a well. Surprisingly, after the long wait, the water was not as refreshing as she had expected.

"Oh, look in the pasture. They've set up an outhouse for us," said Velma. "You want to go first?"

"No, no." She looked with distaste at the portable shack sitting conspicuously in the pasture—and the herd of black cattle some distance off. She doubted if she had the courage to closet herself in such a vulnerable building and waited until all the other girls had climbed the fence before paying a visit.

Mrs. Koch, meanwhile, bid the inspector goodbye and joined the girls along the fence row. "Now when the fields start coming in, we'll have our hands full trying to keep ahead of things." She explained that when the tassels were ready to shoot pollen, the small undeveloped ears deep in the folds of leaves would send out silk threads. "There's a silk for every kernel of corn, and a grain of pollen has to light on each silk and travel back to the ear. I'll show you later—the unfertilized kernels look like fish eggs. But come on now, we've got to get back to work."

Time began slipping by quickly as the routine became

familiar. Gloria had covered a great distance before she realized an hour had passed. This was the thing to do: squeeze time and make the minutes seconds, the hours minutes, the days merely hours; weeks would pass like the flick of a hand.

But suddenly the orderly process stopped. "There's a rogue!" someone shouted. "A rogue!" the girls echoed. "A rogue! A rogue!"

"Where?" called Velma, running forward angrily.

"Up ahead. See him?"

Gloria stood on tip-toe, then jumped in the air. Ten or fifteen yards before her, on her very row, was a tall, queer-looking cornplant which towered at least nine feet in the air.

"Don't leave your rows!" Mrs. Koch shouted. "Keep your places."

But cries of "Rogue! Rogue!" kept passing among the crew, and the girls came running, converging on the cornplant. Gloria ran with them. Several tried to leap for the monstrous plant's tassel, but it was too high. One girl stamped upon its roots again and again, but she could not quiver the stalk, for it was as thick as a young birch tree. They tore at the rogue's leaves; they pulled off its ears, and finally they brought down the stalk. Everyone was enveloped in a faint golden mist—and then Gloria saw the full-sprung tassel in the broken top; it was heavy with pollen, and she sneezed.

"These damn rogues!" said Velma.

"Come now, girls. Back to your rows. Don't get mixed up and latch onto a bull row by mistake. This here rogue was for Gloria to take care of. It was on her row."

Finally Mrs. Koch and Gloria were left alone. "Them rogues get in now and then. They're freaks. You never know what they're doing or what damage you'll end up with. Look here," she said, kicking the flowered tassel contemptuously, "he's shooting pollen already. Well, there's no silks out for him to fertilize, and that's good. Whenever the girls spot a rogue they always jump on him. You can't keep 'em off—and I guess I'll stop trying to. Now, Gloria, go back to where you left off. I guess *he* won't give anybody trouble any more." She stepped upon his roots with her heavy barnyard shoes as if to make sure and then walked away.

At seven-thirty the company truck took the crew back to Kaleburg. The rolling motion lulled them all into silence as they rode along. Gloria's mind was a tired blank, and when the truck stopped in front of the Farmers Savings Bank she looked out upon Main Street as if she had been away for years. Walking slowly down the sidewalk toward home, she felt stiff and a little chilled. In the west the last glow of the spent day was spread across the sky.

Eva Wolbers, wearing a crisp white apron, had supper ready, and as soon as Gloria entered the pastel kitchen, her mother said, "Well, I was starting to worry! You're so late. Jane Orley has been home for an hour, and so has June Schmidt. I talked to their mothers."

Gloria said nothing. She removed her hat, flung it into a corner, and sat down at the kitchen table. "Now I know this hamburger is overcooked," her mother continued, "and what these beans will taste like, I can't say. It's my bridge night you know. I was about to leave it all on the stove for you with a note."

Gloria studied her mother sharply.

"Oh, I'm not having the club here, darling, if that's what you thought."

Silently, Gloria began her supper. The lima beans tasted chalky.

"Well, what was it like? You have a terrible burn. Put some Unguentine on it right away. Are you going back tomorrow, or have you had enough? Say *something*, at least."

"Mother, I'm eating."

"Was it awfully hot out there, dear?"

"Yes, it was hot." What else could she say? She had savored the day minute by minute and hour by hour under the force of that sun. She had seen the earth at work and had been there when the day had died; she had witnessed it all: the dimming light, the cooling air. Her own body had sunk into fatigue as the day fell away. She had welcomed the first cool draughts of evening upon her brow. And now it was over. What could she tell her mother, or father—or Ronald—or anyone, of that? This day in the cornfield could not be elaborated upon or explained. And tomorrow, within the context of her life, she would absorb another living day; she asked for no more. She felt complete and exhausted. She excused herself and hurried upstairs to a bath and the total darkness of her bed, and sleep. She could hardly wait for tomorrow.

A series of thunderstorms swept across the plains in succeeding days, and the detasselers were usually caught in the middle of a field. As the first large drops fell on the corn leaves with a clatter as loud as hail, the girls would leave their rows and race for the meager cover of their blankets. More often, they hoped to reach a grove or they huddled around the trunk of a single oak in a pasture; but almost always, they were drenched in a few minutes. If they were not soaked during the storm, they became thoroughly wet later in the field, for the corn leaves held water like rainspouts, and each plant disturbed after a rain released a small shower of water. The tassels swelled in wet weather and became more difficult to pull; each pop sounded like a cork being pulled from a bottle. The humidity continued to rise, almost as if it had not rained at all, or as if the air still contained its humors, which would have to be let out by another thunderstorm. "More rain tonight, girls," Mrs. Koch would call, shaking her woolly head.

"If you think this heat is bad, wait'll you get out here to-morrow."

As quickly as the brown crust of earth in the cornfields dried, another shower would come, turning the ground into sticky mud. If Gloria wore shoes in the wet fields, she discovered that clods of dirt would form balls under her feet, hobbling her walk. She tried to knock the gathered mud from her soles, but another wedge would build up quickly. Most of the time she abandoned her shoes, although sharp stones often bruised her feet.

The worst was yet to come—this was Mrs. Koch's persistent promise, and Gloria heard it each day with mounting dread. The sun shone with a tropical brilliance and intensity. "Hurry up, hurry up, girls," Mrs. Koch said. "This field is really moving." At the end of a row one day she asked them all to be very quiet. There was no wind, and in the east they heard the distant, angry murmur of a storm that had passed over earlier that day. "Do you hear a snapping noise? A crackling here and there?"

Gloria heard a faint, restless, alive sound. "Is it the corn?"

"That's the *sound* of corn growing," Mrs. Koch nodded. "You come out here on a still night and you'll hear it, too. In this weather the stalks grow as fast during the night as in the day. Now I'm telling you, girls, we'll be in trouble on this field unless we work overtime—or I'll have to call in a boys' crew with a detasseling machine. You wouldn't want me to have to do that, would you? You're not going to let this corn-field lick you! If you're willing to stay on and earn time-and-a-half, we'll work till it's so dark we can't see. I've got a carton of candy bars that should hold you till you get home. If you let them boys get in here with the machine, they'll clean things up—and you won't earn the money you expected to. As it is, looks like the season this year is going to be shorter than usual."

The girls all agreed that the machine should be kept away; they would match their strength against the weather and the corn. Occasionally, during the next hours, Gloria saw the detasseling machine, like a mammoth praying mantis, on a neighboring hill. Six boys rode along between the cornrows in little baskets, and they plucked tassels as they passed. "Listen to that silly two-cylinder job," said Velma. The other girls, too, snorted over the fact that the boys were being carried through the fields. Mrs. Koch was delighted by their scoffing, and she said over and over again that boys weren't as tough as girls. The company records proved it, time and again. There was nothing to match a woman's endurance; a man will always try to get off as easily as he can; he takes his pleasure and gets away. "In this business, you need women to do the job, everytime," said Mrs. Koch, and the girls nodded, with smiles of satisfaction. They returned to the field with renewed zest.

Finally, at nine o'clock, Mrs. Koch said: "Okay, girls, let's go home. And get all the sleep you can. We're starting to hump it now."

But Gloria slept fitfully, disturbed by nightmares of missed rows and condemned fields. She had an erotic dream, too, the details of which were not clear, except that someone touched the tips of her breasts—that was all—and she could not be sure whether it was the inspector or Ronald, or someone she did not know.

Each day, without let up, she trudged to the bench in front of the Farmers Savings Bank, leapt into the truck when it stopped, and together with the other girls, was transported to the fields; Sundays, weekdays—all were the same. She lost track of any other existence. A camaraderie developed among the crew, united as they were in this battle. "Pull faster, girls. Pull faster," Mrs. Koch kept saying.

The corn grew far over their heads, and Gloria often had to jump for the tops. The tassels themselves changed and turned dark green, became thick and erect; the dangerous time was nearing. Once during a rest period Mrs. Koch broke off a half-formed ear, stripped away the leaves, and showed the girls the pale, golden threads of corn silk. "Here's the hair coming," she said. "Won't be long now. These plants are growing up. We'll have to work hard on this field, or we'll end up with a red flag."

Soon the tassels opened wide, spreading tiny branches from which pods the size of wheat grains were attached. When these pods burst open, the pollen would fly. "We're really humping now," said Velma again and again, for she liked the phrase. Glora was now quite used to seeing Velma half-naked in the fields; her breasts were browned the color of pecans.

During these final days, Gloria avoided her mother more than ever. She remained in her room when not in the corn-fields, and she refused, in Eva Wolber's phrase, "to come out of it." The thought of the rest of the summer depressed her—what would she do with herself? What was happening to her life? Sometimes she wept from a racking, unknown sadness. Perhaps she was merely too fatigued. It was hot in her upstairs room, and she would often lie naked on the bed or stand in front of the mirror, studying herself. Her limbs were brown, her hair bleached pale—for she did not even bother wearing a straw hat now. Her breasts and stomach were white, and her body, altogether, beautifully formed. She admired her profile and even looked over her shoulder for a back view. Then, suddenly overcome with shame by her behavior, she would fling her bathrobe around herself and button it up to the top.

Often she was still awake at midnight when her father came home from his meetings at the plant. There he had received reports on the latest victories, and together with his men, he planned the strategy for future conquests. As the area foremen spoke, giving their battle positions, the possible dangerous areas and the sectors under control, he would listen thoughtfully.

Standing in front of his great map of the whole area, he would work out estimates of the time left and the forces needed to finish off the last of the fields. He would move the little colored pins around on the map to new locations, and at breakfast the next morning predict with an arrogant assurance that victory would be his very shortly.

But on the day Mrs. Koch promised to be the last, she discovered a female row in full flower and a male row that had been completely detasseled. "How could this have happened? I told you to be careful. I warned you—but one of you girls didn't listen. Got started wrong." Her sharp brown eyes surveyed them all. "Now what're we going to do about it? These tassels are starting to shoot pollen. I want all of you to go down this row fast. It's a ninety-acre field, and we don't want to lose it. I'll go up to the farmhouse and phone for the boys' crew to work in from the other side." She turned and stalked off.

The girls, shaken by the danger, obediently started down the row, often lunging for the same tassels. Gloria realized, as soon as she entered the field, that the neglected row had been left too long already. Silks tufted the corn ears everywhere, and they were already brown on the end, like paint brushes, for pollen had reached them. This field should get its red flag—but who would be so disloyal to Mrs. Koch as to report it?

Every time a tassel was wrenched from its tight socket a shower of golden pollen dusted down upon the girls, filling their nostrils; it clung to their hair and gilded their skin. "Well, *we're* sure getting pollinated," said Velma, laughing, "and that's a fact!"

The girls speculated with excitement about the crew of boys working toward them from the other side, but after going halfway, there was still no sign of them; the high tassels ahead were unplucked. "Those lazy cobs," said Velma. "They're so used to riding the machine they don't know what it's like to work."

Occasionally, the girls stopped to listen, hoping to hear male voices, and during the lull, tubes of lipstick and small compacts were passed around. They moved on, growing more and more disappointed, until finally they reached the end and found the boys lolling in the shade of mulberry trees. The girls were enraged and let out cries. "Hey, where you been?"

"What's the matter with you cobs?"

"Letting *us* do all the work!"

Unified in their anger, they stormed through the endrows in an uproar, Velma in the lead—but Gloria hung back, watching. The boys hooted and spread out their arms. The first girls to reach the shade were thrown to the ground and pinned there, though they squealed and struggled to get away. A mock battle took place, with Velma shouting the loudest and swinging at the boys right and left. But it was clear to Gloria from the start who would win and what was going on. She turned away hurriedly and ran along the fence row. When she reached the road she flagged the mail carrier, Rusty McIverson, who was heading back to Kaleburg, having finished his route. What a disgusting end to the days of detasseling, Gloria thought as she rode along, and she felt slightly sick to her stomach.

Gloria remained in bed all next day, explaining to her mother that she "didn't feel well," which Eva Wolbers took to be a locution for the menstrual period, and she left a large box of Kotex in the bathroom. The sight of the blue-and-white box only deepened Gloria's anxiety about her health, for she had examined the calendar carefully, and she was already four days overdue. This had never happened before; she was as punctual as the full moon. She lay very still on the sheets and tried to relax; she knew that physical exhaustion from overwork could cause this delay. She waited and waited. Since she could not concentrate on the printed word, she gave up trying to read, and she lay there listening to love songs on the radio. Her mother brought tepid tea at four o'clock and suggested that Gloria get up for supper. "You should be all right by now—aren't you?"

On the second day Eva Wolbers became worried. "What is it, dear? Why do you want to stay in bed? If you're really ill I'll call the doctor." Gloria requested again that she be left alone, and finally, in the afternoon, she locked the door so that her mother couldn't come snooping. Five days! What could it mean? Was there something the matter with her? She had not even kissed a boy the whole month long. There were those rumors about catching a baby from a toilet seat, but Gloria had read the booklet her mother had given her when she was twelve, and she knew such tales were false.

The next day she was running a slight fever, and without delay Mrs. Wolbers called the physician. He was a partially deaf, fumbling old man, and Gloria told him nothing. For a long time he sat and gazed at her, as if his years of medical practice had made him so skilled that he could bypass physical symptoms and probe, instead, the illusive mind and heart for his diagnosis. Gloria turned her face to the wall.

"She's only got a temperature of ninety-nine," he told Eva Wolbers in the hall.

"But is it a cold or what? I'm so afraid of polio."

"We'll keep an eye on her," he chuckled. "But I'll bet she's all right tomorrow."

Dutifully, Gloria swallowed the aspirin he had left her and drank glassfuls of fruit juice. Now that she was fully rested from the long days in the cornfields, she could hardly sleep at night, and her nightmares became crazier. Once she woke up, bewildered, recalling that she had dreamed she was in an obstetrics room, and the pains in her abdomen were mounting rapidly. A doctor and nurse stood by for the birth, and then it happened—horrible, frightening enough to waken her with a gasp—she produced an ear of corn, wrapped neatly in its green husk; it had slipped from her pleasurably, moist and warm. She leapt from the bed and rolled up the windowshade to look at the moon. I'm going insane, she thought. If something doesn't happen soon, I'll scream my head off.

But, finally tired, she went back to bed and slept fitfully the rest of the night. In the morning she came downstairs to breakfast, and although her mother said she looked pale—and she was, indeed, very jumpy—Gloria maintained that she was all right now. She had decided to pretend that this wasn't the sixth day. She would not think about it at all. Maybe this month she was simply going to skip the red-flag time, and if so, that was all to the good. Her mother nagged her about looking up old friends. They were already miffed, said Eva, that Gloria had ignored them this long.

But Gloria had no intention of seeing her girl friends today. She was going to find Ronald, whom she could trust; perhaps he would give her medicine for relaxing and she would feel well again. The doctor and his stingy aspirins had been paltry comfort, but Ronald with a whole drugstore at his disposal could do better, she knew. The problem was: would he do it without a prescription? Only if there were no other customers in the store—therefore, noon was the most likely time.

After skipping out on lunch, she raced up the stairs and opened the big door of Koch's. "Hello, Gloria!" said Mrs. Koch, Ronald's mother, coming forward. "Haven't seen you in a long time."

And so she was trapped. She bought a tube of toothpaste and got out, learning, first of all, that Ronald would be in the store all afternoon. She knew she spoke too rapidly, too loudly, and she kept running her hands through her hair, but she could not help herself. She felt like having a good long cry and hurried home to the privacy of her room. There she sobbed with her face buried in a pillow so that her mother couldn't hear her. Afterwards, although her eyes smarted and she felt exhausted, she was really no better off. Why had she ever allowed herself to get so rundown? The pleasure she had felt earlier in detasseling dwindled away. She thought with loathing of the whole nasty two weeks spent out there, since it had brought her to this pass.

It was nearly six o'clock and closing time when she ran into Koch's a second time. The lights in back were off, and Ronald was just pulling the cord to stop the big paddle-wheel fan that hung down from the ceiling. "Well, stranger, back from your labors?" he called.

She felt the intensity of his interest almost immediately. "Yes, and I've come to—talk.'"

"Fine, fine," he said, and as she moved familiarly to a stool in the center of the soda fountain, he walked behind it and began drying Coke glasses.

"I've—I've had quite an experience," she began, though it was not at all what she had intended to say. "And I guess I'm changed."

"Good," he smiled. "And I assume for the better."

She sighed. "Oh, don't start teasing—I don't think I can take it."

He stared at her very sharply. "Want a Coke?"

"No thanks."

"Are you feeling okay?" he asked, concerned. He walked from behind the counter. "What's the matter?"

Gloria glanced at herself in the mirror, but she was so tanned that the paleness she felt didn't show. "I don't know. I've been in bed. Could you give me something?"

"Such as?"

"I don't know—but no aspirin."

He looked at her measuringly, as if testing for further meanings; and he smiled. "You must tell me more. How else can I help you? We'll have to have a long talk."

"Yes, let's. I haven't talked to anybody for weeks, it seems."

Very slowly, he removed his glasses and set them on the marble top of the counter. Then, mysteriously, he walked to the door, locked it, and pulled the shade over the oval window. "Now, there's just us two here alone."

"Don't start telling me what a ninny I am; too much has happened in the last couple of weeks. I'm different now, though I guess I *was* awfully spoiled. Everything you used to say was true—you at least were honest about what you felt."

He smiled, then laughed aloud. Without his glasses, he seemed undressed, and he was better-looking than she had realized. He picked up both her hands. "Oh, Gloria, how I've lied and lied to you."

He dropped her fingers as quickly as he had taken them up, then threw both arms about her and pulled her from the swivel seat. She was astonished but did not fight him. He kissed her neck and cheek and rubbed her back slowly. "I love you, love you—don't you know that?" Then he kissed her upon the mouth and held the embrace; she felt his hard body against her. A great surge of relief and joy passed through her, and she relaxed against him. Having found this love, all her problems were over.

"Let's not stand up here for the whole town to see," he said huskily, as he guided her to the back room, his arm around her waist. "You said you weren't feeling well. Why don't you lie over there?" He pointed to a cot against the wall, then bent down and opened a cabinet. "I'll give you something that'll make you feel just fine."

The storeroom was lined with brown bottles and white boxes of powder and pills; there was a faint medicinal smell, as if this were an operating room. Ronald, of course, had always wanted to be a physician. She lay down on the cot and closed her eyes, repeating to herself those amazing words he had said to her: "I love you." And he had meant it, too. She heard the clink of glasses, then gurgling liquid.

"Here's a potion for you—it'll either kill you or make you well. One or the other." He had a glass for himself, and he toasted her by touching rims.

They both drank. "Mmmmmm," she said and smiled. "Tastes like wine."

"It's blackberry brandy. I keep it there in the cabinet. Have a snort every once in a while to keep up my spirits—since I don't have you here, or anyone." He leaned over and kissed her ear.

They drank two large glassfuls before they both stretched full length on the cot, their arms about each other. The room was growing dim. He proceeded to make love with a patient sureness, a steady ardor that overwhelmed her. Afterwards, Gloria lay still for a long time, quite stunned. Could she lift her arm? Perhaps, if she tried. She heard him get up, put on his clothes, and move about the room. She knew that time must again be found and engaged, snared into her life, but meanwhile, she enjoyed floating free. She supposed her mother was angry because she had missed supper. Then the first regrets and guilt arrived, awakening her quickly.

Ronald came over when he saw that her eyes were open. He kissed her lips again with passionless gentle touches; it was merely a reminder of what had gone before. "Are you all right?" he asked.

"Oh, yes—but we shouldn't have done it."

He looked at her, puzzled, and then went out in front to get his spectacles. When he returned, he sat on the edge of the cot again, but Gloria pulled the sheets up to her chin. "Go away," she said. "I must get home to supper."

"You're not mad at me, are you Gloria? I told you I love you. I want to marry you. It isn't as if—"

"Go away and let me dress. You've spoiled everything!"

She hurried down the street, trying to fit herself into her life again, and she was afraid to meet the wondering, speculating eyes of her parents. What lie could she tell? She saw that the house was dark, and she was filled with immediate terror. Had they gone to the police? Were they out searching for her right now? It was eight-thirty. She rushed through the back door, almost tripped over a cat, and turned on the kitchen light. There was a note on the table: "Gloria, honey: Where've you been? You knew this was my bridge night, and I wanted to have supper early. You'll find it on the stove. Daddy's playing poker at the Elks. Love, Mother. 6:30."

Gloria sank down upon a kitchen chair, and she felt too weary to rise and turn up the burners under the pots. The emptiness of the house was appalling, but her own hollow spirit, even worse. She put her head in her arms and wept. Then, after finding a candy bar in the cupboard, she went upstairs—and just in time, too, for her red-flag period began. There was a certain relief that it had finally happened, even though for the past hours she had forgotten about it completely.

Without turning on the lamps, she moved through the twilight of her bedroom, put on her nightgown, and knelt upon a pillow by the window; she looked out at the stars and moon with an almost tired wisdom. She felt in her body the dying of the old—a long-delayed emptying of her childhood self. She did not feel that she was yet a woman, but neither was she a child any longer. She had learned the season's lesson, but now, what would she do with it? It was so sad.

XIII

This was a bridal morning if ever there was one, thought Letty Kallsen, with the air faintly scented by mock-orange bushes, the grass sparkling with dew, and the sky cobalt, cloudless. At four o'clock this afternoon when Ronald and Gloria were to be married, would anyone remember the dark events of the weekend? Better, how could anyone forget? She looked across the table at Vernon, who sat unusually still; there was a strange quiver in his eyes. He, too, had not quite recovered from the weekend.

Perhaps the most horrible factor was the planning. Emma Albrecht must have hunted in Hans' tool shed for a rope when Hans himself was not around—or perhaps when he was paying one of his visits to the house across the road. All these years how many people had lifted eyebrows over the Albrechts' peculiar affairs, and how many snatches of gossip had Letty heard about Shirley and Hans? And the speculations concerning Chuck, why he remained in the Navy so long, unable to find his way home. But, as with a host of other tales, some of them even more bizarre—women who were trying to murder their husbands, high-school girls who dropped their dead, smothered babies down outhouse slots, and men who found delight in indecencies—she had listened to be entertained, surely not to act, and never had she given real belief, to be confused with the truths of one's daily life.

In the case of the Albrechts, how mild had been the gossip compared to the actual facts! That is, if current rumors were close to the facts—and Letty was certain they were. She remembered how Emma these last few years had become more wizened and leather-skinned, her pained face in strong contrast to Hans and Shirley's gentle calm. Before the very eyes of everyone in Kaleburg, Emma's grief was displayed—had anyone but the wit to see. On church committees she was simply "faithful, dependable Emma." At every funeral she was a persistent mourner, a regular coffin-clinger. But if her vision of life seemed starkly tragic, did it necessarily mean such monkeyshines in the back bedrooms of her life?

Letty had thought all along that Emma was lamenting the folly of Chuck's wandering and the pretty young wife left home, neglected. In her innocence, Letty had also thought that Hans probably worked Emma too hard, demanding heavy barnyard chores as well as housework, gardening, and poultry care. Now the truth was out! All these years Emma had been eating the liver of her own misery, unable to risk a single confidence in another woman—tied hand and foot to ever-recurring shame, until at last she plotted revenge and threw her own skeleton into that sensuous bed her husband and daughter-in-law were keeping.

Some of the details were still not certain. Official reports in the town newspaper and over the radio held that Emma had been mentally distressed for some time. Hans hastily elaborated for anyone who asked: the menopause, after all, frequently twists a woman's mind. Little did he suspect that Emma's brain was going off kilter. Yes, true, she had said some odd things—wild things, even—and he should have taken her to a doctor at once. He was very sorry, very grieved by it all.

At the wake Letty had observed Hans, and it was obvious from his circled eyes that he had been unable to sleep. Shirley was pale, shy, and clutched Chuck's arm; she did not look at anyone if she could help it. During the days before the funeral the neighbors helped out, as if this tragedy were only a normal one. Though the ritual took place as usual, Hans must have sensed the difference; surely he saw the narrowed eyes and heard conversations drop to a whisper as he passed. He remained in the farmhouse only two days after Chuck's arrival, then departed for California. He had been on the plane out of Missouriville last night. Ah well, thought Letty, it will all blow over.

And yet, it was intriguing to wonder: did Hans and Shirley together—at the same moment—discover Emma's body hanging in the upstairs-bedroom closet of the hired man's house? Only the guilty pair actually knew this fact, but if Emma had carefully planned the whole thing—picking the long weekend of Memorial Day so that interment would be postponed—then, too, she would have planned such a ghoulish detail. Even Ronald and Gloria's nuptials fitted the picture—and what Emma intended by her self-destruction. Oh, how love fled at death's icy breath; how better chill ardor than swing a body before it? What a prelude to the tender ceremony of the betrothed—a funeral sermon! Letty knew the pattern well, for in her own life there had been a certain parallel—Vernon always more eloquent over an open grave than ardent over an open bed, the sheets pulled back, her loving arms ready. Oh, yes, Letty was sure that Emma had deliberately thrust her own corpse between Hans and Shirley's embrace. She had years to plan it, after all: the wretched wasteland of time which is the legacy of the unloved.

It was unfortunate that Ronald and Gloria were innocent victims and that Emma saw in their marriage rites the disease of love. After all the ups and downs of their romance—Gloria even having gone to college for a year, then suddenly returning —they might at least have had the luck to marry each other in untainted times. This afternoon at four when Vernon conducted the ceremony, who would be able to strip the scene of the coffin that had been there only yesterday? Since Emma was supposed to have tended the coffeepots in the Wolbers' kitchen this afternoon at the wedding reception, it was hard to believe she hadn't ruthlessly planned to spoil the festivities. Very likely there was no personal grudge against either the Wolbers or the Kochs; rather, it was the bliss of love itself she made her enemy.

Last night in church the incongruity had seemed awful, although Gloria and Ronald were oblivious to everything but each other. At seven o'clock Vernon began the wedding rehearsal. Custom forbade Gloria herself from stepping down the aisle as the organist boomed out *Lohengrin*—that would court bad luck—and thus the bridesmaids slowly moved down the aisle alone, and Bill Wolbers gave away a substitute daughter.

Then came a curious moment: the dressmaker, who was working on the bridesmaids' hand-clipped illusion-lace veils, called the girls into the vestry to try on their coronets of seed pearls. Vernon, still overwrought by the afternoon's funeral, snapped his knuckles nervously. "Let's continue with the ceremony, anyhow," he said, for Ronald, the best man, the ushers, and Gloria all stood waiting. The rehearsal was primarily for the benefit of Ronald and Gloria, surely. "Come, Letty, you stand in for the bride," Vernon said, his hand out to her.

And so she repeated the marriage ceremony after him, Ronald echoing with proper responses. Letty stood there in a daze while it was happening, almost unable to believe her ears or eyes. "And do you, Gloria Marie Wolbers, take this man. . . ." Vernon intoned.

Letty, dreamily responded: "I do." As she stood there, her

hands clasping an imaginary bridal bouquet, a sudden sentimental feeling swept over her, and she began to weep. Vernon
noticed but continued solemnly, as if he were not her husband at
all. Of course, he stopped short of "I now pronounce you man
and wife." That would have been going too far altogether.
The magic and suspense of the ceremony held them all—
truly, it seemed to Letty, hermetic words were being uttered
which could change destinies.

Before Letty stepped back beside Gloria, who was just behind the mock bridal pair, listening to everything closely,
Carrie Maxwell and two other women of the Ladies Aid
flower committee entered the church and marched up to the
sanctuary, where everyone stood. Then Letty noticed the baskets
of roses, carnations, and other flowers beside the altar—blossoms of the dead, left over from Emma's funeral. The women
of the committee put their heads together. This basket was to
go to Mrs. Sampson, who had broken her hip, and that basket
to the old people's home in Popkin, and the other—what about
that small, ungainly bunch of daisies? It was too insignificant
for a real gift to any of the sick, the lame, the feeble; surely
those partly wilted blossoms would not reassure anyone that the
world of the living was beautiful, and smelled nice, too. "Take
them out to the cemetery," said one.

"Yes," replied Carrie, too loudly, for her raucous voice carried
all over the church. "We'll scatter these on the grave." Having
heard none of the tales flying about, Carrie Maxwell had played
a prominent role in the funeral, quite unaware of her daughter's involvement.

A hush fell over the bridal party, and for a moment everyone
seemed caught in a morbid trance. Then the organist broke the
spell by pulling out all the stops for the marriage recessional.
Joyously, the bride and groom strode down the aisle, accepted
the imaginary congratulations of friends, and were showered
with invisible rice. Then, unable to wait a moment longer,

Ronald grabbed his bride and began kissing her again and again.

Letty thought Vernon called too loudly: "That's all for tonight."

Either he deliberately reached for the light switch or he did not see Ronald and Gloria embracing. No, Letty realized, even if he had noticed them behind the door—these lovers conquering death once more—he could not understand or believe. But Letty felt more sentimental than ever, and as the church emptied of young people, she took Vernon's arm, and they walked back to the parsonage as companionably as an old, contented, long-married couple. Letty knew, come what may, newlyweds had the last word and always would have—a triumph only the living understood. Too bad, not you, my husband, she thought, as they parted company in the upstairs hall and entered separate bedrooms.

The phone rang, disturbing the post-breakfast silence, and as Letty talked to Eva Wolbers, Vernon hastened to his study and closed the door. Nevertheless, after she hung up, Letty knocked and entered. "Guess who's volunteered to percolate coffee for the reception this afternoon?"

Vernon's eyes widened. For a moment Emma's ghost walked through his mind. "Who?"

Letty smiled and sighed. "Shirley, of course."

"You wouldn't think," Vernon began with a frown, "that she would make herself so conspicuous—this soon after yesterday."

"But don't you see? That's exactly why! She's got to pretend nothing's wrong at all. She's going to start right away making people get used to the idea that Chuck's home to farm and everything has always been on the up-and-up between them. Somehow, she's persuaded Chuck that this is the best course."

"Maybe—maybe after all, there's nothing to the rumors."

Letty laughed. "Precisely what you're *supposed* to think. See how easy it works? You know, a person pretends he's such and such, and if he's clever enough, most people will finally believe it. Is that so strange?" she asked, sarcasm coming heavily. "Have you never heard of such a thing before? Oh, I've seen it *often*. Just ask me, and I'll tell you. I've had a long *personal* acquaintance with the whole phony business."

Vernon jumped up from his desk—too quickly for a man of sixty with high blood pressure, and she saw the familiar off-focus dizziness pass across his eyes. He leaned heavily on the desk. "I wish you would stop torturing me. When I've got all of *this* on my mind!" He swung his arm out toward the church, scene of yesterday's funeral, today's wedding—and probably Sunday's baptism.

Suddenly, Letty felt only pity for him. Last night at four A.M. she had heard the regular squeak of the floor boards in his room; he was pacing the floor like a caged bear. She guessed that the hanging was bothering him—and memories of Eugene on the apple tree. During these last twenty years, whenever there was a hanging, she noticed the same awakened shudder within him. And she thought last night, as she thought now, that if Vernon would just trust her to accept whatever poured out, perhaps a bond of some sort could grow between them. She might even yet come to love him as much as she hated him, for there was a wide arc of feeling within her.

Never had she really understood Vernon's quest, following his solitary way, holding himself apart from others as if he considered himself above them. Poor Vernon: what did he know of any of the people of this town? Or of the lives even of his church elders? And in their mirrored images (including the bitter Emma Albrecht) what had he discovered about himself? What, in the final analysis, had he learned from having lived?

Vernon turned away and walked over to the window. He

pushed the lace curtains aside and looked out upon the white, flowering mock-orange. "*She* was a real Christian martyr," he began slowly, as if talking to himself. "Strong in her faith all these years despite her hard lot—fervent, even. The whole town gossips about Chuck and Shirley, and Hans's going off—but who has thought of Emma and her awful life? Maybe even that last act was justified in a way we're not qualified to judge or understand."

Letty was surprised that he had said so much. Her heart beat faster, and she tried to hold back her tongue, but she could not: "Why don't you use her for a sermon?"

"I might—I might do just that," he said, ignoring her sarcasm. "The trouble is, all this speculation is based on stories we've heard, on what the gossips have told you, and none of it might be true."

"You've never wanted to listen to stories, have you? You've always turned away. You've withdrawn from the human race. You haven't wanted to be a part of it—as if *that* will save you in the end."

He looked squarely at her. "I don't like stories because I'm after truth—that's been my whole object!"

"But *this* story you'd like to believe," said Letty slowly. "You're human, too. It comes close, after all, to being your own."

"All I'm saying," he continued immediately, as if he had not caught this veiled reference to Eugene, "is that if Emma's troubles were really what people say they were, then what she did may be justified. Look how many Christian martyrs gave their lives to make a point—underscoring a principle with their own blood—and like Jesus' own suicide, making an unforgettable impression."

"Jesus' *suicide*!" she said, aghast. "God in heaven, why haven't we heard *this* from the pulpit in Lent? You could start a whole new religion."

"You can never resist being clever."

"Oh, why don't you go hang yourself!" she replied in disgust and turned away.

Vernon whirled around, and she saw his eyes widen ominously. She could bite her tongue for having allowed *that* to pass her lips. Those were the same careless words he had flung at Eugene twenty years ago on the fatal afternoon. Clearly, he had never forgotten them. "I'm—I'm sorry," she said.

"That was deliberately cruel."

"I know, but it was a careless cruelty. I'm sorry."

"How often do you think of Eugene?" he asked slowly, his voice painfully thin.

"As often as you do," she replied and closed the door.

XIV 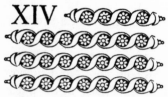 By quarter to four the church was filled, and in the flower-scented air the audience sat in hushed contemplation of the vows they would soon hear spoken again; a revery of marriage memories seemed to hover. To the right of the organ in the sacristy, Vernon and Ronald stood waiting for four o'clock to come. Both of them were too nervous to sit down, and although Vernon tried at first to talk to him about the weather—which happened to be unusually agreeable—Ronald was clearly too jittery to think of anything but the marriage, the difficulties of making a get-away from the reception, and perhaps, the intimate matters of the wedding night. It struck Vernon as a little improper for all of these thoughts to congeal under the church roof—it always had; the social and the sexual had nothing much to do with the religious —at least, not here in Kaleburg.

Ronald kept pushing his shell-rimmed glasses against his face, and he tugged at his cuff links—a gift from the bride—so that they would show. His coat was creamy and flawless, and the lily-of-the-valley spray in his buttonhole was fresh and surprisingly fragrant. Did all of this whiteness truly symbolize sexual purity for him? These days, it was difficult to guess, for although the young were certainly uneasy about a lot of things, the old concerns did not seem to trouble them.

At last the noisy opening runs of the wedding march sounded, and Vernon turned, with Ronald at his heels, and went out front to await the bride. The ceremony itself was like all the others Vernon had conducted, only this time, at the very end as he lifted his right hand to give the traditional blessing, he was suddenly self-conscious of that gesture—and so his hand remained closed, the fingers tight together in a fist. He wondered if anyone had noticed.

Afterwards, Letty spoke to him in the vestry while he was removing his robe. "Oh, come to the reception at the Wolbers', just this once. They've even got tables set up on the lawn, and the whole town'll be there. It'd be so nice if we could go together." She stopped when she saw his taut face. "No, I suppose you never will—ever." She gazed out the window at the mock-orange bushes. "It was such a lovely wedding—and Gloria, so beautiful! Oh, weddings are the best time of all." Then she looked at him again. "I'm going to the reception, I can tell you, and I'll drink champagne, too. If I come home drunk, you'll know why. Goodbye till later—much later."

When everyone had left the church and the janitor had run a vacuum cleaner over the crimson carpet, when the baskets of flowers had been removed and the fallen petals picked up, when everyone had gone, Vernon felt overwhelmingly depressed. This was the inevitable aftermath of the false gaiety of a wedding, only today the widening gulf between himself and everyone else seemed darker and deeper than usual. He had a strange fear of the empty church itself, for it seemed a cavernous projection of himself. Even his mind seemed oddly vacant, the furniture all at rest. How could he spend the hours until Letty's return?

There were, fortunately, a few mechanical things with which to occupy himself, and by working with his hands, he would come to his senses again. First of all, the bulletin board in front of the church must be changed. With a shoebox of metal letters under his arm, he walked out to the glass-enclosed case. Next Sunday's sermon, thus far only partially developed, came to mind; it was based upon the text: "But miserable were they, and in dead things were their hopes, who called them gods which are works of men's hands—gold and silver, wrought with careful art, and likenesses of animals, or a useless stone, the work of an ancient hand." One by one he slipped the letters into place: "A Useless Stone." The title pleased him—in fact, more than the sermon itself, which would be neither new to him nor to the congregation, for he planned to hurl at them the old stand-bys: the tower of Babel, the worship of Baal, and the Lord's displeasure over the golden calf—all stern lessons in the folly of putting faith in false images or creating one's own gods.

Over the years he had frequently enumerated the golden calves of Kaleburg: greed, avarice, pleasure, self-satisfaction, lust, and pride. Sometimes he thought of others—it depended, somewhat, on how far he wanted to go in castigating them. But did anyone really listen? Though each had ears to hear, was a single life changed? This was the terrible doubt which assailed him in moments of depression: all—absolutely every breath, each spoken word, years of effort—might finally be for nothing, and having directed his life to a higher purpose than most people aspired to, could he receive any certain satisfaction, any real comfort, that wasn't colored with wishful thinking? For he, too, was guilty of what he intended to preach against on Sunday: the all-too-human insistence upon embroidery, upon shaping, falsely picturing oneself to oneself. This, indeed, was "a useless stone," for all would finally be revealed on earth as well as in heaven—seen in a flash before drowning, or glimpsed like a stroke of lightning, even by the most self-deceptive! One might attempt falsification, as if there were no God to whom one were finally accountable, or as if one were God himself and could make of life what one wished. To fashion, to shape, to deceive ourselves—this was the ancient hand at work in all our lives, for whatever reason there might be: to hide what we did not want to know, to believe what we wanted to believe, to convince when our deeper selves remained doubting.

Ah, that was it! He closed the glass door and snapped the lock. Only—now what? How should he occupy himself? His gloomy study seemed repulsive, the church, still faintly ominous. Across the alley and up the street at the Wolbers' house he heard music and laughter which seemed to come in waves, rising and falling. On into the evening there would be noisy toasts around the punch bowl, lively clinking of champagne glasses, and the usual round of lewd stories, while out in back the urchins would tie tin cans to Ronald's car bumpers and write obscene words in soap on the hood. Perhaps at this moment the bridal pair were being forced into an automobile and driven around town to be exposed to public smiles. How many such processions had he seen in his lifetime? In the early days the bride and groom had been squired around the streets in decorated buggies; then came the Model T's, and finally the wide cars of the present day, which were too low-slung and enormous for observers really to see into very well. Recently, Vernon had watched a gaily waving couple who had been toted through the streets in the back of a pick-up truck: once again, the bridal couple had been exposed to the half-ridicule, shame, and envy of everyone.

He thought of his own courtship and marriage: a tale both quaint and naïve—he, a graduating seminary student, and Letty, plain but a good cook; what an odd turn of fate had put them together. He had happened to room in her father's house when he could no longer afford to stay at the seminary. How long ago it all seemed, and though he tried to keep himself from thinking of those early years of marriage and the tragic adoption

of Eugene, he knew that more and more, lately, he was unable
to exercise much control in keeping it all firmly from him.
Memories seemed to crowd ever closer—a sign, he feared, that
his grip was loosening, that old age would catch him in the
end and crack him open. There was no one to turn to—certainly
not Letty, who seemed to be waiting, ready to fall prey. She
talked of dyeing her hair and boasted that she had never felt
better.

Sometimes in the middle of a sermon he would snap to—as
if waking up—and he would look down from the pulpit at the
congregation, though he could not for the life of him imagine
what he had been saying, how long he had been talking, or
even remember having entered the church. At such moments,
he could not even conclude a sentence he had just begun. He
simply stopped, grabbed for the Bible, and began reading—but
did anyone know it was a cover-up? By their bland expressions
he could tell nothing.

With the shoebox of jingling metal letters, Vernon walked
back into the church, but he did not feel like putting them away
at the moment, not when the craving for a good long remem-
brance filled him as strongly as it did now. He set the box in a
pew, and in the tower room, which adjoined the entrance,
began to mount a small steel ladder that led up to the belfry.
This was his secret house, and childishly, perhaps, he guarded
his one private sanctuary from the eyes of everyone, including
Letty. When the new church had been built several years ago,
a huge tower had been begun which was to have a steeple reaching higher into the sky than the Catholic church's, but suddenly, funds had run out and the steeple was never built atop
the square shaft that stuck above the church. The belfry was
very roomy, for the congregation had planned to install a
carillon which would be played from the organ—rows of bells
with graded tones. Now, however, a single bell hung in the
tower and a rope led down through a hole to the cloak room

below. Vernon, as he climbed the metal ladder to the belfry, lifted the trap door with his back. Pigeons flew away through the opening with a great whirring of wings as he stepped upon the floor. The wind blew gently against his face; it was private and exciting, like the tree house of his childhood. He peered through the horizontal slats across the openings and saw the town and countryside below him, all laid out before his gaze, all removed from him. He could rest himself here in the upper air; it was the one place lofty enough for pure thought.

Perversely, the image that rose to his mind was that dreadful day he had tried to whip Eugene in the garage, when his son's companions, whom he had banished, cowered behind trees. They witnessed the whole scene and spread an enormously distorted version of the incident throughout Stilton. Even to firm believers in corporal punishment, the whipping had seemed uncalled for, strangely extreme. Some people, Letty reported, were calling him an ogre; others said he was losing his mind. Sunday morning and Wednesday evenings all through the Lenton season the village church was filled to the front pew. Everyone was curious and hoped to catch a clue to the mysterious trouble in one of Vernon's fervent prayers, or in the sermon itself, tucked away among the branches of oratory like a hidden angel's face among the foliage in a child's puzzle.

Letty reported every snatch of gossip, eager to rub raw the wounds of his indiscretion; he suffered silently under her tongue lashing, and Eugene went his merry way—hunting in the fields in spring, fishing in the Stone River. As Easter came, excitement over the whipping died down, and children no longer ran from Vernon's path if he neared them.

Then in May during a summery spell, late on a Saturday afternoon, one of Eugene's closest companions came trudging into town with Eugene's clothes in his hands. He stopped first at the General Store to announce that Eugene had drowned in the Stone River. Then, as the alarm spread, a procession of townspeople, Mrs. Blount and the boy in the lead, headed down the dirt street for the parsonage. Vernon saw them coming, and his stomach turned, anticipating some awful trouble. Letty clattered down the steps from her bedroom and together they went out to the porch.

The boy repeated his story, with Mrs. Blount prompting sharply: "Now the truth, do you hear? Tell us everything!"

He recounted how they had been fishing. Eugene got warm and wanted to go in swimming, though the current was swift. "He dove in, and he must've hit a log, or bottom, or something, because he never came up. I ran all along the shore, but I couldn't see him anywhere. I picked up his clothes and ran back to town."

Letty began sobbing, her hand crumpled like a handkerchief under her nose, and Mrs. Blount quickly put her arms around her for support. "Oh, no, no—it can't be!"

"Look at the clothes—are these Gene's?" asked Mrs. Blount patiently, but Letty turned away and would not look.

Vernon took the bundle from the boy and placed it beside him in the rocking chair. He lifted the blue overalls by the straps, letting the garment fall full length—as if Eugene, invisible, were holding it up. Then he carefully shook out the cambric shirt, measuring with a careful eye to see if the shoulders were broad enough. He picked up each sock and inspected the shoes and underwear. He said nothing, and the audience, now numbering over a score, watched in fascination. At last he looked up. "Yes, these are Eugene's."

Letty cried out, "No, no! I don't believe it!"

Mrs. Blount helped her inside, murmuring comfort words, and two neighbor women joined them. Eugene's friend said to Vernon, "We're all going down to seine the river. Want to come along?"

Vernon glanced sharply into the boy's pseudo-innocent, ex-

cited eyes—and he was suddenly certain that it was all a hoax.
This was The Joker's biggest prank. "No, you go ahead with
the others," he said softly, without betraying himself. "Tell the
men I have to stay with Mrs. Kallsen."

To make the hours pass for the bereaved, neighbors called
and stayed to visit; they sat on chairs in every room on the
first floor, and Vernon had to get extra folding chairs from the
church basement. At nightfall the men returned empty-handed,
ashamed of their failure. The women served coffee, pie, cake,
and cookies. A tableful of food appeared, as if miraculously—
or, Vernon thought, as if the housewives of Stilton were always
ready with bakery goods, constantly anticipating some disaster.
With all the townspeople filling her house, Letty tried to be a
hostess, but she was pale, distraught, and easily succumbed to
grief when sympathy was offered.

Vernon kept moving about through the rooms, his face a
mask, for he was partly amused by it all. He heard the hearty
voices, the quaking sounds of laughter. He realized that they
all seemed much more alert and vital than usual, as if calamity
had pinched their sleeping bodies back to life. Coffee cups clattered, smoke curled around the chandeliers, and Vernon walked
over to a dark window which reflected his own image, like a
smoked mirror. Somewhere out there, Eugene was watching.
Perhaps he had silently sneaked up behind the apple tree and
was now sitting among the branches, looking through the windows—no doubt he was surprised and pleased by all the commotion he had caused. Well, let him see my black silhouette,
Vernon thought. Let him wonder why I'm standing here so
silently, and so long.

At eleven-thirty, when the last friend had finally gone home,
Vernon and Letty wearily climbed the stairs to their separate
bedrooms. Under the light of the upstairs hall they turned
briefly toward each other; their hands met although their
glances did not. Vernon felt a momentary impulse to kiss her

stricken face, to soothe her sorrow away by the touch of his hand, with a word of reassurance—but he turned into his dark bedroom, instead. Once alone, a strange, gaping disappointment possessed him. Loneliness filled his body like a sob: how empty, empty was the world.

Then suddenly, quite distinctly, the floorboards creaked overhead. "He's in the attic!" Vernon whispered aloud, and life seemed to flush through his veins; his heart beat rapidly, and the tips of his fingers tingled with excitement; his face was suddenly hot.

He entered the hall and knocked on Letty's door. Vaguely, he thought he would tell her the news—he would share his discovery of Eugene in the attic. But when she said, "Come in," he entered and saw her in her nightgown—and he forgot his message. With her braids unwound, Letty's rich, dark hair slightly touched with gray, fell nearly to her waist, and in the pink-shaded glow of the bedlamp, her flesh looked young and blooming. She sat on the edge of the bed and kicked off her slippers.

"I was just—" he began. "I was just—lonely," and a tumultuous sense of pity and affection sent him rushing to her side. He drew her roughly into his arms. "Oh, Letty, Letty," and in the embrace, found, familiarly enough, that his mouth was half-open on the tendons of her neck, his teeth bared. He could feel her flesh through the thin nightgown, and he pressed her harder against him. She was crying, but he could not tell if in sorrow or joy. He kissed her mouth and throat again and again. "I want to stay here tonight," he said. "I want to be with you." He snapped off the bedlamp. Clutching the hem of her gown, he lifted it high over her head, as if tearing aside a veil, and then he wrenched off his own clothes, desire hot within him. When they were under the covers together, his body pressed fully upon her naked flesh; he began a passionate rocking that jiggled the casters of the bed, squeaked the floorboards, and trembled the whole flimsy house. On and on he worked, long after she had begged him to stop, as if he would not rest until he had shaken the rafters loose and brought down the whole building upon their heads.

At breakfast next morning he was loath to break the spell. They hardly spoke, but contentment lay between them; never had the morning sun, flushed across the dew-gray lawn, seemed so promising, nor the world so fresh, the days so full of hope. If only this were not Sunday he might delay even longer the revelation of the culprit in the attic. He allowed himself a second cup of coffee; he basked in the sweetness of their accord. Then at last he said: "In the night, it's funny, but I thought I heard someone in the attic. Do you suppose it could be Eugene, hiding up there, playing a trick on—"

"Eugene!" Letty jumped up, tipping the chair over. She raced for the stairs calling, "Eugene! Eugene, are you up there?"

A moment later Vernon heard her muffled voice in the attic and the boy's low-pitched replies. Slowly, he started up the steps to get his whip from the closet. The parental duty facing him depressed him—he had no stomach for such things, and on a Sunday morning at that.

When Letty, stooping under the rafters, saw Vernon climb the attic stairs with the whip, she shouted, "No, no you mustn't. Wait—now don't—don't," she backed away, as if it were she herself who would get the whipping. "I've forgiven him. It's all right. He won't do it again." Eugene, dusty in T shirt and jeans, looked mildly interested in both of them. "Oh, I can't stand this," Letty wailed, "I can't! I can't!" She ran down the stairs, and a moment later the kitchen door slammed as she left the house.

Then the punishment began. Eugene did not attempt to escape; instead, he cupped his hands in his crotch, bent over, and let Vernon do his worst. There were no comments from either of them as the whip slapped across his buttocks. Vernon did not count the lashes—but he did not administer many. He was out of breath quickly. "There," he said, "I hope that'll teach you not to play this trick again." But he doubted it, and his voice revealed the doubt.

Meanwhile, as Vernon learned later from Mrs. Blount and from Letty herself, the terrible scene Letty imagined taking place in the attic made her physically ill. A swirling dizziness stopped her in front of the church; she leaned against an old cement hitching post to keep from falling, was sick to her stomach, and lost her breakfast. Afterward, she hurried on to the General Store. A strange unreality took possession of her—she feared it was the prelude to insanity. She had difficulty controlling the movement of her legs; she hobbled along, having lost the rhythm of her gait. Finally, she pushed open the door of the store, saw Mrs. Blount behind the counter, next to a stack of Sunday newspapers. "He's found! He's found! Spread the news," she cried. "Eugene is alive."

Mrs. Blount rushed forward, put her arms around Letty, and drew her to a counter stool. "Come here, sit down. Now, what's this?"

"Eugene's alive," Letty said, her voice shrill. "He wasn't in the river! He was hiding in the attic all along. Isn't that wonderful?" She began to laugh, and Mrs. Blount sent one of the boys who stood gaping to fetch the doctor.

"You just take it easy. Have a cup of coffee—and now don't you say anything more."

Letty grabbed Mrs. Blount's arm, and with her voice confidential, said: "You know, he doesn't get along at all well with Reverend—that's the trouble. Everybody in town must know it by now."

Mrs. Blount and the three children in the store nodded solemnly.

"We shouldn't have had a boy so old, you know. A little boy

of five or six, that would have been different! We could've handled him. A little boy—and I would dress him so cute."

"Here, drink your coffee," said Mrs. Blount. "Then we'll take you home."

Letty dropped her hands and looked up wildly. "No, no— you mustn't come to *our* home. We're wicked people!"

The doctor arrived a few minutes later, and with the help of Mrs. Blount, they walked Letty to the parsonage. She was given a sedative and put to bed, where she stayed for three days. During her recuperation, Eugene slunk around town, ashamed of what he had done—and he was roundly scolded by his peers, who had heaped praises upon him such a short time ago.

It was a lovely period of peace for Vernon, and townspeople quite frankly told how they sympathized with him, caught with a problem boy like Eugene. "He's not really *bad*, you know," they said, expecting Vernon to be generous in his estimate. "It's just that he's too much for everybody—and that much live-liness is bound to bring trouble." Vernon nodded but said little. He felt that he may have broken Eugene at last but was super-stitious about claiming victory too soon.

After the school term ended, Vernon and Letty saw less and less of Eugene, for he roamed the country with his gun and companions; he showed up for meals, he slept in his bed, but his real life was outside the parsonage, and Vernon did not try to halt his withdrawal. Normally Letty did not worry over Eugene's whereabouts, but one day in the middle of June a sudden, severe storm swept across Stilton, preceded by heavy winds which bent back the trees and ripped off old branches. The air was dark brown with dust and whirling debris. Soon after the wind began, Vernon and Letty ran for the basement, their storm cellar. Anxiously, they looked out at the purple clouds, which were faintly greenish at the edges. "Where do you suppose Eugene is? What could he be doing?" said Letty.

Hail began bouncing on the grass—first a few stones and

then in great numbers; finally, the heavy rain began, and Vernon and Letty moved upstairs to watch the storm through the lace-curtained windows of the living room. They could not see across the street, for the rain was a gray-white shroud enclosing the house. "I'm worried about Eugene," said Letty over and over. "I wonder where he is."

At last the rain stopped, the sun broke through brilliantly, and a large double rainbow arched across the dark eastern skies. Vernon and Letty went outdoors and stood upon the wet sidewalk to watch the display of colors. Vernon could not help but wonder if Eugene had not called "Wolf! Wolf!" once too often and fate had come through with his desire. But he said nothing to worry Letty. Instead, he walked down the garden path past glistening rose bushes and entered the rear door of the church. Eugene, after all, would always be with them; he was as indestructible as the world itself.

For nearly an hour Vernon sat in a church pew and tried to shape his sermon for Sunday, but his ideas were pedestrian; he was still thinking about Eugene and where he might be. At last he gave up trying to concentrate and left the church. A light was on in the kitchen, and, to his shock, he saw through the unshaded window the naked back of Eugene; he was standing facing the stove, as nonchalant and immodest as if he were about to step into a bathtub. Vernon did not know quite what to do. He took only a few steps forward, then saw Letty move toward Eugene with a towel in her hand, and the expression on her face sent a shock through his body. She smiled intimately; they wrestled lightly over the towel. Vernon heard their dim laughter—hers, gay and exuberant as a girl's, his, deep and toying.

Vernon gasped with horror. He rushed forward, up the steps, and threw open the door. "What are you two doing?" he cried.

They whirled about, and Vernon was surprised to see that

now the towel was tucked around Eugene—had he indeed witnessed the scene he thought he had? Letty moved to the opposite side of the kitchen with guilty haste. He detected a blush creeping up from her throat, and she began to stammer that Eugene had gotten wet in the storm. "He—he almost drowned in the river. I just now brought him a dry outfit."

Eugene bent over to pick up the bundle on the chair. He did not even look at Vernon or seem to care one way or another what anybody thought.

"Almost drowned!" Vernon spat out, contemptuously. "Where've I heard that before?" he asked Eugene. "Why not almost shoot yourself—or go hang yourself?"

"Run upstairs and put on your clothes," said Letty quietly.

"Oh yes, we must be proper now. The minister's arrived." With a bitter smile he watched Eugene clutch his dry clothes to his stomach and pad by in his barefeet to the staircase. "Go!" he shouted, just as the boy passed near him, and Eugene jumped.

"A ha ha ha ha ha," Eugene exploded, and his wild peal of laughter carried him on upstairs.

Sorrow and weariness seemed to weight Vernon's shoulders. He looked at his wife. "I might have known all along."

"What are you trying to make of this?" she asked.

"I saw it all through the window—you and the boy," he said coldly, as if she were a fallen woman, beyond hope.

"Now just a—"

"I don't want to discuss it. There's nothing to be said." He turned and left her.

Upstairs in his bedroom he slumped down at his desk by the bay window, which looked out upon the orchard. The gloom of late afternoon seemed too oppressive to bear, and he snapped on the gooseneck lamp. The last rays of the sun flushed an orange light across the clouds, and the garden was strangely illuminated by this indirect glow. Vernon closed his eyes and tried to find peace in prayer; although he formed a rosary of words, they did not seem to connect with anything beyond him.

Suddenly his attention was drawn to the garden below, for he saw Eugene crossing the lawn. The boy glanced over his shoulder at Vernon and cheerily grinned. He was up to more of his devilish tricks, Vernon knew, and his nerves tightened. This boy, his enemy, was omnipresent, reaching even into the privacy of his prayers. He was an impudent invader, forever mocking—and yet, Vernon could not help but watch him.

Eugene was dressed in overalls and a shirt, and he carried a rope that slithered behind him through the grass. Obviously, the whole show was being staged somehow for Vernon's bene-fit; Eugene kept aping toward the upstairs window. For a moment Vernon considered drawing the shade and closing off the scene, but already he was consumed by curiosity. He turned off the light and watched Eugene toss the rope over a bough of the apple tree. The boy made a noose and tied the knot, then shinnied up the trunk and swung out upon the branch from which the rope dangled.

Eugene waved his hand to Vernon and, drawing up the rope, slipped the noose over his head. Slowly, with painstaking care, he lowered himself from the bough, gripping the rope above his head. Vernon sat transfixed and rigid with tension; sweat crept over his brow.

Then downstairs, Letty screamed. Vernon shot up, knocking back the chair. He rushed to the head of the stairs.

"See him! See him in the apple tree!" she shrieked below. "Stop him! Vernon, stop him!"

He hurried down the stairs, but in his confusion, his heel caught on the bottom step. He fell upon the floor at Letty's feet. She pulled on his arms, trying to help him up—a groping, fleeting embrace—and then together they rushed outside.

The light had changed from a saffron glow to dusk, and at first Vernon could not clearly make out Eugene dangling from the tree. And when he got to Eugene, he wrapped his arms around the boy's legs, lifting him in the air to take the strain off his neck. But then he did not know what to do, and he dropped the legs again, for they seemed heavy as weights for a drawbridge. Letty was talking incoherently. Vernon saw as he scrambled up the tree and climbed out upon the bough that the slightly swaying body was oddly inanimate. He moved further on the limb and tried to unfasten the rope. He clawed at it with all his strength and at last got the knot loose. The hemp burned hotly in his hand as it suddenly spun out. He heard the plump of Eugene's body falling upon the earth. Then he noticed the neighbors crossing the lawn. He leaned against the trunk and covered his face with one hand, for tears had sprung in his eyes; he was so weak and tired he felt he could not move.

The doctor explained later that Eugene had not been strangled; the spinal cord had snapped and death had been nearly instant. As people gathered in the household that night, Vernon repeatedly told them: "I watched the whole thing from my window—Eugene was trying a trick. You know how he was, always up to something. He hoped to scare us, but he slipped."

They nodded, mumbling condolences, but he saw the uneasiness in their eyes—half a fear of him. Though convinced it was an accident, the turbulence of this household was known to all, and now this awful thing had happened. Nobody wanted to sit near Vernon, or talk, or even touch his hand.

Letty was upstairs in bed, partially drugged, but not even the doctor realized how unbalanced her mind had become over this grief. And after the funeral, when the effect of the medicine wore off, she recoiled wildly. Vernon had to lock her in the bedroom, or she would have gone raving through the streets. He was afraid to leave the house to fetch the doctor, in case she might try to fling herself from the window. But then he realized that her oaths were directed solely at him, and he stood there outside her locked door and took the full brunt of her wrath. "Infidel! Jew!" she screamed. "You killed him! You killed him! Ah, the Prince of Life, and you hung him on a tree!"

XV 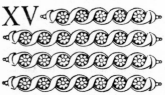 The sounds of revelry from the Wolbers' wedding reception woke Vernon from his trance. He peered through the horizontal openings of the belfry windows to see what was causing the commotion. Horns were blaring, noisemakers whirring, people laughing, and underneath, a murmurous hum of talk, blurred together at this distance to a continual drone. Then a chorus of huzzas—again, and again. Three cheers for the bride and groom. May they find happiness, remain innocent, and always be in love.

Oh, the world's excitements and concerns! How distant it all was, as if he had already passed beyond—yes, beyond normal cares and half out of life itself. All along and all the time, it had been his own destruction he had sought, not Eugene's. But where did this decadence come from? Why, it began with God, who must punish, and sinners, who deserved punishment; and never did a sinner deserve it more than he himself for what he had blindly done to that boy. Even now, twenty years later as he looked back, Vernon felt the sorrow of that struggle, as palpable as his present sense of futility and despair. He knew that even back then it had never been a question of virtue and wickedness. Eugene simply existed, offensive as a weed and as certain to thrive. One either fell upon his neck in adulation or dropped under his heels as he trampled on through life, riding roughshod over everything. He was a bad son only in that he showed no sign of the meek strength of a good son.

The other way: to turn one's cheek, bear humiliation and insults but still rise triumphant, as Jesus had done, this was the Christian way and closer to Vernon's inclinations. Furthermore, it made a virtue of what otherwise might be considered weakness and offered a reward to those who would ordinarily have nothing. These many years he had tried to be a good son to the spiritual Father; he had borne his wife's tongue lashings, hostility from the people of Stilton, guilt over Eugene, loneliness in Kaleburg, and his own sense of failure—and what had all this abnegation amounted to? He felt none of the sweet sense of grace that one should have with spirituality, none of the control or serene confidence, the ineffable pleasure. The other way—to be a bad son—was never his temperament or possible lot in life. He could never bull his way through anything or shake his fist defiantly at misfortune. He could never give that loud, long laugh. Here in the church tower on a waning afternoon, he forced upon himself the bitter knowledge lurking always in his heart: what could arise from the shattered vessel of his life—his self-destroyed life—but the dank emptiness of death?

Like a ghost dreading the morning cock, he now heard with sickening distaste the sound of marriage revelry. All these years he had been marrying young people, putting his cool fingers upon those hot marital hands to chill the lust of their minds, to say wisely, "until *death* do you part." Out of envy? No, surely only to maintain that it was all illusion; the final reality was death. Even in the midst of breathless love-making what lovers did not sense—at least in the aftercalm, in the dying and falling away of their bodies—a prelude to death itself? But, keen as a cock in the morning crowing his lustiness, had any of his bridal couples listened? Had he made his point? Oh, no more than he had ever conquered Eugene. There was always the salty odor of copulation in the air, mingled with the scent from the wedding bouquet. The heady pleasures of the bed were never banished by anything he said, threatened, or promised.

Suddenly another shouting toast from the wedding reception welled up, fell away—it seemed such a hearty raspberry to his thoughts that he turned from the window, half humiliated, half angry. At least one thing was clear: if being alive meant all that mess out there—a drunken wedding reception and a lot of obscenities, then he stuck by the choice he had been following unwittingly. Only, now he knew what he was doing. He had drawn apart from these people; he had created—willful as an artist—a certain image of himself before their eyes. By his creation he had hoped to make the hand of the Lord indelible and unmistakably clear, so that, if only in a small way, his parishioners might exert some measure of control and moderation upon their lives. He had tried to keep constant in their minds a realization of the eternal, against which their earthly lives would be measured eventually.

What was there left for him to do? He could not get over the overwhelming action of a woman like Emma Albrecht—a bold, clear, decisive stroke—and look at the effect! One could envy such magnificent unselfishness, such grandeur of sacrifice.

In the alley of the Wolbers lot, Vernon noticed several figures tying tin cans to the get-away car. Where was the protective best man—or the unlucky, unsuspecting groom? The gang of pranksters proceeded to lift the hood of the decorated car; they were obviously tampering with the spark plugs and coils. There were wild shrieks of laughter from a group on the lawn. The people seemed only thumb-high, and to Vernon's slightly hazy vision, they were blurred to anonymity, mere stick-figures of humanity. More bursts of laughter—it seemed the whole town was present, overflowing the house, filling the lawns. Was everyone having a good time? This, certainly, was the biggest social event in Kaleburg—the largest, the best.

But Vernon knew there would be many more: births and deaths, showers and weddings, family reunions and family fiascos—relentlessly more and more and more. He had gone through sixty years of them, and the thought of an endless continuity was too staggering to contemplate, for what did all of this senseless business mean to him? Get far enough away—as he was now—and those people were mere sticks running on green grass. Some were in skirts, some in suits; there were short ones and tall ones, some quick, others slow. Babies were squalling and old men were drunk. Bound and strapped to the seasons on this midland plain, the years were passing all alike: under the green leaves of spring all creatures that creepeth upon the earth desired mates, wooed and won their loves; there followed the full foliation of summer with the cornfields ripening, with everything under the sun rushing to the relentless conclusion of autumn—a momentary stasis, an Indian summer of the earth, mind, and heart, before winter threw its cover of death over the world, its mask of snow.

Automobile horns began to blare, and the crowd gathering on the front lawn at the Wolbers' grew larger, but Vernon's view was partially obscured by the high shrubbery along the alley. Oh, yes, there they were! The bride and groom ran down the steps and cries rang out. Arms were flailing the air—people were throwing rice. Around the corner of the house raced the newlyweds, out to the alley—little did they know, the car would be no haven. The crowd paused. They could have engulfed the get-away car, for Ronald was having trouble. But, since grooms often do, they waited, giving him a chance to perform. Yes, it started up! Vernon saw the puff of exhaust smoke, and soon the tin cans rattled noisily together. As the car rolled down the alley there was a loud backfire—an answering shout from the crowd, which streamed into the alley. Would the young couple make it? The car seemed to falter. A gang of boys started down the alley, their arms lifted high. But again the car started, spurted forward, and suddenly, in a cloud of dust, the newly-weds disappeared around the corner.

They were off! Vernon turned from the window.

He saw the rope dangling from the bell overhead, and all his memories of Eugene's death returned like the clap of doom. He followed the line of rope with his eyes to where it disappeared through a hole in the floor. Evening was hastening on; end of another day—and with tomorrow, a torment of newly remembered memories; and thus on and on. Why had all of this happened to him, a minister of God? Where was the strength in the right hand of the Lord? Always, it seemed, he was under the shadow of the left. And in all of his blunders, he had been unable to forgive himself, let alone feel the Lord's forgiveness. Resolutely, he had worn this mask before Kaleburg, hoping to engender religious feelings in others, at least, though he had been unsuccessful himself—and hoping, of course, that the countenance he pretended to wear would at last grow upon his face, and he would become what he thought he should be.

But death lifts the last mask. Again he eyed the dark, straight rope which hung down from the iron bell above. Stained by the weather, it seemed more a black cable than a piece of hemp that could be bent, looped, and knotted. He felt suddenly a strange familiarity about the scene—one of those odd illuminations of having been in a place before. He realized that from the very beginning he had been traveling toward this hour of dimming light; there came a time too tightly circumscribed to be postponed. Quickly, as if rescuing a man from the sea, he pulled at the bell rope, reeling it up through the floor and looping it in his hands until he had plenty of slack. The necessity to contemplate seemed to leave him, and as he moved, his only concern was to do it well and do it surely. He saw the small ledge below the slatted window and calculated whether the drop would be enough. Moving to the window, he gauged the distance: four feet—yes, surely, if he did not allow himself too much free line—and why should he? The wooden sill was almost wide enough to stand on, though to perch there he had to anchor himself with one hand. With the other, he worked the rope around his neck. Had he a shears, he would have cut the cord and fashioned a knot, but faced with one long strand of hemp, his only solution was to fling it around his neck several times until he had a coarse necklace that reached to his ears. By holding the bottom end tightly against his chest, when he fell he could count on success. He teetered on the ledge, his back to the openings. And just as he slowly turned to take a last look through the window—before he was ready to proceed —he lost his balance, reached out with both hands for something to grab hold of, but toppled forward into darkness.

Bwong, bwong, bwong.

The enormous clanging of the bell pained his ears. He was choking to death on the floor. He clawed at the coils of rope around his neck, sat up, and again *bwong, bwong, bwong* sounded above him. The very air seemed ridged with sound, and panting with fatigue and wonder, he lay back. A pigeon feather tickled his nose and he brushed it away. *Bwong! Bwong!* The bell seemed to follow his gesture. He looked up and saw the clapper moving in the dark mouth of the bell— the rope swayed beneath it, right down to his very own neck. Every time he moved he rang the bell. Oh, he was alive! An odd, inebriating sensation passed through him. He reached to his throat and began systematically to unwind the rope, not caring if he knocked the bell, or if the noisy ringing continued. Let the sound flood over him; let it wash him, loll him—he was back. Joyfully, he fed the loose rope into the hole in the floor; it dropped below again, where it belonged—getting rid of the evil, putting it out of sight. Accidentally he set the bell above him rocking and ringing again. And in the midst of the last tentative *bwong* he heard a voice below. He listened.

"Vernon! Vernon, is that you up there?" Letty called.

Should he answer? He felt caught—trapped in a curious way, and unable in the least to explain himself. She called again. He thought he heard her foot on the metal rungs of the ladder. Finally, he moved over, and feeling for the latch, pulled up the trap door. Her face below was tilted back, oval as an egg, familiar, yet down there in the dark church, strange, too; everything seemed odd, newly created, and unfamiliar—even himself. For a moment he could not speak, and he simply stared down upon her.

"What are you up to? Don't you know you're sounding the alarm?"

"Alarm?" he asked, his voice husky, off-key. He stood up. Yes, he remembered now—it was civil defense. The town siren was for fires, but the church bell, rung at odd times, other than Sunday mornings or before funerals—was a warning of imminent disaster.

"Vernon?" she called, her voice anxious. "Vernon? Are you on your way down?" And she added, "Please don't ring the bell again—the whole town is coming."

Slowing rubbing his raw, bruised neck, he walked over to the window and peered between the boards. Indeed, people were tramping down the alley toward the church from the Wolbers' reception. Dan Beers was in front, taking long steps, his chin high—mayor of the town, leader of them all. Lagging behind was Herman Johns, red-faced and arthritic; he paused beside a hollyhock bush to rest, though he was nearly knocked aside by Bill Wolbers and his wife—both quite drunk, their arms about each other's waists as they skipped lazily to and fro, making the procession look like a snake dance. Many people kept glancing up, as if they could see him standing there. Carrie

Maxwell frowned, her gaunt, stern face uplifted. Walking beside her was Shirley, who, from this angle, looked squat and unusually hefty. And where was Chuck? Who were these other people?

"What shall I say, Vernon?" Letty called. "That it was all a mistake?"

He turned from the window, and going over to the trap door, dropped to his knees. "Yes, just an accident," he said. Then, leaning back, he carefully rubbed his neck; traces of blood came away on his fingers. If Letty asked about it, he would say he had fallen.

Fallen indeed! But he had been saved; he had risen again. The exultation of being alive filled him with happiness—a joy that was sweeping, satisfying, a general pleasure. The white pigeon fluttering above seemed a thing of wonder. He wanted to speak to it—to someone—to the whole world. He stepped over to the window, but before he could glance down, a touch of vertigo made him close his eyes and cling to the window frame with both hands. He felt that the earth was tipping, or as if he were a captain on the bridge of a ship, the sea stormy under him. Slowly, he opened his eyes. There below on the lawn was Letty, the people fanned out around her, listening to her explanation, looking up now and then, trying to see him. They turned to each other, and finally, their backs showing, they started their return to the Wolbers' party—hoping, no doubt, that conviviality could still work its magic; back to the punch bowl and toasts to the future, to the years ahead for everyone, to love and all the joys celebrated this afternoon. And after the party, Vernon knew, they would go to their separate homes, re-enter their private lives, and encounter once more the elemental stillness which creeps into all our lives.

He imagined Letty and himself at the supper table tonight, and all that she would have to tell: what the bride wore for going-away; what Mrs. Schneider said to Marygold Clausen;

who had been niggardly in wedding gifts and who unnecessarily extravagant—on and on. Perhaps he would listen with only half his attention, as he had always done, though not with despair—not heavy-hearted because the follies of the world choked the surface of life. In one magnificent leap he had been carried into a circle of peace, and he was content to stand here at the window of the church tower and look down.

Easily, he could visualize his old age with Letty as they rode a stream of gossip, ran upon snags of misfortune, and witnessed, finally, more deaths than baptisms—or so it would seem. All along they would be flowing swiftly toward their own ends: that dark unknowable at the confluence where eternity begins. Here in this inland town, far from a river such as the Stone, which had supposedly drowned Eugene—here in Kaleburg, where there was only a sporadic run-off of water after thunderstorms or when winter ended, there was, still, a slight, imperceptible tilt of the soil. And all the gathering of waters finally became the Mississippi, then the Gulf, and at last the ocean itself. This far inland such an end was often difficult to imagine, and even if foreseen, hard to continue to remember. In his old age, he resolved to think of this solid earth, this precious soil, and how little by little it was being carried away—how this planet like his own life and every man's was being slowly ravaged—and not by time alone or the follies of mankind; it was also the work of an ancient hand. With a wonder that seemed to flower inside him, filling him with rapture and a surprising hope, he recognized, suddenly, this new awakening. Aloud he said: "I believe in God."